T

REBI

ARABELLA SEYMC
now lives with her
school, she worked for ten years as a librarian and read plenty of novels before deciding to write one of her own. Her previous titles include *A Passion in the Blood* and *Dangerous Deceptions*.

by the same author

A PASSION IN THE BLOOD
DANGEROUS DECEPTIONS

THE SINS OF REBECCAH RUSSELL

Arabella Seymour

FONTANA/Collins

First published by William Collins Sons & Co. Ltd 1989
First issued in Fontana Paperbacks 1990

Printed and bound in Great Britain by
William Collins Sons & Co. Ltd, Glasgow

For My Darling Daughter, Keturah
and for
Gary and Delena Raymond, with love.

THE BRODIE AND THE RUSSELL FAMILY TREE

ANNA MARIA FLOOD *mistress* — EDWARD BRODIE

ANNA MARIA FLOOD
married
Richard Rowe – no issue

EDWARD BRODIE
married
Lillian Mary Radwinter
|
issue

ANNA BRODIE
married
1 Lionel Tollemache – no issue
2 RALPH, LORD RUSSELL

CLARA BRODIE
married
THOMAS TRADESCANT
|
issue

JAMES RUSSELL
married — *by mistress* — *by mistress*

CORINNA CHARPENTIER — Margaret McAllister — Isabella Ajanti

REBECCAH RUSSELL
married
Rufus Waldo

JAMIE RUSSELL

ALICE RUSSELL

Prologue

LIKE A SLEEPWALKER, she stretched out her arms in front of her and clutched tightly at the edge of the witness box, and hung onto it with all her strength. Her legs felt like water, scarcely able to bear her up; beneath her stark, black velvet gown her heart was racing so wildly that she felt dizzy and sick. She closed her eyes, then opened them and stared all around her, willing herself to be in some other place. But she was not.

Because this was not a dream, but a nightmare that was reality. And she, Rebeccah Russell Waldo, was on trial for the murder of her husband.

There was no one to help her; her family were powerless. She was completely innocent. Only one man could give her the alibi she needed; but to name him would be to betray his identity; and that she would rather die than ever do, no matter what they did to her. Without him, she would rather be dead, anyway.

Hopelessly, she raised her tired, red-rimmed blue eyes and looked around her. No way out. All about her were thronged the audience of anonymous humanity, packing the public gallery; the audience who gaped, whispered, censured, speculated, hanging like scavengers above a carcass, onto every titbit of scandal, every new revelation, every intimate detail of her private life; who had, she was sure, already judged her guilty because they wanted her to be. She had committed adultery, and that sin, in the eyes of the respectable world ranged against her, was a sin worse than the crime of which she now stood accused.

Her eyes moved from the sea of faces above her to the judge's bench, then downwards, towards the barristers, forbidding in their wigs and gowns, even her own man, the best advocate that money could buy. Suddenly, he glanced up and caught her eye, and smiled; a taut, professional smile, the smile he would give all his clients. Small comfort. Her frozen lips moved in response, but they would not obey her. Her eyes had already moved on, fearfully, to the Crown Prosecutor; the enemy. She watched him, head bowed, toying with the thick, well thumbed sheaf of papers in his hands, conversing with his junior in rapid, low whispers. Already, she hated him. A month ago, a week, a few days even, she had not known that he existed. He was a stranger, a man she had never seen nor spoken with in all her life; nor done any wrong to. Yet he had spent every day since the trial began attempting to tear down in shreds every vestige of her good name and character, replacing it, skilfully, with a woman of his own creation who no one, listening, could fail to hate and despise . . . How could she ever prove that nothing he had said was true?

He was getting to his feet now; in the sudden hush that fell upon the court she heard him clear his throat, ready to attack. Her whole body tautened. Her fingers, clammy from perspiration inside her gloves, gripped the edge of the witness box tighter than before, ready for another onslaught. Steeling herself, she made her eyes move level with his . . . and she saw triumph in them.

Deliberately, he waited. Then, never taking his eyes from her face, he held up a package in his hand.

'Mrs Waldo . . . learned Counsel for the Defence has consistently maintained that you, the accused, must be innocent of your late husband's murder, or any part in it, because you had no motive sufficiently strong enough for wishing him dead . . .' A pause, while the whole court became so still that she could hear the sound of her own breath. 'I now believe that the Prosecution has found such a motive.' He held the package up higher for her to see; as she realized what it contained, she gasped, and stumbled forward. All around her, the faces, the benches, the walls began to tilt and spin. Her shaking hands found the solid edge of the witness box again and hung onto it, like a blind woman.

'Mrs Waldo . . . these letters that have come into the possession of the Prosecution are letters written by you to your lover, and signed with your name. The contents, which I shall read aloud to the court, will prove beyond any reasonable doubt that not only did you both hate Rufus Waldo with such an intensity that in itself provides a motive for the crime . . . but that the letters specifically allude to a carefully planned plot to take his life.'

All around her, the whole court erupted into a volcano of deafening noise. From what seemed a long way off, a single voice was calling for silence; but it seemed an eternity before silence fell. In front of her, through the red, hot mist that was burning in her eyes, she saw the figure of her own man rise to his feet, hands raised in plea, looking at her, then back towards the judge's chair.

'My Lord, the Defence objects to the Prosecution's assertion that my client must be guilty of complicity in murder, merely on the production of a bundle of letters whose authenticity must surely be questioned . . !'

'Objection overruled. Let the letters be shown to the accused, so that she may, while still under oath, confirm or deny that they are written in her hand.'

Someone was walking towards her now, holding them out; the words that she had written to him, all the passionate longings and desire, all her hopes and fears, her hatred for Rufus, her craving for his touch, all rose up and hit her, like a stinging blow. None of them would understand, none of them would believe her if she told them how it really was . . .

A voice said, '*Mrs Waldo, do you admit that these letters were written by you to your lover?*' and she opened her lips to speak, but no words came out. Desperately, her eyes sought the face of her half-sister, Alice, among the sea of faces ranged above her in the public gallery; but there was no sign of her.

Before she fainted, all she could remember was to ask herself how anyone else had known the letters existed . . . and how they had stolen them from Alice . . .

PART ONE

The Child

1

REBECCAH RUSSELL was nine years old when she had first found out the truth about her father; the father she idolized, the father who could do no wrong.

She had been playing in the big, rambling gardens at Linnets Hall, arranging her china dolls and teddy bears in a circle on the lawn, pouring lemonade from her porcelain dolls' tea pot into the tiny matching cups, when she had suddenly caught sight of him, with a strange lady; arm in arm, they emerged from the Folly, then walked to the main house through the shrubbery and entered it by a side door; a door which was out of bounds to the servants, a door which she had been forbidden to ever use.

Curiosity aroused, she had paused, stopping to wonder who the strange lady might be. Not an acquaintance of her mother's; for her mother was in Kentucky visiting her American relatives and would not be home in England again for another week. Not her aunt from Epsom, for the lady with her father was too short. Putting down the dolls' tea pot, Rebeccah had left her toys' tea party and run towards the house.

The door creaked when she opened it. Her hands were trembling as she edged it open and went through. She felt both guilt and excitement, exploring forbidden territory. She was also puzzled, for her father had always told her no one was permitted to use this door because the old staircase which ran up from it to the little used side of the house was rotten in places, and dangerous to climb. As she went up step by step, her curiosity heightened; for there was no sign of rot in any of the wood.

At the top she hesitated, her ears straining to catch any sound. That was when she heard the woman's laughter; then her father's.

She stayed where she was for several moments, hesitating, wondering whether to go back to the garden or to go on and find her father. She had intended to wait until he'd finished all his daily paperwork in the stud office, then ask him to join her toys' tea party on the lawn. Maybe the strange lady would like to join them, too.

Smiling, she walked on along the length of the passage, then stopped outside the door from where their voices came. Lightly, she tapped on it, but there was no reply.

Strange, unfamiliar sounds were coming from inside the room, sounds that disquieted and puzzled her, for they were the sounds of someone in pain. When she tapped on the door for a second time and there was still no answer, she opened it and looked inside. It was then that she received the biggest shock in all her life.

Inside the room was an enormous, elaborate bed, all draped in lavender brocade; all her life she was to remember that, in startling detail. On top of the bed lay the strange woman with her father, both naked. The woman's hair, the colour of horse chestnuts in autumn, lay spread across the white linen pillows; her father lay across her; breathlessly, they were whispering each other's names.

Never in her entire life had Rebeccah ever seen a naked man, and the sight stunned and revolted her, without her understanding why. Eyes transfixed in terror and morbid fascination at the scene in front of her, her whole body shook; tears stung hotly, then began to trickle down her face. Holding back the sobbing, she turned and fled the way she'd come, stumbling down the narrow staircase, fighting for her breath when she reached the bottom. As she pushed her way outside again she had to shield her eyes from the sudden stark glare of the afternoon sunlight.

It was at that same moment that she first saw him. A tall, stocky boy of about thirteen or fourteen, with flinty grey eyes and black hair. She had no idea who he could be, or where he had come from, but, instinctively, she disliked him on sight.

He grinned, but the smile did not reach his eyes.

'Well, we are in a hurry, aren't we, little girl?' He laughed, harshly, as if her distress amused him. 'I've come here with my mother, to see papa. Before your mother gets back from America.' He paused, letting each word sink in. 'You didn't know, did you, that he's my father, too. I'm Jamie Russell, your half-brother . . .'

2

'SON OF A BITCH!'

'Corinna, please . . !'

'My God, what a fool you've made out of me!'

'For pity's sake, lower your voice! Do you want all the servants to hear you?'

'Why not? Let them all hear me. Most of them probably know everything already; servants always do. And then they gossip to other people's servants. That's how their betters' private lives get made public knowledge – do you need to be told that?'

'If you'd do me the courtesy of sitting down and listening to me for just one moment . . .'

'Listen to you? Why should I listen to you, James? Give me one good reason why I should believe anything you say.' Tears of rage welled up into her eyes and she dashed them away, angrily. 'But you can believe this. I'll never forgive you for this humiliation. Nor for what you've done to your own daughter! Can you ever begin to imagine how she felt when she was confronted by that boy? Can you?'

'He's little more than a child himself. And what child ever thinks before it speaks? Yes, I understand your anger. I'm angry with him myself for his complete thoughtlessness and lack of tact. He was wrong to reveal his identity to Rebeccah, but can't you see the whole episode was an unfortunate accident? Blame me for ever thinking it safe to bring him here . . . I had things to discuss with his aunt and neither of us dreamed that he'd wander off into the gardens after we both told him not to.' Heavily, he sighed. 'If only Rebeccah hadn't told you . . .'

She stared at him in disbelief.

'Did you really think that she wouldn't?'

For a brief moment, no answer. He ran a hand through his dark, wavy hair. 'I'd hoped to be able to talk to her . . . to try to explain in some way . . . before you came back . . . but then you arrived earlier than anyone expected, and I had no chance to. It was too late then.' He sat down at one end of the long, highly polished table and buried his face in his hands. He was acutely aware of her, watching him, waiting for him to speak. It was a moment that he'd never thought would ever come to him, a nightmare. Before his marriage he had had a long affair with a beautiful young widow; the illegitimate son she had given him had always been the pivot of his life, and always would be. But how ever could he explain that to his wife?

'I was very young, and foolish.' He had all her attention now; everything – their relationship, the future, his control over her money – depended on his words. Taking a deep breath, he chose every word with infinite care. 'I've already explained to you how things were between me and my mother . . . more than ten years on, and little's changed. I was always a disappointment to her, a failure. I lacked my father's character and her drive; and there was no one else to replace me. She had to make do with what she had . . . but not a day went by when she didn't make me feel as if she wished I'd never been born. Perhaps you'll never understand how terrible that was . . . I was lonely, adrift. She refused to give me any proper responsibility for the racing stable, or the stud. To get rid of me more than for any better reason, she sent me to Scotland one summer, to check on the youngstock at a little known stud near Perth – that was where I first met Margaret – Jamie's mother . . .'

'Go on.'

'She was my age . . . gentle . . . modest . . . quiet . . .

everything my mother at the same age was not. I was drawn to her. But she'd been married very young, barely seventeen – to a man much older than herself – and he'd been killed in a hunting accident a few months before. She was still in mourning. It was more than a year after that when we – '

Corinna jumped to her feet, and went briskly over to the window. 'Please. Spare me the details!'

'I was trying to explain . . . I want you to understand the way it was . . .'

She spoke without looking at him.

'What I'm waiting to hear is why you found it necessary to bring your whore's bastard into my house!'

'She wasn't a whore! She came from a well respected family.'

'Any woman who behaves as she did is a whore!'

'She was in love with me.'

'In love with who you were and what she could prise out of you, more like!'

'Corinna, please . . . I would have married her . . . especially when she told me that she was . . .' His voice petered into awkward silence; impossible to tell her the truth, word for word. That Margaret McAllister had stormed and wept when he'd told her they could never be married. That he was marrying, instead, a rich American heiress from Kentucky whose father owned the biggest race horse stud in the southern states – because she was bringing with her an enormous dowry that someone as lowly as Margaret could never hope to have. No, he could not tell her that. Nor could he ever tell her that it was Charpentier money, and not his, that had kept Margaret and her son in comfort and luxury for the past ten years.

'I didn't love her, you see . . . I tried to, but I couldn't. I felt wretched. Guilty. As if I'd used her and tossed her aside. If I'd have met you first, before that ill fated trip to Scotland on my mother's business, none of it would ever have happened. There's no comparison between the two of you . . .' He could still only see part of her face; she was still standing in the embrasure of the huge window, half turned away. But he could see by the way her lips had curled upwards at each corner of her mouth that he had salved her vanity. Relief made him breathe more easily. Inwardly, he, too, smiled. How vain women were, and how easily a man could pacify them, by a few words of simple flattery. Even a woman as educated and intelligent as Corinna.

'Please . . .' he came towards her, arms outstretched. He touched her shoulders lightly. 'I hate it when we quarrel. And there's never any need, is there? You know how much I care for you. Margaret meant nothing to me, not ever. You must believe that. I was just a stupid, ignorant young fool, a boy who wanted to prove himself a man . . . more than most, because of the contempt my mother has always had for me, because of the way she's always compared me to my father and found me lacking. And never hesitated to say so to my face. Margaret's admiration was like incense, like balm on an open wound. It was the only way I could blot out the sense of failure.' Yes, that had been the truth, at least, coupled with the fierce, burning need of physical desire for a woman's body, the fierce desire that had often threatened to take over his life; but he could hardly speak of that to his wife. He had so desperately needed a woman's approval, craved it, treasured it; he would always be grateful to Margaret for giving him that. In his mother's presence, he had always felt inadequate, unimportant, diminished; every time he stood before her and looked up at that massive oil painting of his father, he had come close to hating her; a strange hate, that had always jostled with love and pride. She and his father were great monuments, and all his life he had lived in their shadow.

Across the space of the room, the rich Persian carpet, he looked at his wife and felt not for the first time that it had been a mistake to marry her, an American. Only on the surface had she seemed, when they'd first met, little different from the English society girls with whom he mixed at fashionable society balls and sporting events, like Ascot and the Epsom Derby, sought after because of his father's name and his mother's prestige, the good-looking, amiable, charming bachelor; few had ever guessed that the veneer was far apart from the truth. The Brodie Russell racing empire was one of the biggest in England, but he was a mere figurehead; a puppet who had no power behind the scenes; no authority to make important decisions, who had to ask his mother's permission for the purchase even of a single yearling, almost as if in that she could never quite bring herself to trust his judgement. That lack of trust, the way in which she refused to delegate any but the most ordinary tasks, had reduced him to the status of a messenger boy, a status that, over the years, had made him feel angry and bitter. Was it, then, small wonder that he'd consoled himself with a succession of beautiful women and, on occasion, availed himself of the services of others at exclusive 'establishments' in London's fashionable West End? Only women he could dominate, women who were subservient and meek, could salve his wounded pride, bolster his bruised self esteem. Women like Margaret McAllister, the sweet angel of his youth. If only her father had been as rich and powerful as Corinna Charpentier's, how different would his life have been.

He sensed her still-smouldering anger, and, with his uncanny intuition, his deep knowledge of the female psyche, he understood; her outrage stemmed not only from indignation, but from jealousy. The other woman, the shadowy figure from his past; the past she had no part of, the past she could not share. She was jealous of Margaret McAllister, he could almost read the questions in her outraged mind, the questions she would never ask him because her pride forbade it. Had that other woman been more beautiful than she was, had she been more charming, more amusing, had she been more exciting in bed? Did he regret, these past ten years, the choice he had made in marrying her and not the other? She was watching him coldly, her small, white hands clenching and unclenching, a habit that was curiously identical to his mother's and which had always irked him unbearably.

When she at last broke the awkward silence, her question took him off guard.

'Does your mother know that you fathered a bastard?'

Only for a brief moment did he hesitate, considering the far-flung implications of his answer.

'Yes.'

'And she said *nothing* to me?' Again, her anger flared. 'All these years, and she *knew*?'

'Before our marriage, she strongly advised me to tell you . . . but I refused. The reasons, I've already given you. There are many husbands – and always will be – who have secrets from their wives. Things, people, ghosts from their past. Their wives may sometimes suspect that they have certain things hidden, but discretion directs them to behave as if those things did not exist.'

'I don't believe I'm hearing this!' Her voice had risen to a shout, her American accent, much muted by ten years spent in England, became more marked; a sure sign of her anger. 'You dare to tell me to my face that you slept with a whore and fathered a bastard and I'm not supposed to *mind*?'

'I can't wipe out the past!'

'You brought that slut's spawn into my house!'

'He's my son, for God's sake, my own flesh and blood! Do you think I could just turn my back on him? What would you think of any man who could do that, to his own child?' He ran a hand through his thick hair; he was beginning to perspire, heavily. His silk cravat felt as if it was choking him; with the other hand, he pulled at it impatiently to loosen it. 'His mother's been dead these past three years, he's being cared for by her sister. She has children of her own and little time for Jamie. He's at an age when he most needs a father's guidance. That's why she brought him here. It was impossible for me to make the journey to Scotland; with everything I have to attend to here there just isn't time. She wrote to me more than a month ago, saying that he was becoming wild and unmanageable. I suggested that she make the journey down here so that I could have a stern talk to him. And that's the only reason that she brought him here.'

'You waited till my back was turned!'

'Yes, I waited! Because I knew what would happen if you ever found out. And I was right, wasn't I? Far from feeling any compassion for him, you feel only hate and anger.'

'What did you expect, James? That I'd hold out my arms and welcome him into the bosom of the family? After what he did to my daughter . . . our daughter!'

'He made the mistake of telling her who he was, and I was furious with him for it! I left him in no doubt that what he'd done was cruel and thoughtless . . . but most boys are thoughtless at his age. I'd hoped to go to Rebeccah as soon as I found out what had happened, and talk to her . . . try to make her understand. But she'd locked herself in her bedroom and wouldn't let anyone inside, except her governess.'

'And that surprises you?'

'No . . .' he said, heavily. 'No . . .'

'She's a nine-year-old child, for God's sake! Do you have any idea what this has done to her? Can you begin to imagine how she felt when that slut's bastard told her he was her brother? Her brother! If only I'd gotten back just one day sooner, and got my hands on him . . !'

'Corinna, we have to make an end to this! Jamie is mine and there's nothing you or I can do about that. He lives. He breathes. He exists. I love him. I can't blot him out of my life. I don't want to. And I wouldn't . . . not even for you, not even for Rebeccah.'

For a few moments there was silence. The only sounds were the ticking of the clocks and the birdsong from outside the vast window.

'It's because I haven't given you a son, isn't it? That's why you're doing this to me! You refuse to disown him? You intend to see him again?'

'Corinna! He's my son. Can't you understand that I love him as much as I love Rebeccah . . ?'

'You can stand there and say that, to my face?'

'Please . . .'

'Could you go upstairs, now, and say it to your daughter's? She idolized you . . . she worshipped the ground you walked on . . . yes, more than she's ever loved me, her own mother, more than she'll ever love me . . . it's always been you, you, you!' She looked at him with disgust. 'And all the time you've resented not being able to bring him here, to live with you, that bastard!'

'I could rent a small house for part of the year, halfway between here and Epsom for convenience's sake, and have him with me there . . .'

She was outraged.

'Over my dead body you will! Do you have no sense of shame? *Guilt*? Don't you give a damn what people will say and think? That they'll be laughing not just at you, but at me, too! Do you think I'd stand idly by and let that happen?' A harsh, threatening note had come into her voice now. 'If you ever take a house and live with him in it, I'd take Rebeccah and go straight back to my father . . . and you know what he would do . . .'

There was no answer to what she said, and he made none. Any open scandal was unthinkable, even for Jamie's sake. He needed her, even if what he had once thought was love no longer existed; without Charpentier money, he was nothing but his mother's lackey, a well-dressed errand boy. Besides which, there was not only Jamie's upkeep and schooling to be thought of . . . God forbid that she should ever find out the whole truth . . .

Only one other thought tormented him; had Rebeccah discovered anything else that afternoon besides the presence of her half-brother? Jamie had distinctly told him that they had come face to face at the bottom of the old steps. Though he and Margaret had been careful, he had been too engrossed to remember to lock the door from the inside, as an additional precaution; besides which, none of the servants were ever permitted to enter the house by that way. He had told the household staff, and Rebeccah, that the stairs were old and unsafe. But still the nagging doubt would not leave him.

Only one way to find out. But, since the confrontation with Jamie, Rebeccah had refused to come out of her room.

'I should speak with Rebeccah . . .'

'Yes, you should.' Her voice was tart, scornful. 'But don't be surprised if she won't talk with you. Randall says she's hardly eaten a thing since. That she scarcely talks. Randall heard her crying at night, and had to go in to her.' A sneer. 'I hope you're proud of yourself, James. I hope you think that having your bastard here for those snatched hours, was worth what it's done to your daughter.'

He had never struck a woman in his life, had never wanted to; but he ached to strike now. There she stood, smug, victorious. She had the whip hand, had him over a barrel, and she knew it. One word to her father . . . And he knew better than to look for sympathy from his mother.

'Never marry for money,' she'd said, ten years ago, when he'd first told her about his rich, beautiful, American bride to be. 'You can borrow it cheaper.'

'But I love her,' he'd answered, trying to convince himself, trying to prove, for once, that his mother was wrong. But she was never wrong. She hadn't answered him; only raised one perfectly shaped eyebrow for several seconds. He had never been able to fool his mother, nor did he ever try to, after that.

On the desk in his study there was a letter from her, some weeks old, complaining she had not seen him recently, and even this morning he had been thinking of excuses he could give her to delay a trip. Now, as soon as he had seen Rebeccah, he intended to tell his mother by telegram that he was leaving almost immediately.

He felt trapped, stifled, unable to breathe. Through the open windows he could smell the cloying perfume of honeysuckle, sickly and sweet.

'My mother wrote asking me to go down to Epsom as soon as may be. I shall leave first thing tomorrow.'

'Do as you please. Leave tonight. I shan't pine for your company.'

Their voices were formal, clipped, talking to each other like strangers. The desire to get out of the room and the house itself overwhelmed him. Nodding curtly, he turned and left.

Left alone, Corinna went over to the small cabinet in one corner of the room and poured herself a large double brandy. The rich, amber liquid burned her throat, made her eyes water, but she gulped it down, then poured another. For a few moments she sat there in one of the largest chairs, staring into space. Then she got up and tugged impatiently at the bell cord.

'Prepare me a hot bath,' she said, curtly, 'then ask McGrath to wait on me in the morning room.'

'Yes, madam,' the girl answered, curtseying and going out, thinking nothing of two orders which, had her mistress been English and not American, would have been regarded as extremely unusual. English ladies always took their baths in the morning, after rising and before breakfast, and wrote their letters, answered invitations and went over the day's menus in the morning room after breakfast and before lunch; Corinna Russell did not do either.

She got up and walked over to the window and looked out of it, across the pleasing flatness of the lawns, to the rose bushes and avenues of exotic, flowering shrubs, the typical English garden that she had always loved and thought of with fondness whenever she had been away from it; but she did not feel the pleasure that she always had done in the past; the beauty of the garden had been violated by another presence. An unwelcome, hated presence, the presence of a rival against whom she could never hope to win.

She could have fought another woman. Outshone her, outmanoeuvred her, outlasted her; eventually, James would have tired of her and she would have faded away; straying husbands, her Aunt Ellen Mae had always told her, always went back to their wives. The 'other sort', the women who did the chores that wives found unpalatable and tiresome to do, meant nothing, were nothing. Men had no respect for them. Wives, they were to be cherished, spoiled, put on a pedestal, and nothing any other woman could do would topple them off again. Margaret McAllister was one of the 'other women', someone James had amused himself with when he was young and stupid, when he didn't know any better. She was a game, a cheap diversion. Only when she produced a bastard son, did the picture change.

A child was different, something she couldn't fight. It was like he'd said, his own flesh and blood. Always there, always reminding. Taking, stealing from her, stealing part of James from Rebeccah. Whatever the boy did, whatever faults he had, if he grew up into a thief or a murderer, James would stand by him. At that moment she could not decide which of them she hated most.

She continued to stare into the garden but she was only aware of her own anger and misery, her impotent fury against someone who, a few days before, she had not known existed. She wanted revenge. On the boy, on her husband. Clenching and unclenching her fists, she bit her lip and concentrated, then smiled.

Suddenly, she knew what she would do.

The nursery wing, on the other side of the big house, always lay in shadow in the afternoons. Going from the sunny hallway and landing below, James Russell screwed up his eyes as he entered the playroom, where Rebeccah's old nurse sat knitting and gossiping with two maids. As he approached, they got up and curtseyed. He smiled, without speaking, too much on his mind to indulge in meaningless pleasantries.

'She wouldn't eat a bite at breakfast time, sir,' the old nurse said, laying down her knitting. 'And scarce touched her lunch, even though pudding was her favourite today. I told the mistress that child's sickening for something.'

He thanked her and spoke a few words, then continued on his way to Rebeccah's room. Outside the door, he stood for a few moments, trying to compose himself, trying to dispel his feelings of guilt and awkwardness. He had to remember that she was only a child, that she was only nine years old. That made his task both more easy and more difficult. He thought again, uneasily and with an unpleasant lurching of the heart, how Corinna had burst in on him shortly after her return, spilling out a torrent of outrage.

He gave a single rap on the outside of the door, then let himself in.

She was curled up on the window-seat, staring down onto the terrace below her window, a doll clutched in her arms, dark, luxuriant hair hanging loose down her back. At that moment she looked younger than her nine years; smaller, white-faced, vulnerable. He felt a stab of genuine regret that she had been shocked and hurt to find out the truth about Jamie; but he was determined, as much as he loved her, not to deliberately lie to her about his feelings for his son.

'Rebeccah?' he said, softly.

She had looked away from the window as he'd come into her room; he noticed her stiffen. She made no move to jump down and run to him, as she'd always done, and that hurt. But he stayed standing where he was. Gently, he closed the door behind him.

'Hello papa.' The childish voice sounded oddly older, as if

the unpleasant experience had in some way changed her, made her different from before.

'It's a beautiful day. Too fine to be cooped up in here. Why not get Annie to help you down into the gardens with your teddies and dolls? A tea party, under the chestnut tree! There, isn't that a good idea? If Annie has finished her work, she could stay with you in the garden.'

'I had a tea party the other day. I don't ever want another one.' Her voice was cold and flat, and the look in her eyes terrified him, because it was not a look that should be in the eyes of any child. For the first time in his life, he felt like a stranger with his own daughter.

'Rebeccah, I have to go away for several days, to Epsom. I have to see your grandmama on important business, about the new horses. Before I leave, you and I must have a special talk.' He dragged out each word slowly, painfully, as though shackled by his own inadequacy as a student trying to converse in a foreign language. 'I understand from mama that something happened in the garden a few days ago that you . . . that came as a shock and a surprise to you . . .' He waited for her to speak, to murmur something, to move even. Staying still she fastened her vivid blue eyes gravely onto his face, and the discomfort he had felt on coming into the room became coupled with acute embarrassment, and not a small amount of apprehension. Was Jamie the only stranger she had caught sight of that afternoon, or had she, somehow, seen him and Margaret McAllister, on their way to the door on the unused side of the house, the door that was forbidden the servants, the door that she was told never to use, because of the danger of the crumbling staircase behind it? True, she had said nothing to her mother, but Jamie had told him that they'd come face to face when Rebeccah had come out from behind the garden door. Was it possible that she'd only peeped inside it, out of childish curiosity? True, he had heard nothing himself while he had been making love to Margaret, but so urgent had his lust for her been that he doubted he would have heard anyone on the staircase. His daughter's face gave him no clues; nor could he bring himself to ask her. How could he? Ineptly, he felt his way forward like a blind man, stumbling, groping in the dark. 'It was that sunny afternoon, the afternoon that Annie helped you to take your dolls down onto the lawn . . .'

She spoke, suddenly, unexpectedly, taking him by surprise.

'I saw a boy, and he laughed at me and said he was my brother. Is that the truth, papa?'

Relief that she had finally broken her silence, that she was making the embarrassing ordeal a little easier for him, made his handsome face break into a smile.

'He is your half-brother, Rebeccah, and his name is Jamie Russell. He's several years older than you are; he was born a long time before I met your mother . . .' He went on smiling, the words came easier now. He sat down beside her on the window seat and took her small, pale, child's hand in his. 'Jamie's mother died, when he was little older than you are. His aunt and uncle are his guardians now. Soon, in the autumn, he must go away to school.'

She turned her face towards his, and looked intensely into it, screwing up her eyes as if they hurt her, as she might do by staring too closely at the sun.

'How long were you married to his mother, papa?'

An awkward silence, while he glanced away, his brain racing for the right words. So, it was not to be easy after all.

'Jamie's mother and I were never married, Rebeccah . . . he is what we call illegitimate . . .'

'Did you not want to marry her? Did she not want to marry you?'

'She did, but it was impossible. I had certain pressing obligations . . . too complicated for you to understand.' She was looking away from him now, down into her cupped hands, as if what he had said was too much for her mind to absorb at once. 'One day, perhaps, Jamie can live with us. When he is not away at school. One day, perhaps . . .' He spoke wistfully, almost to himself; Corinna would never permit it. But there were ways, there had to be ways. Wasn't his mother's favourite saying 'There is always something you can do about everything?' Odd, that any words of hers could comfort him, give him hope, now. But thinking of them heartened him. He put his arm around Rebeccah. 'Because Jamie is my son, does not mean that I love you less. You do understand that?'

Without answering in words she looked back into his face, searching it with her beautiful eyes. Those, too, she had from his mother; Corinna's were paler and always cold.

'Is mama still angry?'

He sighed, the smile on his lips vanishing like the sunshine outside the window. There would be rain, later, making his journey to London and then Epsom tiresome and more miserable. 'Yes, I'm afraid she is, because I have never explained to her before about Jamie. She thinks that I may have loved Jamie's mother more than I love her. But she's very wrong to think that. When she realizes the truth, then she'll no longer be angry.'

'I'm afraid when mama is angry.'

'No need to be.' He squeezed her hand, then kissed her cheek, lightly. He stood up, aware of the time and all he had yet to do, anxious to be gone and on his way, yet unwilling to leave her too abruptly. 'Be a good girl while papa is gone.'

She gazed after him, at the empty room; outside, along the passage, she could hear his footsteps dying away, then the distant chatter from the nursery. He would pause for a few moments there, making polite small talk with the three women; she could visualize their faces looking up at him – she had already noticed how all women, even servants, looked at her father – smiling at him while he smiled back, charming them, never speaking to them in the brusque manner that some masters used when speaking to their underlings. Unbidden, the scene in the lavender-draped bedroom came back to her, and she shuddered, trying to shut it out by closing her eyes, by thinking of other things; she wondered what her old nurse, and Annie, and the other maids would have thought of him if they knew the truth, if they'd seen him naked, as she had, doing unspeakable things to the body of that strange woman.

A clock chimed somewhere in the depths of the house. Soon, time for tea. She had no appetite still. She felt oddly, uncomfortably changed since that afternoon in the garden, like waking from an unpleasant dream. Except that Jamie was not a dream; he was real, her father's flesh and blood, and she hated him. Because of him her father was different, because of him everything had changed. Nothing would ever be the same again. And her father had lied to her. He had said the woman who brought Jamie to the house had been his aunt, but she knew that was not true; Jamie had told her who the woman was. The woman was his mother. Her father had told her that she'd died, five years ago, and her childish mind tried to find a reason why he had told her a deliberate lie.

She wondered what he had told her mother. The same lie, no doubt. But she could never bring herself to speak about it to anyone else. The secrets of the lavender-draped bedroom would remain locked away, inside her.

Moving closer to the window she stared down, miserably, into the gardens below; the breeze was gathering strength now. The evening would be chilly, perhaps it would rain. She pressed her face hard against the window pane, and a single tear welled up in the corner of her eye, then ran down her cheek and onto the cushion beside her.

She had always, perversely, wanted a brother, often wondered if she ever would; but not like this. Her mother's son, not some strange woman's; a boy who laughed and smiled, kindly, a boy who would join in her games, not one who sneered and mocked, taunting her. *I'm older than you are*, he'd said, his cold, grey eyes harsh as they'd looked down on her; *I'm the first-born, the most important. Father even made sure that I was given his name. Jamie Russell.* Another sneer. *He loves me best, I heard him say so . . . you're only a girl. One day, this house, all the studs, everything . . . they'll all be mine, you'll see. Father will make me his heir . . .*

She put her hands over her ears and pressed down hard, trying to blot out the hateful voice. The lump in her throat grew bigger, and the tears were burning and hot behind her eyes. Suddenly, across the room, hanging from a nail on the wall, she caught sight of a calendar; last year's, Annie had left it there because the picture was so pretty.

A year ago, a whole year . . . if only she could go back in time to then.

3

OUTSIDE THE DOOR of the drawing room, James Russell hesitated, hand poised above the handle; but he let it fall back against his side. No, he could not face her now; not yet, not so soon after their violent quarrel, so soon after the ordeal upstairs. All his life, he had hated scenes, loathed confrontations; so different from his mother with her fire, her energy, her fighting spirit. Yes, he had been a bitter disappointment to the celebrated Anna Brodie Russell. And, now, he was estranged from all three women in his life.

Dejectedly, he turned away and went to his study. For a long while he sat there at his desk, head in hands, staring down but not seeing the muddle of papers spread carelessly across the top of it; sales sheets, bills of sale for stock to the stud; letters as yet unanswered. Half-heartedly, he began to sort them into piles, into some semblance of order. Then, halfway through, he left them and rang for his secretary. McGrath would see to it. McGrath was always there when he needed him; dependable, clever, thorough. He sighed.

'I'm leaving for Epsom within the hour. I'll take the carriage to London, then finish the journey by train.' He leaned back in his wing chair. 'Are there any papers that need my signature before I go?'

'None that won't keep till your return, my lord. Except these.' McGrath was holding several pieces of paper in his hand, paper that looked like bills. As Russell took them, frowning, he saw that each one bore the printed heading of a fashionable London couturier. 'I was about to bring them to you, when you called for me. They arrived earlier today, and

I would normally deal with them as all the other personal bills are dealt with. Except that I noticed that the dates on which the purchases were made were all dates during which Lady Russell was away in America.'

'There must be some mistake.'

'My feeling also, my lord. Would you care to ask Lady Russell if she knows anything of the matter, or shall I simply return them to the accounts manager, explaining that there must be some kind of error?'

Russell studied them more carefully for a few moments. 'No, I shan't trouble my wife. It's clearly a mistake. See . . . this bill, for a ball gown in amber satin with black lace scallops? My wife hates amber. She would never order any gown in that particular shade.' He handed the bills back to McGrath. 'Return them, with a covering letter, signed on my behalf.'

'Of course, my lord. I'm sorry to have troubled you, but I did think it best to check with you before I took it upon myself to act. Will there be anything else?'

'Only these papers . . .' he pointed to the muddle on the desk top. 'After I've left, if you would . . .'

'Yes, my lord. And I wish you a safe and pleasant journey. Please convey my respects to the dowager Lady Russell.'

Russell smiled, despite the heavy feeling of depression, that weighed on him like a massive stone.

'McGrath, you know how much my mother hates being called by that absurd name . . .'

Corinna Russell placed a marker in the book that lay open on her lap; then she closed it and put it to one side. Beyond the drawing room door, she could hear the usual, familiar sounds of departure; servants' hurrying footsteps, voices raised, luggage being brought down from the floor above and deposited in the hall. Another quarter of an hour, and he would be gone.

She was still too distracted and too angry to continue with her reading; she had only picked up the book, after all, to keep her hands busy after he had left her, to stop the shaking in her wrists, to force her mind to think of what she intended to do. Later, she would go upstairs and see Rebeccah, but not now. Now, she needed to be completely alone, she needed to think. If only she had stayed in Kentucky longer, if only she had never come back; then, she might never have learned the truth. She thought, now, bitterly, of the first time she had ever seen him, how she had given him all her love. How her friends had envied her, how the society newspapers had written about their magnificent wedding, how she, Corinna Charpentier Russell, was one of the greatest acknowledged beauties of the Prince of Wales' select circle, and the Court. How empty those words seemed now, how worthless. Yes, he would pay dearly for this betrayal.

She waited for a short while longer. Then, with a bitter smile playing faintly at the corners of her lips, she left the room and made her way to his study.

It had been useless trying to enlist the help of his private secretary; McGrath was totally loyal. But she would find what she was looking for without his aid; she was not her father's daughter for nothing. Once inside the room, she turned and locked the door then leaned against it, looking around her.

In total contrast to the rest of the house, the study was stark, almost spartan, in its simplicity. White walls, uncluttered mantelpiece that bore only a single clock; plain carpets, plain curtains; not a single print or painting adorned the bare walls. Only the massive oak desk, with its intricately carved and brass inlaid edging, and elaborate cabriole legs, stood out, a single thing of beauty. At one side, stood a heavy gilded inkwell; on the other, a massive silver candelabra.

Slowly, she walked over to the desk and sat down behind it in his big leather wing chair, her hands spread upon the polished surface. Then, carefully, methodically, she went through every drawer, every piece of paper, not even certain of what she was looking for, or what she expected to find; only her instinct spurred her on. The last drawer was locked.

There was no key in any of the other drawers. If she sent for McGrath to ask him where it was kept, he would either say that her husband had taken it with him, or that he had no knowledge of where it was kept; this was, after all, the private study. McGrath would only have access to the papers that were kept in the stud office, relating to the racehorses or the breeding stock. Unlikely that James would hide personal papers there. Where else? She gazed around the room, her eyes lighting on the single cabinet that stood against the opposite wall. But, again, she was to be disappointed; it contained only cut glass decanters of brandy, sherry and liqueur.

She was about to give up and leave when, passing by the desk on her way back to the door, her vast flowing skirt brushed against the gilded inkwell and knocked it to the floor, and, instead of a gush of ink spilling out onto the carpet, the top came off and out fell a single key. With a gasp of surprise and delight, she picked it up and fitted it to the lock. Smoothly, silently, it turned, and the drawer came open.

It was stuffed with papers. Bills of sale for yearlings; stock checks, notes and letters from a host of people; his stud manager, his mother's trainer; statements of account from his tailor, hatter, the secretary of his London club. Again and again she sifted through them, taking care to keep them in the same order in which they were found, reading and re-reading each one in case there was a clue which she had missed. But there was nothing unusual, nothing incriminating, nothing at all to link him to the Scottish slut or her bastard boy.

Angrily, disappointed, Corinna re-locked the drawer and replaced the key.

There seemed no point in staying. Letting herself out, she went upstairs into her boudoir, and rang for her maid.

'Esme? Lay out my gown for this evening, then bring me my jewel box and let me choose something suitable to go with it.' She sat down at her ornate dressing table and stared into the mirror, while the girl, sensing her mistress's mood, busied herself with her usual tasks in silence.

Her own reflection gazed back at her, sad, dull-eyed, another face. Was it only yesterday that she'd been so carefree, so happy, eager to be home with him again? Strange, how fate decreed otherwise; that Rebeccah had, by accident, come face to face with that boy; that he had said what he had said to her; that she had told her mother. If only any of those three things had never happened, how different the expression on the face that stared back at her now would be. If only, if only. She got up, suddenly, unexpectedly, startling Esme, and began to pace the room, clenching and unclenching her fists. She was glad she knew. Grateful. Grateful that now, after ten long years she had finally found out the truth. Had he been laughing at her for all that time? Had he lain with his cursed Scottish mistress and made fun of her, her the foreigner, the American who had only given him a daughter, not the son and heir he always craved, for being ignorant of his past? Other men had bastards, and she could have forgiven him, had he promised her that he would never see the boy again. But the way he had sprung to his bastard's defence, refused to give him up, had embittered and alienated her.

'My lady?' She turned, sharply, at Esme's voice, close to her ear. She was holding out the jewel casket, and as she looked down into the padded velvet depths, each piece that winked and glittered seemed a mockery.

The emerald and topaz wristbands, with matching necklace and small tiara, that he had given her as a wedding present; the sapphire earrings and choker that he had given her on their first anniversary; the gold and emerald choker, with matching ear clips and bracelet, that he had given her for her last birthday. With cold, unfeeling eyes she stared down at the tokens of his love that had once meant everything to her, and felt nothing but a heavy anger. He had lied to her; he had deceived her, and she knew in her heart that she would never be able to forgive him.

There remained the boy. Did he intend, she pondered, to make the bastard Jamie Russell his heir, if anything, God forbid, ever happened to Rebeccah? There was the question of his will; everything, she'd always taken for granted, would be left to her and Rebeccah in trust, with her as the chief executrix of that trust. But she could no longer take anything for granted, for she no longer believed in him. Could it be that he had had the gall to divide his estate equally, between Jamie and his legitimate daughter, leaving Rebeccah with only half of that to which she was entitled? The thought enraged her, only further strengthening her resolve to do what she had already decided to do.

'Will you wear the rubies this evening, my lady?' Esme was asking now, still holding the casket with its bright, glittering contents before her. 'They go so well with your red velvet gown . . .'

Corinna turned and looked at the girl as if she was only now aware of her presence. Then she looked back at the rubies, glistening against the background of the green which lined the casket, like great drops of blood. She smiled, but her eyes were set and cold.

'Yes, the rubies tonight, Esme. The rubies will go very well.'

As soon as she was alone again, she took paper and ink from her small escritoire and sat down in front of it, chewing for a moment on the end of her pen. Then she wrote, in her large, bold hand, '*Dear Papa.*'

4

THE GREAT HOUSE loomed up at him, as it always did, from beyond the line of trees as he gazed, impatiently, from the carriage window; past the gatehouse, along the drive, its mellow brick and welcoming black oak timbers bathed with the gentle, restful light of oncoming dusk. He understood, each time he saw it, why his mother loved it so much and why it was so important to her.

He remembered how, as a child, she would tell him the story of how she'd first seen it, and wanted it; how she'd schemed and fought, against all odds, to make it hers. He could see the drive as once she'd seen it – tangled, neglected, overgrown with weeds and thicket – and as if he was seeing it all again, but through her eyes, more than fifty years ago, he saw the thistles and shoulder-high cow parsley, growing up between the stones, the wood and brick of the house itself moss-covered and rotting.

She would have walked along the overgrown drive, leading her horse by his reins – or perhaps have tethered him at the gatehouse – her long, black hair loose and flowing to her waist, riding crop in her gloved hand, unafraid of the silence and the dark loneliness of the empty building, unafraid of ghosts, of oncoming darkness. Unexpectedly, he felt a lump rising in his throat. If only he had known her then, if only he could have gone back in time. Perhaps, then, they would have been, might have been, close as they were not close now. But it was too late. Whatever she had wanted him to be, expected him to be, he had disappointed her.

As the carriage drew to a halt in the courtyard and her

grooms came forward to attend to the horses, he got out before her butler and a manservant could help him, and began to pull down his own luggage.

It had already started, that old feeling of uneasiness in her presence, that old feeling of uselessness and inadequacy, that he felt that he had to make so foolish and empty a gesture as the getting down of his own baggage.

He politely returned the servants' greetings, politely answered their usual questions about the health of his wife, his daughter, the pleasantness of his journey.

The light in the great hall was soft and restful, as she liked it to be; he looked around him, as if he was seeing it all for the first time; at the polished, heavy oak furniture that she preferred to the light and modern, at the oil paintings of long-dead racehorses in their gilded frames that she had bred and trained and ridden; she had achieved so much and he so little, every time he saw them he felt dwarfed by her; unimportant, unregarded, a nothing. Then he stopped, abruptly, as he always did when he drew level with the bottom of the staircase, and looked up. There, on the wall at the top of the stairs was the lifesized painting of his father, Ralph Russell.

For a few moments he was silent. He stared at it; wistfully, painfully, wondering why, not for the first time, he had inherited nothing of his father's strength of character, none of the things that had made his father the man he was. Turning away, he walked ahead of the butler to the sitting room where, at this time of the evening, she would be.

For a moment he faltered; walking into her presence was always an experience that unnerved him; even as a little boy, he had always been in awe of her. So anxious to please, so adoring, so proud of her, his famous, clever, beautiful mother. The painting of her as she'd been, more than fifty years before, hung opposite the door, above the great wing chair on which she was seated; the beauty of her face as it had been then never failed to take his breath away. She looked up when the door opened, her lips not quite smiling, the blue eyes still piercing and clear. Even in old age, Anna Brodie Russell was striking, the old, powerful presence of her youth still there in an old woman's body.

'I received your telegram,' she said, without any greeting, motioning him to a seat. 'Well, what is it this time? Have you gone and saddled yourself with a stallion you can't breed from, or another barren mare?'

Lightly, he bent forward and kissed her cheek, then sat down, heavily, in the chair beside her.

'She knows.' He looked down at his hands, lying like pieces of flotsam in his lap. 'Mother, Corinna's found out about Margaret and Jamie.'

For a few moments she stared at him.

'How?'

'It happened while she was away, her visit to her family in Kentucky.' He heard his own voice as if it were someone else's; hollow, hesitant. He could not quite look her in the face, for he knew what she was thinking, what she would say. He knew her well.

'You bloody fool James!' Agile as a thirty-year-old, she sprang from her chair and began to pace the room, clenching and unclenching her fists. 'Dear God! Can any son of mine really be that stupid? You brought your mistress and that boy to the house, *while Rebeccah was there* . . ?'

He, too, sprang to his feet.

'Mother . . . I thought it was safe. Rebeccah was playing in the garden. I told Jamie to stay indoors, to stay out of her sight.'

Her angry eyes blazed at him.

'And you really thought he would? You really believe he'd do anything you say?' She looked at him with a kind of disgust, as if he were a clumsy page boy who'd spilled food on the carpet. 'If you weren't so blind, if you didn't think the sun shone out of his no-good arse, you'd see him for what he is! A cold-blooded little opportunist, waiting in the wings for you to do great things for him . . . knowing, as he already does, that he can twist you around his little finger.'

'That isn't true.'

'It is true. James, I've warned you before and I'll warn you again now. That boy will use your love for him to destroy anything that stands in his way. I could see it in his eyes, that time you brought him here, two years ago. He knows what he is, a bastard without an inheritance. And it rankles.'

'Mother, for Christ's sake, the boy's only fourteen!'

'I learned how to hate, long before I was that age. I knew what it was to feed on vengeance and bitterness. But I was different. I had some vestiges of decency and kindness to redress the balance; and my father wanted to marry my mother. James, face the truth. You used Margaret McAllister. And you love the boy so much because you don't have a legitimate male heir.'

For a few moments there was silence between them, broken only by the gentle ticking of the clocks and the crackling of the fire.

'I thought you would understand, that you'd feel close to Jamie . . . because once you had nothing, and you had to fight.'

Her lips twisted into a wry smile.

'That's right. I did have to fight for it. I fought for everything I wanted, everything I had a right to get. The boy is different. He doesn't want to fight for it; he doesn't want to fight for anything. He's too lazy, too stuffed full of his own importance. And why should he lift a finger to get anything, when he thinks, and expects, his doting father to hand it to him on a platter? He reminds me of a man I was once married to, before your father . . . and in spite of what you feel for him, I doubt very much if he really feels the same about you . . .'

Slowly, James turned away and went to stand beside the fire. He stared into it, holding out his hands towards the blaze, watching the leaping, multicoloured flames dart in and out of the piled wood and coal. Wearily, he closed his eyes, conscious of his mother standing behind him.

'Mother, I didn't come here to quarrel with you.'

'You came here because you've quarrelled with Corinna and you want to keep your distance from her for a few days, till she gets over what's happened. Am I right? And, having given your nine-year-old daughter the shock of her life, you don't know how to handle that, either. So you want a haven and you want my advice.'

He spun round; her lips were turned up at the corners in a ghost of a smile. How well she knew him! 'If you were me . . . what would you do?'

'If I were you, do you really think I would be in this situation?'

He stared back down into the leaping flames, avoiding her eyes.

'No, mother. No, you wouldn't. I'm the only fool in the family. I have realized that by now.' His son's face rose up to him through the flames, the grey eyes mocking; he had failed him. So much, he had wanted Corinna to give him a son. But Rebeccah's birth had been difficult, so long, so painful . . . and then, no more children. He had always thought, secretly, to himself, that it would make no difference to him, that it would not matter; he had always reminded himself of what his mother had achieved, single-handed, alone; it was not essential for a man to have a legitimate son. But as much as he loved Rebeccah, Jamie had always been first with him; the first born, the special one. Jamie was perfect in his eyes. If only his mother understood.

'And Corinna?'

He turned back to face her.

'You can imagine how she took it. Badly. She demanded that I have nothing further to do with him . . . my own son! A woman's logic.' He sighed, heavily. 'As if I, more than any man, could turn my back on my own flesh and blood.'

'Does she know that you use her father's money to keep the boy and his mother in luxury?' A sharp note to her voice.

'Hardly luxury! Comfort, yes, but not luxury.'

'That doesn't answer my question.'

'Do you really think I could tell her the truth? She assumes the money has been coming from my own pocket, from the profits of the stud. I don't discuss business with her, nor the state of my personal affairs. She'd be astonished, no doubt, to learn that far from being a shareholder in the company, I have no more status than any other senior employee.'

Anna noted the bitterness in his voice, the strong hint of rebuke; but she ignored it.

'You're my son, James, my only son. And I love you, despite everything, despite the things you've done, despite the many differences between us. But on one subject my mind remains made up. As I've said before, nothing you've ever done in your life has convinced me that I can trust you to manage the affairs of the racing stable and the stud with sufficient skill to merit my turning over one or the other wholly to you. Within a year, you'd go bankrupt. No, don't bother to deny it. I know you, like the palm of my hand. Generous. Extravagant. Wasteful. You don't mean to be. Your intentions, aspirations, they're always good, your motives are the best. But, somehow, nothing you do ever turns out right.' She went over to the little table in the corner of the room and poured two glasses of brandy. 'It took me and your father a lifetime to build up what exists now. I can't, won't, hand it over to you lock, stock and barrel, and risk what would happen . . . for Rebeccah's sake.'

'You mean her to have everything?'

'Don't worry, I've been generous to you in my will. It would be wrong of me not to be. And I've left you shares in both the stud and the bloodstock, with certain limited powers should I die while Rebeccah is still under age. But I've left nothing to chance, James. To leave you with sole control of everything would be inviting disaster. You have no sense of business and no acumen. Your daughter deserves more than that.'

So, Rebeccah was to get all. In silence, he walked over to the window and parted the thick, heavy drapes, peering out into the gathering dusk. He thought, morosely, of the future; the promises he had made to Jamie's mother, his heavy debts, keeping up appearances to Corinna's father. He had always suspected that his mother had never quite trusted him, but he never thought that she would do this. For a moment the shock had robbed him of the ability to speak.

'If you hadn't sent me the telegram,' her voice came to him from across the room, 'I would have written to you again. I've heard rumours, from a certain source . . . about you.'

Swiftly, he spun round, startled.

'Since when has Anna Brodie Russell ever listened to common gossip?'

'Since it said that my son has been gambling too heavily and too often.'

He shrugged, too casually to fool her.

'I don't delude myself that I have no enemies. And I gamble as much as any other man in my position, when the odds are right. But only then. I play the occasional game of cards, yes, but only on social gatherings, when it would be considered churlish and ill-mannered to refuse. One can't be a member of the Royal set and not play cards. Baccarat is HRH's favourite game.'

'HRH has more money to play with than you do.'

He gave her a look of reproach that she interpreted only too well.

'Yes, I made a small fortune in my youth, James. But I didn't sweat and suffer to let you throw it all away.'

'You really despise me, don't you?'

The blue eyes clouded over sadly. How little he understood her.

'You're part of myself, part of the man I loved. All I have left of him. And I wish that you were more like both of us than you are. But never accuse me of despising you. If the best stallion and the best mare I ever had produced a foal that never won a race in its life, do you think that I would care for it less?'

There were tears in her eyes. He could not remember when he had last seen her cry.

Rebeccah sat at one end of the long dining table and her mother at the other, eating in silence, not speaking, even between courses. This was a special occasion, an unprecedented treat, for her to be permitted to sit at dinner with her mother. But the specialness of the occasion was marred by the strained atmosphere, the cheerless gloom that hung about them like heavy curtains.

She could tell from the red marks about her mother's eyes that she had been crying; and she could guess the reason why. She had little appetite for the delicious food, even leaving half of her bowl of strawberries and cream, her favourite dessert. At the far end of the table, she noticed how her mother, too, picked listlessly at the array of rich dishes, scarcely doing justice to the cook's expertise.

Finally, when the meal was over and the servants had cleared away the table, her mother dismissed them.

For a few moments, they sat looking at each other; then Corinna Russell got up and went to stand beside the window. It was dark now, and she could see nothing; but she went on staring into the blackness, as if gazing at something outside that she alone could see.

'Rebeccah? What did your father say to you . . . about the boy?' She turned, suddenly, unexpectedly, as she asked the question and stared into her daughter's face, as if she was willing her not to hide anything he might have said to her.

Rebeccah stood up when her mother spoke.

'He said . . . he said he was my half-brother, that his name was Jamie Russell. He said that one day soon he would be going away, to school.' She sensed her mother's smouldering rage, kept under tight control, and it frightened her, without her understanding why.

'Is that all he told you about him?'

'Yes. Yes, I think so.'

Corinna turned, suddenly.

'Are you sure, Rebeccah?'

'Yes, mama.'

Her mother leaned down and took her by the shoulders. 'I want you to do something for me. I want you to listen carefully. When your father comes back from Epsom, I want you to ask him the date of Jamie's birthday. Tell him you want to know because you want to make him a birthday card. Then try to find out from him where in Scotland Jamie was born. Can you do that for me, Rebeccah?'

'Yes, mama. But I don't understand. I don't want to send him a birthday card. He's mean and hateful, and I never want to see him again. He laughed at me, because I didn't know about him. And I don't understand why you don't ask papa yourself.'

Corinna let go her shoulders and paced the room, her satin skirts swishing like the tail of an angry cat.

'You don't have to understand, Rebeccah; just do as I say. There's something I must find out and I can't do that without certain pieces of information. If I asked your father myself, he'd know what I wanted them for. He'd be suspicious, he wouldn't tell me. Besides which, this is a secret, a secret between you and me.' She knelt beside her daughter and grasped her hard, staring into her face. 'You must understand. This is a secret, Rebeccah. You must tell no one that I've asked you to do this, not even Annie.'

Rebeccah gazed at her mother, so beautiful, so graceful, always smelling of exotic French perfume. She wondered how her father could ever have loved anyone else.

'No, mama . . . I'll never tell.'

5

ANNA SAT BESIDE THE FIRE in her room, one of the hide-bound picture albums that she cherished lying open on her lap and, with a faint smile, she slowly turned the pages, hesitating and studying each one.

There were the earliest pictures, looking muted and blurred, of herself, and her sister Clara, their children standing beside them with false, regimental stiffness, staring into the camera; an old daguerreotype of Jessie, dear Jessie, now long dead, who had had to be cajoled and persuaded to pose for the photographer; she sat there, heavy jaw set in disapproval for this silly, new-fangled photography business, glaring at the camera as if it held a loaded gun pointed at her head. Smiling, Anna turned over the page.

James, as a child; James with her, with her and his father; with his father alone. James on his first pony, James dressed in soldier's uniform with his cousins, all standing proudly to attention. James at fifteen, eighteen, twenty-one. James on his wedding day. The smile faded, the hand that held the picture album shook very slightly. The face that stared back at her from the photograph betrayed nothing, like a mask. The eyes were blank, sightless, showing neither happiness nor sadness, not even indifference; what, she wondered, had he been thinking? That he was free of her, that he could manage alone, that the marriage of convenience with an American heiress who thought he had married her for love would solve all his problems? He would never tell her; not then, not now. Ever since his first act of recklessness and stupidity, a gulf had come between them, and only become wider with the passage of time.

She remembered her own anger, her own sense of impotent outrage when he had first told her about Margaret McAllister and the boy; not from any sense of old fashioned morality because that had never been her way. But the endless implications, the problems that she could foresee in front of him because of that single act of youthful folly. Not from Margaret McAllister, that gentle, unambitious simpleton, but from the boy Jamie, as hard and as unyielding as the rocks from his native Scotland. Jamie would become a force to be reckoned with. And her son was too blind to see it.

For a long while she sat there, gazing into the fire but not seeing it, her thoughts running wild and unleashed. Then she reached over to the small rosewood cabinet beside her bed and took out a small ivory locket.

Originally, it had been gilded and set with small diamond chippings, but with the passage of time the gilt had become worn and faded and some of the minute stones were missing; but the painted miniature inside seemed as bright and as fresh as the first time she had ever seen it. She opened the ivory top, and laid the picture side by side with one of the photographs in the hide-bound album, struck again by the startling likeness between them; the miniature had been of her mother as a young girl; the photograph, of her granddaughter, Rebeccah. She continued gazing at them for a long while. Then she put the ivory miniature back into the drawer of the rosewood cabinet and the picture album back in its place on the little table in the corner of the room, and got to her feet.

The house was shrouded in peace and silence at this time of night; most of her servants had long been in bed. Pulling her dressing gown closer around her, her long hair, silver-grey, loosely hanging down her back in a single, thick plait, she made her way along the wide landing to the other side of the house, where the light still showed beneath her son's bedroom door.

She knocked, then went inside before he had time to answer.

'You're still awake, then?'

'I couldn't sleep.'

He was lying fully dressed on top of the big, brocade-hung four-poster bed, paper and pen on the small table beside him.

'Your conscience, James?'

In a moment he was on his feet.

'Mother, I don't want another argument with you. About anything. I had my fill of arguments with Corinna before I left Suffolk.'

She closed the door and sat down.

'James, you have problems and you won't solve them by running away from them. No man can hide from himself. I'm your mother and I love you; I'll help you if I can. But you know as well as I do that your wife is different from an Englishwoman because she isn't one. I warned you when you told me that you intended to marry an American, and now you can see that I was right. If she were English and she'd found out about Margaret, Jamie and your past, she'd grin and bear it; she'd keep a stiff upper lip and her mouth shut, gliding through house parties and Royal Ascot as if nothing had happened and neither of you would ever speak about it. The English aristocracy never wash their dirty linen in public. Adultery, bastards and buggery are all swept firmly under the carpet, and that's where they stay. But not with Corinna Charpentier of Kentucky. I told you before you married her and I'm telling you now . . . unless you provide for Jamie and then put him firmly out of your life, she'll never give you a moment's peace. Believe me. She won't forgive and forget. She won't knuckle under. She wasn't brought up that way and nothing you can do or say to her will ever change her mind. Look at the other American heiresses that have married into the aristocracy over here – Consuelo Vanderbilt ran off with a Frenchman because she was bored with her husband, and Livia Van Treevenburg made a scene in the middle of the Ambassadors' ball because she found out her husband's ex-mistress had been included on the guest list. She took all her money and went back to New Jersey. Do you want that to happen to you?'

Beads of sweat had appeared along his forehead.

'For God's sake, mother, she couldn't leave me. She can't. It would cause a scandal!'

'Do you really think she'd care about that?'

'She'd never do it. She'd never leave Rebeccah!'

'What's to stop her taking her own daughter with her? It's been done before.'

'I wouldn't allow it! She can't take Rebeccah out of the country without my permission.'

'On a visit to her family in the United States? Come, James, don't be so naive. All she has to do is let it be known that she and Rebeccah are going to the Charpentiers for a holiday. Nothing more natural. What you won't know until it's too late is that Corinna won't be coming back.'

'She couldn't get away with it. I'm Rebeccah's father and I have sole jurisdiction over her. To take her away without my permission would be against the law!'

'And if you instituted proceedings in a court, what of the publicity you fear? Everything you're fighting to keep a secret would be public knowledge, you know that.' She got to her feet, and began to pace the room. 'You're a fool, James! Instead of rushing here to me to lick your wounds because your wife has found out you've been cheating on her, you should have used your head and stood your ground; she'd have thought more of you. Don't try to tell me that you're not used to charming and lying to your women – and I long ago lost count of how many there've been – couldn't you have swallowed your bloody pride and lied to your wife? After all, you've been lying to her for the last ten years!'

'I told her that Jamie's mother was dead! God forgive me, it was the only way. I told her that the boy is being brought up by Margaret's sister . . . in case anyone saw her that day at the house and wondered who she was. But I couldn't renounce Jamie. Is that what you expected me to do? Mother, he's my own flesh and blood. When you were his age you told me that you and your sister were renounced by your father. Are you telling me now that you think that is the honourable thing to do?'

She looked at him hopelessly.

'I'm not Jamie, and you are nothing like my father. The circumstances were different, James. My father met my mother after his marriage – not before. If Jamie meant so much to you, you should have married his mother and not Corinna Charpentier. You did so for the basest of reasons . . . money. And I warned you what the consequences would be if you went ahead and made a marriage of convenience instead of one for love – even though other men have been doing it for the last few hundred years – but you wouldn't listen. You knew what you were doing. You had it all worked out. Except that it didn't work out the way you thought it would, did it, James? You caught a fox. You thought she'd be putty in your hands, that you could do anything you liked and she'd never find out, or that, even if she did, she'd be so grateful that you'd married her, she wouldn't care. You were wrong about that, too. You'd never take advice from me or from your father, you only have yourself to blame. And if you reckoned on that yankee girl you were so anxious to marry because she came in the same package as her father's dollars, knuckling under to the notion that she was playing second fiddle to other women and keeping your bastards into the bargain, then you never made a worse error of judgement in all your life.'

Despite his weariness, temper flared.

'I didn't just marry Corinna for the money. You know that! If I hadn't wanted her as well, it would never have worked. And we've been happy for the last ten years!'

'Is that why you've never broken off your affair with Margaret McAllister, and slept with more women that I care to think about?'

'That isn't fair! How could I turn my back on Margaret when she'd given me Jamie? When she'd stood by me, through thick and thin? Never making demands, never nagging, never threatening to tell my wife? She deserved more than that!'

'And you gave it her. Don't think I don't know about the cottage you bought her, the generous allowance for her clothing and food. And your plans to send her son to an expensive public school!'

He wheeled round on her, stunned.

'How did you find out about that?'

'I still have my contacts in Scotland, James. Remember that it was on my business that you were first sent there, and where you met her. The Perth stud is still one of the finest in the country. I hear things.'

'So somebody is spying on me. Is that what you're saying?'

She gave him one of her maddening smiles.

'If the cap fits.'

'You would say that, wouldn't you? You're taking Corinna's part!' Suddenly, a suspicion dawned, and he stared at her, trying to read her thoughts. 'You want her to find out everything, don't you? All the other women, the affairs, even though most of them mean nothing to me. You want her to leave me and come here with you, because you know she'll bring Rebeccah! Rebeccah . . . that's all you really care about!'

'How little you understand me, James.' There was sadness in her voice now. 'You think I would ever take sides against my only son? Yes, I care about Rebeccah. She is the innocent one, the one who will be hurt the most if there was ever an estrangement between you and her mother. I don't ever want her to suffer. And, while there is breath in my body, I don't ever intend that she shall.'

He sank onto the edge of the bed, his head in his hands. He was tired, weary through and through. The journey, the violent quarrel with Corinna . . . desperately, he needed to sleep, though he knew that he would not.

She was standing near the door now, her hand on the latch, the dim light of the lamps on the mantelpiece and beside his bed picking out the threads of silver in her long hair. She had often stood like this, he remembered, when he was a little boy and she had come to kiss him goodnight. The picture he had of her was frozen in time, framed in his thoughts. The slim, graceful figure, with the black hair falling to her waist, the startling blue of her eyes. Unexpectedly, he felt a lump, big as a fist, rising in his throat, and he could not speak. Somewhere, in the passage of time, he had lost her.

'I suppose the fault is mine,' she said, opening the door, going further away from him, 'I always thought that, if I had a son, he would be exactly like his father. That was my mistake, James, and I'm sorry for it. I've always expected too much of you.' Without saying goodnight, she went out, closing the door behind her. And the room was empty; he was alone.

Rebeccah lay there in the darkness of her room, listening to the ticking of the mantel clock, to the sounds of the branches of the trees outside beating restlessly against her window. There was a strong wind now, blowing in from the bleak flatness of the fens. She could picture how it would make the huge shrub bushes in the gardens bend and shake, like green-fronded, frenzied dancers, scattering their heavy, sweet-scented blooms, how it would whip and toss the line of trees that stood like sentinels along the winding drive.

She wondered where her father was now; what he was doing, whether he had reached Epsom and her grandmother's house, the house she missed, the house she loved and longed to live in once more. It seemed so many months since she was there, wandering in and out of all the rooms, the secret passages and the cellar, the cellar that had so many hiding places and nooks and crannies. She missed riding out with her grandmother onto the windswept Downs, watching the horses at exercise, listening to the stories that she never tired of hearing, of her grandmother's youth, when she was a fifteen-year-old girl who once worked as a rough rider in Sam Loam's yard, over Mickleham way. She had taken Rebeccah there, once, to show her where the breaking yard had been, the lines of stables that had housed the unbroken youngstock and the big house. Nothing remained of any of it now, not even rubble. Without speaking, for she had sensed her grandmother's need to look upon the scene in silence, she had let her eyes wander over the empty spaces.

'He was a good man, Sam Loam,' Anna Brodie Russell had said, still staring straight ahead of her; but Rebeccah had seen the brightness of tears in her blue, still-beautiful eyes. 'A good man. And Kate Loam . . . the first morning I came here, ragged, dirty, pleading for work, they took me in and she cooked me a breakfast that I never forgot.' A wistful smile. 'I can see it now, on that big, earthenware platter that she put in front of me . . . and I was that hungry I all but forgot my table manners. I'd not eaten such a meal in all my life.'

'What happened to them, grandmama?'

'He died and there was no son living to take his place . . . Kate Loam went to live in Spitalfields, with a niece. The stock was sold, the buildings fell into disrepair . . .'

'Didn't anyone want to buy them, or the house?'

'Epsom was beginning to change, even before Sam died. Kate Loam sold the land to a newcomer, one of the new rich who thought to build himself a fine house and stables, like all the other Epsom gentry. But he was a gambling man and lost everything in the Leger that year. That fine house never was built.'

'And the big house that grandpapa used to live in when you first came to Epsom . . . tell me what became of that.'

She remembered the way her grandmother had paused, her face dark, before she had answered.

'That was never a happy house. It had too many bad memories for both of us, so he came to live at the Old Brew House, and we had Russell Hall razed to the ground.' Something in her expression, in the tone of her voice, had prevented Rebeccah from asking any more questions. And she had never asked about the house again.

She sat up, suddenly, her sharp ears having caught the sound of a woman crying.

It was faint, a long way away, but she had not imagined it. Throwing back her covers, she got out of bed and tiptoed across the room to the door, opening it quietly. Beyond her room was where the maid, Annie, slept, in a small, black iron bed with a patchwork quilt. Pausing on the threshold of the room, Rebeccah could hear Annie's snores, and, as her eyes became used to the darkness, she could see the covers rise and fall as Annie slept. Softly, holding her breath, she went to the furthest door and let herself out onto the landing.

The sound of the woman crying was coming from the floor below. Holding her long, white, trailing nightgown above her ankles, she made her way down the stairs, then along the landing, past the rows of doors that opened onto unused bedrooms. The sound of the woman crying was coming from the bedroom of her mother.

She hesitated outside the door. The crying was muffled now, each sob stifled, as if her mother's face was half buried in her pillows. Kneeling down, Rebeccah tried to peer through the keyhole.

For several moments she stayed where she was, undecided what to do. It was dark and cold kneeling there on the landing, despite the thick carpets, and she shivered, hugging her body through the thin cotton of her nightgown. Slowly, half afraid, she turned the brass handle on the door. As it came open and she looked past it into the room, she froze with shock.

On the big pink silk hung bed, lay her mother; dark hair wild and dishevelled, her beautiful face wet and bloated with tears. Her eyes were swollen, almost unrecognizable. When she heard the sound of the closing door, startled, she pushed the mane of wet hair away from her distorted face.

'*Rebeccah!*'

'*Mama . . . mama!*'

She threw herself into her mother's arms. Then while her mother clung to her, she too burst into tears.

'Your father doesn't love me any more,' her mother burst out, fighting for breath between giant sobs. 'He loves someone else . . . that boy's mother. Even though she's dead, he still loves her better than he ever loved me.' She was shaking, hysterical. 'He wanted a son and I can't give him one. That's why he won't give up that misbegotten bastard of his! I pleaded with him, I begged him, but he refused!' She grasped Rebeccah by the wrists and held them so hard that it hurt. 'I know what he wants – ' Her pale eyes wild, she suddenly let Rebeccah go and began to walk distractedly about the room ' – to marry you off, when you're old enough, to some rich man, with a big dowry, and let Jamie Russell have everything else! But he can't, he can't do it. The title of Viscount he'll never have. No bastard can inherit that. The racing empire . . . that's what he wants for his precious boy to run. But I won't let him!' Her voice had risen to a scream. 'Nor will your grandmother! As God hears me, he'll get this house and what goes with it over my dead body!'

'Mama, please . . . please don't cry!'

'I'll make him sorry. Sorry he ever touched that Scottish trash. Sorry he didn't smother that bastard as soon as he drew his first breath!'

'Mama . . .' Clinging to her mother's hand, Rebeccah

hesitated. It came back then, the image that would not leave her, the picture of the forbidden door, the flight of steps to that lavender-draped room, in its centre the massive oak carved bed; the naked bodies, doing terrible, inexplicable things. She shuddered.

Corinna knelt down and held her firmly by the shoulders.

'Remember, Rebeccah, think back. What else did that boy say to you? Did he say anything else that you've forgotten to tell me?'

She stared into her mother's tear-filled, swollen eyes, and swallowed.

'No, mama . . . I can't remember anything else.'

Slowly, Corinna let her daughter go. She leaned against the carved post of her enormous bed and closed her eyes. Her head throbbed with pain. Sleep. If only she could sleep, untormented, and wake to find everything had been merely a dream.

Rebeccah stood there, afraid, uncertain; she had never seen her mother like this. Her serene, self-possessed, beautiful mother; who always looked so immaculate, so perfect. What her father had done had reduced her to a creature with bloodshot eyes and tangled, unkempt hair, pacing the room like a mad woman. She reached out and gripped her mother's hand, and the coldness of it seemed to permeate her own.

She had always loved her father; adored him, idolized him . . . before she had opened that forbidden door and climbed the flight of steps to the lavender-draped bedroom.

She loved him still. But he had ceased to be perfect in her eyes.

6

HE HAD FORGOTTEN what an early riser his mother was. He overslept, after lying awake into the dawn hours. Ahead of him, the thought of inescapable tasks and duties without ending, made him groan and turn over, pulling the bedclothes over his head.

As he dressed and made his way downstairs, he thought of the new confrontations ahead of him, the ball at Clarence House in four days' time that he could not now avoid attending; Corinna on his arm, both of them acting out the pretence that all was well, that nothing had changed. He could picture how it would be, moving together through the glittering throng of guests, smiling false smiles, feigning happiness, laughter. He was James Edward Russell, Viscount Russell, and appearances must always be kept. He owed it to his mother, to his father's name, to the wife he'd lied to; everyone but himself.

His mother looked up at him as he entered the dining room, waiting till the servants serving breakfast had gone and he was seated before she spoke.

A pile of unopened letters lay beside her plate.

'Here.' She pushed one of them across the polished table towards him. 'This has been forwarded to you by your secretary. I'd recognize McGrath's handwriting anywhere.'

He thanked her and took it.

'He's conscientious and efficient, as always. He makes it a practice to send on any personal mail, in the event that it might be urgent.' He sipped his coffee, feeling the hot liquid revive his spirits. From the big oak sideboard the delicious aroma of fresh eggs and bacon tantalized his nostrils.

'You'll serve yourself,' his mother said, between mouthfuls, more of a command than a suggestion. 'My staff get up early enough to prepare the food and cook it, then bring it in to us; I don't expect them to wait on me as if I were a baby or an invalid.'

Filling his plate, he smiled, amused; nothing about her would ever change. He remembered, as a child, how she would wash his soiled clothes in the scullery in the big wooden tub, with her own hands, even though any domestic tasks bored and irked her. 'You're my son,' she'd say, rolling up her sleeves and kneeling on the hard stone floor. 'I had you by choice . . . I can't expect other people to do my dirty work for me; nor should you.'

She went on talking as he resumed his seat, about this and that; the stud, the new stock, the sale of some of their choicest yearlings.

'I'm keeping the Iroquois filly; she stands out like a beacon light . . . just wait till you clap eyes on her. If she isn't an Oaks and 1,000 Guineas winner in the making, then I never knew a winner in all my life . . .'

'Isn't that the filly foal out of Quicklime, that John Porter was raving about?'

'Yes . . . and Quicklime was only half a length a loser to Shotover in the '82 Derby . . . you remember that? Besides which, she'd lost her form twice in the last eight weeks before the race, because of some virus or other that was going round the stables . . . bad luck.' She finished the last piece of bacon and laid her knife and fork sideways across her plate. She leaned back in her chair. 'Shotover hasn't been the great success at stud that everyone thought she'd be . . . Quicklime has done much better. Half a length away from winning the Derby . . . crazy, when you think about it. Three feet from a place in posterity.' She smiled. 'When I look back over the years, at all the Derbys I've seen, there were so many that won by the skin of their teeth and shouldn't have . . . unfair. More often than not, the first past the post hasn't always been the best.'

'No prizes for being second.'

'No, no prizes for being second. When I look back and think of how things used to be . . . how much was luck, and chance . . . horses nobbled, jockeys taking pulls, bribed judges and starters . . . how a whole field could be held up for more than an hour for some trifle, then be given the off when half of them were facing the other way! Your father and Lord George Bentinck did more than anyone will ever know to clean up the turf.'

Slowly, he began to tear open the letter. 'Do you remember how you used to tell me about that villain, Jacob Hindley, and the Tollemache brothers? About how you bid for your filly Hope at Tattersalls, and set all the men on their ears?' He laughed, and she laughed with him. 'And how you outwitted the Jockey Club so that you could beat their ban on you and go on running your horses in Tollemache's name?'

'Oh, how they hated me!'

'What did it feel like . . . when Bloodstone won you the Derby? When you rode him in, when all the Epsom crowds were there around you, cheering you because you'd got the better of the powers that be?'

She laughed, softly, her blue eyes bright, remembering.

'They loved it! And their cheering well nigh deafened me and the horse as well. Not that it lasted long, mind you . . . not when Henry Dorling found out that there was no proper entry for the colt, and that your father had just backed me up in pretending it was entered for the race in his name . . . they gave the Derby to Amato, instead . . . but it didn't matter. It was my colt who passed the post first, my colt that they all cheered. On paper, he was disqualified from the race . . . but they all knew who was the best in the field that day.

Bloodstone. When he died after eight years at stud, I cried my eyes out as if he were a human being. He was brave, that horse of mine . . . as brave as a lion . . .'

For a few moments there was a silence between them.

'And so were you.'

Anna looked at him from across the long table.

'Are you happy, James? Are you really happy? Have you ever been? I've often wondered if you took over as stud manager when your father died, just to please me. I never thought of asking you. I should have, I suppose. Horses have always been so much a part of my life that I always assumed they would be part of yours, too. Maybe I was wrong about that. Maybe you would have done better in something else.'

'No, I wouldn't have. What you and my father started, I always wanted to carry on with. If only you'd give me more responsibility, more trust . . . maybe then I'd find it easier to do better.'

'Is that a rebuke James?'

'No, mama. But it was you who told me yesterday that you've decided to leave everything in trust for Rebeccah because you think I might gamble away her inheritance.'

'You do me an injustice by saying that. I told you that I'd arranged matters so that Rebeccah's interests are protected. From anything that might happen.'

'I'm sorry . . .' He took out the single sheet of crested paper inside the envelope he'd torn open, and laid it on the table in front of him, then felt every drop of blood drain suddenly from his face.

'Bad news?'

'N . . . No . . . nothing . . . it's nothing at all . . .' His fingers shook as they refolded the paper and replaced it inside the envelope; the newly digested bacon and eggs rose up, in a heavy, concentrated lump in his throat, and he fought down the wave of nausea that accompanied it. 'Just a . . . note to remind me of a meeting I'd arranged with John

Loder, about the two-year-old he wanted me to look at on my way back . . . I'd completely forgotten about it . . .' He knew she was no fool, and he poured himself more coffee so that he could avoid her eyes. 'It means I shall have to leave by this evening, I'm afraid . . .'

If she was suspicious about what he'd told her, she made no sign.

'Leave whenever you like, after you've seen the young-stock in the breaking yard. Benjamin can drive you to the station.'

He left his single travelling case at his club in Grafton Street, and instructed the doorman to call him a hansom cab to the Savoy Hotel. When he reached his destination, he tipped the driver, went straight inside to the reception desk, and approached the clerk.

'I understand my cousin, Saul Tradescant, is staying in the hotel . . . would you be kind enough to give me the number of his room?'

The clerk pulled the huge gold-tooled ledger towards him, and looked down the list of guests.

'No Mr Tradescant, sir. Do you have the date that the gentleman arrived here?'

James craned his neck so that he, too, could see the names of the new arrivals. And, there it was, just as he thought. So she had arrived nearly five days ago, with not a word to him. No message. No warning. How like her that was.

'Thank you . . . I am sorry to have bothered you.'

'My pleasure, sir . . . might I suggest . . . do you have the correct hotel . . ?'

'On second thoughts, his letter may have said the Connaught. I shall take a cab there.' The clerk moved away to attend to more new arrivals, and James moved back into safe anonymity, among the groups of chattering people and potted plants. For several minutes he stood there, his top hat pulled well down over his forehead to hide his face, looking about him to make certain that there was no one here that he knew. As a bell boy suddenly came rushing past him, he touched him lightly on the sleeve, and produced a sovereign.

'Kindly show me to suite 413.'

He stood outside the double entrance doors, listening to the faint sounds that were coming from within the room. He could picture her, moving about, pacing impatiently, cursing in her native tongue, knowing that he would come, even against his will. Already, he was anticipating what she would say and what his own answers would be, for part of him already knew, and dreaded, the new demands she would make on him; and he had no doubts whatsoever that she would. Like a leech, a clinging vine, Isabella Ajanti would never release her hold on him, never let him go.

The deep anger that had been smouldering in him all the way from his mother's house at Epsom, suddenly boiled over and spilled into red hot rage. He raised his walking stick and rapped loudly, impatiently on the door.

Almost instantly, the double doors swung open and a short, stout, olive-skinned Italian matron was staring into his face with small, black, suspicious eyes. Before he could speak, she stood back so that he could see into the room . . . and there she was.

There was no surprise written on her face; she was expecting him to come. Her dark, shiny hair was piled high on top of her head, and held in place by sequinned combs; her dark eyes mocked him. She was wearing, on purpose he knew, the amber satin gown trimmed with black lace that he had been sent the bill for from his own wife's couturier. And at her throat and ears and around her wrists sparkled the garnets and diamonds the Bond Street jewellers had charged to his account.

'So, James, you have come.'

'How dare you . . .' His voice shook. 'How dare you do this to me . . !'

She made a single sign with one hand, an almost imperceptible nod of the head, and the Italian matron vanished noiselessly into the adjoining room.

'*Dare*? You ask me how I dare? All these months, and not a word. Not a single letter. Not a message. Nothing. You send not even a line, to ask me of the welfare of your daughter . . . just the money. You hand over the money to buy my silence, as if I were nothing more to you than a whore!'

He strode across to her and waved the envelope that had arrived that morning in her face.

'What in God's name do you think you're doing to me? Today I received *this* – sent on to me by my private secretary – £3,000 worth of jewellery, charged to my personal account, and the gowns ordered from my wife's couturier in Brunswick Square – a total of more than £4,500! What else is to come? Furs? Milliners' bills? The cost of your suite of rooms in this hotel? Do you think that I'm made of money?' He struggled to contain his anger. 'And what are you doing here in England, Isabella? Why have you come? You promised me that you'd never come without letting me know first . . .'

Her own rage matched his.

'Bastard! You begrudge the mother of your daughter a few pieces of finery, when your rich American wife can order whatever she wants? *Basta*! *Finito*! I will have those things, I will come and go as I please! You lay with me, first . . . before her! You belong to me . . . me, do you hear, James? My daughter, our daughter, was born three months before hers . . ! And in the sight of Our Lady it is I who am truly your wife . . . deny it if you can! I know that you only married her for her father's money!'

'What are you doing here in London . . ?'

'I bring your daughter to see her father, the father she has a right to see, the father she has a right to be with, yes? You think that if you ignore her, it means that she does not exist. But she does exist, James. And she needs you, more than she needs me. Every day, for more than a year, she asks me about her father . . . and I tell her, I tell her all about you. I tell her that one day she will come with me to England, and we will be together.'

'You have it all worked out, don't you?' His voice was harsh, bitter; what a fool he had been! Italy, Venice, so long ago, more than ten years back in the past. A chance meeting, a wild, youthful infatuation, and she had snared him forever. Like the Devil, she had him in her power.

Yes, she was very beautiful, a different, more earthy beauty than Corinna's. He remembered the nights they had spent together, when her passion and uninhibitedness had astonished him, shocked him, even. Then, he had never given thought to the consequences. If his mother, if Corinna ever found out the truth . . .

She came slowly towards him, her eyes dark, glittering, inviting; there was a smile on her lips . . . was she laughing at him now? He could see the gleam of her olive skin as her breasts strained against the bodice of the amber satin gown; when her hand touched his, he felt his desire for her leap and heighten, weakening his anger at what she had done, and he hated himself for it.

He opened his lips to speak, to tell her that it was late, and he must leave her when, suddenly, the door to the adjoining room opened several inches, and a small girl stood there, gazing at him. The likeness to Rebeccah, save for the long, sloe-coloured eyes, was so striking that for a moment he could not speak.

Isabella Ajanti turned, and saw her, too.

'Alice, *bella filia* . . . come here, to mama.' She held out her hand and the child came forward. 'Come here and see your papa.'

The little girl did as she was told, hesitantly, staring at him, stopping opposite where he stood but several feet away. She glanced first at her mother, then back towards him, fixing her large, glowing eyes directly on his face.

Slowly, carefully, but feeling awkward and ill at ease because it was so long since he had seen her, James knelt down and held out his arms. For a long moment the child made no movement, only continued to stare at him with her dark, brilliant eyes that did not seem like the eyes of a child; then, at a nod of the head from her mother, she moved closer to him and threw her arms about his neck.

With a lump in his throat, James buried his face in her abundant dark hair. Above her bent head, his eyes met and held with Isabella Ajanti's, and she knew that she had defeated him. He would find a way to pay for the jewels; he would find a way, too, to keep his daughter with him in England. She smiled; slowly, self-assuredly. She had always known how to get what she wanted from men.

At that moment the woman who had opened the door of the suite to him reappeared from the adjoining room. Isabella spoke a few rapid words to her in Italian that he could not understand, and she went to the wardrobe and brought out a child's hat and coat.

'Maria will take Alice out for a walk now, while we talk.' Gently but firmly, she disengaged the child from his grasp. 'There will be time for spending with her later, when they return.'

'Goodbye, papa.' It was the first time she had spoken, and the clearness of her childish voice, with no trace of an Italian accent, impressed and surprised him.

'She is a daughter to be proud of, yes? Always, at home, I speak only English with her. Only English. Yet she can speak Italian too. She will show you, later . . .'

When they were alone, she went over to the large window

overlooking the square outside, and pulled the heavy velvet drapes together; then she turned and looked at him.

'Maria understands that I wish not to be disturbed when I am with you . . .' She came towards him, sensuously, her voice soft, liquid, like warm honey running through his brain. 'James, make love to me . . .'

7

THE LATE AFTERNOON SUNSHINE was fading fast now, as they rode back towards Linnets Hall, past the four mile starting post, along Devil's Ditch, laughing gaily as they wound their mounts skilfully in and out of the forest of trees at Hare Wood; then, on the brow of the hill, they paused, and the two girls dismounted.

'Let's have a rest before we ride home!' Rebeccah shouted over her shoulder to her cousin, Lottie Tradescant, and her father's head groom, Mahler. 'Then we'll see who can reach the stable yard first . . .'

Mahler shook his head, respectfully. The girl was a wonder in the saddle, and that was a fact; it was born and bred in her, the skill with the horses. And she had a way with them, too, he'd seen it for himself, first hand. But she was still barely ten years old and she was his master's only daughter. If there was an accident, if anything happened to either of the girls, he'd get the blame. After all, they'd put him in charge.

'No racin', Miss Rebeccah . . . Lord Russell's orders. Now, you don't want to get me into trouble, do you?'

She smiled, with that winning way that she'd always had, trying not to look disappointed.

'My grandmother was a rough rider when she was only fifteen . . . did you know that? She worked for Sam Loam over on Banstead Downs . . . before she left Newmarket, she used to get a ride on a cart up to the Heath and bribe the stable boys to let her exercise the horses!'

'Yes, miss . . . I knew it. That's quite a lady, your grandmother, Lady Russell.'

Lottie sat down on the soft grass, and spread out her velvet skirt to straighten the creases. 'When I grow up, I want to go on the stage . . .'

Mahler laughed.

'Well, that's as may be, young lady, but neither of you'll be in one piece to do anything if you ride those horses too fast over that pot-holed ground down in the dip.' He shaded his eyes against the last rays of the sunlight, and gazed towards the house ahead of them. 'Time to go back now . . . and no racing each other . . . like I said, your father's orders . . .'

Rebeccah swung herself back into the saddle without his help, and stared in the same direction.

'Why, look, Lottie! The carriages are already arriving!' Her blue eyes danced, excitedly. 'Have you ever seen the Prince of Wales?'

He watched them from the window, silently, as they rode back on their cobs to the hunter's yard; he watched Mahler help both girls down, then doff his cap to them as all three mounts were led away to be brushed over and watered. His mother stood beside him, also silent, thinking her own thoughts; how much that small, slender figure with the wild tangle of thick dark hair reminded her, poignantly, of herself, so long ago. She remembered wooding, with her sister Clara, near Frogs Hall and Denham Thicks, scrabbling for the loose twigs and pieces of dead bark that every day they searched for, to take back to her mother and Jessie in the ramshackle cottage at Lidgate, meagre offerings for the nightly fire. She remembered how cold they'd been, clinging together on the straw pallet that passed for a bed, shivering beneath the single threadbare blanket; she remembered the scant food, the patched clothes, the bitterness and the hatred for her father that had, sometimes, been all that had kept her going. And now she wanted for nothing. Lady Russell. How often the irony of that title she bore had struck her, and how many times she had sat, thinking on it, rocking with silent laughter.

How much she missed him, how painfully each day, each month, each year dragged by without him, the man she'd loved. Paradoxically, time had only heightened her sense of loss rather than diminishing it; every day she went on living without him, she missed him more not less. She wondered when she would reach the limit of her sorrow.

She glanced at her son, so like both of them to look at; so unlike each in what he was, and sensed, as she'd sensed from the moment of her arrival, his barely concealed unease. Knowing him as well as she did, she sensed that he was troubled, distracted, restless; that his mind was far removed from her, Rebeccah, the preparations for the Moulton Cup Ball that evening; but, knowing him as she did, she knew, too, that if she asked him why he would only lie to her.

'It's a great pity,' she spoke into the silence between them, 'that Rebeccah is an only child. Don't you think?' He only half looked at her, as if there was something in his expression that he did not want her to see. 'She's been a different child since Lottie's been in the house. Anyone can see it. With things between you and Corinna as they are, it isn't good for her to be alone.'

'You know what the doctors said, after she was born. Corinna shouldn't have any more children. It would be dangerous.'

'And that is why you've amused yourself with other women for the last ten years?' she answered quickly. His face paled, he looked away. 'She hasn't forgiven you for Jamie . . . a blind man could see that. Two months ago, she found out the truth. The instant I walked into this house, I could have cut the atmosphere between you with a knife.'

'It isn't my fault.'

'Oh? Then whose fault is it? It's you, not her, who has the bastard child.'

'You're being as unreasonable as she is! It happened a long time ago, before we were married, before I'd ever set eyes on her or heard the name of Corinna Charpentier. Every man sows his wild oats, every man makes mistakes.' He came away from the window, abruptly; why couldn't she forget it, why couldn't either of them let it alone. Jamie was his son and nobody could do anything to change that.

They stopped talking while two maids came into the room to light the fires. Then James continued, 'You can't forgive him, can you, for blurting out to Rebeccah that I was his father? You still think that he did it on purpose, purely out of malice and spite . . .'

'Why, don't you? Come, James, open your eyes. I asked her myself to repeat exactly the words he said, and they were no accident. If you can't bring yourself to blame him for what happened – and if he'd kept his mouth shut Corinna would never have found out – blame yourself. Where were you when he was with Rebeccah that day . . . making love to Margaret McAllister in your wife's bedroom?'

'I was with her, yes . . .'

' . . . My God, James! Sometimes I ask myself how a son of mine could be so stupid . . !'

There it was again, the sudden gulf between them; the moment he had almost seized upon and clung to, passed. '*It's a pity, don't you think, that Rebeccah is an only child* . . .' Almost, but not quite, he had started to tell her about Alice . . . almost; now it was too late. Already she had lost patience with him, was telling him that it was time to go down to the stud to look over the new batch of young horses. Always, it was the horses first.

Out into the pleasant summer evening together they strolled, side by side, along the terrace, across the rose-scented courtyard, barely speaking. So much, he wanted to be close to her, he needed her to listen to him; so many times in the past, since that first, youthful mistake he'd made with Margaret McAllister, he'd longed to break down and tell her everything. But it was too late.

'It's him!'

'Hush, they'll hear us!'

'Look . . . there's Mrs Langtry!'

'Annie says she's the most beautiful lady in the whole Court . . .'

'She isn't half as beautiful as mama.'

'Neither is the Princess of Wales. People just say she is, out of politeness, because she's married to a prince. And because all her clothes are beautiful, and she wears lots of jewels . . .'

'People always say princesses are beautiful . . .'

Both girls huddled together, pressing closer to the banister rails on the first floor landing, gazing in awe down to the hall below them where the guests were arriving; they were already in their nightgowns, washed and ready for bed, but Corinna had allowed them to watch from above as a special treat. Behind them, Annie the maid hovered, as fascinated as they were.

'That's it, you young ladies . . . bedtime now . . . the guests are all here . . .'

'What did you think of the Prince of Wales, Annie?'

'He's got a big stomach!'

'Hush, hush, the pair of you . . . do you want someone to hear?' She giggled, her hand over her mouth. 'Now, that's not a nice thing to be saying about your future king.'

'He has got a big stomach, Annie.' Heaving up her trailing nightgown, Rebeccah took her cousin's hand and, reluctantly, they moved away. The big marble hall was quite empty now, except for the footmen, the lights from the huge chandelier casting a golden glow on their polished brass buttons, on the buckles of their shoes. Beyond the big double doors, they could hear the sound of the orchestra playing, the laughter, the clatter of champagne glasses. How strangely lonely and silent the nursery floor seemed in comparison.

At the turn of the stairs, Rebeccah glanced over her shoulder for one last, lingering look.

'Lottie . . . I wish we could be down there, too . . .'

'When you're older, Miss Rebeccah,' Annie said, hurrying them up the stairs. 'When you're older you will . . . and, I dare swear, you'll be the belles of the ball . . .'

He hated every minute of it. The false smiles, the meaningless pleasantries, the charade he was being forced to play, he and Corinna. Through the chattering, laughing groups of guests they moved, her hand on his arm, smiling, nodding, pausing now and then to speak; pretending, hiding behind the cheap, shoddy veneer of make believe and civility.

He knew he must make an effort; normally, he enjoyed the company of his friends, he had always liked HRH, better known as the Prince of Wales; Princess Alexandra was charming, sweet, interested, as always. Moving away from her, he stopped to discuss odds on the Moulton Cup field with a group of friends from his London club, all the time half of him somewhere else; strained, ill at ease, longing to escape. Once, he caught his mother's eye, and saw her looking at him with that sharp, quizzical expression which always maddened him, but which he understood so well. Then he'd turned away, moved in the direction of another group of guests he knew he must pause and talk to, and found himself staring straight into the cool grey eyes of Edith Dysart, one of the acknowledged beauties of the Marlborough House set, with whom, many months ago, he had had a fleeting affair.

She had been watching him for some time; her sleek, corn-coloured hair glittering behind the sapphire tiara, the Dysart family jewels glinting about her swan-like neck. She smiled, almost imperceptibly, a different look in her eyes than the blank, nonchalant glance she had given him earlier, when she and her husband had been greeted by himself and Corinna at the door.

Against his will, courtesy prevailing, he edged his way towards her through the glittering press of people, footmen balancing silver trays of canapés and wine.

'Good evening, Lady Dysart. May I compliment you on your appearance. Beautiful, as always.'

She smiled, and her pale eyes twinkled.

'Why, how kind you are, Lord Russell . . . you must speak to my husband, later on in the evening . . . he's anxious to ask you your opinion on who's most likely to win the Moulton Cup.'

His laugh was genuine.

'If I knew that, I'd be one of the richest men in England.'

Was it only his imagination that they were being watched, was it his guilty conscience, his secret knowledge that he feared would show in his face, that he and this woman, the wife of a trusted friend, had lain together, naked, in her bed? He could scarcely bring himself to look at her.

'James,' she said, in a muffled, urgent whisper, 'I must speak with you . . .'

He gazed around him, his eyes moving swiftly over the mass of heads, making certain that Corinna was not looking their way.

'For God's sake, Edith . . . not here . . . not now . . .'

'It's too important. It can't wait.'

'We haven't seen or spoken to each other for more than four months. What could possibly have happened since then that you need to see me about so urgently?'

'I can't tell you here.'

He cast a quick glance all around him for a second time, then ushered her, as nonchalantly as he could through the crowded ballroom to the buffet tables, covered with starched, snow white linen cloths and silver salvers full of every variety of food. A large, ornate silver punch bowl surrounded by crystal punch cups stood on an adjacent table; taking two of them, he began, slowly, to ladle punch into each one.

'Well, what is it?'

'I'm pregnant.'

'Congratulations, Edith. Dysart must be delighted that you're going to give him an heir – or an heiress – after three years of marriage.' Smiling, he handed her the crystal cup brimming with punch. 'So much for that silly theory of yours that you might be barren, and the line would come to an end! I told you it was nonsense. Where will you lie in . . . at the London house or in the country?'

She put down the punch cup and looked straight into his eyes.

'It isn't his.'

For a moment, the whole room reeled; the chandeliers, the mirrors, the walls, the people, everything ran into one long, blinding mass of colour, began to tilt and spin. He stared at her, trying to take in the enormity of what she was suggesting.

'Then whose in God's name is it?' He had forgotten everyone around them, forgotten that he needed to be cautious, circumspect. He had forgotten, even, to lower his voice.

'It could be any one of five different men,' she answered, coolly, 'except that I looked in my diary and knew that, on the day I conceived, it could only possibly have been one of them.' A momentary pause. 'You, James.'

'It isn't true!'

'Please, keep your voice down . . .' anxiously, she glanced about them. 'I'm telling you the truth . . . do you think I don't know the father of my own child?' There was anger in her voice now. 'Richard was away for the whole of that week, visiting his manager . . . some business connected with the estates . . . you were the only man I slept with while he was away!'

With difficulty, he kept his voice low.

'We went to bed twice, the last time on the Friday when he returned on the Saturday evening; don't tell me you didn't sleep with him then. The child is his.'

'We'll soon see, James, after it's born. We'll see which one of you it favours most!'

Almost heedlessly, he swung round on her.

'And what the hell do you expect me to do about it? Tell my wife? Divorce her and make myself a social outcast? Or create a scandal that'll ruin everyone involved . . . is that what you want?'

For a moment she glared at him with cold, furious eyes; then she swept away without another word. He watched her as she effortlessly attached herself to another group, tossing her blonde, bejewelled head, fluttering her silk and ostrich feather fan. She was so two-faced, shallow, selfish, vain; he wondered what it had been that had ever attracted him to her. His eyes suddenly caught sight of Corinna in the midst of the crowded room; moving gracefully among the guests, her flowing, off-white gown of organza and silk twinkling, as the tiny seed pearls and sequins sewn onto the bodice caught the light. He thought, more puzzled than ever before: you're elegant, rich, beautiful . . . so why don't I love you?

8

REBECCAH GAZED in excited, avid wonder at all the noise and bustle and colour of the lively scene down in the paddock below them, as she and her cousin Lottie craned their necks from the side of her father's private box in the members' grandstand to get a better view.

Everywhere, the whole place teemed with a multitude of people, all moving in different directions: jockeys coming to and fro from the weighing room; trainers, stable boys, owners, racing managers; fashionable ladies strolling with their escorts, parasols shielding them from the brightness of the early afternoon sunshine; grooms with blankets and armfuls of tack, rushing to the saddling enclosure; bookmakers shouting the odds from the row of betting stands in the public ring. Here and there, she and Lottie recognized many of the rich, aristocratic guests who, only a few days before, had attended her parents' Ball back at the Newmarket house, to mark the beginning of the Moulton Cup meeting.

There was Lord Richard Dysart, his wife nowhere to be seen, who had two runners in the first race and another in the Moulton Cup field itself, the most important and prestigious race of the day; the Marquess of Hartington, Louise, Duchess of Manchester – 'no one knows how beautiful a woman can be who did not see the Duchess of Manchester at thirty' – the Duke of Portland, with entries in every race on the card, and staying at his suite of rooms at the Jockey Club, straight from Welbeck Abbey; the Duke of Westminster, one of her father's closest friends, one of the biggest and wealthiest owners and breeders in the whole country; and there, among them all, her grandmother, Anna Brodie Russell, on her father's arm, moving sedately through the press of humanity, drawing everyone's eyes because of who she was and what she was . . . 'Your mother is the most remarkable woman I've ever met,' she'd overheard Westminster say, once, to her father, at one of the many lavish houseparties he'd held at Linnets Hall, 'By God, I do admire her . . .' Then, his eyes moving to the large equestrian portrait of her, painted nearly half a century before, 'Heavens, she was a beautiful woman, Russell . . . that young daughter of yours has a strong look of her, to be sure . . .'

Rebeccah remembered how her cheeks had stung with pleasure, and she'd slipped away, unnoticed by either of them.

'Look, Rebeccah, look . . !' Lottie was tugging at her sleeve now, 'It's the Royal party . . !' She giggled, conspiratorially, 'And Mrs Langtry is with them . . . there, in the lavender dress.'

Lavender. Lavender. How much, how violently, she loathed that colour. For a moment, her cousin's face and voice, the crowds beneath the grandstand, all receded, and she was alone again at the foot of the winding stairs. In her tortured imagination she was climbing them again, the strange, unfamiliar sounds from one of the bedrooms above wafting down to her; then she was standing outside the door of a room, and turning the handle in her hand. Tightly, she closed her eyes, screwing them up so that they hurt her; willing away the sight that kept coming back to her in dreams.

'Rebeccah? *Rebeccah*!'

Slowly, blinking, as if she had just woken from a deep, troubled sleep, she turned in the direction of the voice, and looked into her cousin's face.

'Rebeccah . . . I've just noticed something . . . why isn't your mama here today . . ?'

For a moment she tried to collect herself, trying to remember the reason why.

'She has a headache. A bad headache. She had to lie down. If she doesn't feel better by this evening, Annie says she won't be able to accompany papa to a party at the Grange.'

'Oh, what a pity! I wish we could go.'

'We can have our own party, Annie said. With jellies and icing cake and lemonade. And strawberry ice cream! And you can sing and play the piano.'

When the last of the carriages had left the house, Corinna got up swiftly from her bed and peered down into the empty courtyard. No one in sight. She pulled on her lace and silk dressing gown, rang the bell for her maid, then seated herself at her dressing table.

Esme came in hurriedly, carrying a breakfast tray.

'Never mind that now.' Their eyes met and held in the mirror. 'Lay out my royal blue velvet day gown, and the lapis lazuli choker and earrings. I'm expecting a visitor at two o'clock.'

Two o'clock, the time of the first race. He had a runner in that, and in the second, before the big event at three thirty, the Moulton Cup itself. No, James was safely out of the way. Nor would anyone else be likely to return to the house.

As Esme brushed out her long, waving, dark hair, she gazed back at her reflection in the mirror, feeling elated, self-assured, more happy than she had felt in months, since she had found out about the bastard boy. She would show him. She would teach him a lesson. No man, least of all her own husband who she'd trusted and loved, would ever get away with making a fool of a Kentucky Charpentier.

Her mouth was hard and set as she reached down into a nearby drawer and took out her father's letter. She smiled, and saw Esme's expression of puzzlement in the mirror.

'Today is the day of reckoning, Esme,' she said, getting up and holding onto the bed post while the girl tightened the laces of her stays. 'I must look my best today.'

'Yes, my lady.' Esme took hold of the voluminous blue velvet and drew it gently over her mistress's head; how soft, how luxurious the material felt beneath her fingers! She knelt down on the floor, and smoothed down the fringed hem. 'But what of the house party over at the Grange tonight, my lady . . . will you still go to that?'

'No, Esme. I have other plans.' She stood before her massive floor length mirror, admiring her reflection. Yes . . . she looked her very best. A brief glance at the mantelpiece clock. Two o'clock; the first race of the meeting would be starting; James would either win or lose. The former, she hoped, not for his sake but for the esteem and prestige of the Russell stable; her father owned more than three-quarters of it.

When there was a tap at her door and a message that she had a visitor downstairs in the little drawing room, she smiled, without surprise.

On her way out, she turned her husband's photograph in its ornate, silver frame, to the wall. Ten years of marriage, ten years of falsehood – nothing but Rebeccah to show for it all. Only then, did she understand how close love and hate really were.

'Mr Eardhardt?' She stood on the threshold of the little drawing room, and studied his sharp, clever face with her penetrating blue eyes. She sensed he was a fellow American, even before he spoke; but not a southerner. His polite, soft accent was either Boston or New York.

'Lady Russell, the pleasure is all mine.' No Englishman, she'd warrant, would say that. She could tell at a glance, that he was overawed, impressed, by the opulence of the surroundings; amused, she saw the way his quick, small, darting eyes moved over the pictures, the porcelain, the collection of rare, gilt clocks. She motioned him to a seat.

'My father has sent you here,' she said, without preamble, 'I received his letter a few days ago . . . so let's not beat about the bush.' Another rapid glance at the clock; ten minutes past two. Why, when she knew that he had no reason to return, had she developed a sudden obsession with time? He would be in the saddling enclosure now, with Mahler, his head groom, giving the jockey instructions for the next race. Still, her heart, beneath the skin-tight velvet bodice, was beating wildly. 'You have some information for me, I believe?'

'Yes, my lady . . .' His small, childlike hands reached into his jacket pocket, and pulled out several pieces of paper, and he stood up and gave them to her.

'The moment Mr Charpentier received your letter, he contacted me. He was outraged. His concern for you is his one overriding priority. Under his instructions I came here to England and initiated my enquiries on his behalf, all my findings have been reported directly back to him, with a copy of everything I've found out, which you now hold in your hands. Each piece of information has been double checked, I can assure you.'

She went on staring at the first page.

'My husband's bastard son, the boy Jamie . . . he was born before our marriage?'

'Yes, my lady. Copies of his baptism at his mother's local parish church near Perth, and a copy of his birth certificate from the register office in Edinburgh, are enclosed with the other papers. No doubt about it. As you'll see, your husband was present at the baptism, and also permitted his name to be stated on the birth certificate . . . unusual, I understand, when the child is illegitimate and the father is a person of note and standing . . .' Relentless, toneless, the voice went on and on, 'Nine months before the boy's birth, Lord Russell arranged for his solicitors in London to send, as you can see, a very generous sum of money to the expectant mother . . . the allowance all but doubling, after the birth. Over the last ten years, the size of the allowance has steadily increased.' For a brief moment he paused, as if to give her time to take in what he was saying. 'Two months ago, your husband sent Jamie Russell to an exclusive and most expensive boys' public school . . .'

Her rage was choking her, burning at the back of her eyes; the room suddenly seemed unbearably stuffy, hot, airless. Her whalebone corset was a suit of armour, crushing her lungs . . . she spoke, and the voice she heard seemed someone else's instead of her own.

'And have your extensive enquiries uncovered the source from which my husband has been financing these things?' She almost knew the answer, before he gave it; until his father's death, his income derived, almost wholly, from his investments in his racehorses and his bloodstock, and from the enormous interest on her dowry, together with fifty per cent of the winnings from the stable, three quarters of which bloodstock were in her father's name. And he had been using her money to keep his misbegotten bastard son and his mistress, Margaret McAllister.

'Your father was more than generous in your marriage settlement, my lady . . . apart from your dowry, he permitted Lord Russell to have exclusive use of all the monies derived from the syndicated bloodstock, sales from the Russell Stud, and winnings from the animals that he owns, though these are raced in your husband's colours . . . no doubt, of course, that Mr Charpentier's generosity was so lavish because it was based on absolute unconditional personal trust . . .'

'Trust!'

'. . .Unfortunately, at the time of your marriage your father had no knowledge of the existence of this woman and her son, or that Lord Russell would abuse his trust and generosity by using monies which were clearly meant to be used for your own benefit, and that of your legitimate daughter, for the direct benefit of two persons who were not entitled to it . . . however, that is the position. And in answer to your question . . . yes, your money has been used for the upkeep of Margaret McAllister and your husband's illegitimate son.' He cleared his throat. 'I also discovered that Margaret McAllister is not the only lady to have enjoyed your husband's favours . . .'

'*What* . . ?' She tried to keep her voice steady, under control. The wad of papers felt hot and sticky in her hands. Margaret McAllister was alive, not dead.

'. . . Lord Russell has conducted several . . . many . . . clandestine love affairs during the course of your marriage . . . if you would care to look at my report, my lady, I have put down a list of names . . .'

Woodenly, she turned the pages and stared down at them . . . After the first half dozen, she stopped, and glanced up at him incredulously. 'Are you sure there is no mistake?'

'No mistake, my lady . . .'

Slowly, she willed her eyes to turn back to the list; names of women she had counted among her friends, names of women she had liked, and trusted. How ignorant, how naive, how complacent she had been! Thinking herself so special, so different, that he would never want to stray away, like other men; never want to indulge in those accepted, cynical, but discreet society affairs between married people, which had always been commonplace among the English aristocracy . . . how little she had really known him! Disbelieving her own blindness, she thought, bitterly, ironically, of the countless times she and Esme had laughed about the society hostesses who placed their house guests in adjoining bedrooms, so that they could carry on their illicit affairs under the very noses of their spouses . . .

'Lady Russell . . .' his quiet, unobtrusive voice broke suddenly into her tumult of thoughts. He was standing close to her now. 'Lady Russell . . . would you care for me to pour you some brandy . . ?'

Angrily, she fought down the need to cry. To wail, to collapse, to scream and shout and smash things. She was a Charpentier and a Viscountess, she owed it to herself, her own good name, to see this through with as much dignity as she could muster. Slowly, she shook her head.

'I'm all right, Mr Eardhardt. Thank you. I don't need to take a drink.' She swallowed. 'Is there anything else you have to tell me?'

'One thing only . . . the most recent discovery.' He saw her stiffen, but there was no way to soften the blow. 'For the past several weeks, a certain Italian lady by the name of Isabella Ajanti, has been staying at the Savoy Hotel in London with her daughter . . . ten years old. Enquiries have established that your husband is paying for the considerable expense of a large private suite there, and there have also been gifts of gowns, furs, and highly expensive jewellery . . . as you know, my lady, your husband has an account with Tattersalls, who hold all the considerable monies from his racehorses' winnings – horses almost wholly owned by your father, Mr Jerome Charpentier. I've managed to establish that the jewels, and the cost of the Savoy suite, have been paid for out of this account . . .'

She put a hand to her head.

'But a large percentage of that money is meant to be transferred to the trust fund set up by my father for Rebeccah!'

'Lady Russell, I already know that, from Mr Charpentier himself; I also know that your husband has been betting heavily, outside the stable, ostensibly to recoup the money from the Tattersalls account that hasn't found its way into your daughter's trust fund. I also know, from certain indisputable sources, that his losses from unwise betting have mounted to a considerable sum.'

She spun round.

'Who *is* this woman staying at the Savoy? Is she another

of his society sluts . . . or is she his mistress? And the child. Whose is this child?'

Every word he spoke was an arrow, being plunged into her heart.

'Her baptismal name is Alice Russell, my lady . . . and she was born in Venice three months before your own daughter . . . the bottom piece of paper in your hand is a copy of her birth certificate from the city hall . . .' Woodenly, Corinna turned back each one until she was looking at it. 'The name of the child's father is James, Lord Russell . . .'

9

James Russell took each girl by the hand and together they made their way into the saddling enclosure. This was a rare treat. Through the vast, gorgeously attired mass of the crowds, pausing every now and then while he nodded or chatted with an acquaintance, a trainer, another owner he knew, Rebeccah looked around them and saw that they were the only small girls to be allowed inside the exclusive paddock.

Standing there, bursting with excitement and pride, they stood silently and overawed, gazing at their father's runner for the Moulton Cup, at the jockey in his colours, at the titled and rich and famous, massing all around.

No other sport appealed to the Marlborough House Set and their ilk so much as thoroughbred racing; with plenty of money and more than enough time for leisure, they found the excitement and glamour of the turf irresistible. They patronized it with rigour, relish, and, at times, huge extravagance, spending fortunes – whether they could afford to do so or not – on buying, breeding, building studs, training stables, on lavish house parties and gambling; more money was spent and lost with the bookmakers during a single season than was available in prize money for the whole year. Great magnates like the Dukes of Portland and Westminster were interested, first and foremost, in breeding and owning the best racehorses of the day; like her grandmother, they combined rare knowledge and vast financial assets to achieve startling, often spectacular results. To others, racing was merely a means to an end . . .

knowing the heir to the throne's passion for the sport, ambitious hostesses had at their disposal a whole season's variety of racing events to which they could both invite and be invited to, throwing costly and extravagant balls and house parties to accompany each one, each host and hostess vying with one another in the lavishment of their entertainment. The Prince of Wales loved it all. And, what had previously been the indulgence of a handful of sporting aristocrats and magnates . . . not to mention the livelihood of a frightening array of vagabonds and criminals . . . was rapidly becoming a national pastime.

Gazing up at her father, Rebeccah felt pleasure and pride in being with him, delight in his company, acutely aware, everywhere they went, that his dark, striking good looks drew the admiring glances of every passing lady. This was the father she knew, the father she idolized.

She stood there, side by side with Lottie, while he talked; first to the Russell trainer, to his racing manager, to the jockey, the head lad; and she watched, fascinated, as the colt stood there, nostrils gently flaring, chestnut coat glimmering like amber satin in the strong afternoon sunshine, waiting to be mounted and ridden away. The saddling bell sounded, the jockeys were up . . . the head lad led the colt away behind the others, and the enclosure looked suddenly empty and bare, bereft of everything that made it important, leaving only people.

'Papa . . .' Gently, she squeezed his hand in hers. 'Do you think Paradox will win the Cup?'

He looked down at her, suddenly, almost as if he had forgotten she was there. He smiled at her, then at her cousin Lottie.

'I hope so. I have a great deal of money riding on him today. So, both of you . . . say your prayers.'

After Eardhardt had left, Corinna went upstairs to her room

and changed her dress. She dismissed Esme, needing to be completely alone. For a long while she lay there, fully dressed on her bed, staring blankly at each sheet of paper he had given her, reading and re-reading every line until she knew each one by heart. But there was no need. Nothing that soft, clever, feather-light voice had told her downstairs would ever be forgotten, as long as she lived.

She looked bitterly around the large, luxuriously furnished boudoir, with heavy, pain-laden eyes; at all the cherished, loved, familiar things, the trinkets he had given her over the years, the photographs in silver frames that each held a memory, a special moment from her life; now everything, every one of them was meaningless. And, in that moment of realization, she knew she could never stay with him.

She was too hurt, too stunned, too angry to cry; tears would come later; when she had left him, when she had left this house, when she had left England. With a sudden stab of anguish and pain, she thought of Rebeccah, and knew that if she left James Russell she must be prepared to leave her only daughter, too.

Again, she glanced at the mantelpiece clock; near half past five now . . . soon, they would be returning, and she must be ready.

She went over to her window and opened it wide, letting in the fresh, warm, sweet-scented air; it would be a beautiful evening. They would have supper alone, together, in the dining room, with the french doors wide open and leading onto the south-facing terrace; he would chat idly about the day's racing, and she would pretend to listen, answering only when necessary; and, when he suggested a stroll in the grounds among the rose bushes and scented shrubs she would go willingly, smiling, holding onto his arm. And while he talked, she would go on pretending, pretending to enjoy his company, pretending she loved him still. Her pretence would fool him as his had fooled her.

She still stood there, feeling the cool air on her face, savouring the peace and the stillness. This, the part of England that she loved, would be sorely missed. But that was only a small part of the sacrifice she would have to make. She thought of her daughter again, and tears pricked at her eyes. Dashing them away, she went over to the bell rope and tugged it firmly. Seconds later, Esme came bustling into the room. Corinna had brought her over with her from Kentucky, and would take her back again . . . what an irony it was, she thought, with added bitterness, that she could take her maid but not her own daughter.

'Are you feeling better, my lady?'

She did not bother to force a smile; there was no need to pretend to Esme.

'No, I'm not . . . but no matter. My husband and the girls will be returning to the house in the next half hour . . . help me to dress for dinner.'

'And Lord Russell's mother?'

'No, she won't be with them, not tonight. She has an invitation to dine with the Duke of Portland at the Jockey Club. I doubt if she'll be back before midnight.'

'Very well, my lady.' She went over to the enormous, mahogany wardrobe, delicately inlaid with mother-of-pearl, and opened it. 'Have you decided what evening gown you wish to wear?'

Corinna went over to where she was standing and looked inside, at the rows of organza, velvet, silk, satin and lace gowns, then pulled one out.

'This, I think.'

It was pale ice-blue, the colour of her eyes; a full skirt and bodice of fan-pleated tulle, the hemline trimmed with thick, delicate scallops of Nottingham lace. She pointed to her jewel box. 'The diamonds, I think, will go well with this.'

When she was dressed, and Esme had gone, she stood in front of her full-length mirror and stared at her reflection. The image that looked back at her was of a still-young woman of considerable beauty; stylish, elegant, self-assured. She thought of the names of the women he had cheated on her with, the names on Eardhardt's list, more than half of them, women who had no particular quality that she could think of, without being uncharitable; not one of them, any of them, she thought bitterly – but without vanity – in her class. So why had he done it? What had he found missing, what had he found lacking in her that he had found in their arms? Despite her beauty, her vitality, her charm, he had found it necessary to take them to bed. The thought enraged her more because she could not answer her own question, and it was the one question now that she would never be able to ask him.

When they returned from the racecourse, she made much of Rebeccah before Annie finally took both girls away to bath them and give them their tea.

'Corinna, what's the matter with you? You were clutching the child as if you were never going to see her again . . .' James asked.

Deliberately, Corinna harnessed her anger and made her lips curve with a tight, false smile.

'I've missed her, that's all. You've been gone all day. And by the look on your face I can see that it wasn't a good one.'

He poured himself a brandy.

'I'll say. Paradox led the whole damn field right to the mile and a half post . . . then, when Cannon asked him for the effort, he just died away in his hands. It's inexplicable!'

'Didn't your mother tell you that if he were hers she wouldn't have run him past his best distance? She said he was a mile-and-a-halfer and that anything up to that distance wouldn't have a hope in hell of catching him . . . but you insisted on running him for the extra quarter of a mile past his best . . . against her advice and your own racing manager's. Are you surprised that the horse didn't win?'

'The head lad said that he'd stayed for two miles on the training run . . . he led the whole string from the first furlong marker to the two-mile post up on the Heath . . . and I've seen him gallop, with my own eyes. He should have stayed the distance.'

'Maybe he didn't feel like it. Maybe he didn't like the heat.' She was acutely aware of his mood; guessing, rightly, that he had bet heavily on the race and lost heavily on it. But, despite her own smouldering anger, she was determined not to provoke a quarrel. Not now. Not yet. The time and place would be of her own choosing, not his.

'I'm sorry he let you down . . . maybe next time . . . over another course, a shorter distance. Did you lose much?'

'Enough. As usual, Westminster and Portland cleaned up. Portland's face, when they led his colt in . . . he has enough cups and trophies at Welbeck Abbey to start a business.' Unlike his mother, he was a bad loser.

She kept her voice deliberately light.

'He's never won the Moulton Cup before, has he? He must be delighted. At least, he'll have plenty to talk to your mother about at their dinner tonight.'

He finished the glass of brandy, and poured out another one.

'If the rest of the meeting goes like today, I shall be pawning the silver,' he said, morosely, leaving her wondering whether or not she was supposed to take his remark as a joke.

'And your mother's horses . . ?'

'All winners, except her Galopin two-year-old, that she only entered for a trial run . . . and even that came second.'

Corinna could not stop herself from smiling.

'Like they say, she certainly has a way with horses.'

'A pity I haven't inherited it, then.'

There was a lengthy silence between them, then he changed the subject and began to speak of something else. As they sat alone at dinner, looking at each other from opposite ends of the long, polished table, she was not listening to what he said, but imagining him with each of the women he had made love to, the women on Eardhardt's list.

As she toyed with the food on her plate, making only a pretence at eating, she stared into his face as he talked, and wondered why she had never suspected him; why she had never seen a sign, a gesture, that might have told her he had betrayed her. She had thought that he loved her; that the stud, the racing stable, all the voluminous business connected with the estate would have taken up all of his time; but that assumption, too, had been merely an illusion.

She wondered if he had thought about her, while he lay in bed with his other women; if they had talked about her, laughed about her, been amused by her ignorance and naïveté; she momentarily closed her eyes, trying to change the relentless trail of her thoughts, part of her secretly exalted with the knowledge that she had finally found him out.

He had stopped eating, and was gazing at her.

'Are you feeling better? In all the disappointment about the race, I forgot to ask when we got back . . .'

'Oh, my headache . . . no, that's gone. I lay down on my bed all afternoon, with the curtains drawn . . . that usually does the trick . . .'

'You're certain you feel all right?' He looked at the half-full plate, the untouched dish of chicken gelatin and smoked salmon, that she'd pushed to one side. 'You've scarcely touched a thing.'

'It's the heat. It always did play havoc with my appetite.'

'As long as you're sure . . . maybe it wouldn't do any harm to have a word with the doctor, if you keep getting headaches and going off your food . . .' There was no note of real concern, no note of solicitousness; he spoke in the same matter of fact tone that he might have used to one of his stable boys. Again, she forced herself to smile. The smile hung there, on her lips, like the necklace of diamonds that glittered at her throat; as cold, and as little a part of her.

'Don't fuss, James. I never felt better. I'm not very hungry, that's all. Perhaps later . . . Esme can fetch me up some supper, on a tray.'

'Incidentally, Richard Dysart's sent us an invitation to their houseparty at Cheveley Park Hall, on the thirteenth . . . it's a double celebration, by all accounts.'

'Oh?' Deliberately, she kept her voice light.

'Yes. After three years of marriage Lady Dysart is expecting an heir . . . or, at least, he hopes it'll turn out to be a boy! His younger brother's something of a black sheep in the family . . . old Dysart would have a fit at the thought of him inheriting.' He paused, while a manservant refilled his glass with wine. 'More than a hundred and fifty guests are being invited to Cheveley, including the Prince and Princess of Wales.'

She looked up then, her smile at last genuine. Friday, the thirteenth of July. One hundred and fifty guests. The Prince and Princess of Wales . . . anyone who was anyone would be there. James, herself . . . and Lady Edith Dysart. Lady Dysart, one of the names on the list . . .

'They must both be delighted, James . . . I hope you gave Lord Dysart my congratulations.'

Slowly, he sipped his glass of wine.

'Yes, indeed I did. He was sorry to hear that you were indisposed . . . you and Lady Dysart both. She was unable to go to the Moulton meeting too, he said, since she's suffering from morning sickness.'

'I'm so sorry to hear that . . . and I can sympathize.' She was astonishing her own self, with her act of cool, calculated hypocrisy. 'When I write accepting their invitation, I must put in a note congratulating them and wishing her better.' A sudden, unpalatable thought, 'You don't think this might prevent her from attending her own ball?'

'Oh, no, I'm certain not. Not when HRH and Alexandra are the guests of honour . . . she wouldn't miss that for all the world. She's far too much of a snob for that.'

Corinna stared at him, wondering if she had heard him right; she thought, *And yet you slept with her*! She leaned back in her chair, and made a pretence at peeling a nectarine and a small bunch of grapes. Lady Edith Dysart. Yes, she could see her face now, dredged from the sea of other, just as mundane ones, who had made up a large number of their own guest list less than a week ago . . . she recollected, vaguely, a thin, arrogant face, topped by the pile of corn-gold hair, the too-slight figure, the cold, haughty, pale grey eyes. If only she had known the truth then, if only she had already seen the names on Eardhardt's list, she would have watched her closely; studied her, followed her every movement. She could not even remember seeing her talking to James.

Into the silence between them she said, suddenly, 'I should like to go to London for a few days, while the meeting is on . . . and take Rebeccah . . .' He stopped eating and stared at her. 'I'm in no mood for watching racing . . . I feel that a change of scene would do me good. And I wanted to visit my couturier and be fitted for a new wardrobe.'

'But you can't . . . not take Rebeccah! Lottie's here, for God's sake!' Yes, she had forgotten Lottie. How foolish of her. 'I could take both of them, with Annie and Esme to help me manage. A music hall matinée! That's what Lottie would love to see! Both of them would adore it, James!'

He looked appalled.

'But what about the Moulton Cup meeting?'

'Today was Cup Day, the most important day of the week . . . they've seen all the colour and glitter, all the Prince's party parading in the Royal Box in all their finery . . . everything else is bound to be an anti-climax. A few days in London, before Lottie has to go back home, will do both of them good.'

He pushed away his dessert plate.

'Oh, as you wish . . . I'll have a word with McGrath in the morning, and get him to make the travelling arrangements.' He got to his feet. 'Now, if you'll excuse me, I have some accounts to go through.'

She still sat there long after he had gone, sipping her wine, deep in thought. In a moment, she would go upstairs and kick off her shoes, and let Esme brush out her long, waist-length hair while she sat before her dressing table mirror; and, while the girl brushed, she would collect all her wild tumult of plans and thoughts, and set them in order. But before that, she would go to the floor above and spend as long as she could with Rebeccah.

She swallowed. She closed her eyes, gripping the edge of the table to stop her hands from shaking. Leaving her, for even a little while, would be the hardest, the most devastating thing of all . . .

10

THE HANSOM CAB clattered along the crowded, busy thoroughfare of Devonshire Street, then turned left as it swung into Portland Place and then left again, before finally drawing to a halt outside Park Crescent and the Portland Hotel. Seeing its arrival, a liveried doorman rushed to help Corinna and the two girls down onto the pavement, followed by her maids and their trunks and baggage.

She tipped the hansom driver and the doorman generously, before shepherding the girls inside.

'Lor, stone me!' Annie gasped beneath her breath, never having been in a grand hotel in all her life. 'This is a swell do and no mistake!'

'You haven't seen anything yet, Annie,' Lottie Tradescant said, tossing her coal black corkscrew curls. 'Has she, Rebeccah? Wait till we go to the matinée at the Curzon Street music hall!'

'I can't,' Annie said, still staring, mouth agape, all around her. 'Look at that, will ya?' She nudged Esme in the ribs and pointed to the head doorman, standing stock still, not moving, in the middle of the entrance hall. 'Is he real, or is he like one of them wax figures I heard about, at Madame Tussaud's?'

'I don't know, Annie,' Rebeccah said, 'why don't you poke him and see?'

Corinna turned away from the reception desk, having signed their names in the register.

'No, Annie . . . don't touch those heavy trunks and suitcases . . . the porter will take those . . .'

She left the maids to unpack the luggage while she stood at the window of their suite, staring down into the crowded street below. So many people, hurrying to their destinations, all busy, all going somewhere. Like her.

Despite the number of people she could see, she could hear almost no sounds; their suite was set back on the east side of the hotel, and only faint, disjointed noises, now and then, reached up to her: a flower seller's raucous cry, the music from a distant barrel organ; horses' hooves and carriage wheels clattering on the road; behind her, in the big, light, airy room beyond, the louder sounds of Lottie and Rebeccah's childish laughter.

She let the lace curtain fall back into place, and turned back from the window and the street scene outside.

Perhaps she should wait until tomorrow to do what she had come to do; now, she was tired, travel-worn, her head ached and she would need to change everything she was wearing; this was one time that she was determined to look her best. But tomorrow was too far away. If she waited, it would mean another night of lying awake, tossing and turning, tortured by her outrage and self-doubts.

She called to Esme in the next room.

'I have to go out . . . please help me change my clothes.' She had already decided what her costume would be. 'The damson velvet walking dress, with the matching hat and short cloak. Annie can take the girls for a stroll in the Park while we're gone, we can have lunch up here together, afterwards.'

Esme bobbed a curtsey.

'Yes, my lady.' She went away to fetch the change of outfit.

'Mama . . .' Rebeccah was in the doorway now, frowning, her blue eyes clouded. 'Why do you have to go out? Are you going to see someone?'

'Yes, I have to see someone. No one that you know.'

*

She took a hansom cab to the Savoy Hotel and went straight into the foyer, where she left Esme. When she had found out the suite number and the floor that she wanted from the reception clerk, she tipped the bellboy to take her there. When he had gone, she stood outside the elegant double doors for a long while, her heart hammering wildly, a gnawing, sickly sensation fluttering in the pit of her stomach.

It would be so easy to turn round and walk away; to leave her father to deal with it, the task that was unsavoury and unpleasant; but she was not his daughter for nothing. And, besides, she owed it to herself. Taking a deep breath, she knocked firmly on the door.

There was no answer from inside the room, and she knocked again, more loudly. She stood there listening, straining her ears for any small sound. She knew that the suite was still occupied; the reception clerk had told her so. After a few more minutes, when she knocked again and nothing happened, she grasped the handles of the double doors firmly and opened them wide.

The inside of the suite was luxurious, exquisitely furnished and opulent, as she had expected it to be. There was a massive, antique couch, upholstered in deep pink brocade, with matching armchairs; Meissen porcelain figures were dotted here and there about the room. The carpets were Persian, the huge mantelpiece, in the middle of which stood a large, gilt, ornate French clock, was white marble, with a heavy brass club fender surround. Everywhere, gowns and undergarments were strewn about the room.

She closed the doors silently behind her and leaned back against them. From the adjoining room, which she took to be a bedroom, she could hear the sounds of someone moving about. Still, she stayed exactly where she was, waiting. And then, suddenly, a young woman in a long, trailing, lace dressing gown, appeared through the half-open doorway. As she caught sight of Corinna she stopped, abruptly, and stared at her.

'Who are you?' She came closer, her dark eyes narrowed, her face wearing an expression of indignant outrage. 'What do you want? What are you doing in my rooms?'

'Your rooms, Miss Ajanti? I think not. Seeing as how the bill for them, ever since you arrived here, has been paid for by my husband . . . with my money!'

'*You* . . . you are James's wife . . ?' She stepped backwards, pulling the lace of the dressing gown closer across her half naked breasts, as if she feared for her safety. The dark eyes flashed. 'He has told you about me!'

'No, he has told me nothing at all. But I know everything . . . and I found out by myself.' She moved further into the room. 'I've come here today to tell you that if you wish to stay on at this hotel, then you must find the cost of doing so from your own pocket . . . James can no longer pay your bills. The money he's been using to support your extravagant lifestyle since you came to London was my father's, and he had no right to use it.' She looked past her, around the disordered room. 'Where is the child?'

'You know of that?'

'Yes, I know of it. Where is she?'

Isabella Ajanti turned away, dark hair tumbling untidily across her shoulders; distractedly, she began to pace the room. 'You would not turn us out into the street . . . James would not allow it . . . hate me, yes! I am used to other women's hatred and jealousy! But my daughter, my Alice . . . you would not do this to her . . . you have a daughter, too, the same age . . .'

Corinna hesitated. She thought, bitterly–he slept with this woman, he gave her a child, almost at the same time as he gave one to me . . . he slept with her, after he first met me, he was sleeping with her while we were engaged . . . Yes, she was beautiful; looking at the olive skinned, flawless, proud face with its small, exquisite features, Corinna could understand why he had wanted her. She looked about her, searching the tables and mantelpiece for evidence of a child's presence, but there were no photographs, no childish knick knacks, not even a single toy.

'For your daughter's sake, you can stay here until the end of the week. After that, your bills will be unpaid. I strongly suggest that you take your child and your belongings and go back to wherever it is that you came from.'

Isabella laughed; suddenly, loudly, harshly.

'You, rich American heiress . . . you think you are so grand, so important in the world! Because your rich father made a big fortune selling horses! You think your money can buy anything, anybody . . . including your husband's love! But you're wrong. He never loved you . . . it was always me. He told me so. He married you only because your father is a great power in the horse-racing world, because your father's money would get him where he wanted to be.' The wide, full lips smiled, cruelly. 'Do you know who my father was? Count Ajanti! We are one of the oldest, most noble families in the whole of Italy . . . only misfortune made him lose everything . . . the *palazzo* in Venice, the estates, the lands, the fortune . . . only the name remains. But in spite of all that we are still what we always were, and what you never can be; true aristocrats. You? You are nothing but *nouveaux riches*!'

Strangely, the gnawing sensation in Corinna's stomach, from anxiety, from nervousness, had stopped; she felt deadly calm. Coolly, calmly – so calmly that she astonished even herself – Corinna reached down into her leather purse and took out the receipted bill from the Bond Street Jewellers. She held it up.

'*Nouveaux riches*? As you say, that's what I am. And you are a Venetian aristocrat . . . no doubt that's true. And this, as you can see, is the bill for the three thousand pounds worth of jewels that my husband gave you. Dress it up in any fancy words you care to, Miss Ajanti – or do you prefer to be called *Countess*? But, from where I come from, *nouveaux riches* or not – we have a certain name for women who take expensive presents from married men – and I think we both know what that name is. Good day to you.'

Before the other woman could retort, before she could even recover from her surprise, Corinna turned and walked out of the room. She slammed the double doors behind her. She walked down the richly carpeted staircase and back into the foyer, where Esme was waiting.

Without speaking a word, she went outside into the crowded street, where the liveried doorman whistled them up a cab.

Inside, jolted to and fro on the bumpy road, she put her head in her hands and burst into tears.

11

ANNA WALKED BRISKLY along the path leading from her gardens to the grazing paddocks beyond, her head groom alongside. Despite her age, he never ceased to be amazed by her tireless energy; her thirst for success, her love for her horses; every one, from foals to those gone to stud seasons before, she knew by name; their sire and dam, their breeding, to five or six generations back; their faults, their form, their wins and losses. She rarely spoke of the past; something that had always surprised him, since all her spectacular achievements over the last fifty years had come about because of her spectacular achievements in her youth. But, knowing her as he did, he guessed, rightly, that she considered the past a very private thing, something unique and special that she did not wish to share with anyone else.

At the paddock fence, she paused and leaned against it.

'The Galopin two-year-old . . . do you think we should enter him in the Cavenham Stakes? I have another three weeks, before the entry form needs to be sent in . . . he's worked more than well, these past four months, don't you think?'

He nodded his agreement, his eyes on the sleek, beautifully proportioned brown colt who stood, grazing, on the other side of the grassy field.

'He was early coming to hand; easy to break, with the temper of a doe . . . yes, I'd say the Cavenham would be a good first race . . . the right distance, testing enough company, and the journey to Newmarket, no doubt, he'll take in his stride.'

She smiled, her sharp, blue eyes fastened on the same place.

'He can stand at my son's stables the day before the race. As usual, we'll send him by train and take a first class compartment ourselves.' Her eyes took on that deep, far-seeing look he knew so well. Yes, she was thinking back. 'I wonder what we ever did in the days before the railways came . . . horses travelling by steam train . . . whoever would have dreamed that it could happen?' She laughed, and he laughed with her. 'When I think of all the horses we've walked, from one end of the country to the other, to get them where they were supposed to be going to . . . on foot, walking beside them with a leading rein, stopping at every public house and posting inn to rest our feet and give them feed and water . . . how many pairs of boots did I wear out doing that?'

'Can you see Westminster or Portland doing it?'

'They'd have dropped dead beat in their tracks! And so I told Portland, too, to his face, that night after the Moulton Cup when he invited me to dinner with him at his Jockey Club rooms!' She laughed again, softly. 'But he does have a sense of humour . . . he didn't take offence when I told him that if it weren't for his money, the furthest he'd ever have got with being a racing man would be mucking out the horse manure from some rich man's stables!'

Mordaunt looked at her sideways; yes, only Anna Brodie Russell would have had the nerve to say that to the Duke of Portland's face.

'Does His Grace have a runner declared for the Cavenham?'

'The old bastard has two; I told him, save their rail fare and leave them at home in their stables . . . they won't win. My Galopin colt'll race the piss out of the pair of them.'

They began walking again, slowly, along the perimeter of the fence. 'I never thought I'd get that special feeling again about any horse . . . not since Bloodstone, not since my filly

Hope . . . or Priam, in the 1830 Derby . . . a lifetime ago. But that one . . . he has the look I've been waiting to see for the last fifty years . . . just something, something extra, something besides the good breeding, the good temperament, the speed . . . something that marks him out, something I've never even been able to put a name to . . .'

'I know. I feel it, too. And I always did rate Galopin's stock.'

'His sire, Voltigeur . . . that was a racehorse and a half; you never saw him run, did you? Before your time. He was foaled in '47, by Voltaire out of Martha Lynn, a Mulatto mare . . . Robert Stephenson of Hartlepool bred him . . . when he came up for sale as a yearling, he failed to attract a bid . . . can you credit that? I was out of the country then, with Russell, buying two-year-olds in Tennessee . . . the Merrick Company, the best there is, who bought Priam . . . Lord Zetland's private trainer, Hill, I think his name was, tried to get him to buy the animal, but Zetland wasn't interested . . . bloody fool. A year later he was persuaded to change his mind, though, by his brother-in-law, of all people . . . he paid a thousand guineas for him and only ran him once as a two-year-old, when he won the Wright Stakes at Richmond; he was never given any other race or even a trial before he ran in the Derby, and even then the betting on him was as far out as 16 to 1. The touts were down on him, because they'd seen him give an unimpressive trial gallop on the Downs before the race. If they'd had an ounce of common sense between them, they'd have realized that that was because he'd travelled all the way down from Yorkshire, and he was stiff and tired.

'He won the Derby comfortably from Pitsford . . . and he should have won the St Leger. He met with such bloody gross interference from Chatterbox that his jockey had to take him to the front sooner than he wanted to, and Russborough got up in the last furlong to force a dead heat. But Voltigeur won the run-off. He was a tough horse, that little colt. He had to be to come out two days later and beat the Flying Dutchman in the Doncaster Cup.'

'He wasn't long at the stud, more's the pity.'

'No. He was kicked by a mare and died soon after that . . . what a loss! But he sired Vedette, who sired St Simon. That's good blood, Mordaunt. Good blood. And guts, too. That horse'd run his heart out if it killed him.' There were tears in her eyes, as there often were when she talked about certain of her horses; and, he'd noticed, at certain other moments, too; when a special foal was born; when one of her horses was first past the post, especially if it was a close finish; when one of her horses was alongside another in a race, fighting neck and neck. Yes, she was clever, ruthless, and tough . . . but her humanity had made everyone who ever worked for her love her in a way that was unlike any other. Mordaunt looked at her and fought down the need to put his hand on her shoulder, to offer her a handkerchief. That would have angered her.

Instead he said, after a few moments' silence, 'It was bad luck Lord Russell lost out in the Moulton Cup . . . the word on course before the race was that his colt Paradox would walk it . . .'

'Only if the other runners had had their fetlocks tied together. I told him. I gave him my advice . . . not that he ever listens to it. Up to a mile and a half the colt would have distanced nearly everything in that field . . . but that's his maximum distance. The extra quarter of a mile, another furlong, even, and he hasn't got it in him. Nobody was less surprised than me when he shot his bolt and faded out . . . I told James that he'd never stay . . .'

'I hear his American two-year-olds are the best that his father-in-law's sent over, yet; I wonder if he'll save them for the three-year-old season, or give them a couple of easy races this year, to try them out.'

'Don't ask me. I'm only his mother.' She smiled, and sat down on the huge stone seat that stood under a nearby tree. 'Jerome Charpentier has his own ideas about what he thinks his horses ought to do; no doubt James will have to take account of that. But, by and large, from what he's told me, the old man usually leaves the final decision about what to do with them, to my son.'

'And your Iroquois filly, my lady?'

'Ah . . . now you're talking. She's special, like the Galopin colt . . . it stands out a mile. I knew it the minute I saw her . . . just a feeling I had; it's not often my instincts have let me down.' He thought, amused, they never do. 'When you see a horse with that something special, you know it. They stand out from all the others, as if there was a kind of aura around them . . . it doesn't happen often, just sometimes . . . no doubt if I'm right and she cleans up with the Oaks, the Guineas and the Leger. I reckon she's got the right breeding in her to stay for at least two miles . . . the Jockey Club will try to dig up some hybrid from her pedigree in the past to use to disqualify her. They always were suspicious of American-bred horses. If Iroquois hadn't been trained by an English trainer at an English stable and ridden by Archer, his winning the Derby in '81 would have caused an uproar. You know as well as I do that the English racing fraternity never did take kindly to outsiders.' There was a twinkle in her eyes; her lips curved in a wry smile. 'But I reckon I fairly beat them at their own game. That was more than fifty years ago . . . we've had a truce, of a sort, for quite a while . . .'

It was almost dark now, and she was ready. Esme had turned down the lamps in her room, and the single, solitary piece of luggage, all she intended to take, lay secreted beneath her bed. All last night she had lain awake, thinking about Rebeccah. Then, unable to sleep, she'd got up, pulled on her dressing gown and gone quietly up to the floor above to her daughter's room. She'd opened the door of Rebeccah's bedroom and stood there, for several moments, watching her sleep. Then she had gone back to her own, cold bed.

She looked at her own, dazzling reflection in the full-length mirror without vanity or pleasure. The new gown, from the fashionable London couturier, would suit the occasion well, with its full, floating layers of white tulle, overlaid with delicate gold lace. The lace twinkled and glittered now, in the soft, muted light of the room; in the bright, chandelier-lit ballroom at Cheveley, it would create a sensation.

The jewels he had given her glowed in her hair, at her ears, about her wrists and throat; this, the last time she would ever wear them. When Esme came into the room to tell her he was ready and waiting, downstairs in the hall, she gave one final glance in the mirror, then left.

He was already at the door, waiting impatiently, being helped on with his top coat by his butler, when she reached the top of the stairs, and paused. She knew he would hear the rustling of her ballgown and turn to look at her, which he did. And she knew, too, from the expression in his eyes that he found her desirable, and beautiful. But it was too late. Jamie Russell, Isabella Ajanti and her bastard child, all the other women he had slept with during their marriage, the lies he had told her down the years, all rose up and came between them; she knew she would never be able to forgive him.

They spoke little during the half hour carriage ride to the Dysarts' country house; as they arrived outside the massive stone portico, she glanced up, from the carriage window, and caught sight of Edith Dysart standing in the brightly lit hall, busily engaged in the greeting of their guests.

Other carriages had arrived with theirs, and, as she took James's arm and waited in turn to be received by their hostess, she kept her face a false, pleasant-smiling mask. When it was their turn to be announced, she noticed how neither James nor Edith Dysart made the slightest sign that they were anything more to each other than neighbours and slight acquaintances.

Heads turned as she accompanied him into the huge ballroom, her unique, white and gold gown standing out amongst the collection of pinks and pale blues and yellows; but other men's admiring glances, and the women's envious whisperings from behind their fans, meant nothing to her now. Holding her glass of pink champagne and sipping it, she looked around her on the glittering, opulent, lavish scene, and found herself thinking what a waste it all was; when there were thousands upon thousands of poor, and hungry; children in rags in the back streets of London, with rat-infested hovels for homes and little to eat; families in slum dwellings, with no proper sanitation, where scarlet fever and cholera were rife . . . she looked at the huge, linen-covered buffet tables, groaning under the weight of the food; smoked salmon, fillet steak, oysters, caviare; food that thousands of men, women and children had never seen in all their lives, much less tasted, and she suddenly felt sick. Sick with disgust, sick with shame, sick with anger at the greed, the hypocrisy, the selfishness of what she herself had become a part of. When the assembled guests stopped talking to turn and applaud the arrival of the Prince and Princess of Wales, Corinna simply stood there, without clapping them, her hands at her sides.

She stayed where she was for several more minutes, watching the chattering groups of people, the royal couple as they began to move among the guests, stopping here and there to exchange greetings before going on; then, catching sight of James ahead of her with the Dysarts and a group of others, she began to make her way slowly towards them.

Oddly, she felt none of the nervousness that she had at the Savoy Hotel; her mind was deadly calm; there was no shaking in her hands. As she came into their midst, all she was aware of was Edith Dysart's pale, narrow face, turning from James suddenly to look at her.

Theatrically, she put a jewelled hand to her head.

'All these heaps of congratulations! I can't think what people will do when the child is actually born!'

This was it, the moment Corinna knew would come from the first time she looked down at that name on Eardhardt's list.

She smiled, coldly.

'Congratulations? Which man should I congratulate? Certainly not your unfortunate husband. It could be anyone, wouldn't you say, since you've slept with most of the men here in this room . . .'

A sudden dreadful silence. All around them, simultaneous gasps of horror.

'*How dare you!*'

'How dare I? How dare you, you whore, sleep with my husband behind my back when you've been a guest in my house. Were you planning, perhaps, to honour him with the dubious distinction of fathering your cuckoo in the nest?' Her voice carried clearly across the room. She looked at Dysart with genuine pity. 'It's you I feel sorry for; truly . . . it's a wise father who knows his own child.'

With that, she walked out.

It was the same dream as it always was; ever since that fateful afternoon that she would never forget; the sun was bright overhead as she left her toys on the lawn, and wandered towards the terrace where she had caught sight of her father and the strange lady, walking arm in arm; the forbidden door, the door which led to the unused side of the house, loomed there in front of her, and something compelled her, against her will, to follow them inside. She could feel the coolness of the rusted latch beneath her fingers; then it swung open and the bare, dark steps towered up to the landing, and the row of doors.

Like a sleepwalker, she was suddenly ascending them without effort, and another door, a door from behind which she could hear sounds strange and unfamiliar, stood before her, willing her to open it and step inside. She reached out, but suddenly it swung open of its own accord, and there they were, her father and the strange lady, naked and horrible, writhing, twisting, gasping for breath obscenely on the big, ornate, lavender-draped bed . . .

She woke up, seconds later, still screaming.

Her own bedroom door was open; standing silhouetted against the light beyond and the darkness inside she could see a ghostly, shadowy figure. For a moment she thought that it was still part of her dream . . . then the figure moved silently towards her and she heard her mother's voice softly whispering her name.

She sat bolt upright, staring into the blackness.

'Mama!'

She had never seen her mother look so beautiful before. The white tulle rustled as she came towards her, arms outstretched, the gold lace fronds that covered the overskirt winked and glittered in the poor light.

She took Rebeccah in her arms and hugged her, so tightly that it almost hurt. Then, grasping her by the shoulders, she knelt down beside the bed.

She had been crying. Her blue eyes were brimming with tears; her cheeks were wet.

'Mama, what is it?'

'Rebeccah, you must listen to me . . . there isn't much time . . .'

Somewhere, a clock chimed in the depths of the house; deep, resonant, the last chime shivering eerily on the still air.

'Rebeccah, I have to go away, back to America . . . I can't explain why, not now, because it would take too long, and you're not old enough to understand . . . but I will explain, one day, I promise . . .' The tears in her eyes welled up and coursed down her cheeks. 'I want to take you with me . . . I desperately want to take you with me . . . but I can't, because the law says that you must stay with your father . . .'

'No!'

'. . . Please, Rebeccah . . . don't make this harder for me than it already is . . . it isn't forever, just a little while, till I can fight him for custody through the American courts . . . I promise, I give you my word . . . as soon as I can, I shall come back to get you . . .' She pulled her into her arms, hugging her, kissing her, sobbing; Rebeccah could feel the wetness of the tears on her face, the feel of the tulle of her ballgown against her body; the sweet, subtle fragrance of her French perfume was the last thing she ever remembered. Then she was gone.

Throwing back the bedcovers, crying, hysterical, she ran after her shrieking for her; then, suddenly, she stopped abruptly in her tracks as the front door slammed and she heard her father's furious voice.

'What in hell do you think you're doing, you bloody bitch? Do you know what you've done to me? Do you have any idea what damage you did tonight . . . right there, in front of them all, right in the hearing of the Prince of Wales!'

'Get out of my way!'

'I'm finished . . . do you know that? Finished because of you!'

'Finished because of me? Because I had the guts to speak the truth? Do you deny it, that you slept with that Dysart slut? That the bastard she's carrying, the bastard that that pathetic cuckold thought was his own, might well be yours?' Her voice was mocking. 'She might as well lay it at your door as any man's, don't you think? After all, one more Russell bastard won't make much difference!'

'What the hell do you mean by that?'

'Don't bother to lie to me any more, James . . . I know it all! Jamie Russell, your Scots whore's son, sent to the most costly boys' school in the country, on my father's money; and the pair of them, him and his mother, who's very much alive and well, I've found out, living in the lap of luxury for the last ten years on money meant to be used for Rebeccah and me.' He stared at her, mouth open, unable to believe his ears. 'Your Italian slut's bastard, Alice, staying with her mother at my expense in a luxury suite of rooms at the Savoy Hotel, ordering gowns and jewels from Bond Street, and sending you the bill . . . which you promptly settled with money that you had no right to touch! What happened to the £10,000 in the Tattersalls account, James? Where did it disappear to? Or, should I rather say . . . in whose pocket did it end up? Yes, I see it surprises you that I know about that, too . . .'

'How in God's name did you find out?'

'I wrote to my father when I discovered the truth about Jamie Russell . . . and he hired a private enquiry agent to make investigations . . . the man certainly knew his job.' She smiled, bitterly. 'Everything you've done to me, every time you've cheated on me with another woman, every lie you ever told . . . what I did tonight, James . . . that makes us even.' She walked over towards the door. 'And now, I'm leaving you.'

'You can't!'

'Do you think you're man enough to try to stop me? Get out of my way, James . . . I never want to see you again as long as I live . . !'

From one of the side rooms, as if on cue, Esme appeared, suddenly, carrying her single case.

'You'd walk out and leave your own daughter?' he shouted after her, furiously. 'What kind of woman are you?'

She spun round on him, tears streaming down her face. Up above them, clinging to the banister rails on the landing, she caught sight of Rebeccah, sobbing, her small hands shaking as they clung to the bars.

'You dare say that to me? You're the only reason I'm leaving this house! And as soon as I can I'll be back with my father's lawyers, to take her away from you . . . legally! You're not fit to bring up a child!' Wildly, she dashed the tears away with her hand. 'Don't think it isn't tearing me apart to walk out of here without her . . . but you haven't left me any choice. In English law, a mother has no rights over her child . . . if I took her with me you'd call the police and we'd be stopped before we even reached Southampton.'

'*Mama*!' cried the small, strangled voice from the landing above. Her face wet with tears, Corinna looked up.

'Rebeccah, I love you. And I'll be back.' Then she was gone. As the front door slammed shut, Rebeccah began to scream. Slowly, hanging on to the banister rail, she came down the stairs, shaking, sobbing, calling for her mother. When she reached the bottom, her father ran to her and picked her up.

'Mama doesn't mean it . . . she'll be back, very soon . . . I promise she'll be back . . .'

'I want her!'

She clung to him, trying to stem the desperate flow of tears, but it was no use. She was shaking, demented, hysterical. Panicking, he let her go and yelled at the top of his voice for her maid. As Annie came running, still in her nightclothes, but already wakened by the noise, the front door bell rang loudly.

'I'll go, sir, I'll go!' Letting go of Rebeccah, Annie rushed forward to open it, then received the shock of her life.

Standing on the doorstep with a short, dark, foreign woman, was a little girl of about Rebeccah's age, immaculately dressed in a white velvet dress coat and feathered hat. The likeness to Rebeccah, save for the glittering sloe-coloured eyes, was so striking that she was momentarily too stunned to speak. James Russell strode forward.

'My lord?' The woman's accent was thick, guttural. She pushed the child forward towards him while they all stared at her. 'My mistress has returned to Venice . . .' she held out an envelope, with the crest of the Savoy Hotel engraved on the back of it '. . . she has asked me to give you this . . . with your daughter.'

'*Wait*!'

A hired carriage was standing outside; James could see

the driver's shadowy figure, silhouetted against the moonlit night sky. Ignoring what he said, the woman walked down the steps and climbed into it, then the driver whipped up the horses and it was gone.

White-faced, with numb fingers, he tore open the envelope and took out the single page.

There was no beginning to her note, and she had not signed her name; there was no need. The tall, arrogant, spiral writing could only have belonged to her. Two lines only.

'*Alice is your daughter; it is her right to be with you.*'

He leaned back against the wall and closed his eyes. The envelope fluttered from his hand. Then he looked down at her, into her small, heart-shaped face, then across to where Annie stood, her arms around Rebeccah.

The two girls stared at each other, both struck with the uncanny, almost extraordinary, likeness between them. Rebeccah had stopped crying; Alice Russell still stood there, like a little statue, waiting for him to speak.

He sighed, deeply, heavily. Then he reached down and took her by the hand. He walked over to the staircase, sat down, and pulled them both towards him, into the crook of his arms.

'Rebeccah . . . this is your sister, Alice.'

PART TWO

The Girl

12

'GIVE THAT BACK to me, it's mine! If you don't, I'll tell papa!'

'Tell him, brat. I doubt if he'll take any notice. He's too busy, out on the gallops with Jed Mahler, watching his runners for the Mickleham Cup.'

'Give it back to her, Jamie. Or I'll tell him, too.'

Jamie Russell laughed, showing strong, white, even teeth. Teasingly, he flung the magazine across the room towards Rebeccah, where it hit her in the face.

'You did that on purpose!'

'An unusually bad aim, that's all.' His voice was mocking. 'You're not going to cry, are you, brat? There, there! I thought you were supposed to be a big girl, now!'

'Why don't you get out of here, Jamie?' Alice said, angrily. 'You've finished your breakfast. I thought you were meant to be up on the Heath now, watching the horses with papa?'

'They were all up and away before six o'clock this morning,' he said, throwing himself onto a chair and putting his feet up on the table. 'And last night I didn't get back from town till nearly three . . . I can go and watch them with him tomorrow morning, or the next day . . . we've got all week long . . . and I need more than four hours' sleep!'

Alice glared at him.

'You mean you're too lazy to get up at six o'clock, more like!'

'Watch that wicked tongue of yours, black eyes. Or I might have to teach you a lesson and put you across my knee.'

'You wouldn't dare!'

'Try me. Serve you right for cheeking your elders.' He heard the sound of the returning horses, and got reluctantly to his feet. 'Well, looks like father is back . . . I suppose I'd best go out into the yard and show willing.' He stopped at the dining room door. 'And don't either of you let him know that I've only just got up . . . or you'll be sorry.'

Both girls stared sullenly after him.

'Did you hear him when he got back last night?' Rebeccah said, angrily. 'He was drunk. Luckily papa didn't hear him. And none of the servants will tell on him, I think most of them are too terrified . . . unpleasant things seem to happen to people who get on the wrong side of Jamie . . .'

'Yes, I've noticed.'

'I heard him being sick in the bathroom when he got back . . . it was disgusting.'

Alice went over to the big bay window and moved the lace curtain, looking out over the courtyard.

'Sometimes, I wish we could go and live at Epsom, at the Old Brew House; I'm always so happy when I'm there. Near Lottie Tradescant. Closer to London. Away from this place and Jamie.'

'Papa spoils him.'

'He says papa spoils us! He's jealous, that's all; resentful because grandmama doesn't like him, and she hardly ever asks him there.'

'That's true. Jamie never did forgive her for having us stay at the house for last year's Derby, when he had to put up at the local hotel.' Rebeccah laughed. 'He was furious. But she told papa that if he couldn't treat the servants with common courtesy then he could stay away. And she wouldn't have him in her private grandstand box!'

Alice turned away from the window.

'Do you think papa knows that he still goes about with that Mottram crowd, after he promised not to?'

'I think papa knows a great deal about Jamie that he doesn't even care to admit.'

'So you're up, then?'

'I've been up since seven!'

'I thought you were coming with us?'

Jamie fell into step beside his father, reaching out to pat one of the sweating horses that the grooms were busy rugging up. 'I'm sorry, father . . . I woke up with the devil of a headache. And, yes . . . I know what you're going to say . . . I was in too late last night.'

'I heard you come in myself . . . it was nearly three in the morning. You knocked over a piece of furniture. That woke me up.'

'I'm sorry . . . but I met a few friends down at the White Hart and we got talking . . . you know how it is . . .'

A few moments of silence, while they walked on. James Russell gave out the day's orders to his head lad, and then carried on in the direction of the stud office.

'Did they give a good showing on the gallops?' Jamie asked.

'If you'd been up there with us you'd have seen them for yourself.'

'I said I was sorry.'

They had reached one of the paddocks now, and James Russell paused, and leaned against the fence. 'Jamie . . . you know how hard I'm trying to establish a good yard so that, in time, you can take over . . . we've discussed it, often enough, for times on end. You want to train, you told me. You want people to think of the name Jamie Russell and know that your yard is right up there at the very top of the ladder, turning out winners with the best. You can only do that by hard work. By watching. By learning. You can't achieve anything by lying in bed.'

At last, his true feelings broke through the thin veneer of politeness.

'Oh, you would say that! And I already told you the reason I wasn't there. I had a bloody bad head! But you don't believe me, do you? If it was the brat, that'd be different, wouldn't it? You'd believe anything she said!'

'Jamie, I've told you before and I'm sick of telling you. Don't speak about your sister like that.'

'Why not, it's true, isn't it?' The bitterness had already crept into his voice. 'She can do no wrong. Nor can sweet little Alice. It's easy for them; they don't have to work at doing anything; they don't have anything to prove . . . Rebeccah gets the Brodie inheritance and old man Charpentier's empire as well, and when Alice is old enough in a year or two you'll marry her off to some rich, idle aristocrat with a nice fat dowry, and she can live in luxury for the rest of her life.' He looked at his father with cold, hostile eyes. 'But what about me? What about the bastard, Jamie Russell . . . what do I get, father? Nothing from the Brodie inheritance – we both know she hates my guts! Nothing from yours worth counting – Jerome Charpentier still owns the lion's share of the stud and the racing stable . . . and we all know who'll get that!'

'Jamie, why are you so bitter?'

'Bitter? Bloody hell, can you ask me a question like that and really not know the answer?' He turned away from him, angrily, and stared into the paddock to the group of horses on the far side, idly cropping the grass. 'I'm sorry. I shouldn't have said that. After all, I'm only a bastard, aren't I? I should really be grateful for anything.'

A thick, heavy silence fell between them. James Russell sighed. Why had Jamie turned out the way he had . . . morose, resentful? He had done everything that a man could do, everything in his power, to make life easier for him; the best clothes, the best schools, a lavish allowance of money. He'd gone out of his way to make him feel that there was no difference between him and either of his daughters, particularly Rebeccah, that the fact he was born illegitimate was unimportant.

'What do you want from me, Jamie?'

For a moment, there was a pause.

'What I want, you can't give me. It isn't possible. I don't suppose I could even make you understand if I wanted to. And there isn't any point. Rebeccah. Rebeccah gets everything that ought to be mine, everything I'd have if you'd married my mother instead of that rich, spoiled, horse-dealer's daughter!' There was real hatred in his face, and James was stunned by it. 'If it hadn't been for the brat, you could have married mama four years ago, after her mother died . . . and I would have been legitimized.'

'For God's sake, Jamie! We've been through all that! You know it wouldn't have made any difference to anything! It was too late. You're the eldest, yes . . . but Rebeccah is my legitimate child, she'd still take precedence in law . . . besides which, even if I left you and you alone everything that I possess, it wouldn't amount to much, in comparison with the Brodie inheritance and what Jerome Charpentier will leave her. You know that.'

Like a dog with a bone, he wouldn't let go.

'Damn Jerome Charpentier to hell. It's my grandmother I'm talking about! I thought she was the great stickler for fair play . . . and her father left her and her sister nearly everything he possessed, even though the pair of them were bastards! I'd have thought she'd have been on my side! You've never properly explained to me why she isn't leaving the Brodie inheritance to you instead of to that half yankee brat! You're her son and heir, aren't you?'

'Jamie, if you speak once more in that way about your sister, I'll have no choice but to ask you to leave the house!'

'Oh, I see . . . that's the way it is, is it? What has she been doing behind my back . . . telling more tales? Alice isn't any better, either, the underhanded little bitch. They make a good pair! All right, you might as well hear it from me as from them . . . no doubt they'll sneak on me anyway. I had a skinful last night and I came home drunk. Well, are you shocked?'

Wearily, James Russell sighed.

'I was your age too, once, believe it or not. And drunk more times than I want to remember.'

Jamie leaned forward on the fence and covered his eyes with his hands.

'Look, I'm sorry. Let's leave it, shall we? You already know how I feel. No point in my going on about the injustice of it all, is there? I won't get anywhere.'

His father slapped him gently on the arm.

'Come on, come with me to the stud office and we'll go over the stock reports together, then we'll have lunch.'

'Very well. I'm persuaded.' They continued walking, side by side.

'When we go down to Epsom next month, my mother will be meeting with the representatives of the Merritt Bloodstock Company from Philadelphia, and the Belle Mead Stud of Tennessee – you know the reputation of the Merritt – the most prolific importers of English bloodstock in the United States . . . if you prove to her that you're capable of hard work and the kind of dedication she admires, you can get her to change her mind about a lot of things by yourself . . . will you do it . . . for me, Jamie?'

He looked at his son and wondered why there seemed no trace in him of his gentle, self-effacing mother; Margaret McAllister, always so grateful, so warm, so undemanding. If only she had given him a little more of herself. Perhaps the fault was his, perhaps all the attention, the spoiling, the easy hand-outs of money whenever he asked for them, had made him into what he was.

'Of course, father. Of course I'll do it. And I'll make you proud of me; you'll see.'

James Russell smiled, his anxiety, his misgivings, appeased.

'I'm proud of you already.'

They reached the stud office door.

'Oh . . . father . . . one more thing. I don't like to mention it, really . . .'

'Something wrong?'

'No, not exactly . . . but . . . when I was out last night, at the White Hart, I got into a card game with some friends . . . you know how it is . . . I lost, rather heavily. I was wondering if you could possibly let me have – '

'How much?'

'Two hundred would cover it . . . well, say two fifty. I'll let you have it back.'

'There's no need – this time. But you did give me your word that you weren't going to get roped into any more games with cards.'

'Oh, don't lecture me, father. I know I was a bloody fool! But when you're with friends, all rich men's sons with huge allowances – a hundred to them is like chicken feed – I could hardly sit there on the sidelines, they'd have laughed at me. Besides, I did feel lucky . . .'

'But you weren't.'

'Look, I won't play again, all right? Do you want me to take an oath on the family Bible?'

'There's no need to be sarcastic. Of course not. Just keep your word to me in future.' As he spoke, he went over to the safe in the corner of the room, twisted the mechanism to and fro several times, then opened the door as it clicked open. He took out a wad of banknotes and counted several into Jamie's hand. 'Take three hundred. And have a care how you spend it.'

Jamie smiled. 'Why, thank you, father,' he said.

13

REBECCAH SAT, perched on top of the straw bales at one end of the big barn, watching her grandmother's head lad as he worked, something that had always fascinated her since she was a little girl; going the rounds of the breaking yard and racehorse stalls, up on the gallops, at Tattersalls Corner for the bloodstock sales; watching, learning; not only because she felt it was expected of her, being who she was and what she was, but because, after the news of her mother's death, only by keeping her mind and body working until she was exhausted, could she unburden the weight of her grief.

For many nights after it had happened, she'd lain awake, thinking, wondering, the tears wet on her cheeks; she'd lain there, staring at the same door that her mother had left by, the memory of that floating tulle ballgown, white and gold, shimmering in the dim light of her room, so clear that she could almost have reached out and touched it.

She had watched her father, carefully, in the long days that followed the news from Kentucky, watching for a sign that he felt the same grief and pain, the same emptiness as she did; but he had stayed dry-eyed. Somehow, the gulf that had gradually come between them since her mother had left that night, had widened over the years. They never spoke together as they used to; they would never laugh, joke, tease. She had been just twelve years old and her childhood was over; the adoration of the little girl who had played with her teddy bears and dolls that fateful afternoon in the gardens of the hall, had disappeared, never to come back again.

But she was luckier, her grandmother had told her, than her sister Alice; for Alice's Italian mother had left her of her own volition, and gone back to Venice; not once had she written. Everything that had happened to both of them had brought them closer together; only their mothers had been rivals.

She shifted her position on the bale of straw.

'Ezra . . . does doing that so hard make your arms ache?' He stood up, dandy brush held in midair, casting his eye over the sleek, chestnut coat that shone like satin. 'Ay, miss, it sure does . . . and me back an' all! But come the time when this'n appears in the paddock, you'll see how worth the slog it all was!'

'He's never lost a race, has he . . . how many times has my grandmother won with him, this season?'

'Five times, so far. Great Foal Stakes, Ashenden Cup, two wins at Alexandra Park, and his last time out, the Champion Cup at the Crystal Palace. She'll have him in the Guineas, this summer, you mark my words.'

'Not the Derby?'

'No, miss. He's a miler, this one . . . won't ever get 'im to stay a yard over . . . Lady Russell, she knows every one of 'em like she knows the back of 'er 'and.' He rubbed his aching back and went on with what he was doing, studiously. 'This one, 'e's a Guineas 'orse . . . long time since I seen a miler as fast as 'e is.'

'I wish I could ride him!'

'I doubt if 'er ladyship'd let you do that. Never twice alike, this colt, you mark my words. Gentle as a sheep one day, 'e'll be . . . the next . . . why, he might take a bite right out o' my arm!'

Rebeccah slipped down from the straw bale and went closer to him. This, it seemed, was one of his good days. She held out her hand and he nuzzled it.

'Well, I'll be damned; 'e likes you, Miss Rebeccah!' He smiled. 'Can't say as I can blame 'im for that, neither!'

Rebeccah blushed. 'Lady Russell, she always gets 'em eatin' out of 'er hand, just like you do!'

'They know who likes them, that's all.'

'An' they know who they can take liberties with; 'er ladyship, now, she's always kind but firm wi' every one of 'em . . . got the magic touch. Maybe you've got it, too . . .'

Making her way across the stableyard, Rebeccah suddenly caught sight of a carriage standing in the courtyard by the front door, and broke into a run. Alice was back, early, from her visit to the Tradescants, over at the big Hall. She'd missed her this morning, first thing, having got up at the crack of dawn to watch her grandmother's horses out at exercise, up on Banstead Downs.

She ran on into the house and then upstairs, calling Alice's name; but there was no answer from any of the usual rooms where she might be. Going down again, she made her way to her grandmother's study, where the sound of muffled voices wafted out to her in the hall.

In the carefree, happy atmosphere of the Old Brew House, Anna never insisted on the two girls bothering to stand on ceremony, and knock before entering the rooms; Rebeccah burst in, as always, full of what she had just been doing when she realized, suddenly, that her grandmother was with strangers.

Two, well-dressed gentlemen in dark suits and holding top hats were with her in the study; one, seated in a chair beside her desk; the other, half-turned from view, had been gazing out of the window into the gardens outside. Rebeccah scarcely looked at them for more than a fleeting moment. Embarrassed, acutely aware of her untidy appearance, her blue eyes were fastened on her grandmother.

'Oh, I'm sorry . . . please forgive me . . . I didn't realize that you had visitors.' Slowly, she stepped backwards. She glanced at the nearest of the two men. 'I do beg your pardon.'

Anna laughed, amusement playing at the corners of her lips in a ghost of a smile.

'I think we can forgive you, this time.' She turned in her huge leather chair towards the two men. 'Gentlemen, this is my granddaughter, Rebeccah Russell . . .'

The dark-suited man in the chair had got to his feet, holding out his hand towards her. But she could hardly keep her eyes steady on his face. For his companion, taller, darker, younger, had suddenly turned away from the window and was gazing at her with thick-lashed, piercing brown eyes.

'Rebeccah, these gentlemen come from the Merritt Bloodstock Company of whom you've often heard me talk. The biggest and most prolific importers of British bloodstock in the United States . . . Mr William Ten Broeck, their vice-president, and his chief bloodstock assessor, Mr Rufus Waldo.'

He had stepped into the space between them already, his hypnotic dark eyes transfixed unblinking on her face.

'Why, Miss Russell . . .' his eyes flashed swiftly from hers to the portrait that hung above the fireplace '. . .what a striking likeness between you – uncanny, almost – .' The dark eyes moved onto Anna. 'May I ask who she was?'

'My mother, Anna Maria Flood, in her youth.'

He looked back into Rebeccah's flushed face. Then gave her a smile that made her heart lurch and begin to hammer wildly, as if she had run a long way too fast; her stomach turned somersaults. 'She was very beautiful.'

'Thank you,' she heard herself whisper, barely audible. 'Have you . . . have you come here to buy some of our horses?'

'Indeed, we have . . .'

William Ten Broeck said, turning towards her, 'The Merritt Company only trade in the best, Miss Russell . . . and the Brodie Russell connection with our company is one that's been established for quite some time.' He smiled, and glanced at Anna. 'In 1835 we bought Priam from the Earl of Chesterfield for fifteen thousand dollars . . . quite a sum of money to pay for any horse, back in those days.'

'But you got yourselves a bargain, nonetheless,' Anna answered, smiling.

'If only you'd sold your colt Bloodstone to us, too,' Ten Broeck went on, amiably, 'I reckon that nag'd have made American bloodstock history. You bred yourself a gem in that one, my lady.'

'Don't I know it . . . leading sire for every year he stood at stud.' The blue eyes clouded over, momentarily. 'I still miss him.' She looked over towards where Rebeccah stood. 'While I finish going over some details with Mr Ten Broeck, maybe you could take Mr Waldo here over to meet Mordaunt, and introduce them; then he can show him the two-year-olds we have for sale.'

Flustered, trying to make her voice sound calm and normal, Rebeccah nodded, her answer barely above a murmur.

'Yes, of course. If you'd care to come this way . . . I'll show you where he is . . .'

He went ahead of her, opening the doors so that she could pass through. Outside, he suddenly reached out and plucked something from her hair; a single strand of straw. Her face burned like fire.

'Now, I wonder where this came from?' The thick-lashed, brilliant brown eyes lit up as they rested on her face. 'Tell me . . . what's a beautiful girl like you doing mixed up with pieces of straw?'

She stared back at him, wondering if he was making fun of her.

'I was in the barn, watching one of the horses being groomed. I like to take an interest in everything that goes on in the stables . . . even the mundane things. When she was a girl, my grandmother did that, too.'

'She's a remarkable woman. Still striking. And a head on

her shoulders that any sharp man might well envy . . . I admire a woman like that, a woman that started out with nothing and built up an empire . . . and beat everything and every obstacle that got in her way. You must be proud of her.'

'Yes, I am.'

'Anyone can see that you look like her; do you have the same fire in your blood for your horses that she did when she was your age?'

They reached the front door and he held it open for her to walk through.

'When she was fifteen she worked for a well-known rough rider, up on the Downs. Then her father died, and left her and her sister Clara most of his personal fortune . . . but not his prize bloodstock, which was all that she wanted! She started with one filly that she bought at Tattersall's auction, and went on from there . . . if I only ever do a quarter of what she did, out of so little, then I'd think myself clever. There'll never be anyone like her.'

They walked on, across the courtyard, side by side. Waldo deliberately slowed his step to keep in pace with her.

'And your father . . . does he take over the reins of Brodie Russell, when the time comes? Or will that gigantic responsibility fall to you?'

She laughed. 'I'm not sure if I can answer that question, Mr Waldo. As you must be well aware, in England the law gives a woman very few rights, even over her own property . . . as my grandmother found fifty years ago, to her cost. She found her own way round all the difficulties – I may have to do that, too. My father has no son to carry on the family name.' Only Jamie, she thought, bitterly, to herself; Jamie who had always envied and hated her. How much he had always resented the illegitimacy that barred him from inheriting the entire estate . . . his illegitimacy and his grandmother's dislike. 'I'll never be what my grandmother was . . . nobody could ever be . . .'

'Perhaps you underestimate yourself.' The dark eyes looked down at her, sideways, and her heart skipped a beat. Why wouldn't it stop, this feeling that set her cheeks on fire and turned her legs to jelly? For the past year, she had noticed how men had suddenly begun to look at her; differently, lingeringly, appraising; at Alice, too; and she had got used to it. But nobody had ever made her feel like Rufus Waldo did, not ever before. She stole a sideways glance at him.

'How long have you been with the Merritt Company, Mr Waldo? Do you work mainly in the United States?'

'I've worked for them since I was twenty . . . six years and two months.' So . . . he was ten years older than she was. 'And America, of course, is our home base. My own job takes me to any destination where there's bloodstock worth buying, which means in practice England and France.'

She tried to slow down her steps, as they drew nearer to the paddock where Rebeccah knew John Mordaunt would be working, exercising the unbroken yearlings on the running rein. There was one, unanswered question in her mind that she was longing to ask him, and she was desperately trying to think of the right way to ask it without seeming forward and impertinent.

'I suppose . . . I suppose your family must sometimes see very little of you? When you're travelling abroad?'

He looked down at her, amusement in his eyes, as if he had guessed what she was trying to find out. She felt her cheeks grow hot again.

'I'm not married . . . if that's what you're asking me.'

'Oh . . .' Flustered, feeling suddenly very young and very foolish, she tried to avoid those bright, liquid, penetrating eyes. 'At last,' she pointed, to hide her confusion. 'There he is . . .' She raised her hand and called to him, and he waved back. 'John Mordaunt, my grandmother's head groom. And a groom in a million . . . her words as well as mine! What he doesn't know about young horses isn't worth knowing.'

Rufus Waldo smiled. 'So introduce us, then.'

She walked and ran back to the house, and went straight upstairs instead of going to Anna's study. She raced up the huge staircase in twos and threes, then burst into her bedroom and threw herself on the bed. She lay there for several minutes, trying to gather her wild tumult of thoughts.

Then she got up and went over to her dressing table, sat down, and stared at her reflection, hard, in the big ornate mirror.

Her face looked no different from how it had looked this morning, nor yesterday, nor the day before. A pale, clear, creamy oval with striking features; long-lashed, brilliant blue eyes. Her cheeks still burned but there was no sign of redness reflected in the mirror; slowly, she put a hand to one side of her face. So, he had looked at her and found her attractive . . . a man ten years older than she was; worldly, experienced, sophisticated, puffing up her pride and uncertain self-esteem. She glanced harder at herself, wishing that she had known they were coming and could have put on one of her very best gowns, not the plain, dark, serviceable day dress that she always wore when she was helping in the stables.

She ran to the window and peeped out of it, trying to see if he was still with John Mordaunt; if her grandmother and Ten Broeck had gone out to join him from the house.

There they were, in the distance, standing in a group beside the paddock.

Quickly, she rushed over to her wardrobe, flung open the doors and looked inside. All her best gowns. She reached out for one of her favourites; then, reluctantly, slowly, biting her lip, she replaced it on the rail. No, she would not change her clothes now. It was too late for that, too late to go out of her way to impress him. And, if she did, it would look too obvious, and she would feel a fool. She closed the door, and leaned against it. That was when she heard the sound of the carriage clattering into the courtyard outside, and ran across to the window to look down below. Alice, dressed in her best, had come back early from the Tradescants.

Rebeccah ran down to meet her, almost banging into her halfway down the stairs.

'Heavens above! What's got into you?'

'I'm sorry.' She paused to get her breath. 'But grandmama has two visitors, people from the Merritt Bloodstock Company . . . I was on my way out again to see them . . . she's with them in the exercise paddock, introducing them to John Mordaunt . . .'

Alice was already unfastening her bonnet.

'Oh . . . so it's their carriage outside . . . I wondered who it belonged to . . . what's so special about them, anyway? Do you think she's invited them to stay to lunch?'

Rebeccah went on down the stairs, curiously reluctant, for the first time in her life, to share something with her sister Alice. 'I don't know, I'll go and find out.'

'You don't have to go racing back across the yard to find out; just ask one of the servants. They always know everything.'

'It doesn't matter. I want to ask Mordaunt something, anyway.' It was a deliberate lie, and she felt a stab of guilt. 'Do you want to come with me and be introduced to them?' she went on, already knowing what Alice's answer would be.

'No, I won't bother, I don't have time; the Tradescants' Ball is on Saturday and I want to try on my new dress. Just in case it needs altering.'

Rebeccah watched her wearily climb the remainder of the stairs; then she went down into the great hall and paused, checking her appearance, before she let herself out and made her way back across the courtyard, greeting anyone she passed, humming to herself to stop her nervousness.

She saw him look up as she approached them, almost as if he had known she was coming. Their eyes met and held, and another sensation, a sensation she had never felt before in her life and did not understand, washed over her, leaving her stomach twisted into knots and her lips parched and dry. Self-consciously, she wiped the palms of her hands as unobtrusively as she could along the skirt of her gown, to wipe off the perspiration that had suddenly made them hot and clammy.

He smiled at her, and the single look went straight through her like an arrow.

Anna turned, and saw her.

'I see that Alice is back.' A swift glance to each of the visitors. 'My other granddaughter. A pity that you can't stay with us for longer, Mr Waldo; then we could have continued our conversation over lunch.'

Her eyes never left his face.

'You have to leave us?'

'Regrettably, yes . . . though my colleague is not so unfortunate.' Again, the smile that went straight through her. 'I have some other business to take care of this afternoon . . . but I very much hope I shall have the pleasure of seeing you again, Miss Russell . . .'

She watched him walk away towards the waiting carriage, making herself hang back with Ten Broeck and her grandmother, though she longed to run after him. Unthinkable. He climbed inside and slammed the door, while the driver got up onto the box and shook the reins across the backs of the horses. Then he turned and looked at her, tipping his tall silk hat.

An idea came to her then. Her heart raced faster. As the carriage clattered off along the drive she turned and ran as fast as she could to the other end of the stables, where she caught sight of Ezra, on his way to the smithy.

'Ezra!' She fought to get her breath. 'Has Aaron exercised Spitfire yet? You didn't take him up on the Downs with the rest of the string, did you?'

He stopped walking.

'No, miss, 'er ladyship said not to . . . an' she knows what she's talking about. Temperament o' that one, he'd take a lump out of the nearest moving thing.'

'Saddle him up for me, will you? I'll take him out and put him through his paces.'

'Did you clear it with 'er ladyship, then, Miss Rebeccah?'

'Yes, of course I did.' She kept her face straight, not a flicker of an eyelid. Anna would be angry with her later, she knew . . . when she found out. But only because of her concern for her own safety . . . she knew Rebeccah could ride as well as anyone in the stable.

'It'll take two of us, I reckon,' Ezra said.

As soon as they left the paddocks behind them and reached the open ground, she felt him fight for his head; beneath her saddle, she could feel the concentration of power, every moving part of him driving forward; testing her own strength and her control of him; he knew she was not afraid; she had ridden him once before, though never alone, and, cannily, he sensed that he had met his match.

She fondled his ears and spoke to him in a soft, coaxing voice as they slowed down while she leant from the saddle and unlatched the gate which led to the path on the Downs, and he responded by standing perfectly still while she edged it closed again, before spurring him on.

Only when they had climbed the steep embankment and reached the brow of the hill, did she let him go off the bit.

His speed took her breath away; cantering downwards, flung forward in the saddle, it took all her strength to hold herself firmly in her seat. Then, when he at last got into his stride, she galloped him forward and let him have his head, and she cried out in exhilaration as the wind flung back her long loose hair, and great clumps of turf flew away in every direction as his hooves pounded the grass.

She caught sight of the carriage up ahead. Guiding the colt deftly in a wide semi-circle between the trees, she rode across its path and then around its rear, so that whichever way he was looking, he had to see her. She was right. As soon as he caught sight of her he ordered the driver to stop, just as she had hoped he would, and she rode, laughing and breathless, up alongside.

Removing his top hat, he leaned out of the carriage window.

'Well . . . you're quite a girl, aren't you?'

'This is one of our savages . . . he has to be exercised away from the other horses.' She smiled, disarmingly, her head on one side, knowing by the expression on his face that he thought she was pretty. 'My grandmother's orders!'

'Savage? He's as gentle as a sheep!'

'You should have seen him in the Chesterfield Cup. He bit one of the other runners and the stewards disqualified him. On the way back to the unsaddling enclosure, he tossed his jockey over the rails!'

The dark eyes twinkled; her cheeks felt like fire.

'Of course. No wonder he's behaving himself. So would I. If I was being ridden by a jockey as beautiful as you.'

They stared at each other.

She longed to ask him, 'When will I see you again?' Instead she said, as casually as she could, 'Will you be returning later to collect Mr Ten Broeck?'

'I regret not. Unpalatable duties call . . . but they have to be done, more's the pity.' His sharp eyes saw the disappointment in her face that she was trying so hard to hide from him. 'Lady Russell very generously offered to have him driven back to Epsom, to the hotel.'

'I see.' Beneath her saddle, the colt began to grow restless, tossing his head and stamping his feet, and she soothed him with her hands.

'But I hope I'll have the pleasure of seeing you again sometime . . . maybe at the Surrey Stakes?'

Her blue eyes lit up too eagerly.

'The Surrey Stakes? You'll be here, in Epsom, for that?'

'Yes. We don't sail for America until after the race meeting.' Again, the smile that went straight through her. 'I shall look forward to the pleasure of seeing you.'

Her heart fell. But then, of course, he would have to go back. She had known it, all along.

'Do you often come to England?'

The dark, thick-lashed eyes glinted.

'In the future, I hope to come to England much more.'

14

In the crowded, smoke-filled taproom of the Rutland Arms, Jamie Russell sprawled idly against one of the wooden benches, puffing on a borrowed cigar. When his turn came, he put down one of the cards from his pack onto the table, then cursed aloud when one of his companions beat him with a Queen and two Kings. Shouts of commiseration went up around the benches.

'Bloody hell,' Jamie said, waving his hand at the landlord for their glasses to be refilled. 'If I didn't know better I'd swear this poxy deck was marked!'

'Bad luck, Jamie!'

'I told you it wasn't your night! You'll have to go running to your old man for some more brass . . .'

Jamie's handsome face turned sullen.

'Chance'd be a fine thing. All I'll get is another lecture.'

'Don't whine, Jamie . . . all governors are the bloody same! I asked mine for a loan of a thousand guineas and he turned me down flat. Now I can't pay my damned tailor's bill or have a bet on the Surrey Stakes . . .'

Jamie took his refilled brandy glass from the landlord without thanks.

'Stand me another brandy after this, Motty, and I'll pay you back on Saturday, after the race . . .'

'How many times have I heard that? You still owe me from last time.'

'For Christ's sake . . . I've told you I'll pay up! Take my IOU for the next game, and I'll see you all alright after the Surrey Stakes . . . I told you before, I've got bets riding on more than one certain winner!'

'Why don't you let us into the secret, then, and we'll tear up your tab!'

Jamie glanced all around him, then cupped his lips and lowered his voice, at the same time speaking loud enough to be heard above the din.

'My grandmother's filly, Chenille, she's a dead certainty for the fourth race . . . she's only had one run before, at the Crystal Palace, but she came second to Westminster's Pelisse, rated the best filly of her year . . . she's been raring to go on the gallops, and her form's never fallen below par yet. I tell you, she's a dead certainty . . . I'd get skinned alive if my father knew I'd put it about . . . if it gets known before Saturday, her odds'll shorten so far that she won't be worth backing . . .'

'All right, you're on . . . but if she doesn't pass the post first . . .'

'She will, I tell you, she bloody well will! Don't you think I know what I'm talking about, for Christ's sake?'

'Look. We can't all place big bets on her, otherwise there won't be enough profit if her odds go down less than three to one . . . each of you put up a stake, and I'll add it to mine . . . I'm putting it on my account at the Beaufort . . .'

'You belong to a betting club?'

'It's operated on credit . . . although if you go down you still have to pay up after the race . . . I still do ready money gambling, if I can get it! My father's come down on me like a ton of bricks lately, when I had to go to him for a sub and he found out I'd been losing at cards.'

'He sounds worse than my gov'nor, Jamie . . . landlord! More brandy all round! All right, Russell . . . you're on. We'll give you our share and you can add it to your own, then place the bet. But if the filly goes down . . . you'll have to pay up!'

'She won't go down, I tell you!'

'What's her starting price likely to be? Did Pelisse beat her a long way off?'

'Half a length; and she was gaining all the way. Another furlong and she'd have had the race sewn up . . . it was only run over the mile, and she needed the extra quarter to put it away. From what I overheard my sister saying to our head groom, she could gallop at full speed for another mile, and still stay!'

'Your sister . . . now there's a filly I'd love to lay something on more than my bets!' Guffaws of laughter from around the crowded table. 'And he's got two of 'em! Bloody lucky dog!'

Jamie scowled, and swigged back the remainder of his brandy.

'They're bitches. Both of them. Get everything they want. Anything they ask for. Neither of them can ever do wrong in my father's eyes . . . or my grandmother's!' He swore. 'If either of 'em wants a new ballgown, or hat, or some such rubbish, father'll stump up with no questions asked . . . if I put my hand out for a few lousy sovereigns to cover my losses at betting or on the cards, he lectures me like I was still a bloody schoolboy . . .'

'Hard luck! The women always wheedle what they want; my sisters are just the same . . .' Mottram lit up a cigar and threw the match on the floor beside him. 'They could buy up half of London if they liked, and nobody would bat an eyelid. Me? If I gamble my allowance away and get stuck for cash till the end of the month, my trustees won't advance me a penny!'

'Come on, fellows, stop whining and let's get on with the next game of cards!'

'Double the stakes this time!'

'I'm in!'

'And me!'

Jamie lounged back against the bench, his face sullen. 'Take my IOU and I'll settle up on Saturday . . .'

'Five hundred then . . .'

'Done.' He took up his cards and shuffled them, then spread them out, against his open hand. Two sevens, a nine, a Jack, a single Ace. He could have done worse. He could have got better. He frowned, sulkily. Luck wasn't with him tonight any more than it had been for all the other times, since they'd come to Epsom. If his father didn't keep him perpetually short of ready money, he could have gone back, alone, to Linnets Hall. His grandmother only had him in the house on sufferance, anyhow.

'Jamie?' Mottram leaned over, glancing at his mediocre hand. 'You've played this all wrong, you know . . . if you take my advice, there's another way to get what you want . . .'

'I'm listening.'

'Your sister. Why don't you ask her to get you the money? She can make out that it's for something of her own, with nobody any the wiser; it's worth a try. Blood thicker than water, and all that.'

'Rebeccah wouldn't give me a glass of water if I was dying of thirst!'

'She doesn't strike me as being that way. You just don't handle her right, that's all.' A pause, while he dealt his hand. 'Anyway, what about Alice?'

'Much of a muchness. It's a them and me situation; always has been. Me, I'm just the black sheep of the family, because I don't have any status or any rights. The bastard son. They're all against me . . . even father, sometimes, especially if I have to go to him to borrow money when I've been hitting a losing streak, betting on the horses or getting unlucky at cards . . . I've already told you.' His turn came, and he banged his own cards down on the table, viciously. 'Nothing goes right for me. Nothing. It's like a curse. A damned bloody curse!' He grasped a piece of paper and scribbled down an IOU. 'When I think of all that there is, my grandmother's whole racing empire and my father's stud . . . nearly every brick of it, every sovereign, every bloody horse in training . . . it's hers, one day. The whole damned lot! A woman, to inherit all that; while me, five years older . . . the firstborn and a son . . . me, I'll tell you what I'll get. Nothing. Sweet damn all!'

'Rebeccah?'

'They'll see Alice all right, too . . . you mark my words! She'll get a fat dowry and be married off to some rich man with a big estate and a title . . . someone who doesn't even need the money she'll bring with her! What will I get? Nothing from my grandmother; she hates the sight of me, always has done. Father might give me his shares in the stud . . . the lion's share of that belongs to Jerome Charpentier, Rebeccah's yankee grandfather . . . and we all know who he'll leave that to! But how much do you think what I'll get, the leftovers, is likely to amount to?'

'But your father's got money of his own; he must have. I mean, Linnets Hall . . . the estate near Newmarket . . .'

'It belongs to my grandmother . . . anything that doesn't is Jerome Charpentier's. And that means Rebeccah's.'

'But she'd make you a good living allowance out of the estate, when she comes into it?'

'You really think so?' His voice was bitter; he kept his eyes on the cards. 'You don't know her as I do.' He threw down the remainder of his cards in disgust, as one of his companions trumped his single Ace with two. 'Damn it to hell! That's my last three hundred gone . . . with the IOU's another two fifty as well!'

'Never say die . . . the filly'll win it all back for you. Come on.' Mottram slapped him on the shoulder. 'For putting the bet my way I'll stand you a free visit to a certain establishment I know, off the London Road . . . how do you fancy sampling the delights of some real choice ladies?'

Jamie's eyes grew bright.

'As long as they don't send my father the bill.'

Rufus Waldo sat at the small writing desk in his room at the Boar's Head, and rubbed his eyes. It had been getting steadily darker for the past half hour, and he had gone on with his letter, covering each sheet with his large, upright, flowing hand, his eyesight fighting the lessening light.

Although there were gaslamps on the flower-papered walls, there was none close enough to cast sufficient light over the desk top. Re-reading carefully every line he'd written, he at last got up and went over to the door.

No servants were in sight. Impatiently, he walked along the narrow passageway until he came to the top of the equally narrow staircase leading to the crowded taproom below, and called to the landlord behind the bar.

'See that an oil lamp is brought up to my room, if you please. Straight away. And be sure that it isn't half empty!'

The man had come running to the bottom of the stairs.

'Why, yes sir. Very good, sir. Right away, sir. At once. An' will you be wantin' your supper in your room, an' all?'

'No, I will not. I'll take it downstairs, as usual, with Mr Ten Broeck.'

The man touched his forelock, then barked an order at one of the boys helping him behind the taproom bar.

'Oil lamp for Mr Waldo . . . filled up, mind! Take one to 'is room, straight away. Look lively!'

Rufus Waldo turned round without thanks and went back along the passageway to his room, leaving the door ajar. While he waited for the boy to bring the lamp, he took up the last page of his letter and read it again beneath the glow of the gas light beside the bed.

> '. . . *as you supposed, the Brodie Russell bloodstock is by far the best . . . the woman has a rare, perhaps a unique talent, for producing four-legged magic from a combination of ingredients that she alone knows how to pick and blend together . . . like a witch casting a magic spell . . . despite her age, she takes an intense and passionate interest in every aspect of the running of her self-made empire, that one can only be astonished at, and admire . . . but, since she is no one's fool, I must tell you that what you have in mind would not be possible under any*

circumstances, if the races you intend to manipulate should include any horses from her stable . . . indeed, in my opinion, it would be dangerous to do so . . .

I will not write more in this letter, as Ten Broeck is expecting me soon downstairs where we will share supper . . . only to say, before I close, that since coming here I have begun to formulate some interesting plans of my own . . .'

He smiled, and walked over to the writing table where he replaced it inside the blotter, moments before the boy sent by the landlord appeared in the half-open doorway, brandishing the lamp.

'Shall I light it for you, mister?'

Waldo gave him a sarcastic glance.

'I would hardly have asked for a lamp to be brought up here unless I wished for it to be lighted.'

The boy lit it without saying anything further, then went away. As soon as he was alone again, Waldo brought the lamp over to the writing table and set it down, then reseated himself and took a fresh sheet of writing paper.

'My darling Mary-Ellen . . .'

Rebeccah had sat in virtual silence, all through breakfast, toying with the food on her plate, fiddling with the unused cutlery. When she heard the sound of horses' hooves coming along the drive, she almost knocked over her tea cup in her haste to rush over to the window.

'Oh,' she said, half to herself, in a flat, disappointed voice, 'it's only Jamie.' She looked round at Alice. 'He's been away all night . . .'

'Rebeccah, what's the matter with you? You've been acting strange ever since yesterday . . .'

Their grandmother lay back in her huge, high backed carved chair at the head of the table, her blue eyes twinkling and bright. 'I think Rebeccah has certain things on her mind,' she said, wryly, looking into her face and seeing that she had guessed aright. Rebeccah's cheeks coloured.

'Oh?' Alice said.

Slowly, avoiding Anna's eyes, Rebeccah went back to her chair and sat down again. 'Jamie's for it, now. Wait till papa sees him!'

'Serves him right.'

Jamie entered the room, hair standing on end, his eyes red-rimmed and bloodshot, his chin dark with the stubble of unshaven beard.

'Good morning, ladies all. Another fine day!'

Coldly furious, Anna got to her feet.

'How dare you come into my house in that filthy state, without so much as enough decency to put a comb through your hair!' He stared at her, completely taken aback, unable to believe his ears. 'Where the hell have you been all night? . . . I'm told your bed hasn't been slept in! Not that I give a damn . . . I don't; it's your long-suffering father who's been worried!' Her voice was tight with rage. 'I told him where I reckoned you'd be . . . and I daresay I'm not far wrong, either! Lying drunk in some London Road whorehouse, or losing money that isn't yours to start with in card games with your idle, ne'er-do-well friends!'

His eyes blazed at her. 'I'm old enough to stay out all night if I choose to!'

'You can stay out and not bother to come back, for all I care! Good riddance. But when you're a guest in my house, living on my hospitality, you dare walk into my dining room where I'm eating with your sisters, looking and smelling like you've spent the night in a pig-sty, then I'll kick you out on your arse whether you're old enough or not!'

His face turned white; he was rooted to the spot. He was

angrily, acutely aware of both girls' eyes watching him, witnessing his embarrassment and disgrace.

Anna looked over him with disgust.

'Your father's waiting to see you. Now get out.'

He turned and barged his way out of the room, banging the door, striding across the hall. One of the ante room doors came open and his father came out of it.

'Jamie!'

Ignoring him, he strode into the morning room and shut himself in, while his father ran after him. 'Jamie!'

Standing there at the window, staring out into the gardens but not seeing anything, gripping the window ledge so tightly that his knuckles showed white, he clenched his teeth with suppressed rage.

Behind him, he heard his father come into the room and close the door.

'Jamie! Did you hear me calling you? Where the devil do you think you've been?'

Jamie spun round, furiously. 'That bloody woman! Did you hear what she said to me? How she spoke to me, right there, in front of them? On purpose, I know she did it on purpose. I saw their faces, Alice and Rebeccah, smirking at me . . . the little bitches! They loved it, every bloody humiliating minute of it!'

'Don't be absurd!'

'She hates me. I told you so. She's always hated me, just me, Christ knows why. Those two girls, they're all she cares about!'

'Stop talking rubbish. And when you speak about your sisters or my mother, you speak about them with respect, do you understand? I asked you a question, Jamie . . . and you'll answer it. Right now. Otherwise as old as you are I'll give you the thrashing I should have given you a long time ago! I asked you . . . where the devil have you been all night? Well?'

Jamie glared at him, his eyes as cold as flint.

'I knew you'd take their part against me . . .'

'The girls have nothing to do with this. It's you we're talking about.' A sudden suspicion. 'Have you been gambling again? Playing cards? After what you promised me!'

'I wanted to win back what I'd lost! I felt lucky, more lucky than I'd ever felt before. I felt that if I took just one last chance, it'd pay off . . .'

'You bloody fool! Won't you ever have the brains to learn by your own stupid, irresponsible mistakes? Sometimes I despair of you . . . Who were you with? Dungannon's coterie and that no-good wastrel Mottram? I thought so. It's a small wonder their fathers don't turn in their graves!'

Jamie's fury matched his own. 'They accept me as one of them. As a Russell. Bastard or not. Which is more than I can say for my own grandmother!'

James Russell darted forward and grasped him by his collar.

'Your grandmother is a woman in a million; a woman who's been through more suffering and hardship than your mind can ever begin to imagine; and she never treated anybody unjustly, not once, in all her life! There isn't a grain of badness, or selfishness in her. And she's got more guts in the tip of her little finger than you'll ever have in your whole body!'

For a long, painful moment, they stared into each other's faces; then Jamie's gaze fell away.

'I'm sorry . . . I was out of line. But I have good reason. The only thing that made me go back to the card table was desperation.' His face wore its humblest look. 'I'm in debt, father. Up to the top of my head. I can't break free of them, I couldn't see any way out except to try one more game and get back everything I lost before . . .'

'Them?'

'My friends . . . they've been lending me money. Lots of it, so I could repay the bookmakers . . .'

'Bookmakers!'

'. . . I've got gambling debts, from the last few Newmarket and London meetings . . . I tried to clear them up! It was no use. I hit a losing streak and just plunged deeper and deeper . . . I don't even know how much I owe . . . not any more . . .'

James Russell turned away and slumped down into the nearest chair.

'For God's sake! Why didn't you come to me before, when you first got into trouble? I could have done something then!'

'I didn't want to bother you, I know how much you despise people who back recklessly and then have to welsh on their bets. I know you're not able to lay your hands on big sums of ready money, that it's all tied up in the stud . . .'

'How much do you reckon would clear up the lot? To the bookies and your cronies? No lying, Jamie!'

He had the grace to look ashamed. 'I don't know . . .'

His father lost his temper. 'For Christ's sake you must have some idea!'

'All right. All right! Say five thousand . . .'

'*Five thousand*? You're in debt for five thousand and you still borrowed money from me to play cards with?'

'Look. I know it was foolish. I know to you it doesn't make any sense. But I thought if I could win, just once . . .'

James Russell put his head in his hands.

'Father, I'm sorry. I truly mean that . . . when it got out of hand, I just didn't know what to do, who to turn to . . . and I knew you'd be angry if I confessed . . .'

'How much do you need to pay back Mottram and the rest?'

'A thousand or so should do it . . .'

'I'll take care of it. For the rest . . . it'll take me a day or two to make the necessary arrangements with the bank . . .'

Jamie frowned. 'Does the bank have to be brought into it? I mean, banks always ask questions . . .'

'Leave this to me, if you please . . .' James got up, stiffly. 'This time, I can pay your debts off for you. But only this once. Jamie, if you ever bet recklessly again . . . if you throw away money that you haven't even earned . . . if you get into trouble ever again . . . I shan't lift a finger to get you out of it. I mean what I say.'

'Yes, father. I'm very grateful . . .'

'Never mind your gratitude to me. Have you apologized to your grandmother for coming back to the house in that disgusting state?'

'She didn't give me the chance!'

'Do it now.'

'Do you want me to go back in there and be humiliated like a schoolboy in front of the two girls?'

'Wait till they've left the room, then. And then apologize. I'll come with you. But if you ever behave this way again, Jamie . . . I swear I'll have nothing more to do with you!'

He followed Jamie out of the room into the hall. From inside the dining room they could both hear the sound of voices, and laughter.

'I suggest you go upstairs to the bathroom and make yourself presentable. When the girls have finished their breakfast, come down again. I'll be in here, waiting.'

Jamie went, sullenly, without another word.

In the big, modern bathroom that his grandmother had put into the house less than five years ago, he stared at his dirty, unshaven face and unkempt hair in the wall mirror, then smiled. His father had always been a soft touch, where he was concerned. Five thousand, in cash, before Saturday! Pay back Motty Mottram and settle his IOU's, and he'd be laughing; a thousand, say, for odds and ends; the rest of the brass, nearly three thousand of it, for betting on the Surrey Stakes. He'd clean up, this time, he was sure of it. Besides, he felt lucky.

He reached out and picked up his badger's hair shaving brush, worked the soap into a lather in his mug, then dipped in the brush, spreading the white, creamy substance over the dark stubble on his face. As he picked up his cut throat razor, Alice Russell poked her head around the half-open door.

'Mind the blade doesn't slip, Jamie. What a pity that would be!'

'You little bitch!' he snarled after her. He could hear her light, delicate footsteps along the landing outside, the peal of her laughter. He hastily finished shaving, washed, combed down his thick hair. Then he went to her room and let himself in.

She caught sight of him in the mirror, and spun round, startled. 'It's customary to knock before entering a lady's bedroom!'

He sneered. 'Oh, you think you're a lady, then?'

'Get out of here!'

He bit back a rude retort; this wasn't what he'd come for. Remembering Motty Mottram's words, he changed his tone of voice. He smiled. 'Can't you take a joke?'

'I'm busy, Jamie. I want to pick out a special gown for tomorrow night; we've got visitors.' She went on going through her wardrobe, looking at each gown, then pushing it back again. 'What do you want?'

He tried to look humble; he could see her looking at him in the mirror.

'Look. I can see you're busy, so I won't beat about the bush. I'm in a spot of bother . . .'

'When are you in anything else?'

'I'm serious, Alice . . .'

At last, she turned round and faced him, her chosen gown over one arm. 'What is it? What's happened now?'

'Father lent me a couple of hundred, and I promised to pay him back tomorrow. Trouble is, I can't. I got into a card game with some friends last night, and lady luck wasn't smiling my way . . . father doesn't know, of course. I promised him I wouldn't gamble any more. If I tell him the truth, he won't trust me again and he won't help me out when I get into any more trouble . . . if you could lend me the two hundred . . . well, maybe three . . . just until Saturday evening, I'll pay you back double. That's a fair profit, isn't it? Look. I know you've just got your allowance for the month, so it's not as if you'll miss the brass for a few days . . .'

'You've got a nerve! How do I know you'll pay me back at all?'

'I've given you my word, haven't I?'

She gave him a look of disgust. 'And how much do you think that's worth? You gave father your word that you wouldn't gamble again, and you've broken that!' She turned away, and laid the bright, yellow silk gown down carefully, almost lovingly, on the bed. 'What happened to your own money, the money that father gives you? No, don't bother to tell me! Frittered it all away, as usual! Well, I'm sorry, Jamie. No use running to me, bleating on about how hard done by you always are. You can't have any of mine.'

'You've got no sense of loyalty, have you? I'm your brother, for God's sake!' He was trying to keep rein on his spiralling temper. 'We should be sticking together, you and me . . . don't you realize that?' He lowered his voice. 'You always take her part, don't you? Against me. Always against me, both of you. Well, try using that brain of yours, Alice. Just for once. Work out what your position is going to be when there's just the three of us left. And guess who's going to be nothing – and who's going to be top dog?'

Her dark eyes glittered, angrily. 'Get out!'

'She'll get everything, don't you know that already? The lot. And us? When the old woman dies, what do you think your slice of the cake is going to be worth compared to Rebeccah's? A pittance, that's what. Do you really mean to tell me that you don't care?'

'You're jealous of her, aren't you? You always were. Not just because of the money . . . it goes a lot deeper than that. Because you're a failure you hate anyone else who's got more than you have. And because you can't stomach the thought of being rated second to a woman! Rebeccah'll see me all right!'

He glared at her. 'You'll be sorry for this . . .'

She turned her back on him and went on with what she was doing, as if he were a servant.

'Not as sorry as you'll be when father finds out you've blown every penny of your allowance!'

'Bitch! Rot in hell!' The door slammed and she heard his heavy footsteps dying away.

She waited in her room for several more minutes, guessing, by his ablutions in the bathroom, what his intentions were most likely to be. She went out quietly onto the landing outside and leaned over the banisters, careful not to let him see her. Her father was already waiting for him in the hall. Together, they went into the dining room; a moment later, Rebeccah came out.

Alice leaned further over the banisters and called to her.

'Rebeccah! Quickly! Up here!'

Rebeccah glanced up and smiled. Then, lifting the hemline of her gown she rushed up the big staircase in twos and threes. Breathless, she reached the top.

'I almost felt sorry for Jamie. Now he's got to eat humble pie.'

'Serves him right.' They walked along the landing towards Alice's room, arm in arm. 'He's always trying to make trouble. And borrow money because he's gambled away his own. Guess what? Five minutes ago he was in here, whining about the injustice he has to suffer from everyone, trying to scrounge two or three hundred pounds off me!'

'But he only got his allowance from papa two weeks ago!'

'That's all gone. Three guesses where to!'

Rebeccah frowned. 'Maybe we shouldn't laugh about it, Alice. Maybe we ought to do something to help him . . .'

'*What?*'

'I don't mean lend him more money . . . that wouldn't do any good at all. He'd just fritter it away like he always does. I mean, maybe we should speak to papa, or grandmama, about it . . . not telling tales, just see if they can do something to stop him . . .'

'You'd be wasting your time. Don't you think papa's already lectured him about throwing away money on gambling and drink? Those idle ne'er-do-wells he runs around with . . . Mottram and the rest . . . they all have carte blanche from their fathers or their trustees . . . much more money than Jamie's ever likely to see in all his life! They're legitimate heirs; he isn't. And that's what rankles; he can't bear it! That's why he's always been so envious of you. Besides which, he thinks the world owes him a living.'

'I know.'

Inside her room, Alice changed the subject.

'Let's not talk about him any more! Tell me about the two men who are coming to dinner tomorrow night, from Merritt and Company . . . are they young?' She picked up the yellow silk gown, held it against herself, and admired the reflection in the mirror. 'I've decided already . . . this is what I'll wear . . .'

'I don't know how old William Ten Broeck is . . . but he's young-*ish* . . .' She gave a conspiratorial smile. 'Rufus Waldo is twenty-six.'

'Rufus Waldo? Only an American could have a name like that. And how do you know so precisely how old he is?'

'He told me.'

'Why should he tell you something like that?'

Rebeccah seated herself on the counterpane of Alice's bed. 'It just came out when we were talking, that's all.' She kept her face straight, without smiling, unwilling to share even with Alice the thrill that she'd felt when he was near.

Her first infatuation; she hugged herself, thinking how delicious it felt, a secret known only to herself.

'But are they good-looking?' Alice persisted. 'None of the men who come here to dinner ever are.'

'You'll have to decide that for yourself.'

15

HER PLACE AT DINNER had been set opposite him; throughout the whole meal, she could never afterwards remember what she had eaten, nor what they had talked about. Every mouthful stuck in her throat; her stomach, as if it had ceased to exist, would not digest a single morsel. Most of the food on her plate was left untouched.

She remembered taking a small sip from her glass of wine; then, he had turned aside from his conversation with Jamie and smiled at her, and the whole room spun.

Afterwards, in the big drawing room while he stood beside the fireplace, dominating the whole company, she sat, side by side with Alice; but when he turned to speak to their grandmother she could indulge herself in the thrilling luxury of looking at him, her eyes transfixed upon his face. Eagerly, she devoured every word he spoke.

'I notice you have no youngstock in your yards sired by Ormonde . . . the Great Ormonde, as I believe he's better known. Is there a significant reason for that?' He was cradling his glass of brandy in both hands, and Rebeccah noticed how long and tapering and beautifully shaped his fingers were. 'Breeders on our side of the Atlantic, considering his outstanding reputation here, will flock to buy any yearling that has his name in their bloodline; yet not you.'

Anna smiled, and sipped her own brandy. 'Mr Waldo . . . I always have reasons for everything I do. Ormonde was a great racehorse . . . yes. Who in their right mind would deny it? The Dewhurst Plate, the Criterion Stakes, 2,000 Guineas, the Derby in '86; the St James's Palace Stakes, the

Hardwicke, the Great Foal, the Champion and the Leger . . . all in his three-year-old career alone. And he had the best of temperaments to boot. A pity his career at stud was only a disappointing anti-climax; but, with great horses, it often happens that way . . .' A look of sadness crossed her face. 'It may be that if the Duke of Westminster hadn't sold him abroad, he might have proved himself at the stud here after all . . . that, none of us will ever know. After he stood for his first year at Eaton, where he sired Orme, he was leased to Lord Gerard and stood at Newmarket, then he caught a severe chill and for the rest of that year served only two or three mares.'

'I didn't know that.'

'He returned to Westminster's Eaton stud a very sick horse, and the Duke sold him for £12,000 to the Argentinian breeder Boucau; an action that got him much criticized, rightly or wrongly. Westminster said then that the only reason he'd decided to sell such a great horse was that Ormonde was a roarer and a descendant of roarers; and that to keep him in England might well prove detrimental to English bloodstock. That we'll never know. The last I heard, he'd been resold to a Californian breeder for £30,000; but I reckon that his procreative powers, whatever they were, have been much impaired by his illness, and his good foals few and far between. We shall see. But it wouldn't surprise me in the least to hear that he might have to be put down, as a last act of kindness.'

Rufus Waldo exchanged glances with William Ten Broeck.

'In the United States, his reputation as a great racehorse has gone before his failure at the stud over here. The reputation of his son Orme, for instance – who I understand has great things hoped for him – tends to overshadow any doubts American breeders might have about the quality of the blood.'

Anna smiled.

'True, Orme has so far shown exceptional ability; his dam Angelica was a sister to the great St Simon . . . now, there's a horse! As a two-year-old he won the Richmond and the Prince of Wales' Stakes at Goodwood, the Middle Park and, like his sire, the Dewhurst; he only lost in the Lancashire Plate when he was narrowly beaten by Signorina . . . but then he was competing against three- and four-year-olds, while he was still only two. Understandable. Whether this year he can take the Derby and the Guineas, is anybody's guess; but then, if he does win, who is to say that it isn't his dam's bloodline, not his unpredictable sire's, that gives him the victories? We all have our own opinions, Mr Waldo.'

The dark, thick-lashed eyes glittered. 'And your opinion, Lady Russell?'

'In my opinion, he won't do it; he's not a true stayer. I've seen him run in all his races except the Middle Park, and I don't reckon he can go much beyond ten furlongs.'

'Then I won't bet my shirt on him.' He glanced across at where Rebeccah sat, and she felt her colour rise. 'While we're on the subject of greatness, do you think there'll ever be a jockey to replace Archer?'

'A great tragedy,' someone said. 'What a loss to racing!'

'Nobody, however great, is indispensable. Archer was great but I dispute the title of The Greatest. When I was a girl, there were three jockeys that I reckon could have beaten him in any race on any terms.' Anna's mind went back, like an unseen hand turning the pages of a dusty book. Jeremiah Chifney; dear, faithful, sad-eyed Chifney, winning on Hope, on Bloodstone . . . even now she felt the lump rising, unbidden, in the depths of her throat. '*Anna . . . this is the only way to go . . .*' She was kneeling on the grass, his torn, bleeding head cradled in her lap; she remembered the cold hand, held tightly in her own, as the tears had blinded her and she'd tried, desperately, to will him back . . . she closed her eyes. Little Nat Street, the genius who never had the chance to live to greatness, his small, pitiful, dead body hanging from the rafters of the wooden hut, a pathetic, long-forgotten victim of turf villainy . . . William Devine, the Irish boy with the magic hands, who'd died, coughing up his lungs, before he, too, could rank with greatness . . . somehow, the memories of all of them were sacred; for a long moment she did not speak. 'Yes, it was tragic about Fred Archer . . . all he ever cared about was winning races . . . it was a terrible struggle, all his life, to keep down his weight. Especially for a man so unnaturally tall; too tall, really, for a jockey. Taller than the tallest rider I ever knew . . . in winter he was eleven stone; by the time of the Lincoln and Liverpool he'd be down to eight stone ten pounds . . . an enormous feat. He had a Turkish bath installed in his house at Newmarket . . . James once saw it . . . and a doctor called Wright there used to concoct some wicked brew to purge him before he rode races – "Archer's Mixture", it was called. One of my boys tried it, once, for a joke! Dynamite, he said it was!' She smiled, sadly. 'He had a wonderful intuition about horses . . . marvellous hands, and seat . . . but there was always a kind of brooding melancholy about him . . . a strange man. He adored his wife, Nellie – Mat Dawson's niece – and when she died in childbirth it was the beginning of the end for him . . . that and the wasting he endured to make the weights . . .' She sighed, and put down her glass of brandy. 'I wasn't surprised, really, when the news came that he'd shot himself. Like a horse that's got a broken neck, he put himself out of his own misery.'

For a few moments there was a silence in the room.

'And your American jockeys, Mr Waldo? Who do you rate among the greatest of them?'

Another quick, fleeting glance at Rebeccah, with the dark, charismatic eyes. 'Oh . . . I don't think you'll have heard of them even if I told you their names . . . but that may well change for the future; I heard, before we left, that some of our trainers have a mind to try their luck over here.

Johnny and Lester Reiff, though, I can tell you now, those brothers certainly have something special . . .'

'But are they honest?'

'As the day is long.'

'I'll look forward to watching them, Mr Waldo. If they're everything you say they are, maybe I'll engage them to ride for me . . .'

Rebeccah excused herself and left the room. It was cool and quiet in the great hall, the clocks ticked soothingly, in unison, as she made her way slowly to the front door, and let herself outside; the cold, fresh air fanning her hot face, she wandered across the courtyard in the direction of the stables.

It was dusk now, and everywhere was quiet; the lads would be at supper, in the big room over the barn; the horses had been watered and fed. Too early, yet, for them to be locked away for the night. As she walked towards the loose boxes, several of them, their heads poking out from the top of the stable doors, turned and looked at her.

She stopped at the first stall, and petted the animal; whispering to it in a soft, low voice, fondling the long soft ears.

Then a door slammed shut in the distance, she heard footsteps crunching on the gravel, and she turned round, quickly. And there he was.

He came casually towards her, a lighted cigar in one hand. As he came up to her and smiled down into her flushed face, she leaned back against the stable door to keep herself steady. Her heart hammered.

'Is it not too chilly for you out here at this time in the evening?'

She shook her head. 'No, I often walk about the stable yard after dinner, either with my father or my sister . . .'

'A remarkable likeness between the two of you . . . you and Alice.' He smiled, and dotted the ash from his cigar on the ground. 'Do you mind if I smoke?'

'No. No, of course not.' She felt unbearably shy and painfully young. 'And, yes, we are alike; most people remark on it . . .'

There was amusement in his eyes now.

'But your voices are very different. And your mannerisms; in fact, every other thing about you.' Another smile. Almost imperceptibly, he moved closer. 'And blue eyes, in a lady, are so much more beautiful than brown . . .'

She swallowed, and caught at her breath, not knowing how to answer him. She felt her cheeks colour. And she wished, passionately, more than anything in her life, that she could be like the suave, sophisticated, self-assured professional beauties that decorated Society and the Court, women like Lily Langtry and the Duchess of Manchester, not a raw, inexperienced, tongue-tied sixteen-year-old girl.

'You're very kind . . .' the words came out breathlessly, tumbled, one after the other, like a deck of falling cards.

'Just truthful,' he said, nonchalantly, drawing deeply on his cigar. He leaned against the stable building with his easy grace. 'My father always did say that honesty, invariably, is the best policy. Especially in dealing with the ladies.'

She half turned away and began to pet the nearest horse, to hide her growing confusion. By rights, she knew, she ought not to be out here, alone, in the growing dusk with an almost total stranger; although her grandmother never stood on the ceremony that governed other households, she knew that her father would be angry with her; yet, despite her gaucheness and embarrassment, the last thing she wanted to do was to shatter the magical moment, to go back inside.

She said, trying to make her voice sound normal, 'Will you . . . and Mr Ten Broeck be here for the Surrey Stakes?'

'Indeed, yes; neither of us would miss it for the world. Your grandmother has a filly entered and we'd be most interested to see how she runs . . . her half-brother is among the youngstock Merritt and Co. are buying in the sale.'

'Chenille. Yes, she ought to do well. Though this is only her second race. But she has the class. And both her sire and dam were notable stayers.'

'You think we could risk a bet on her, then?'

She smiled. 'I would think that you could . . . that is, if you don't mind the gamble . . .'

'Sometimes it is necessary to gamble.' The dark eyes were serious now. 'Without the occasional risk, wouldn't you say, life would be very dull . . ?'

For a moment she stared into his face, trying to read something else in the lightly spoken words, but he did not add to them. Before she could answer, she caught sight of her sister, Alice, waving to her from the other side of the stable yard. Rufus Waldo saw her, too.

'It's too chilly out here now for a delicate girl; shall we go back inside?'

'Rebeccah! What in God's name were you thinking of, alone with him outside? And it was nearly dark!'

'Dusk, papa. And he isn't just anyone, either. He was a guest; a gentleman. From the fuss you're making anybody would think he was some ruffian who'd climbed over the wall, or an escaped convict.'

'Don't answer me back! Your behaviour was thoughtless, foolish and the height of impropriety!'

'That isn't fair and you know it! All I did was to go outside to see the horses, and he came out to smoke a cigar. He saw me and we began talking. If it had been Jamie instead of me you wouldn't have said a word!'

'Jamie's twenty-one years old, five years your senior. And a man. Girls of sixteen aren't permitted the same levity.'

'But, papa,' Alice interrupted, springing to Rebeccah's defence. 'You're being completely unjust! Rebeccah wasn't gone more than twenty minutes! Besides, Americans are much more free and easy than we are . . . he wouldn't have thought anything of it!'

Her father turned on her angrily.

'I wasn't aware I'd asked for your opinion, miss . . . nor do I wish to hear it! Whether or not Americans observe the same social conventions as we do here in England is of no interest to me whatsoever. My concern is what other people think of the personal conduct of my daughters!'

'When my grandmother was my age she did exactly as she liked!' Rebeccah shouted. 'She was a rough-rider up on the Downs when she was even younger than me! She competed against men on their own terms, and she beat them hands down! She never allowed herself to be stifled and trampled underfoot with stupid, meaningless, hypocritical conventions and empty rules!' It was the first time she had ever fallen out with her father, and she was shocked by her words. 'I did something I do every evening . . . walk around the stableyard and see the horses before the lads bed them down. Rufus Waldo came out of the house and he began talking to me, and you're outraged. Well, I'm sorry about that.' She was a little girl again, walking in the big gardens at Linnets Hall, her toys behind her on the lawn; the forbidden door opened, and above her towered the flight of steps . . . in her imagination she was being propelled upwards, till she stopped, abruptly, outside the little used bedroom door, and then reached out and opened it . . . 'I'm sorry if you think talking to a guest in grandmama's house is the height of impropriety. How wicked I am! Well, as Jesus said to the mob who wanted to stone the harlot to death beside the well . . . Let he who is without sin cast the first stone!'

His reaction to her words was instantaneous. For a few moments he stared at her, stunned both by her temerity and her insolence. He strode across the room to where she stood, and slapped her, hard, across the face. Behind her she heard her sister gasp.

'*Papa!*'

'How dare you speak to me like that! And you,' to Alice, 'are scarcely better than she is, taking her part when you should have the decency to know better! For a punishment, neither of you will be allowed to attend the Surrey Stakes meeting on Saturday, nor will I permit you to go to Chilworth Manor and the Tradescants' Ball! Now go, both of you!'

Alice fled, but Rebeccah stood her ground. Biting back the tears, she faced him.

'That's unjust, papa! Punish me if you think I deserve it, but not Alice! She was just being loyal!'

'I will not be accused of injustice or immorality by my own daughter! Nor, I hasten to add, have I any intention of changing my mind! Go to your room and stay there!'

She turned and ran. Through the hall, up the stairs, into her bedroom, where she flung herself on the big, damask covered, four-poster bed.

He had ruined all the beauty and the magic of her evening. He had spoiled everything. Saturday was Rufus Waldo's last day in England, and now she would never see him; not even to say goodbye. The injustice of it all overwhelmed her.

'He didn't mean it, I'm sure he didn't! It's so unlike papa. He wouldn't stop us from going to the Surrey Stakes, or over to Chilworth Manor for the Ball! Look at the way he rants and raves at Jamie, when Jamie steps over the line and does something wrong; he isn't angry for long. It all boils over and then he's all right again and everything's forgotten. He just lost his temper, and said the first thing that came into his head, to save face . . . he knows how much Saturday means to both of us!'

'He meant it when he slapped my face!'

'He shouldn't have done that, whatever you said. But you did goad him, Rebeccah . . . when you said about "Let him without sin cast the first stone . . ." I could scarcely believe my own ears when you said it . . . I wouldn't have had the nerve . . .'

Rebeccah rolled over on the bed, slowly rubbing the side of her face. There were tear stains on her cheeks, her eyes were red-rimmed from crying.

'I hate him for treating me like a child!'

'He's probably sorry, he's probably more upset than you are. And grandmama. I'll lay you a hundred to one on she'll take our part against him . . . if I know anything about her, she will!'

Rebeccah sat up, leaning back against the thick, oak carving on the bed. 'He had a look about him, a look I've never seen before. It was my fault, what I said . . . I could bite my tongue off now, for your sake! But I was right . . . he was making a mountain out of a molehill, and I won't apologize for saying that!'

'When people are in the wrong, and they don't want to admit it, like papa, it just makes them more stubborn when someone else points out the truth.'

'He always forgives Jamie!' Her voice was uncharacteristically bitter. 'Jamie doesn't get slapped and sent to his room like a ten-year-old. No matter how badly he behaves, he always gets forgiven.'

'That's because he's a man, and five years older than we are.'

'Old enough to know better!'

Alice's dark, beautiful eyes took on a far-seeing look. 'You know . . . a thought just occurred to me . . . no. No, it's just my imagination, I'm sure . . . a wild shot in the dark . . .'

'What is it? Go on, tell me . . .'

'The way papa lost his temper tonight . . . over something so trivial . . . hitting you; he's never lifted a hand to either of us before . . . I wonder . . . I wonder if he realizes, during all the talk about the stables and the stud this evening . . . if he realizes that one day, when you're as old as Jamie, you'll have more than he has . . . from the Brodie Russell inheritance. Grandmama always did say that men couldn't bear to be upstaged, especially by a woman! Maybe papa's resentful of what you'll have one day; maybe he doesn't even realize that he resents it. But, it could be true . . .'

The thought, even the suggestion, appalled her. Yet Alice's words had a ring of truth about them.

'And Jamie. He's always been the apple of papa's eye, you know that. Maybe papa resents him getting nothing from the estate more than he resents it for himself.'

'Jamie won't get anything because grandmama sees him for what he is. Papa knows that.'

'But love is blind, don't they say . . . and papa loves Jamie more than he'll ever love either of us . . . yes, it's true. He's the son, the heir who won't inherit because he isn't legitimate. The fruit of the idyllic little love affair with his first, long-lost love . . . he'll always be special. It's unpalatable, I know, to have to admit, Rebeccah; but you can see as well as I can that papa always puts Jamie first.'

Rebeccah hauled herself angrily from the bed. 'He always said that he loved the three of us just the same! All I did was walk outside, and speak a few words with Rufus Waldo, and he makes me a prisoner . . !'

Alice's expression changed.

'He's very handsome, isn't he? And different. Not like anyone else that we've ever met, at all . . . but then, I suppose that's because he's an American . . .'

'So was my mother.' A ghost of a smile.

'But he is different, not just because of that . . .'

Dull-eyed, heavy-hearted, Rebeccah touched the delicate lawn of her ballgown that Annie had draped across the foot of the bed, the gown that she'd never worn and would not wear, on Saturday night. So passionately, for so long, she'd looked forward to that; her disappointment was so acute that it made her feel physically sick.

It seemed so childish, so futile, so impotent, to cry; there was no point now. Her father would never forgive her for what she'd said, and she would never apologize, because it had been the truth.

But Alice; she couldn't let Alice suffer.

'I don't want him to punish you, too. I told him that, after you'd gone out of the room. But he just ordered me upstairs.' She turned and looked at her sister. 'I'm sorry.'

'It doesn't matter.'

'It does matter. If you go and find him and tell him you think I was in the wrong, he'll let you go. Then I won't feel so guilty.'

'I couldn't. It wouldn't be the same if I left you behind.'

'I'd be happy, knowing that you, at least, were enjoying yourself. Don't worry about me.'

'Rebeccah . . .'

'. . . Give him time to calm down, then go and look for him. He'll be doing the last rounds of the stables, no doubt. Take a shawl, the wind's turned cold. Say that you took my part out of loyalty, but you want to apologize . . . he'll forgive you, I know he will.'

'Why don't you come down too?'

'He told me to stay in my room.' A pause. 'He's still my father. Until I'm of age or until I marry, I have to obey him.'

Alice was hesitating at the door.

'Shall I tell him you want to see him? Shall I say that you're sorry? It won't hurt to eat humble pie and get what you want. Rebeccah, he'll never guess. You'll wave the olive branch and pacify his anger, and he'll let you go to the racecourse and the Ball.'

Rebeccah sat down on her bed again. Slowly, she shook her head.

'I can't, Alice. I can't do it. It was right, what I said.'

When she was alone again, she wondered if standing on her principles was worth not seeing Rufus Waldo for one last time.

*

'You've done what?'

'I've sent her to her room, mother. And there she'll stay until she apologizes. Please, I beg of you, don't interfere. She was unpardonably insolent and said things to my face, my own daughter, that shocked me to hear. Don't go against me and take her part.'

Anna lay back and looked at him from the depths of her wing chair.

'Unpardonably insolent doesn't sound at all like Rebeccah. And what, after your dear son's behaviour, could be left to shock you to hear?'

'Please, let's leave Jamie out of this argument. Besides which, he's old enough to take care of his own reputation; Rebeccah isn't.'

The curved eyebrows arched. 'Her reputation?'

He gave a brief, halting, angry account of the episode in the ante-room.

'Oh, come, James, for God's sake! What a fuss over nothing! And you'd stop her going to the Surrey meeting and Saul Tradescant's ball just for that? Alice too. If my mother had chided me at their age for talking to any man – respectable or not – I wouldn't have taken the slightest notice.'

'With respect, mother, I prefer to bring up my daughters as I think fit. You were different; you always were. You were independent, you always made your own rules . . . and broke everybody else's. That was fifty years ago and you got away with it. Yes, I've no doubt you'd do the same thing all over again, and get away with it again too. But Rebeccah isn't you. I won't tolerate being lectured by my own sixteen-year-old daughter, quoting Jesus Christ's words at me from out of the Bible, and I'd be grateful if, just for once, I received some backing up of my authority from you.'

The striking blue eyes narrowed as they went on looking at him.

'Don't raise your voice to me, James. Especially in my own house. I may be old . . . but not hard of hearing.' She leaned forward, and he could see the anger in her face. 'A few days ago I heard you and Jamie quarrelling in the library. Don't bother to deny it. Yet you saw fit to forgive him and send him on his way . . . no doubt with a few extra hundred for him to squander, as he squanders all the rest. No doubt, either, that he said things to you that he ought to get a hiding for, as old as he is. And wouldn't I love to give it to him! Your daughter spends less than a half hour talking politely to one of my guests, and you give her a lecture on morality and send her to her room!'

'Mother . . .'

'. . . I'm warning you, James. Whether she's your daughter and you have jurisdiction over her, or not. You can't make fish of one child and fowl of the other. That's bloody unfair. The girls get punished but Jamie gets away. As usual. You know you can get them to obey you just by telling them to do something, while what you say to him, the lazy, no-good waster, goes in one ear and out of the other. Don't you ever dare try making a whipping boy out of either of those girls, or I'll see you regret it!'

It was always useless to argue with her; she always won.

'Mother, I'm sorry. I don't want to fall out with you over this . . . especially as, after the Surrey Stakes, I'm taking the girls back with me to Newmarket . . .'

'They're both happier and better off here!'

'Mother, they're my daughters and they belong with me. I won't have them disobey me. And if they grow up thinking they can flout the conventions, no man will want to marry them, however much of the estate they bring with them. Maybe fifty years ago they might have got away with it, like you did; but they're not you. Now, any man of breeding and good family looks for other qualities in a wife. Rebellion is not one of them.'

Anna got up and went over to the small table that stood in one corner of the room, and poured herself a brandy.

'Any man worth the name would want a woman with a bit of spirit, not a whimpering woolsack frightened of her own shadow. And you overestimate the value of money; not all men are so mercenary. True, a woman with money of her own is better than a woman with nothing at all, if only for her own sake; it's humiliating for any wife to be entirely dependent on her husband's bounty, however much she loves him. We all need it, whether we despise it or not; money, like other things, is merely a means to an end. But if a man marries a woman only for what she brings with her, he's not worth marrying. He should have enough of his own not to care whether his wife is wealthy or not.'

'Marriages in society today, even out of it, rarely take place without some consideration for a woman's dowry.'

She smiled, but without warmth. 'Just because you married for money, James, it doesn't follow that every other man does. Or wants to.'

'I did what I had to do.' Her barb had gone home, as she'd intended. But it served him right. Looking at the expression on his face, the resentful anger in his eyes, she knew exactly what he was thinking.

'Go on, James, let's have it out here and now. It's always stuck in your throat, hasn't it, that your father left everything to me and not you? You've never got over it. And you're thinking, now, as you've done ever since you first set eyes on Corinna Charpentier, that if I'd handed everything over to you lock stock and barrel and spent the rest of my life in a rocking chair, knitting charity socks, you could have married some hare-brained, amiable simpleton like Margaret McAllister, and lived happily ever after. Well, real life isn't like that. You made your bed and you have to lie on it. You wanted the money that came with Corinna because I wouldn't give you any of mine. And why should I? You were fourteen years old when your father died, a raw, unworldly boy; did you think you were capable of running a racing empire? An empire that I built up, with sweat and toil, against all odds, that I fought tooth and nail to keep going, even when I nearly lost everything. Your father trusted my judgement as much as he loved me. And he wanted to leave the decision to me as to how much or how little you were capable of handling. I made that choice. And your behaviour, your way of life since that day has made me more certain now than ever that I made the right choice.'

'Because of the scandal when Corinna left me? Because people found out about Jamie, and then Alice? Scandals can be lived down . . . you, of all people, should know that.'

Nobody had ever got the better of her; nor had anyone succeeded, in all her long life, in cheating her of the last word. She smiled at him, like a gambler who, at the end of a long game, produces the winning card.

'Scandals, like time, eventually heal. But you remain all your life what you are, James. As you have. And you know, as well as I do, that a man can run away from almost anything except himself.'

16

LONG BEFORE the first race, the whole expanse of the racecourse, and beyond it, Epsom Downs, was filled with a milling, noisy, colourful mass of people, from the common public and the rag-tag assortment of fortune tellers, gypsies, beggars, tumblers and organ-grinders with their monkeys, to the prosperous middle and upper classes, lined up in their sumptuous carriages and plush landaus, the finely dressed ladies gazing towards the paddock and the course with silver opera glasses, or entertaining guests in the lavish privacy of their grandstand boxes.

Down at the saddling enclosure, Jamie Russell, his off-course betting with the bookmakers already done, leaned against the paddock rail to watch the preparations beginning for the final race.

'I don't see Chenille,' Motty Mottram said, screening his eyes against the glare of the late afternoon sun. 'Or, come to it, that good-looking sister of yours. What gives, Jamie?' The others were crowding round them now, having caught sight of the Russell filly, being led into the parade ground by her lad, who was now busily removing her rug. She was a sleek, strong-boned chestnut with a beautiful head, round, moulded, deep shoulders, and a magnificent tail. 'That's a winner, just look at her! I can smell 'em a mile off!'

'She looks like Stubbs' painting of Eclipse!'

'If the race was on looks then she'd distance the whole bloody field!'

'Who's riding her, Jamie?'

'McHeath, my grandmother's favourite jockey. He knows her like the back of his hand.'

'Didn't he ride Youth, over two miles at Ascot?'

'That's the one.' Briefly, Jamie let his narrowed eyes rove over the rest of the paddock as the jockeys got up. 'He was riding a 40–1 shot in the Blaybury Stakes, and he played a waiting race; but not with the usual waiting tactics, bunched up at the back of the field . . . he kept the nag near the middle, just behind the front runners, till he was ready to deliver his challenge at the last quarter of a mile . . . it was pure bloody artistry! He gave the nag its head two furlongs out, when both the front runners and the favourite had shot their bolts, and sailed past the post like a yacht with the wind behind it. The crowd gave him a standing ovation.'

'He'd better win today!'

'I've put five thousand on at the Beaufort!'

'If I lose any more at this meeting, my trustees will bury my bloody brass and throw the key away!'

'Fillies. I never did like fillies, can't trust 'em. Like any female. Unreliable,' Mottram said.

Jamie sneered, 'She'll walk it, didn't I tell you? With McHeath up she can't lose!'

As soon as they'd begun the slow canter down the centre of the field, McHeath knew there was something wrong.

She'd looked magnificent back there in the paddock, but now, bowling along on the soft turf, he could feel something amiss and jerky in her action; instinctively, he slowed down.

A brisk trot, then a stately walk. Tossing her beautiful head with its long, silky luxuriant mane, she seemed to have suddenly got back into her stride. McHeath was puzzled. Turning to glance back over his shoulder at the way they'd come, he checked to see if there was some unevenness about the turf which might have caused her to stumble, and jolt. Nothing that he could see with the naked eye. A stone, perhaps.

When they reached the starter's chair he slipped lightly down from the saddle, and checked the underside of each hoof. A minute chipping, lodged between the nearside shoe; just as he'd thought. When it was prized out, he got himself back into the saddle and took his place among the other runners in the field.

Away to his right hand side, he could see the mass of waving, dancing blobs that were human beings, spread across the lushness of the grass; the sunlight, almost harshly, bathing the greyness of the grandstand brick; the lines of carriages, bursting with their occupants, all eyes riveted on the waiting field.

As soon as the flag was down he sprang forward in the saddle, guiding her deftly between the second and third horses; his favourite waiting position in a race. As if she had wings, the filly sped along with the sure, swift smoothness of a bird of prey in flight, until they were halfway around the wide, undulating course. Then, he felt her stumble beneath his hands and lose speed. Lame! Cursing, he'd bet his life on it.

Courageously, stretching her neck forward, she tried to go on, but McHeath knew better. Pulling her gently to a standstill, he slipped down from the saddle and examined her foreleg, which confirmed his fears.

Well, sometimes it happened to the best of them. Who was that Derby winner who'd been lame both before and after the race, and never won another in the whole of his life? For the life of him, he couldn't remember now. Lady Russell had told him.

He patted the filly on the neck and drew her reins over her head, preparing himself for the long walk back.

A good thing, he thought, hearing the disappointed groans from the crowd, that Lady Russell hadn't laid out a big bet this time.

*

'The bloody horse has gone lame!'

'She was under Starter's orders, we've lost the lot!'

'Russell, I've gone down five thousand on this goddamned race! You owe us full cover on our bets!'

'I gave you a tip, that's all! I said if she ran she was a certain winner!'

'But she didn't run. The bloody jockey drew her up halfway!'

'How the hell was I to know? The best racehorses have suddenly gone lame! It happens . . .'

'It's all your fault. You said it was a certainty that the filly'd run!'

'McHeath should have pulled her out before the start. Then we'd have got our stake back!'

'What about the brass you owe us, Jamie?'

He stared round at them, the anger and hostility in their eyes. Friends indeed. Anger, rage, consumed him.

'She was a sure winner. You can't blame me for what happened, any more than if she'd suddenly reared up on her hind legs or tossed the jockey over the rails!'

'You promised to pay up after this race, for the loans and the IOU's . . . and you'd better.' Motty Mottram's sly, pale, hatchet-like face looked suddenly menacing. 'We don't like people who welsh on their debts.'

'All right. I heard you. But I can't give it to you now.'

He turned away, abruptly, boiling inside, and pushed his way roughly, rudely, back through the milling crowd. He knocked people out of the way, not bothering to tip his hat for the ladies, his face set in grim, hard, uncompromising lines. If he couldn't lay his hands on some ready money, things might just get ugly. And he'd been stalling them for weeks now over the money that he'd borrowed and still couldn't pay back.

His only hope was his father.

There was no chance of seeing him alone until much later. He'd be here, with everyone else from the Russell yard, until long after the crowds had gone away; talking to officials, jockeys, other owners and training managers, seeing that all the Russell horses had been safely rugged up and ready to be walked away. No chance then, back at the house, to have a private word with him; the Tradescants' Ball, over at Chilworth Manor, started at seven o'clock and by six everyone in the house who was going would have to be ready, with the carriage waiting to drive them away. No time to talk.

Sullenly, kicking a stone beneath his foot, he stuck his hands in his pockets and walked heavily, sulkily, through the gradually thinning crowd.

He was glad, at least, that he'd come on horseback, and not in the open landau with all the others. In the mood he was in, he needed to be alone. And he needed a drink.

He rode off in the direction of the Boar's Head, on the road leading from the Downs.

'Why, Mr Russell.' A soft, accented voice, strongly familiar to his ears, spoke from behind him. 'Don't tell me you've come here to drown all your sorrows . . .'

He turned, sharply, and found himself looking into the sharp, clever face of Rufus Waldo. The dark, thick-lashed eyes glittered in the bright light of the taproom bar, and there was thinly-disguised amusement in them. 'I watched you walk back from the paddock after the last race . . . by your expression, I'd say you lost.'

'Too right I did. And so did my friends!'

Waldo sipped his glass of brandy. 'What a pity your jockey didn't pull up on the canter down to the post . . . instead of halfway through the race.' He smiled. 'Then nobody would have lost a cent on it.'

'Bloody jockeys! Not worth a shovelful of horseshit, the whole lot of 'em! Over that distance he could have pushed her to the end of the race! It's been done. She had the stamina, and the speed. Lame horses have won before; I've seen it done!'

'But invariably if that happens, then they can never run again.'

'Who cares? As long as I got my brass back and paid off my friends . . . I gave them the tip for the Surrey, and they're all at my throat!'

'Pressing you, no doubt?' The soft, silky voice was insistent, probing; but Jamie was too miserable to care.

'Pressing! That's putting it mildly! I'll have to ask my father to stand me another loan . . . Christ knows what he'll say when I tell him. Not only the brass; he'll know then that I gave them the tip . . . and I'm not supposed to give out secret stable information under any circumstances. If the old woman finds out she'll skin me alive!'

'Lady Russell?'

'She already hates my guts. She'll probably throw me out the house. Not that she'll need much of an excuse, anyway. She only has me there, once in a blue moon, for father's sake.' He swigged back the last of his drink and fished in his pocket for another sovereign. 'Well, I won't give her the satisfaction! If I can get something off father to throw to the pack of wolves, I'm leaving first thing in the morning for Inverness . . . my mother lives there.' He peered closer into Waldo's face. 'Anyhow, what's your interest? You're going back to America tonight, aren't you, you and that colleague of yours . . . Broke, Boke, Boek, something or other . . .'

'William Ten Broeck.' Another charming smile. 'Jamie . . . I may call you Jamie? Perhaps we could talk . . . there's a private room, reserved for the guests, at the back of the Inn . . . it's more quiet in there . . .'

'Talk? What about?'

'You'll see. And do let me buy you another drink . . .'

She lay there, propped up against the bedhead, a book open on her lap, staring into the gathering darkness with sore, tear-swollen eyes. Only the ticking of the clock on her mantelpiece soothed and comforted her; inwardly, she still seethed against her father.

He had known what today had meant to her. How long she had looked forward to it; the meeting, the big race with her grandmother's prize filly, the Tradescants' Ball. It was so many months since she'd been over to Chilworth Manor, so long since she'd seen her cousin Lottie. She thought of her now, a faint smile on her lips; Lottie, her childhood friend and companion before Alice . . . Lottie, with the voice like a nightingale and a face like an angel with dark hair; Lottie, who wanted to go on the stage and sing. With that glorious voice, she would, too.

In a minute, she would ring for Annie and get undressed. Nothing else to do, now, but to go to bed. The house was so still, so peaceful, now that everyone had gone over to the Manor for the Tradescants' Ball.

Her eyes moved stiffly, almost unwillingly, to the place where her unworn ballgown still lay, ready to be folded and hung back. The tears, fresh tears, burned behind the back of her eyes. There was a lump in her throat, big as a fist, and she swallowed, willing herself not to cry. It was then that she heard, almost imperceptibly, the faint tapping at her door.

'Come in, Annie,' she said, struggling to hide the break in her voice.

'Well, well,' said Jamie, letting himself in and closing the door behind him. 'All alone in the dark, I see . . .'

She started to struggle up.

'What are you doing here . . ? The others left more than an hour ago for the Tradescants' Ball . . .'

'As you can see, sister dearest, I didn't go with them.'

'But . . . why not?'

'I'm not in the mood for jollities, not today.' Uninvited, he sat himself down on the end of her bed. 'I lost a packet on the Surrey, and so did my friends . . . for which they blamed me. And they're insisting, none too gently, that I cover their losses.'

'The filly lost?' There was disbelief in her voice.

'As good as. She went lame halfway through the race, and McHeath pulled her up. Under Starter's orders. All bets lost, null and void. I'm sick and tired of the bloody bookies getting fat because of me!' With considerable difficulty, he stifled a stronger oath. 'If she hadn't gone lame she would have flown it! There was nothing else in that field to touch her!'

'She's never gone lame before.'

'I've never backed her so heavily before!'

She looked at him through the growing darkness, wondering why he had come to see her. They had never been close; and now he was almost friendly towards her.

'Have you told papa that you've lost money?'

'I haven't had time to. Nor the chance. When he got back from Epsom, he went straight to his room to get ready to go over to Chilworth Manor. No time for me. Still, I daresay his reaction will be predictable, don't you think? Especially since he's already in such a foul mood. I don't know what's got into him, these past few days . . . you could have knocked me down with a feather when Alice told me what he'd decided to do to you. I'm sorry. I know how much you wanted to go to the meeting; and to Saul Tradescant's Ball. Lottie will be more than disappointed.'

She stared at him, at a Jamie she hardly knew. He seemed so altered, somehow. And he was sympathizing with her.

'Jamie . . . have you been drinking?'

He looked surprised that she should ask. 'I had a couple of brandies at the Boar's Head to drown my sorrows, yes. And give me some Dutch courage in case I decided to tackle father when I got home . . . but there'll be no point in that. He won't give me an advance on next month's allowance; I've already had two. Not that I asked for the money for myself . . . it was just to repay some old debts.

But he doesn't understand. Motty Mottram, Bedford, all that tribe . . . all they have to do is ask their trustees if they want more brass; and they spend it like water! But me, Jamie Bastard Russell, I have to make do with father's small change!'

For a moment Rebeccah didn't answer, being uncertain of what she should say. Somehow, when he spoke about his illegitimacy so blatantly, it embarrassed her, almost made her feel guilty, as if it were her fault, not her father's.

'These so-called friends of yours . . . if they have that much why do they care whether you can repay them or not?'

'Greed, like everyone else. They say they're sick and tired of playing banker, and me welshing on the stakes. I also try to pay back what I owe. On what father gives me, that isn't easy.'

'Do you mean that they're threatening violence if you don't pay them?'

He shrugged, casually. 'How should I know?'

'But that's illegal!'

'Plenty of things are illegal, but they still go on. Nobbling horses, prize-fights, and certain other activities I could mention . . . what matters is if you get caught.'

'But Jamie . . . what are you going to do? You'll have to tell father what's happened!'

'Don't worry about me . . . I'm off to Inverness first thing tomorrow morning, to pay a visit to my mother . . . and I plan to stay there for quite a while . . .'

Inverness. She had never been there, but had heard him and her father talk about it. Mountains, heather, wandering sheep, idyllic, tranquil. She sighed, and cupped her chin in her hands. Two days from now and she and Alice would be back in Newmarket.

'Will you be all right? I mean, have you got enough money to get there?'

'A little. Enough to last me for a while.' He smiled, something he rarely did when he was with her, astonishing her still further. 'Oh, by the way . . . when I was drinking in the Boar's Head, I ran into that American fellow . . . what's-his-name . . .? Yes . . . Rufus Waldo.' Even in the semi-darkness, he saw her expression change. 'Not bad, for a foreigner. He asked me to send you his very best regards.'

Her heart suddenly began to beat very fast.

'Did he say anything else?' Deliberately, she kept her voice noncommittal and light, almost uncaring, while she hung on his every word. 'He's going back, isn't he?'

'Yes, he is. They travel to Southampton this evening, I believe, to board their ship. Rather them than me; I always get sea-sick, even in a fishing boat.'

She longed to question him further; to ask about small, unimportant details, such as how he had looked, if he had said when he'd return, whether he regretted the necessity of having to go back at all, but she left all these questions unsaid; Jamie would only be suspicious. Yet in leaving them unasked, her vivid imagination began to fabricate, and torture her with images that she could not bear to think about. If he would forget her; if, when he returned home, he might meet someone else . . .

As if her fear were a real, physical pain and not in her imagination, she clutched her hands to her chest.

'Are you all right?'

'Yes. Yes, I'm all right . . . it must be something that I ate . . .'

He was getting to his feet now, this new, unfamiliar, kind-faced Jamie. It seemed to her ironic that their father's present anger at them both, had somehow brought them, unexpectedly, together. A strange alliance.

'Well,' he said, going back towards the door, 'I'd best go and see about packing my baggage for Scotland.' Then he was gone.

Rebeccah sighed, slid down from the bed and went over to the window, pulling aside the lace curtain to look down into the gardens below. It was a sight, at this quiet, tranquil time of the evening, that usually brought her a feeling of happiness and calm peace; but not now.

How long, she thought, miserably, would it take Rufus Waldo to forget her?

It was a sparsely-furnished, uncluttered room, thick with the lingering odour of stale tobacco smoke and beer, with a single battered table, a desk in one corner, and three plain chairs. On the desk, the top one open at a half-written page, lay a stack of hide-bound books, their spines ink-stained and worn.

There was a huge swivel chair with enormous back and arms beside the desk, the once-bright scarlet hide upholstery faded to a drab maroon. In it sat a tall, thin-faced man, with pointed ears like a ferret, a short, hand-rolled cigarette held casually between his fingers. He took a quick draw on it, and glanced at his companion.

'So. When do you reckon the time is right for us to go over? Not now?'

The difference between him and the man seated opposite could not have been more startling. Their height, the only thing they had in common. His companion wore a dark, plain cloth suit, immaculately cut, the crisp linen of his shirt beneath a spotless, brilliant white. His silk top hat gleamed with newness. Enoch Wishard, in his long, crumpled, tattered working coat and dusty shoes, looked as if it wouldn't have been an impossibility that he had slept in all his clothes.

Rufus Waldo smiled, and shook his head.

'Too soon. Besides which, Gates and Drake still need you here . . . for the time being. Loose ends, and such like. They have another dozen betting coups planned for the remainder of the season, and it makes sense to let any scandal die a natural death, then lie low, until the new

English flat racing season begins next March. That's when we make our first move.'

Wishard nodded slowly, drawing on his cigarette.

'That's almost another year. Not that that's likely to worry my owners; they can wait for what's worth waiting for . . . but you, Rufus . . . you wrote in your letter that you had plans of your own . . . will they keep that long?'

'Like the best wine, they'll improve with keeping.'

Wishard's light, shifty eyes twinkled. 'Something to do with the Russell girl?'

'The apple of her grandmother's eye.'

Wishard smiled knowingly. 'And yours?'

'I'm not the falling in love kind.'

'But she's taken your fancy?'

'Any woman with looks could do that . . . this one's something special. Striking beauty, and the family fortune when the old woman dies. An irresistible combination.'

'Irresistible to plenty of others as well as you! And you're not on the scene, watching, keeping an eye on things; don't you think you're making a mistake?'

'I don't make mistakes.'

'There's always a first time. And pride comes before a fall.'

'Not mine.' He made himself more comfortable on the battered chair. 'Use your head, Enoch. Merritt's business in England is finished until next spring; until then, I don't have a strong enough excuse to make a return journey so quickly on top of the other. It would look too contrived and too suspicious. And I already told you . . . the old woman is nobody's fool.'

'What about the plan you have in mind for the forged ownership papers of the Belle Mead Stud in Tennessee? Can't you put that into action earlier and use it as your excuse for going back now?'

'No. It wouldn't work. And there's too much at stake for this to be a rushed job . . . no sense in ruining the ship for a hap'orth of tar, so the English say. The girl wouldn't be suspicious . . . but her father and the old woman might. I can't afford to take that chance.' The dark, liquid eyes beneath the thick lashes took on a calculating look. 'Then there's Jerome Charpentier. He's been ill, for some time . . . the talk is that he won't live much longer. How would it look, then, if as soon as he was dead and buried – and his only grandchild inherits the lot – I turn up on the scene, offering condolences in one breath and asking her to marry me with the next . . . what do you think I am? An amateur?'

'You know what you're doing.' Wishard came to the end of his cigarette and tossed it on the dusty floor. 'You always do. Just one thing you don't appear to have made allowances for . . . what if the Russell girl forgets you?'

'No woman ever forgets me if I don't want her to.'

'And the risk you're taking by leaving it so long till you see her again? How will you know what's happening, when you're not there to see? Some rich Englishman with a small fortune in one hand and a title in the other might suddenly appear on the scene . . . and then what will you do? While you're on the wrong side of the Atlantic ocean, you're just moving in the dark.'

Rufus Waldo smiled, as if it were of no importance at all. 'A spy inside the walls is worth an army outside them. I have someone, perfectly placed, who can tell me anything I want to know.'

PART THREE

The Woman

17

THE ST SIMON COLT, the early morning sunshine glinting on his glass-bright brown coat, moved swiftly through the main group of galloping horses, expertly guided by McHeath; then, as he drew abreast with the leaders, streaked ahead and passed out of sight behind the trees.

An ecstatic, half-disbelieving cry went up among the small group clustered on the edge of the gallops.

'It's a record!'

'He gallops like Eclipse!'

'I've never seen a faster two-year-old! You'll surely enter him in all the two-year-olds' races for this season, my lady?'

Anna smiled. Nearly eighty years old, she was still out of breath from the short walk from where one of the lads waited by her two-wheeled curricle.

'He isn't mine to enter in anything.' She turned to Rebeccah, and placed a scroll, tied with red legal ribbon, into her hand. 'Happy birthday.'

'*No!*'

Anna pressed the rolled up documents tighter into the shaking hands.

'It's my present to you, Rebeccah; I want you to have him.'

'But I can't . . . he's your pride and joy . . .' Behind her eyes, she felt the faint, hot-pricking of unbidden tears, acutely aware of the others standing around her. She fought them back.

'Yes, he was. But I've lived a long life, and I've already had my share of prides and joys . . . now it's someone else's turn.' She smiled, and her blue eyes, still beautiful, were soft. 'I might not be here to see it; but he's a Classics colt, if ever I saw one. And when he wins the Derby next year, he should win it in your colours, not mine.'

'I can't bear it when you talk this way!'

'I'm an old woman, Rebeccah. None of us, however much we want to, can beat time. And I'm a realist . . . I always was.' They were back at the house now, in the warm, welcoming drawing room, with its tall gleaming panels of dark polished oak, and roaring fire. 'When I was young, like you, I had a favourite saying . . . There's always something you can do about everything. I said that in the self-assurance and arrogance of youth. But two things I've learned since then, two things that nobody can ever change. Old age. Death. None of us, whoever we are, can escape either of them . . . unless, like my mother, they die young.'

Her eyes moved upwards, and rested on her own portrait; the portrait of herself, a wedding present from her beloved Ralph Russell, the face in its suspended, time-locked state of youth and beauty. The sadness that she felt was not from vanity; Anna Brodie Russell had never been vain. But that because, within the aged and worn-out outer shell, beneath the tired body and the face that drooped with wrinkles, the young Anna still lived and breathed. That was the ultimate tragedy of old age, she realized; the body became a prison from which only death would set the inner youth free.

She looked at her granddaughter, the living image of Anna Maria Flood; the mother she still thought of; the mother who had died too soon. Anna Maria had never grown old, never watched her youth and beauty slowly, year by year, disintegrate piece by piece; she would never sit beside the fire as Anna did, feeling the stiffness in her limbs and the shortness of breath when she rose. Her mother, like her own portrait, would remain just the same for all time.

She understood Rebeccah. Old age and death were as remote to her as snowfall, on a hot summer's day; when she had been her age her whole life had stretched way ahead of her, like a long, undulating road that had no ending. Now, when the ending was almost in sight, did she realize, at last, there was no such thing as immortality.

No need for morbid thoughts; that, too, had never been her way. But the inevitable must be planned for, and Rebeccah's, and Alice's futures secured. A sizeable sum of money for Alice, the rest of the estate to be inherited by Rebeccah. The stud, at Newmarket, to go to James. From that, he could make his own provision for Jamie Russell.

Rebeccah was looking at her intently; so much beauty in her fresh, flawless face. Above all, she wanted her to be happy; not to struggle, bitter and alone, as she had. Few women, left alone in the world, could have made as much as she had out of nothing. In sharp contrast Rebeccah, and Alice, had never struggled, had never wanted. Her only wish was that neither of them would ever have to; she intended to see to that.

'When I was coming back from the gallops, yesterday,' Rebeccah said, earnestly, 'I saw the doctor leave . . . did he come to see you?'

Anna smiled. No need to tell her now; some truths were best left unsaid. The sharp, crunching pain that had passed briefly across her chest, now and then for the past few weeks, could safely stay her own secret, and his.

'Do I look as if I'm ready to be wrapped in my winding sheet?' she quipped, laughing. 'If I hadn't been so stiff up on the gallops this morning, I'd have ridden that colt instead of McHeath.' They laughed together, both, equally, knowing it to be untrue. So many years, now, since Anna had been able to sit a horse. So many years since she'd felt the unique thrill of riding at a gallop, the wind in her long, loose hair, fanning her face, taking away her breath, feeling the thudding of the pounding hooves beneath her as they bit into the turf, clods of grass and earth flying out behind her in all directions. But the girl who had watched Priam's Derby sixty years ago, the girl who had ridden the filly Hope and rescued the colt Bloodstone from his burning stable, who had outwitted and outmanoeuvred the Jockey Club and all the turf villains, would never ride again; she was gone, somewhere, lost between then and now, the only remains in the gold-framed portrait that hung proudly on the dark, polished oak wall.

'I had a letter from Jamie this morning. From his mother's house near Inverness. He said that the Earl of Dunroven has a castle nearby, and that when he heard Jamie was staying there he'd invited him to dinner.'

'No doubt that appealed to his never inconsiderable vanity. Dunroven . . . isn't he a racing man?'

'He has a large stable . . . yes. Jamie wrote about it at some length. He has horses entered for all the big northern races, and entries for all the English Classics this year. He also has a sister, Jamie says, about my age. And she's unmarried.' Amusement came into her face. 'Reading between the lines, I think Jamie definitely has hopes in that direction.'

Anna put back her head and laughed. 'Hopes, I'd wager, that are likely to remain unfulfilled, unless Dunroven's sister is out of her mind.'

'He seems to think not.'

'I guessed there was some stronger motive for his suddenly spending so much time in Scotland, other than a curiously belated devotion to his mother.'

Rebeccah was silent for a few moments. She gazed into the leaping flames of the big log fire.

'Did you ever see her, Jamie's mother?'

'I met her father, more than once. He was stud manager at Perth, over twenty years ago. I sent your father up there to conclude some business for me, never dreaming that he'd seduce McAllister's daughter.' She, too, let her eyes wander to the fire. 'She was a young widow, then; had married a man much older than herself. James was young and foolish. Even so, I'd have credited him with better sense. No doubt she thought he'd have to marry her, when she found out that she was pregnant; how little she knew him then. He had other ambitions, and other pies to dip his finger in. And no intention of bringing her south, which was what she wanted. As wildly beautiful as Scotland is, an unending diet of hills and heather has its limitations, even for someone as unambitious as Margaret McAllister. Perhaps that was her attraction for him; sloppy-minded, undemanding, as comfortable to fall back on as an old feather pillow. Unlike all the others. And he always has gone back, despite everything. Over the years, she's the only woman in your father's life that he's still maintained any contact with. And not just for Jamie's sake, either. Maybe I should be grateful to her for that.'

'And Alice's mother?'

'The Italian woman?'

'She rarely speaks about her. And I never ask. In case it's too painful for her to remember; and I think it must be.' Her mind went back to that cold, cheerless, brightly-lit marble hall in the house at Newmarket; reluctantly, painfully; the memory of that night when her mother left, still raw and vivid in her mind. Alice's childish face, the big dark eyes brimming with tears, the woman Maria walking away without a word, leaving her standing there; a small, diminutive figure in white velvet, all alone. 'My mother had to leave. Papa left her no choice. But I knew she was coming back. She promised, and she'd never broken her word to me. She would have come back, if she hadn't died in the accident . . . Alice's mother deliberately abandoned her. Left her alone among strangers. She couldn't have cared for her, for how she felt. How could she have done that? How could any woman do that to her own child?'

Anna looked at her gravely.

'You ask me a question that I have no answer to. I don't know. But I think I know about Alice . . . what she would feel. Like you, I'd never ask her. When my sister Clara and I were little girls, we were in the market place one day at Bury St Edmunds with our mother. Our father came by with his wife and two sons, riding in a big fancy carriage. He looked, and he saw us, but he pretended that he didn't know who we were. I've never forgotten that. The way he averted his eyes from our faces as they drove by; the mud that the carriage wheels splashed up from the road over our mother's gown . . .' A pause. 'I always think of that, what he did, when I look at Alice. I know how she felt that night.'

'But your father tried to make amends. He left you everything. And he'd tried to find you, when he knew that he was dying. Alice's mother went back to Italy and never wrote. Not one letter, in all these years . . .' A sudden thought struck Rebeccah, and she spoke it aloud. 'Your father's two sons . . . they were Brodies, too. Did you never hear of either of them again?'

'I heard they both died, some years back, without issue. Clara and I were the last of the line. And now, only me . . .' Anna thought of her younger, dead sister, without pain now. Not the mottled, anguish-marked face in its last illness, but of another, lost Clara; a girl of twelve, sitting, legs dangling, on Ralph Russell's wall; a young woman with dancing black curls and bright blue eyes, her lovely hands moving lightly, lovingly, over the keyboard of a piano; Clara in white, on Tom Tradescant's arm, laughing together as they walked out into the sunshine from Chilworth Manor's grey stone chapel . . . that was the Clara that she would never forget. Unexpectedly, she felt hot tears spring up into her eyes. Blinking them quickly away, she pulled herself up.

'Grandmama . . . are you all right?'

She could still laugh, even at herself. 'Take no notice of me, Rebeccah.' A disarming smile. 'I'm nothing but a foolish old woman.'

It was growing dark in the little flint built house that had once been a hunting lodge to local Scottish gentry long since gone; since their departure it had stood, silent and neglected, for several years until James Russell had bought it, together with several acres of land, as a gift for his mistress, Margaret McAllister.

It was only a mile from Inverness; tolerable in winter, pretty and picturesque in the summer months; all around it, a landscaped garden that he had also paid for, of climbing roses, violets, rhododendron bushes, honeysuckle, and native heathers.

He paid the wages of her three servants, which he had continued to do for the past twenty years; a manservant, who also doubled as a gardener and a groom; a personal maid, now more of a companion; and a cook-general who, as her name implied, did the rough work and everything else in the kitchen.

For the past year or more, Jamie had spent more time with his mother than he had ever done, since finishing his schooling; since he never did anything unless it was of direct benefit to himself, his lengthy stays at the hunting lodge had little to do with any new-found affection for his mother; the proximity of Dunroven Castle, and the Earl of Dunroven's unmarried sister, were the only inducements he needed to bury himself for months at a time in the wilds of Scotland.

He had quickly found out that Dunroven, a man with a passion for horse racing, had invited him to dinner at the family seat on the strength of his name . . . he was the grandson of the celebrated Anna Brodie Russell. During their conversations, he also discovered that Dunroven was under the impression that when she died, Jamie would inherit a large slice of wealth, bloodstock, and property, from her will. He did nothing to suggest that this was untrue, and, consequently, continued to be a frequent guest at the castle. But back at the hunting lodge, slouched moodily in a chair beside the fire, his veneer of pleasant charm soon gave way to reveal his true self.

'Dunroven only sends me invitations because my name is Russell,' he said, bitterly, and in his usual, self-pitying tone, 'because he thinks, like everyone else, that when the old woman dies I'll come in for a fat slice of the estate. Some chance. She wouldn't give me the drippings of her nose.'

'Jamie! I won't have that kind of talk in my house. Whatever would your father say if he heard you? Anna Brodie Russell is a remarkable woman, a woman whose blood you should be proud to share. That in itself is an honour.'

He glared at her in silence, but said nothing. No sympathy from that quarter! No point in arguing further, that was self-evident. Instead, he let his thoughts turn in the direction of Louise Dunroven, the thoughts that had over the past few months developed from a pleasant daydream into a violent obsession. He, Jamie Russell, a bastard born, married to the sister of an Earl; heady ambition. But what was any man without it, he'd asked himself over and over again? Anything worth having was worth fighting for. In marrying Louise, he would elevate himself to her status, the status he had always envied and aspired to; and his own illegitimacy need not be a stumbling block; everyone knew that sufficient wealth, hand in hand with bastardy, was enough to make it respectable. Night after night, sitting beside his mother's fire, his grandiose schemes had grown ever more larger.

Margaret McAllister seated herself opposite him in the large, comfortable chair, and took up her embroidery, a habit that irked and irritated him unbearably. And he was furious that she hadn't immediately sided with him in his grievances; had she been buried so long out here in the back of beyond that she couldn't think for herself any more, or remember the shoddy way his father had treated her, how he'd got rid of her while he went off to woo the heiress Corinna Charpentier. Truly, love was blind! He felt restless, impotent, cooped up in the lodge that was no bigger than his grandmother's drawing room and hall combined. He had no choice but to stay on longer, even though he was desperately short of funds and his allowance from his father was not due for another week; before she left for a holiday in Paris, he wanted to see Louise again.

His mother glanced up from her needlework to smile at him.

'I'll miss your company, Jamie, when you decide you must leave . . . and, I've no doubt, so will Lizzie . . .'

'Really, mother, have you no sense of dignity, making an equal out of a common servant? You let her take liberties. Sitting with you in the evenings, eating meals at the same table. Give any servant an inch and they'll take a mile. You ought to know that.'

She gave him a look of stern rebuke.

'Lizzie has been a good and loyal friend to me through thick and thin. And I'll thank you to remember that.'

'As you wish, mother. I'm just pointing out to you that you're making a rod for your own back. Just wait and see. Let her do exactly as she likes and she'll end up walking all over you.'

'Jamie, sometimes I despair of you. So much hate. So much contempt for other people. And bitterness, like over what might or might not be in your grandmother's will . . . so much bitterness isn't good for any man to have inside himself . . .'

'If I'm bitter, it's only because I have good reason to be. Wouldn't anyone, after the way I've been treated? The girls, always the two girls before me.' He looked down at her.

'And you've been a fool, mother, do you realize that? You gave him what he wanted too easily, and he played you for a fool! You let him buy you off, bury you up here in the middle of nowhere, so that no breath of scandal would rear its ugly head to disturb the fine, ordered tranquility of his cushioned life . . . and I'm the one who's suffered from it. If you'd made a fight of it, if you'd stood up to him and demanded that he married you and not that rich, spoiled American Charpentier bitch, I'd now be his son and heir, and inherit the old woman's entire fortune.' He was almost foaming at the mouth in his anger. 'But did you do that? Oh, no! You didn't like to worry him, you didn't want to make any demands, in case he went and tired of you! Or was it that you were just too polite to argue? Well, it doesn't matter any more, does it, because it's too bloody late!'

'Jamie! I won't have you use that language in my house!'

'Your house? Is it? Make sure he's put it in your name, or mine, because otherwise you'll lose that too! He could have bought me a house, somewhere in London, the least I'm entitled to. Not a hope in hell! All they think I'm fit for is the crumbs from their table!' His light, cold grey eyes narrowed, as if he was thinking of something else. 'But I'll show them . . . All of them . . . I'll make them sorry yet!'

Something in his face, in the tone of his voice, made Margaret McAllister look up.

'Jamie, what do you mean by that? What are you up to?'

He smiled, but not pleasantly. 'A little trick, mother. A little trick up my sleeve. I promise you . . . you'll see.'

18

ALICE STROLLED with her father through the gardens, watching the men at work: weeding, hoeing, digging, replanting for the spring; their large, calloused, earth covered hands and soil encrusted nails, bent over the plants, as tenderly, almost, as a mother bending over the crib of her first child. As a child one of her favourite places had been under the gnarled oak, where one of her father's carpenters had built a circular seat. Alice's castle, she'd called it. It was the place where she would come to think or to cry, a toy clutched tightly in her arms, a book lying open on her lap, a place where she had sat for hours in the hot afternoon summer sunshine, wondering about her Italian mother.

The letter had come two days ago; but only yesterday had she been able to open it. She had spent an almost sleepless night, wondering what it might contain; foolish, perhaps, not to have torn it open at once, and stilled the churning in her stomach, the shaking in her wrists and hands.

She had not wanted to be alone when she had opened it. Never, in all her life, had she wished so much that Rebeccah had been there; but her sister was away in Epsom, staying at the Old Brew House. Finally, she had taken the letter to her father.

Neither of them had spoken while she opened it with his desk knife; she remembered how still it had been in the room, how loud the ticking of the single clock had sounded, and the sickening, ripping noise as the blade had sliced its way through the crisp white paper.

The envelope contained a single, large page, covered with

tall, flamboyant black script. Her mother had signed her name at the foot of the page with a proud, italic flourish. *Isabella Ajanti.*

She had looked up into her father's eyes without speaking. She had simply held out the letter towards him, and he had taken it. When he had glanced up, at last, Alice had asked him the question that was foremost in her mind with a single word.

'*Why*?'

'After all these years of silence? Only your mother can answer that. But if you want to reply to her letter, or visit her in Venice as she suggests . . . don't feel that you can't do either out of loyalty to me. She is still your mother.'

Yes, she'd thought, bitterly. She is still my mother. The mother who used me as a bargaining counter to get what she wanted; the mother who abandoned me when I was nine years old. It came back to her, then; the cold, brightly lit marble hall; her father's astonished, appalled face; Rebeccah clutching the banister rails; the woman Maria, pushing her inside and letting go her hand . . . leaving her alone in a house of strangers.

'I don't owe her anything.'

'Only respect for who she is, Alice.'

He had looked down again at that tall, upright, arrogant script that he remembered so well; at the stark, almost savage pen strokes, where the nib had bitten into the paper, the long, elegant loops of her letters. Emotional, passionate, ruthless, and self-assured.

He'd said, gently, 'You don't have to make a decision now. Why not think about it?'

That had been yesterday. And now, here they were, strolling in the gardens among the bushes and flowers, and she was still undecided.

'I couldn't sleep last night. I kept thinking about her. What she did, how she left me. And not a word. All these years, and not a single word. How could she do that if she truly loved me? How could any woman do it to her own child if she really cared? She wants something, I know it. I can feel it in my veins . . .'

'Why not write back to her and find out?' He, too, had his own suspicions; Isabella never did anything without a reason of her own. Every word, every caress, every love letter, always calculated, like a money-lender, to secure her own ends. Could he really believe in his heart that the last ten years had changed her?

Maybe he did her an injustice. Maybe all she really wanted was to see the daughter she had abandoned so long ago. Only time would give both of them the answer.

'I can't decide now. I can't even think clearly. If I do write her an answer, I don't even know what I can say. Or what she expects from me, after what she did. Forgiveness? Love? It's like writing a letter to a stranger . . .'

They sat down, side by side, on the wooden seat beneath the tree.

'Wait a few days, then make up your mind. She won't expect you to answer straight away. You need not write a long letter. If you want to make the journey to Venice, then I'll make all the arrangements for you. You might find it easier to talk to her face to face.'

Alice looked down at her hands, folded neatly in her lap. 'Can Rebeccah come with me?'

She saw his hesitation.

'Do you think that would be wise?'

She sighed, understanding. 'Yes, I see what you mean. But they need not even meet. I want her with me. I don't think that I could face it, not alone.'

'Why not ask Lottie Tradescant?'

Her face lit up. 'Of course!' Then, 'But do you think she'd come?'

'Why shouldn't she? With her love of music Venice is the ideal city. Their opera house is world famous . . . and the place itself is very beautiful.'

His mind went back to the Ajanti *palazzo* on the canal; the huge, sparsely furnished, gilded rooms, the echoing passages; Isabella's room, hung with tapestries and cloth of gold. How long ago it seemed when he was young; another world, another lifetime. He remembered the first time he had seen Alice, cradled in her mother's arms; he recalled the anguish and the guilt, the dark, accusing look in Isabella's eyes. He had already married Corinna Charpentier.

His mind came back, slowly, to the present. He could feel Alice's eyes intent upon his face.

'Shall I ride over there, then . . . this afternoon, and ask her? Do you think Uncle Saul will let her come?'

He smiled, and touched her cheek.

'Yes, of course. And I'll come with you.'

She glanced away again, her eyes brighter; but he could still see that something else was troubling her.

'The invitation, to the Clanradines' castle . . . Rebeccah and me . . .'

'Yes . . ?'

'I can't help wondering . . . that there's something else behind it . . . the way Duncan Clanradine keeps looking at me . . .'

He laughed, lightly. 'And why shouldn't he look? I have a very beautiful daughter!'

'He isn't married. And I can't help thinking . . . he keeps following me about. Staring. I hate it.'

'Clanradine is a very sought-after young man. The family are well in with the Prince of Wales; he invariably stays as their guest when he isn't at Sandringham; and they're wealthy. Is there something you dislike about him?'

'Not exactly. Well . . . he isn't the most handsome man I've ever seen, that's for sure.'

'Looks aren't everything, Alice. You should remember that.' Bitterly, he thought of her mother, the angel's face hiding the heart of stone. 'It's the character of a man. What he is. That's what counts. Think about it. And, if you really want me to tell you what's in my mind . . . he's just the sort of good, honest, reliable husband I'd want for my daughter . . .' He reached out, took one of her hands between his, and cradled it between his palms. 'A handsome face and dashing charm alone, are worthless.'

She was silent for a moment. 'I suppose you're thinking that I ought to be flattered that he's interested in me; that I ought to be grateful for what I can get.' A harsh tone came into her voice. 'After all, bastards can't be choosy, can they?'

Her words hit him like a slap in the face.

'Alice. That wasn't what I was thinking at all. Whoever you decide to marry, now, in the future, whether you decide never to marry at all . . . you'll always be well provided for. I can promise you that.'

Well provided for. She almost smiled. If she never married anyone she would live where she had always lived, an allowance made from the estate, a continual guest in someone else's house, with nothing of her own, the years stretching out ahead like an unending limbo, her looks fading as time passed by. No, that was not what she wanted. Better to be married to safe, dull, boring Clanradine, than a lonely, placeless spinster. She knew what choice her mother would have made, too.

'Maybe if I go to Venice, he might forget me. He might marry somebody else while I'm gone.'

'If he's already made up his mind, he'll ask you before you leave. And, even if he doesn't, he'll consider that you're well worth waiting for.'

She glanced away, back at the distant figures of the gardeners. 'It's almost like a business, isn't it? Marriages among the upper classes. Everybody knows the rules; everybody keeps to them. He couldn't go beneath himself and marry a costermonger's daughter . . . what *would* people say? I'm illegitimate, but I'm a Russell. Anna Brodie Russell's granddaughter. My grandfather was a Peer. And she'll give me something to take with me, won't she? A slice of the estate for my dowry, big enough to make it all respectable. Not that the Clanradines need it; it's just the done thing. Keeping one's end up. None of us must ever break the rules.' Her words shocked him; the streak of cynicism he had never heard before. He had never guessed that she felt like that. 'I know what everyone will say, if he does ask me. That I should count my blessings. That I don't know how lucky I am. It's true, isn't it, father?'

'Not in your case, no. He wants you for yourself.'

She gave a short, sour little laugh. 'Won't that give some people something to think about? Me, Countess of Clanradine!'

'The only thing that matters is that you are happy. What other people think doesn't count . . . not that it's any of their business.'

She turned and looked at him. 'I wonder what Rebeccah would do. If she were me.' She smiled. 'I wish she were here, now. But then I suppose I ought to know her well enough to know what her answer would be. She wouldn't marry him.'

'It isn't your sister he's interested in, is it?'

'I know what you're trying to say, papa. That she'll inherit everything and if all he was concerned about was the money, then he wouldn't choose me. That is it, isn't it?'

'That's obvious, don't you think?'

She didn't answer him. She simply went on gazing towards the gardens, and the line of trees that bordered the drive, beyond them.

'I've decided. I will go to Venice and see my mother. I think I should. If I didn't, then I'd always wonder why she wanted to see me . . . after all these years.' A smile. 'She'll be surprised, won't she, if I tell her that I might marry Duncan Clanradine . . . me, an Italian girl's love-child, a Countess.' A lengthy pause. 'Do I look like her? I've never asked you.'

His eyes rested gently on her face, and he smiled.

'Yes, you are like her. In looks. She was very beautiful.'

'You never wanted to marry her?'

Words raced about inside his head, each jostling with the other.

'I couldn't marry her. I was already married to Rebeccah's mother.'

'But you met my mother first. And that wasn't what I asked you.'

'It wouldn't have been a suitable marriage. We were worlds apart, it would never have worked. I loved her but I could never have lived with her. She would have driven me insane.'

'Did you love Rebeccah's mother more than her?'

'I don't know how to answer that. I don't even know if there is an answer. They were both so different.'

'If Rebeccah's mother hadn't been the daughter of an American millionaire, would you still have married her then?'

'I don't know. Not any more. She was a strikingly beautiful woman . . . but in a completely different way to your mother. Corinna was like a painting, a piece of classical sculpture. Beautiful and cold. Something to wonder at, something to admire without touching it. Something that you never took down from its pedestal. Your mother was never like that. She was all warmth and passion and fire. Yes . . . I suppose I did love her more . . . more than any of the others . . .'

'And Jamie's mother? You still see her, don't you?'

'He would have told you that! Yes, I still see Margaret McAllister. Not that there's anything between us now. Only Jamie.' Nostalgically, he thought back. 'I was only a raw young man when we first met, all those years ago. She was a fresh-faced, pretty Scots girl who took my fancy. And that's how it all began . . . my mother was furious, of course, when I told her that Margaret was pregnant; Margaret's family were appalled, being strict Scottish Presbyterians. I was afraid they'd cast her off; but that didn't happen. I couldn't marry her; that was selfish, I know. But I had to marry into money. She was heartbroken at first . . . but she did understand. I was always grateful to her for that. I honoured my obligations, and I bought her the house near Inverness, where Jamie was brought up till I sent him away to school. Never once, in all these years, has Margaret asked me for anything . . . so I was always happy to give. My one regret is that Jamie hasn't inherited any of her qualities . . . but this past year, since he's been spending so much time with her, he at least seems to be changing a little for the better. It must be her influence.' He smiled. 'But what I felt for her, once, was nothing compared to the passion I felt for your mother.'

A silence.

'Would you like to see her again, ever?'

'I don't think that would be very wise, do you? It would only stir up old grievances, old quarrels. Nothing would be gained by it.' At last, he stood up, and Alice stood too. 'But I think you should see her . . . and I'm glad that you've decided to. I'm sure she'll be very proud of you, when she sees you at last.'

They began walking, side by side, back towards the house.

'Do you want me to give her a message? Is there anything that you want to say?'

He paused, and thought for a while. 'Only that I thank her for my beautiful daughter. And that I shall always wish her well.'

19

THE OLD, DESERTED WAREHOUSE, lying midway between Wapping and the Surrey Docks, loomed up from the blanket of darkness around it, its unsightly, partially demolished roof sticking out like an obscene, pagan landmark into the stormy night sky.

Thunder still rumbled menacingly somewhere in the distance; now and then, forks of lightning flashed in the darkness, like a nightwatchman's torch in the smoggy, dank air. As the small boat glided almost soundlessly through the murky Thames water, Jamie drew his thick double-breasted coat closer around his shoulders, and peered into the darkness.

'How much further is it?'

'Nearly there, Gov'nor!'

Impatiently, he shifted his weight on the uncomfortable wooden seat, ears strained to catch any sound from the riverbank. They had been rowing for the best part of an hour, and his hands and feet were frozen stiff, his face numb with cold. He fished in his waistcoat pocket for his gold fob watch and stared at its face in the darkness; a few minutes to ten o'clock. Then, across the ink-black water, he saw it; the first, faint ripples of light from the deserted wharf.

'There they are, Gov'nor!' The little cockney boatman stopped rowing, and let the boat begin to drift forward of its own accord, slowing down as it eased its way towards the jetty. He stood up, expertly moving a single upright oar to the side of him in the water, then threw the rope attached to the little boat to one of the shadowy figures waiting on the wharf.

'You made good time,' said Rufus Waldo, moving forward.

'If we'd been any longer I would have frozen to death,' Jamie answered irritably, holding onto his outstretched hand and hauling himself ashore. He stood up on the jetty, stretching his cold, stiff, aching limbs. He glanced furtively all around them. 'Waldo, you are sure there's no chance the beaks might have got wind of this fight?'

'Of course I'm sure.' He turned to his two companions and made brief introductions. 'You worry too much, Jamie.' The dark, thick-lashed eyes glittered in the murky light, 'Besides, mostly the law turn a blind eye; they know the nobs patronize it. When have you known them not to look after their own . . ?' He paid the boatman and told him to wait. 'When you've secured the boat you can follow us, if you've a mind to. Just make sure that it's tied up out of sight.'

He took Jamie's arm and propelled him in the direction of the warehouse, from which light seeped through the narrow cracks in the building and through the half closed main doors. As they came closer, the hum of voices from a large gathering of people assaulted Jamie's ears.

'Bloody hell, they'll be heard a mile away!'

'Stop worrying . . . the place is deserted at this time of night! Why do you think the organizers picked this spot for the venue?'

'I'll take your word for it.'

At last, the four of them reached the warehouse doors.

'You'll enjoy it. There'll be plenty of blood spilt tonight. A real grudge match, this one is.'

The first thing that hit him was the heat, in stark contrast to the freezing night air outside; then, the stink of human bodies; too many crushed together in a small space. As he stared over the noisy, cheering crowd, he saw gentlemen in frock coats and top hats side by side with rough, working men, all pushing and shoving each other, shouting bets, everyone trying to get as close as they could to the edge of the makeshift ring.

Because prizefighting was illegal and a venue could be raided by the police at any time, the date, time, and place were kept strictly secret, and often had to be switched at a moment's notice; because of the risk of discovery, there had been no previous preparation for the match, such as putting up posts and ropes, except for a hasty scattering over the hard, dirty floor, of large quantities of sawdust.

Rufus Waldo spoke a few whispered words to the lookout who had been posted outside, then, with Jamie and his two companions, shoved his way to the front beside the makeshift ring. There were hardly any proper chairs. Fusty straw bales, upturned boxes, sacks of mouldering grain, all had been dragged in a rough circle, twenty times deep, to serve as seating. He motioned them to sit down, while he stood up, looking around him, waving a wad of notes in one hand.

'I've got five hundred riding on the Iron Man,' he said, shouting to make himself heard above the din. 'I've put the same on for you. It'll be a close run thing, you'll see . . . but he'll put the bastard away before midnight . . .'

'I haven't got five hundred to put on; I'm broke till father sends me my allowance for the month . . . I'll tell you why, after the fight . . .'

Waldo smiled. 'It doesn't matter. I told you. The five hundred's on me. You can pay me back later, the way I said. The way we already agreed.'

Jamie shrugged. 'I'm satisfied with the arrangement if you are.'

His last words were lost in the sudden roar of the crowd. From the other end of the warehouse, flanked by their seconds, the combatants were coming into sight. Bare chested, with skin-tight ankle length pants that hugged their thick legs obscenely, they faced each other from either end of the makeshift ring, eyes full of hatred. Naked flesh glistening with sweat, their huge fists clenched, they pummelled savagely into each other's bodies, to the screaming, yelling cheers of the crowd, each blow of their fists echoing thuds; the fierce, ceaseless rain of punching increasing with every moment, soon both men's faces were covered with blood.

Jamie surged forward from his seat, shouting to the man his money was on as wildly as the rest of them.

The other man was down. His aggressor stood over him, menacingly, held back by the referee, spitting on the sawdust beside him and mocking him, insulting him with crude obscenities. The crowd went wild with glee.

'Get up, get up!'

'Give it to him!'

'Punch his face in, the bastard!'

Excitedly, Waldo grabbed Jamie's sleeve.

'I told you, the Iron Man's a dead certainty! But he won't finish him yet. Like I said, it'll be a bloody close thing . . !'

'How can he see through those cuts over his eyes? They're swelling like hell!'

'He doesn't have to see, he can smell him! Look at that right hand!'

The other pugilist was on the floor again; but up on his feet quickly again, cursing, dashing the sweat and blood from his coarse, ugly face.

'I told you it was a grudge match. Look at those punches flying!'

'Suppose one of them kills the other?'

Waldo laughed, his eyes transfixed on the two big, heaving, bloodstained bodies in the ring.

'Too bad. They'd toss his body in the river, and his backers'd lose their shirts. It's all in the game.' His voice was lost in the sudden burst of cheering as the Iron Man delivered his knock-out punch. It crashed into his opponent's battered, bloody face, knocking him to the ground where he lay motionless, his bruised, sweat-soaked torso stuck all over with sawdust, oblivious to the screaming and shouting around him.

The shaven-headed conqueror raised his two arms in victory, and the crowd went wild.

Waldo turned back to Jamie, his face showing delight.

'What did I tell you. Out cold.' He laughed, callously. 'That's the quickest way to triple your stake money that I know!' He grasped Jamie's sleeve and began pushing him through the noisy crowd towards the men on the other side of the floor who had been taking the bets.

'Where are we going?'

Waldo smiled. 'To collect our winnings. Then, a little ride across the river to the other side, and we can enjoy the company of the ladies of a certain establishment I know . . .'

The whore lay shamelessly across him, her plump body and big breasts glistening in the glow of the dim red light in the richly furnished room. Expertly, her hands ran up and down his body, darting away, every now and then, to wind themselves in his thick, wavy dark hair; then, she leaned forward and kissed him.

He lay there for a few moments with his eyes closed while the exquisite sensations made his whole body burn and tingle. Then, suddenly, he reached out and grabbed her, roughly, almost savagely, and flung her onto her back. She teased him with her lips, pouting, pretending to resist. Then he jerked her legs apart and entered her, thrusting a dozen times, before his whole body exploded into a climax. Afterwards, when she reached out her arms to embrace him, he shoved her off the bed.

'Get out, you whore. And send someone in with a bottle of brandy when you go.'

His clothes still lay where he had left them, draped across the back of the upholstered love-seat, his top hat perched beside them on the floor. When he was dressed again, he poured himself a large brandy, drained the glass in one gulp, then went into the bedroom next door to find Jamie.

He lay there on the big curtained bed, still naked, stretched full length on his stomach, while two prostitutes massaged his shoulders and his back. One look from Waldo, and they both scurried away.

'Well?'

Jamie rolled over, slowly, and looked at him in the dim, red glow of the room.

'I've had whores before . . . but not like these. How the hell did you ever find this place?'

Waldo smiled and sat down. 'A recommendation from a friend. He knows my tastes.'

'Expensive!'

Another smile. Waldo lay back, and lit a cigar. 'We get what we pay for, don't you think?'

'What I've had was worth every penny.'

The long, blue column of smoke from the cigar wound its way upwards towards the ceiling.

'I think we should talk.'

Slowly, Jamie sat up. Waldo passed him his clothes and he began to get dressed.

'About my sister?'

'Has anything changed since your last letter?'

'Not as far as Rebeccah's concerned. Plenty after her . . . who wouldn't be, with her looks and my grandmother's money?' He sat down on the bed and began to put on his shoes. 'The way's clear for you to make your move . . . but be careful; the old woman's no fool. And I'd wager she can smell a fortune hunter a hundred miles off!'

'I know how to handle her.'

'My sister Alice, that's another matter. The Clanradine heir has got his pale, white-lashed eyes on her, and he isn't particular about whether there's any money. He's got it badly, all right!'

Waldo lifted one eyebrow, quizzically.
'Is she going to marry him?'
'If she's got any sense she will. An Earl with a castle in Scotland, plenty of brass in the family coffers and a hundred thousand acres thrown in . . . and to boot, he thinks the sun shines out of her arse. Not bad going for an Italian harlot's bastard.'
'You're not jealous, are you, Jamie?' There was amusement in his voice.
'It's nothing to me who the hell Alice marries. She can marry the devil for all I care.' He stood up. 'What I care about is who I intend to marry . . . and I need your help. I told you there was something I wanted to talk to you about, urgently. Well, this is it. If I can show I've got enough property and brass behind me, I can go cap in hand to the Earl of Dunroven's sister.'
'How did this come about?'
Talking continuously, Jamie finished dressing. He adjusted his necktie in the elegant mirror.
'Dunroven invited me to the castle because I'm a Russell. And he knows the size of the Brodie-Russell estate. What he doesn't know is that the old woman won't be leaving me any of it . . . and what I inherit from father wouldn't keep Louise in Paris gowns for a season. If he finds out that I don't have the brass to back the name, I can kiss his sister goodbye.' His mouth was set in a hard, ill-tempered line. 'And that wouldn't suit my plans at all!'
Waldo smiled. He drew deeply on the cigar and inhaled the smoke.
'I told you before, that day in Epsom, after you lost on the Surrey Stakes. I need someone close to Rebeccah, inside the house, watching, listening . . . do exactly what I want you to, and you can propose to Louise Dunroven as soon as you like.'
Jamie's eyes looked unnaturally bright.
'How soon? On my next visit to Scotland?'

'Ask first for Dunroven's permission to court his sister. Leave the rest to me.'

'But he won't agree to the marriage unless he has proof that I'll inherit a substantial share of the estate.' He looked sulky. 'I don't even have a house of my own . . . except the hunting lodge when my mother dies. I can scarcely take an Earl's sister to live in that rat box!'

'You won't have to. When I've finished my business in London, I'll come north on some pretext or other; and, unexpectedly, pay a visit on you. Make it known to Dunroven and get me an invitation to the castle. Then I'll do the rest.'

'How?'

Waldo had finished the cigar. Reaching over, he stubbed it out in an ornate seashell tray.

'Trust me.'

20

'HE'S BACK? Rufus Waldo? Here, in England?'

'Yes . . .' Deliberately, Jamie kept his voice casual and light. He went on eating his breakfast, slowly, leisurely. His slowness maddened her. 'I ran into him when I was in London; it was quite a coincidence. I was getting out of a hansom cab in Grosvenor Square, and he was coming out of the Grosvenor Hotel. He took mine!'

'What did he say?'

He went on eating, barely troubling to look at her. 'Not much. There wasn't time. He had an appointment. I had a train to catch. He's in London on business, something about buying a big stud from a syndicate. I didn't really listen. But he did say that he had business in Scotland, too, so I mentioned that I was going up next week, to visit my mother. He might call in on me, if he has the time.'

Her heart had begun to beat wildly again.

'Did he say anything about . . . about coming here?'

For the first time, Jamie glanced up. 'No, he didn't. Why should he? I expect when his business is done he'll just go back to America. If he's bought a big stud there, he'll most likely spend all his time running it. Wouldn't you?'

She was silent for a moment. 'I haven't heard of any big studs up for sale.'

'Not here, no. After ours, and Welbeck and Westminster's . . . and the Royal Stud at Sandringham, of course, there aren't any. I meant, a major stud farm in America.' He paused, letting the words sink in. 'He must be rolling in it, to make a purchase like that. And just like that, too. Like nothing.' He was pretending to read the newspaper, but he was watching her face carefully from behind it. 'He talks about a million dollars as if it was a handful of sovereigns. Wouldn't I like to have his brass!'

'Was that all he told you, that he was going to Scotland after London . . . nothing about his plans afterwards?'

'Like I said, we were both in a hurry. I didn't bother to ask.' Finally, he laid down the newspaper with perfect timing and looked at her. 'What's it to you, anyway?' A sly smile crept across his face. 'You're quite taken with him, aren't you? Don't think I haven't noticed! Every time anyone mentions his name, your face turns red.'

'That isn't true!'

'Then what are you so angry with me for?'

'Oh, shut up, Jamie!' She got up, cheeks flushed, scraping back her chair and flounced out of the room. Gathering up the folds of her riding habit, she ran upstairs and into Alice's bedroom, where her sister was busy packing.

'You didn't come down to breakfast.' She paused in the doorway, getting her breath. 'Father's still in his study with McGrath. I had Jamie all to myself.'

'Lucky you!'

'Will you come for a last ride, before the carriage comes round to take you over to collect Lottie?'

'I'd like to, but I can't.' She held up one of her new London day dresses and admired it. 'Annie did most of the heavy packing yesterday . . . but these are all my special things . . . I wanted to see to these myself.'

'I'll miss you, Alice . . .'

'And I'll miss you. It's only three months, though. And time has a habit of flying.'

'It'll seem like three years!' She closed the door, flopped down on the bed and sighed. 'This house isn't big enough for me and Jamie!'

Alice stopped what she was doing. 'I thought he was

better now. You said so, not so long ago. Has he fallen from grace already?'

'He has this morning. I suppose I shouldn't take any notice. One thing, though; he does seem to have renounced all his evil ways . . . gambling and frittering away his money. When he came back from London and the carriage driver brought him to the house, he gave him a sovereign as a tip. And when he took out his wallet, it was crammed full of banknotes!'

'He must have listened to papa's last lecture on the virtue of thrift. I'll bet it goes against the grain!'

'I think Motty and his cronies were a bad influence on Jamie. They always had much more money than he did, and he tried to keep up with them. He wanted to be accepted by them as an equal, and they led him into bad ways. I know he's stopped seeing them now . . . no doubt about it; he's all the better for it.'

Slowly, Alice laid the last delicate garment in her trunk, and gently lowered the lid.

'Rebeccah . . . you do think I'm doing the right thing, don't you? Going to Italy . . . agreeing to see my mother?'

'What's wrong? Are you having second thoughts?'

Alice sat down next to her on the bed. She drew up her knees and hugged them.

'I don't know . . . I've had long enough to make a decision . . . I thought I knew exactly what I wanted to do . . . I discussed it with papa, just after her letter first came . . . now I don't feel so sure . . .'

Rebeccah put a hand on her shoulder, gently.

'You mean you'd rather not see her?'

'I want to . . . out of curiosity, if nothing else. To see what she looks like, if she's changed from the woman I remember . . . it's so long ago . . . for years, I felt bitter. About her, for what she did to me. I've always wanted to see her again and ask her why.'

'And now you can, you don't want to?'

'I'm nervous, if you want to know the real truth . . . foolish, isn't it? Afraid to meet my own mother? I felt all right until a few days ago, when the preparations all began . . . I was even looking forward to it. Travelling across France, Northern Italy, arriving in Venice. I was born there, and lived the first nine years of my life in the city . . . but I scarcely remember anything special about it at all . . .'

'You'll feel different when you get there. And you'll have Lottie with you. I wish I could be. Once you've met her, you won't be nervous any more.'

'I wish I could believe that.'

She got up and walked over to the window. For a few moments neither of them broke the silence.

'I couldn't sleep last night. I kept tossing and turning. Thinking about the journey. Thinking about her. Wondering what I can say to her when we meet. Like being with a stranger, isn't it? I wonder if she'll apologize. Beg for forgiveness for abandoning me. Do you suppose that's why she wants to see me, after all these years? Her conscience?'

'Alice, how can I answer that? I wish I could. For your sake. You can only wait and see.'

'I might hate her. I might even tell her to her face all the things I've wished on her, down the years, for leaving me. The Ajantis. They're Catholics, of course. No doubt she's lit a few candles for me and said her prayers, and she thinks that grants her absolution. Not in my book.' There was bitterness in Alice's voice that Rebeccah had never heard before. Bitterness that only appeared when she spoke about her mother. And she almost never did . . . until the letter from Venice came. She suddenly surprised Rebeccah by laughing. 'Do you know what? When I lay there before it was light this morning, thinking, turning everything over in my mind . . . I wondered what would happen if you and I changed places, and pretended to be each other instead of ourselves! You would go to Italy, and I'd stay here. We might even get away with it, except for the difference in our eyes. Yours blue, mine brown.' She smiled. 'Everyone would notice that at once, wouldn't they?'

Rebeccah came over to her and hugged her. 'It'll be all right, Alice. You'll see. It'll be all right.'

The dour, grey turrets of Dunroven Castle, pointed like four witches' hats, rose upwards into the cold, cloudy spring sky, flanking its square central keep like sentries; from across the loch that ran beside the castle, travellers could glimpse it, nestling between a mass of trees, casting its huge, elongated shadow across the spread of grass.

Even in winter, when the snow fell deep and the castle might be cut off from the outside world for many weeks, it was a beautiful and impressive sight; a fairy tale castle dusted with snow, icicles hanging like stalactites from the crenellated tower, the evergreen bushes clustered around its base sprinkled with white.

It was at its most striking during the early springtime, when the gardens that stretched from the rear of the castle downwards towards the deep, undulating loch, came alive with blossom and early blooms; when the ice broke and flowed downstream, and the first leaves began to appear on the thickly wooded bank that divided the castle from Dunroven Loch.

The interior of the castle was no less magnificent. There were massive stone fireplaces in every room, and rich tapestries decorating every wall. There were exquisite clocks, handwoven carpets of breathtaking beauty, marble statues imported from Italy, and delicate porcelain, glass, and French furniture from Versailles. In the splendid, huge dining room, by complete contrast, there was a colossal carved oak table, twenty feet long, proudly topped with matching silver candelabra at each end, and surrounded with high backed, carved oak Scottish chairs, the biggest Jamie had ever seen.

Though he had dined with the Dunrovens twice before, the striking contrast between the austerity of the stone walls, decorated with ancient shields, dirks, daggers and swords, and the richness of the furniture and silverware, never ceased to impress him. He gazed around him as they sat there, looking at the weapons adorning the walls as if he were seeing them for the first time.

He turned in his chair and looked at Rufus Waldo beside him.

'I told you the castle was magnificent. And this has always been my favourite room.' A smile towards Dunroven's pretty sister, Louise. 'Were you telling me last time I was here, Dunroven, that the swords on this wall were used by the Dunroven Clan at the battle of Culloden?'

'Indeed they were. And the shields on the north wall. Fortunately for us, we were on the side of the King and not the Pretender's rebels.'

Rufus Waldo continued to stare around him. 'You must forgive me for spending so much of my time admiring your castle instead of talking business.' A smile that could melt ice, directed at Louise. 'But in America we have so little true history. Your home is a delight.' Slowly, he sipped his wine. 'Tell me, is it true that you once had a broadsword with a bloodstain that could never be removed?'

Dunroven smiled. 'An old family legend, dating back for four hundred years. The sword was reputedly used by one of my ancestors to murder his brother; they were both in love with the same woman. Because of his wicked crime, the perpetrator was cursed by his father to suffer in torment for all time, unless he could remove the blood of his brother from the blade. A grim tale. Legend has it that, no matter how he scrubbed it, or what he did to try to remove it, the indelible mark remained. And his soul has reputedly wandered in purgatory ever since.'

Across the massive table, Lady Louise Dunroven shuddered. 'When I was a little girl, I was always afraid of wandering in the castle alone, without my nurse or my personal maid. I fancied at night I heard groans and screams of agony . . . always, they came from the same place. The Old Scots Room, in the East tower. It's very sparsely furnished now, not much used. But in the sixteenth-century it was used as a nursery. It just has a simple tapestry on the wall now, a chair, and an old, handcarved child's rocking crib.'

Waldo smiled. 'And you think the room was haunted?'

'I did then. Especially on the long, dark, winter nights, when the light faded early in the afternoon, and everywhere was alive with dim corners and moving shadows.' She began to laugh, softly. 'Robert would tease me unmercifully about it. And I used to go crying and telling tales on him to my mother.'

'I remember well!' Dunroven said. 'Tell me, Mr Waldo. Do you plan to stay in Scotland for long?'

'I have business is Edinburgh; then I return south, to London.'

'Jamie tells me that you've recently acquired a large stud farm in the southern states . . . purchased from two well known American owners. Have you always had such a deep interest in racing and breeding horses?'

'Always. I love them in their own right. As a businessman, I've always been attracted by the value of them as investment. Few sports are so popular. None has the enormous potential of breeding bloodstock for the racetrack.'

'Do you intend to buy extensively from English stock, such as the Brodie Russell stable, or will you concentrate on home bred animals, like Iroquois?'

'A half American horse, and he won your English Derby. That would be my ultimate ambition, yes, to breed another Iroquois. I shall still retain my connections with Merritt and Company; I'm one of their major shareholders.' A brief, knowing glance towards Jamie. 'As is Jamie. Of couse, with his own interests to pursue in the bloodstock line, we were only a few days ago discussing the possibility of his purchasing his own stud in America, a project that has interested him for some time.'

Both of them could see Dunroven's mind working, cog on cog.

'I suppose your grandmother, Lady Russell, will want you to eventually take over the reins from your father? With his own stud based near Newmarket, he must have plenty to keep him busy . . .'

Jamie hesitated before answering, knowing that his chances with Louise depended on it.

'My half-sister Rebeccah, of course, will have a token share in my grandmother's estate, and also my sister Alice. When Rebeccah's grandfather Jerome Charpentier died, she inherited his entire fortune, which is held in trust until she marries, or until she reaches the age of twenty-one. My grandmother knows, of course, that when both my sisters marry, they'll live on their husband's estates, and she wants a man's hand at the helm of the Brodie Russell ship.'

Dunroven had the answer that he wanted from his carefully disguised question. He smiled, and Jamie knew that he had won.

'A remarkable woman, your grandmother. A legend in her own lifetime. You're no doubt very close to her.'

'I always have been.' He kept his face a mask. 'The family tradition in bloodstock was born and bred in me. I want to take what she already made famous, and make it more famous still. My father's role in the organization has always been a much more passive one. He's never shared my passion for the turf . . . something, between us alone, of course, that I think has deeply disappointed my grandmother. For her, racing was always such a passion in the blood.'

Beside him, he could feel Rufus Waldo's hidden mirth, and with difficulty he stifled the impulse to laugh. His mouth turning up traitorously at the corners, he quickly picked up his empty wine goblet and hid the bottom half of his face.

When he had regained his self-control, he put the goblet down, before him on the table, and let his eyes linger on Louise. While her brother talked across the table to Rufus Waldo, he enjoyed the silent, visual foreplay, smiling at her without words, in his expression a hint of things to come. Yes, he would ask Dunroven later, before they left. There was time enough.

But as they rose from the table when the meal had ended, he was careful to draw Dunroven, briefly, to one side.

'A few moments of your time, Dunroven, in an hour or two, before we leave for Inverness . . . a matter I should like to discuss with you in private . . .'

'It seemed almost too easy . . . do you really think he believed me?'

'It's your guilty conscience, Jamie; why shouldn't he? Dunroven takes you at face value . . . you're a Russell. You're the last in the Russell male line. And your grandmother is the head of the Brodie Russell empire, most of which he thinks you'll inherit when your sisters have been provided for. The bar sinister doesn't matter. Money eradicates even bastardy, if it's plentiful enough . . . I've told you that, often enough, before. He's consented to your marriage with his sister, and, I'll wager, since there's just the two of them and he's a widower without an heir, you'll most likely be in for the lot!'

Jamie sank back on the ancient bed, and stretched, lazily.

'I can scarcely believe it! Me, marrying Dunroven's sister! Wait till I get back home!'

'Tread warily. You're not home and dry yet. But you will be, with caution, a little astute juggling here and there . . . and if you continue to listen to me.'

'I owe you more than I can ever hope to repay . . .'

'Generous words. All I want you to do is get me Rebeccah.'

'You can do that for yourself. She already wants to see you again, I told you what she said when I pretended I'd met you in London. She never stopped plying me with questions.'

'What of the competition?' Waldo lit a cigar. 'And don't tell me that there isn't any. A girl as beautiful as that and who stands to inherit a fortune, is never short of ardent admirers, all pressing their claims. Anyone serious?'

'Not that I know of. And I would know.'

The complacent smile vanished from Waldo's face.

'Don't be flippant, Jamie, not with me. This isn't some game I'm playing. I've planned and schemed and waited for too long to be thwarted now. I told you to listen, to watch carefully. If she's invited to some ball or other function, make certain that you're invited too. Do I make myself clear to you?'

'Of course. I've told you. You've no need to worry. Yes . . . there are plenty who want her, for all the reasons you've said. But she isn't interested in them, not any of them. I've watched. I've listened. And there isn't anyone you need worry about. Rebeccah has a mind of her own, anyhow; my father couldn't force her into any marriage of convenience, even if he wanted to. She'll only marry who she wants.'

'Still keep watching. And remember. If there are any complications, your marriage to Louise Dunroven goes out the window.' He drew slowly on the cigar, filling the air around him with the thick, acrid, pungent smoke. 'Until I get Rebeccah, and what comes with her, you'll need enough brass to show around to impress the Dunrovens, to prove that you're truly a man of means. Do exactly as I say, Jamie, and I'll keep you well supplied.'

'Tell me more about Enoch Wishard.'

Waldo stretched out his long, elegant legs. 'He's a top trainer back home. And he's crooked. So far, he's made a fortune for his two employers, William Gates and James Drake. They're both millionaires. But, since you're a bright boy, you'll know that however cleverly horses get nobbled and however good anyone is at covering his tracks, it's only a matter of time before the authorities dig up the truth. This is what's starting to happen, and it's time for Wishard to get out . . . where better for him to start up business all over again than merry England?'

'But it might not work this time . . . things are different over here. If he starts trying to fix big races, the Jockey Club'll smell a rat and be onto him like a ton of bricks. Not to mention other watchdogs.'

'He isn't an amateur. And he doesn't use the old, obvious, crude methods . . . he's made doping horses a fine art.'

'*Doping* them?'

'Fixing big races isn't his game; he's more interested in betting coups. Handicaps, not top class animals. A certain substance is injected into the horse before the race, with a hypodermic needle . . . Enoch's own brew. Not too little, not too much. A mistake either way can be fatal. A shot of the magic mixture will turn a no-hoper into Eclipse's double . . . for just long enough to turn over the form and win the race . . . you're beginning to get the picture?'

'But any widespread doping of horses would play havoc with the handicapper!'

'Exactly. It can still be done, occasionally, in a big race. But it's much more risky, for several reasons. First and foremost, the sudden burst of unexpected good form for some second rate nag running in a handicap up north, wouldn't cause many eyebrows to lift; but if it happened in, say, the Oaks, or the Derby, people would start talking. Enoch knows what he's doing.'

Jamie sat there, chewing his fingernails, deep in thought. 'And Rebeccah and the old woman?'

Waldo stubbed out his cigar. 'When we leave here, I'll go on to London; you'll spend a few more days with your mother at the hunting lodge, then return home. There's a big meeting at Epsom the week afterwards, the Diamond Cup, when you'll accompany your father and Rebeccah and stay there at your grandmother's house. Once you're there, you'll let slip that we bumped into each other again in Edinburgh or Inverness, where I had business, and that we were both guests of Dunroven's at the castle.

'You'll then let it be casually known to the old woman that I'm coming down for the Diamond meeting, and you'll get me invited to the house.'

'And then?'

'Just leave the rest of it to me.'

21

AS THE GONDOLIER slowly approached the *palazzo* steps, all the half-faded memories of her childhood came back, bitter-sweet, almost unwillingly. A lost world, so different from England. When they drew alongside the stone landing stage, Alice looked up at the tall, crumbling walls of the *palazzo* Ajanti that she remembered, the long, narrow windows that looked out over the waters of the canal, like a Canaletto painting. She wondered if her mother stood behind one of them; watching, waiting. But she could see nothing, no sign of life.

The boatman helped her to mount the steps, but a boy was already waiting, hands outstretched, to take her into the *palazzo* entrance above them. He spoke no English. So many, long years, since she herself had spoken Italian with her mother. But, surprisingly, she found that the words came back with unexpected ease, almost as if she had never learned to speak another tongue.

'*Grazi*,' she murmured, as he stood there beside the high arched entrance, waiting for her to pass through.

Without speaking, he led her through endless corridors and musty-smelling, almost bare rooms, long since divested of their furniture and treasures. Their footsteps echoed, eerily, on the floor of the marble hall that she remembered, the plinths that once, long ago, held priceless statues, now stood empty, like an abandoned museum.

There was no sign of any other servants, except the boy. Little sunlight filtered into the sad, dreary, naked rooms, giving her a crushed, joyless feeling of acute depression. Had she really lived here, in this once-grand, but now sadly neglected, crumbling place? Had she once been happy? She shivered, drawing her long, richly furred cape closer around her body, to ward off the atmosphere of dampness and chill.

They had reached the end of another long corridor. The boy went forward and opened the huge, tall, double doors, to reveal the room inside. Looking past him, Alice could see that this room was lighter, and more furnished than all the others; a different room, a lived-in room. There were large, faded tapestries hanging on the walls; French furniture, once magnificently upholstered, but now as faded as the tapestries and the gold fringe ragged; the rugs scattered on the polished woodblock floor were worn and in some places, threadbare.

She held her breath. Her heart suddenly began to lurch, and beat faster, for there was someone there inside the room. Obsequiously, the boy stepped forward with a little bow.

'*Contessa Ajanti, la signorina Alicia . . .*'

Her limbs wooden, Alice walked forward into the room, and looked into the proud, still beautiful face of her mother.

Behind them, the doors closed.

'So, my Alice . . . you have come at last . . .'

Alice went on staring at her. The face was almost as she remembered it; the skin flawless, unlined. Her dark hair, swept upwards in the French style, was thick and glossy, with no sign of grey. The dull, gold velvet of the gown she wore contrasted, strikingly, with the smooth, olive perfection of her shoulders. Topaz glittered around her throat, and on her ears.

'Well, do you have nothing to say to me after so long?' She smiled. 'Was your journey along the canal a pleasant one?'

Alice's dark eyes, the beautiful, glittering dark eyes that she had inherited from her mother, flashed.

'How can you stand there, smiling, speaking to me as if you saw me only yesterday? Ten years. Not a word. Not a single letter. You left me. I was a nine-year-old child in a foreign land, and you walked away and left me.'

There was no surprise, no sorrow, on her mother's face. She merely shrugged.

'You do not understand, Alicia; and how can a child ever understand the things that a mother must do? I was alone in the world. We were noble but poor. There was no money left with which to give you the start in life that was your right . . . only the Ajanti name. You were your father's daughter. A Russell. It was only right that you should go to him, for I knew that he could give you what I could not. It was a duty that I owed to you. My own feelings did not matter. Now, when I look at you, I see that what I did was right.'

Alice could only go on staring at her, in disbelief.

'Is that all you can say? After all these years of silence, not knowing, even, whether I was alive or dead? That what you did was right?'

Isabella Ajanti smiled. 'You have inherited my temper, Alicia. That, at least, pleases me. I am glad that you have the Ajanti spirit. But what you accuse me of is unjust. I did care. I have always cared. You are my flesh and blood. Because I did not wish you to be brought up here, in poverty, because by leaving you with your father I gave you what I could not, does not mean that I stopped thinking about you. Or wishing that things could have been otherwise.'

Alice looked into the dark, long-lashed eyes – replicas of her own. She thought of a small, frightened little girl in white velvet, standing alone in a big, strange, brightly lit hall, stared at by strangers.

'Didn't you feel *anything* when you went away and left me?'

'Of course. Sadness. Regret. Pain. Yes, I shed tears because of what I had done. Because of what I had to do. But I knew that, when you were a woman, you would be grateful for the sacrifice I made.'

'Grateful?'

'The world in which you now move is what I always wanted for my daughter. When you were a child, living here with me in the *palazzo*, I felt much bitterness when I realized that your father would not openly acknowledge you, because he was afraid of his rich, spoiled wife, his rich, spoiled wife's father. He only married her for her money. With us, it was all love, and passion. Never would he get any woman to love him as I did. But because to have much money was so important to him, he chose to leave you here, with me.'

'I already know that.'

'What you do not know is that I begged him, many times, to take you into his care, to give you what I alone could not give . . . but he always refused. I knew that to make him do what I wanted, I would have to force his hand.' A pause, a long moment of silence. 'That is why I sent you to him that night, before I left to come back to Italy.'

'Are you saying it was all his fault?'

'Whose fault was it if not his?'

Her anger spent, Alice did not know what else to say. So, he had lied to her. Not quite a lie, but more a clever twisting of the truth.

'You mean that he didn't want me?'

'He did want you, Alicia; but he is an Englishman. Englishmen care most for money, and their reputations . . . if they are of your father's class. That is something that you would be wise to remember, and learn.'

After a long silence, her mother went over to the big, faded French couch, and sat down.

'Are you not pleased to see me? And, if you are not, why did you come? You could have ignored my letter. Yet you did not.'

'I don't know why I wanted to see you. Curiosity. I wanted to see what you looked like, I suppose; if you were exactly as I remembered you.'

'And am I?'

'Yes.'

Another smile. The dark eyes glittered.

'I am glad, Alicia, that you did not forget.'

'Most of all, I wanted to ask you the question that I've wondered inside for all these years. I suppose I have my answer to that now.'

'Will you not sit down beside me? Or, over there, if you choose . . .' Alice sat down, awkwardly, self-consciously, uncharacteristically, without her usual easy grace. She looked across at where her mother sat. 'Tell me. You are nineteen now, yes? You should be married. Are there many rich young men who want to marry you?'

'One in particular.' She forced her mind to think with a semblance of normality. 'But I haven't decided to accept.'

'One should never accept the first offer, unless it is irresistible. Many men will desire you, because you are my daughter and you are beautiful. Your father will see that you have a good dowry. But that is not enough. The choice you make, Alicia, must be the right one; you must not make a mistake. That single choice will affect the rest of your life.'

'He's very wealthy. A Scottish Earl. Duncan, Earl of Clanradine.'

Isabella Ajanti's perfectly curved dark eyebrows lifted. 'Then marry him.'

'You haven't even asked me if I love him.'

A knowing smile.

'Love, in such a marriage, is irrelevant. He is rich and he is titled. You will be his wife and you will want for nothing. And, one day, you will be a rich and titled widow.'

'If I don't die of boredom first!'

'You can always take a lover. If you are discreet.'

Alice was astonished. 'You really mean that, don't you?'

'But of course. Your father did it. Why not you? He married Corinna Charpentier for her money, and found love elsewhere.'

Alice looked down at her clasped hands, lying motionless in her lap.

'There's someone else. Someone I really want. Ever since I first saw him, I haven't been able to get him out of my mind. But it's hopeless. He wouldn't marry me without money. What father would give me wouldn't be enough.'

'An ambitious man? With a head that always rules his heart. You would be wise to forget him, Alicia . . .'

'I can't forget him.'

'To love so, it is dangerous. Imprisonment. He will bind you with chains and you will never break free. I know this, for it was with that kind of love that I loved your father. And it brought me only heartache and misery.' She got up, and began to pace the room. 'Many men have desired me; before I met your father, and afterwards. But I could never marry any of them, he was in my blood, a fever that nothing could ever quench. My love for him tortured me. In the end, it made me bitter.' She stopped pacing and turned to face Alice. 'What I lost, I want for you. What I should have had, you must have. That is all I have left, the desire for revenge; the desire to see you have everything that should have been mine.'

Slowly, Alice rose to her feet. 'What do you think I should do?'

Her mother came to her, and placed both hands on her shoulders. Alice felt the pressure and the warmth of them through the velvet of her cloak. The first time she had touched her mother for ten long years.

'If I were you . . . I would marry this Duncan, the Earl of Clanradine. And then I would wait, and watch, and listen.' A pause, while she thought. 'Is this man that you cannot forget to marry someone else?'

Alice broke away from her strong grasp, unable to meet even her mother's eyes. 'Yes.' She turned and gripped the worn, carved lion's heads that decorated the massive arms of the faded chair. 'I knew he wanted her, from the first time

I ever saw them together. And I had to pretend that I didn't care.' It was a struggle to go on. 'I could almost read his mind, sense, feel what he was thinking. The Brodie Russell fortune . . . and her as well . . . I hated him for wanting it. And I hated myself for wanting him . . . I watched her, carefully, without her even realizing it . . . and I could see the way her face would change, her eyes light up whenever he was there, how she'd colour, if anyone mentioned his name . . . that's when I knew. Before any of them . . . it was almost uncanny, some sort of magic . . . like a soothsayer, or a witch . . . like looking through a mirror into the future . . .'

Isabella Ajanti was astonished, for the first time. 'Alicia . . ? You say he wants the Brodie Russell fortune . . . *and her too* . . .? By that, you can only mean one other person . . .'

They stared at each other.

'Rebeccah.'

There was a sudden, deathly silence in the room. For a moment, neither of them spoke. Alice felt suddenly appalled at her own thoughts, the harboured, bitter, angry thoughts that had festered for so long without her even realizing that they existed, the thoughts she had, at last, put into words.

'I started hating her when I first saw them together. It was at my grandmother's house, near Epsom, a dinner party. Everyone was there. Then she got up, and went out into the stableyard as she always does in the evening, after we've eaten . . . and he followed her.' She looked up at her mother, with dark, furious eyes. 'I knew then. It was just a feeling; a feeling that he'd be back. I can't put into words the way I felt. Just that I hated her, because he wanted her and not me.'

'The money, Alicia . . . it is the money, not Rebeccah . . .'

'If you'd seen her, you wouldn't say that. She's more beautiful than I am. Different. A different kind of beauty. Maybe that's the kind he wants.'

'She is like her mother, the American bitch? I saw her,

once . . . you never knew that, did you? She found out about me and came to my hotel. She wanted to hurt me. Insult me. Pretend that the love between your father and me was sordid, and cheap.'

'You met her? Corinna Charpentier?'

'She was very beautiful, yes. But cold. Like a marble statue. Those blue eyes. So striking. So rich a colour. But no warmth. No passion, no fire. That is not what a man wants, a woman of stone. However beautiful, he would soon tire of such a woman. This, I know; believe me.'

'Do you really think it was only the money?'

'You would know the answer to that better than I would, Alicia. What did his eyes tell you when they looked at you?'

'I don't know.'

'Then you must find out.'

Alice walked away, slowly, around the room; the faces on the faded, threadbare tapestries that hung about the walls looked down on her, sightlessly; the cherubs on the ornate plaster pillars, once gold, now a dull yellow, seemed to mock her as she passed. Her bastardy had never seemed to matter to her, to anyone, before; her father, her grandmother, everyone, had always treated them the same. But now it mattered. It mattered because Rebeccah would get everything, including the man she wanted for herself. The injustice of it so overwhelmed her that she wanted to be sick. To shout, to scream, to smash things. But it was no use. She was a bastard, like Jamie, and what she wanted didn't matter at all. For the first time in her life, she understood why Jamie had always been so bitter.

When she spoke her voice was quiet, controlled. She was glad, after all, that she had answered her mother's letter. She was glad, after all the doubts and the misgivings, that she had come.

'I never realized how I truly felt. Not ever. I thought we were equal, all of us. But that isn't true, is it? Because Jamie and I are nothing. Everything is hers. Jerome Charpentier's fortune, my father's house, my grandmother's self-built empire. It's strange . . . I never thought of it like that before . . . I don't know why. It wouldn't matter what she had, if I could have Rufus Waldo.' She looked into her mother's eyes. 'I'll take him away from her, I swear it. Any way I can.'

Isabella Ajanti smiled. 'You need only be yourself, and he will come to you.'

22

'ONE OF THE LARGEST STUDS in Tennessee, you say? Yes, of course I'm impressed . . . who wouldn't be?' Anna glanced up from the letter she was writing to look at her son, seated opposite. What a pity James had never been born with that same fire, that relentless energy and thirst for achievement, that she, in her youth, shared now with the young Rufus Waldo. From the first time they'd met she'd felt, far transcending the quick, clever brain and the magnetic charm, the affinity between them. 'He's been Merritt's chief bloodstock assessor for the last five years; not usually a job they'd entrust to a young man. That by itself proves his mettle. He knows what he wants and exactly how he aims to get there . . . a man after my own heart.'

James Russell nodded, slowly, wondering if it was merely his imagination that heard the hint of regret in his mother's voice. He quickly changed the subject.

'What I'm grateful to him for is that he seems to have done Jamie a power of good. A steadying influence. They've met, by accident, once or twice, and now Jamie tells me that they bumped into each other in Edinburgh. At first, I thought it was just a coincidence; but it isn't. Ever since Jamie first met him, he's made strenuous efforts to change his ways. And he's done it. No more gambling. No horses. No cards. Not even a guinea's worth. And as far as I know he hasn't been within a mile of old Mottram's ne'er-do-well heir . . .'

'You know why Jamie's changed for the better, don't you? Rufus Waldo made him look at himself, and he didn't like what he saw. Waldo is everything Jamie's always wanted to be and isn't. Successful. Wealthy. Clever. And the people who matter respect him. Whatever else Jamie is, he isn't a fool.'

'He's been living well within his means, at long last. That, I never thought to see. At times, I almost despaired of him . . . yes, mother, I admit it now. But he's my son and I felt it was my duty as his father to stand by him, whatever he did. Maybe there's more of Margaret in him than I ever realized. For more than a year he's been a changed man about money . . . he hasn't asked me for a single penny.'

'That surprises me almost as much as it did when he wrote to you saying he was going to marry Dunroven's sister. There's a right royal fortune there. And if Dunroven never remarries, his sister will inherit the lot. Jamie, king of the castle. Whoever would have thought it?' She glanced down at her letter. 'Talking of the Dunrovens, since the engagement was announced, I thought it only politic to invite them and Rufus Waldo down here for the Diamond Cup meeting. With Alice due to come home in the middle of it, we might as well make it a family gathering. We'll have the Tradescants over for the Diamond Cup Ball, too. Then young Lottie can sing to us all before she goes off to London.' She smiled, with a touch of sadness and a touch of pride. 'She's my sister Clara to a tee. The same looks. The same voice. But tougher. And she'll need that if she's going to sing in the music halls in the big city.'

'If she were my daughter she wouldn't go. Saul must be out of his mind!'

'That he isn't. Lottie'll be well taken care of; she'll be living in the Shaftesbury Avenue house with his brother-in-law's family, and properly chaperoned everywhere she goes. Besides, do you think he could stop her from doing what she's always wanted to do? She's wanted to go on the stage ever since she was a child.'

'I still wouldn't let her do it.'

'Is that a fact? She's got Brodie blood, James. We always do what we want to. Saul couldn't stop Lottie singing any more than you could stop Rebeccah wanting to ride a horse.' He fell silent. 'Now, let me finish this letter to Dunroven. A house party for the Diamond needs a lot of planning and there's little more than two weeks left to go. Rebeccah's running the St Simon colt for the first time, did she tell you?'

'Yes, she did.' He was frowning. 'But I still think it should be entered under a pseudonym, like Mrs Langtry uses; not her own name. Whatever you say, mother, it isn't the done thing for a lady to run horses . . . even now.'

'Rubbish.' She dipped her pen in the ornate inkwell and didn't bother to look up. 'Just tell her to hurry up and give him a name.'

'He's a truly handsome colt. One of the best I've seen.' Dunroven turned to Rebeccah and smiled. 'You must be very proud to own such an animal. I know I would be. And I always did have a profound admiration for St Simon's stock.'

'Yes; he is beautiful, isn't he? A birthday gift from my grandmother . . . the kind of gift that only she would think to give me.'

They went on watching the colt as he stood, like a burnished statue, beside the clump of oak trees in the centre of the paddock. His lad had done him proud.

'Louise, my sister, has never shared my passion for the turf. More's the pity. My father and my uncles were all great racing men. A family tradition. Five years in a row, Dunroven stock took every major northern race. Quite an achievement.'

'Before my grandmother's time or after it?' They both laughed. 'I'm sorry, I shouldn't have said that.'

'By no means. Anna Brodie is a name I was brought up to take notice of. Truly a one and only.'

'I wish I'd known her then, when she was a young woman.' They began to walk, slowly, around the fence of the paddock. 'Or that she'd live forever.' The smile had vanished from her face. 'She's almost eighty . . . did you realize that? And she's looked pale and drawn these last few days . . . not herself. I know she's had a few visits, on and off, from the doctor in Epsom; but when I asked her about it, she says it's nothing.'

'She's probably right,' Dunroven said, quickly, to reassure her. 'Eighty is a great age, you know. A simple check up every now and then, which I'm certain the visits were, is nothing untoward.' They walked on, Rebeccah still silent. 'My grandfather was over ninety when he died . . . and he saw his doctor from Inverness regularly, twice a week. They had a dram together and played cards!'

She knew that he was trying to set her mind at rest, and she was grateful. There was something peaceful, and reassuring, about being with Dunroven. She had wondered, ever since the news of the engagement came, what his sister Lady Louise Dunroven, ever saw in her brother Jamie.

'Your sister Alice is still in Italy, I believe? Venice. A beautiful city. I visited it once with my father and my tutor, when I finished my schooling. I've always meant to go back there one day . . .'

'Alice should be home in time for the Diamond Cup. And, I hope, to see a Russell horse win it.'

'Does she share your passion for the turf or not?'

'We're both Russells; I think it runs in the blood. But I do feel guilty having my own colt when she doesn't.'

A pause. She could almost hear him thinking.

'I don't mean to pry, of course . . . I did know that she . . . that she was only your half-sister . . .'

'Her mother is Italian. But we were brought up together, exactly the same, from the age of nine. Her mother and mine both left England at the same time. The very same night, so it happens . . .' She thought back, of the great marble hall, and two little girls, both in tears, being comforted by Annie. So long ago. 'Neither of us, I suppose I should say, has really ever been close to Jamie . . .'

He said something then that surprised her.

'It'll be quite a feat for him, when he and Louise are married, living in Scotland and here too; forever travelling back and forth. Not that that will be likely to bother him; Jamie takes everything in his stride. But I should imagine that your grandmother, being the meticulous lady she is, will still expect him to look after his own interests in the bloodstock in England.'

She said nothing. But later, when she found Anna alone, she mentioned their conversation.

'I didn't correct him, of course . . . it wasn't my business to. But he seems certain that Jamie has a large controlling interest in your bloodstock empire. I know that he doesn't have. Do you think that he agreed to Jamie's marriage with his sister because he believes him to be a wealthy man of means? Do you think Jamie has been lying to him purely to get his permission to marry Louise Dunroven?'

Anna lay back in the huge wing chair. Yes, of course, it all fitted. Like the missing pieces to a jigsaw puzzle, every persistent, nagging question in her mind fell neatly into place.

'Nothing that Jamie did would ever surprise me. Lie to Dunroven to mislead him? I wouldn't put it past him. I've been wondering, ever since your father broke the news to me, how a ne'er-do-well like Jamie, who's never done a day's work in his life, managed to hook such a big fish as Lady Louise; something must have tipped the scales in his favour, because, outside of royalty, she's one of the biggest catches, marriage-wise, in the country. Admittedly, Jamie's got more than his fair share of looks, and he can turn on the charm when he chooses to. But for a man like Dunroven, it'd take a whole lot more than that for him to agree to the marriage. On the principle of like marries like, Jamie's the last man on earth he'd want to marry his sister to.'

'You think Jamie told Dunroven that he owns a big slice of your estate?'

'Something like that. There's no other explanation.'

Rebeccah bit her lip.'Do you think he'd go so far as to stop the wedding taking place if he found out the truth?'

'Anything's possible. Besides the fact that Jamie has nothing but an allowance to his name – there's the question of Dunroven having been made a fool of. If I judge him rightly . . . and I'm a pretty fair judge of men . . . he won't take kindly to that.'

'What can we do?'

'Nothing. No point in interfering. Jamie's old enough to manage his own affairs. Not that I'm condoning what he's up to; and after what you've told me, I'm pretty sure he is up to something. After the wedding when he gets his hands on Louise's dowry, nobody will be any the wiser. The fact that he has no property of his own at all won't be discovered until much later. Anyhow, I don't think it matters, and I won't play God. The Dunroven girl clearly thinks your brother is wonderful; let's not spoil her fun.'

'But do you think Jamie really loves her?'

The smile faded from Anna's face. The blue eyes looked grave.

'Jamie's never loved anyone but himself.'

Jamie watched from an upstairs window as Dunroven and his sister parted company, and each walked in a different direction. He stayed where he was and watched them go. Rebeccah into the house. Dunroven in the direction of the exercise yards, where his father was giving Lady Louise an escorted tour. He knew Rufus Waldo was getting ready to join them. Quickly, he went along the corridor to his room without bothering to knock.

Their eyes met and held in the mirror. Then Waldo went on adjusting his necktie.

'Rufus? I think we're going to have trouble. And lots of it. That bloody Dunroven . . !'

'What about Dunroven?'

Jamie shut the door and leaned heavily against it. 'He's after Rebeccah. I'd stake my life on it.'

Waldo spun round.

'What?'

'Ever since they got here, he hasn't taken his eyes off her. Then I thought it was my imagination, the way he kept looking, and following her around. After all, the men are always ogling her. Her and Alice. But this is different. And it could ruin everything . . . for both of us. If Dunroven took it into his head to ask my father for permission to court her, where would you be? A title's still worth its weight in gold, you mark my words. And if she married Dunroven and they had children, where would that leave me? Louise wouldn't get anything!'

Waldo had gone very pale. A nerve ticked away furiously in his cheek.

'Where's Dunroven now? And Rebeccah?'

'She came indoors. He went off in the direction of the exercise yard, probably to look for my father and his sister. What are we going to do?'

'We'll play it by ear. Keep watching him. But remember what you said to me . . . Rebeccah wouldn't marry anyone unless she wanted to. Do you really suppose she'd prefer that Scottish boor to me? Or are you only worried about yourself?' The dark eyes twinkled harshly. 'You don't give a damn who your sister marries, so long as you get what you expect from Louise?'

'We're in this together, Waldo. If you marry my sister and I get Dunroven's, we each profit. You get the entire Brodie

Russell inheritance; I get Dunroven's. If Rebeccah marries him instead, you get nothing, and so do I. Except Louise's dowry. And I want far more than that.'

He could almost see Waldo's quick, clever, cunning mind working, cog on cog.

'All right. Listen. This is what we'll do. Leave Rebeccah to me. I first met her over a year ago, and I've only just come back . . . so no one can even have the glimmer of a suspicion of what's in my mind. Certainly nobody would ever suspect me of being a fortune hunter. I've covered my tracks too well. Drop a few hints to Dunroven over dinner that she's particularly taken with me. Since it's true, you won't even have to lie about it.'

'You're bloody sure of yourself, aren't you?'

'I know women.'

'All right. What then?'

'That'll dampen his ardour. Set a date as soon as possible for your wedding to Louise.'

'But he's here for another week. That might make complications. And whatever I say, he might take the view that all's fair in love and war. He might not take any notice at all.'

Waldo turned back to the mirror and finished adjusting his necktie.

'He's already invited us back to Dunroven Castle for the shooting, hasn't he?'

'And Rebeccah's included in the invitation!'

'It doesn't matter. Because at the end of that weekend Dunroven won't be able to marry anyone at all.'

Jamie stared at him. He was about to ask him what he meant. And then he understood.

When Rebeccah had left her, Anna continued to sit there in the big wing armchair, deep in thought.

She was no longer thinking about the artful machinations

of Jamie; they were no more than she expected of him. But the question of what Jamie had been up to in Scotland had brought other, more urgent, questions into her mind. Questions that, for now, had no answers.

She recalled the previous conversation with her son. She heard his voice over and over again, as if he were still there with her in the room. '*What I'm grateful to him for is that he seems to have done Jamie a power of good . . .*' She recalled, too, her own words, words of liking and praise; was it, could it possibly be, true, or was it a figment of her imagination, this sudden, totally unexpected flicker of suspicion in her mind? Was she being unjust to Rufus Waldo, a man she had been instantly drawn to and impressed by, she, who had never been taken in by anyone in the whole of her life? She could see, too, how much Rebeccah had been drawn to him; how, all that time ago when he had left, the girl had moped around, for weeks afterwards, for a long time only a shadow of her former self. She had got over it, as Anna had known she would. And now he was back again. Should she read something suspicious or sinister in that long absence? An absence during which he grew rich and Rebeccah grew from a girl into a young woman . . . were those missing months merely nothing more than that, or were they used for some other purpose, a preparation for which only Waldo knew?

She got up, as well as she was able, for her joints lately had been growing more stiff and she was often in considerable pain. But pacing had always helped her think. For a moment she looked up; at her own huge, lifesized portrait; if only she could be, for a short while, that young, vital, agile girl, long enough to find out the truth, instead of an old, pain-racked woman who could barely climb the stairs without assistance. She winced, suddenly, as the sharp, stabbing pain that had knotted her chest and brought beads of sweat to her brow, came back again. With difficulty, she clawed her way back to the safety of her chair beside the little cabinet, lowered her body into it, and lay there, head back, eyes closed, fighting for her breath. After a few moments, when the pain had subsided, she reached into the cabinet drawer for the pills the doctor had left her. Then she swallowed one, and lay back again, her hands gripping at the sides of her chair.

Her head began to swim. Round and round, wildly, as if she was on a merry-go-round and the whole room was spinning.

Jamie. Rufus Waldo. Had they really met so many times, coincidentally, purely by chance? London. Edinburgh. What, she wondered, had Jamie been doing there? Then, both guests at Dunroven Castle. Not, on the face of it, much to make her change her mind. *A man after my own heart* . . . her own words. Not much to justify that tiny, fleeting suspicion. Just that old, inexplicable feeling that she'd always had when something was not quite right, that feeling that had never, in all her long life, let her down.

When the dizziness and the pain had passed, there was a letter that she must write . . .

23

SINCE LONG BEFORE DAWN when the rain had begun to fall, the nervousness had begun to attack her.

Rebeccah lay there in bed, tossing and turning, unable to fall back into sleep. Then, still before daylight, she had got up and got dressed without calling for her maid. So much was to happen today, almost too much. Gold Bridge, her St Simon colt, was to run in the Hambletonian Stakes; Alice and Lottie Tradescant were due home from Italy; at the Diamond Cup Ball tonight, Jamie and Louise Dunroven would announce the date of their wedding; and she would be able to dance with Rufus Waldo.

She sat curled up on the window seat, staring down onto the lawns and the countryside beyond, but seeing none of the trees and hedges and flowers, only his face.

He seemed different to the Rufus Waldo she knew before; more distant, his mind somehow half occupied when he was with her, as if only part of him was listening to what she said, the other part elsewhere. She wondered what he had done in the time that had gone by since they last saw each other; if there was some other woman, back home, in his life that he had not spoken about, yet longed to return to; she had already noticed how women would watch him, how their eyes would follow him as he passed by, and the stab of jealousy that she felt made her think of the evening ahead as an ordeal and not a pleasure.

She took extra care with her appearance as she dressed; for the racecourse she chose a rich, grey velvet, fringed with ermine, and a matching hat, decorated with a single spray of feathers. She wore her dark hair in ringlets. Gazing at her reflection in the long mirror, she had cause to smile.

For the Ball that evening, a very special gown. Ivory Spitalfields lace, over a flared, multi-layered skirt of organza, the matching bodice decorated with minute seed pearls, and cream satin ribbon bows. She went over to her wardrobe and gazed at it; reached out and touched it, softly, reverently, with her outstretched hand. The faint aroma of rose petals, from the tiny sachets of dried petals that Rebeccah had hung among her gowns, wafted out to her, and clung, almost imperceptibly, to the folds of the ivory gown. Slowly, she closed the door of the wardrobe, and pulled the heavy velvet curtains aside from her bedroom window. It was daylight now, but still dull outside, the grass thick with dew and last night's rain.

For a while longer she paced her room, every few moments glancing at the clock. How slow the hands were moving. How much time seemed to drag. Finally, as quietly as she could, Rebeccah went downstairs and into the library.

Rufus Waldo was already there.

'Good morning,' he said, getting immediately to his feet. 'Up so early?' The dark eyes were transfixed on her face.

'I couldn't sleep. I kept thinking about the race. About Gold Bridge. The going was good yesterday morning. With the rain that fell last night, it'll be more than soft.'

He smiled his slow, easy smile, the smile that made her heart hammer and lurch.

'You don't think the ground will suit him?'

'I can't be sure. He's been trained on all goings. Firm, good, soft. Downright quagmires. That's the way my grandmother always trains all our horses. She reckons that if they can run on every type of going, it's easier to see what they're made of. She hasn't been proved wrong yet.'

'I've been watching him, on the gallops, while you've been occupied with entertaining the boring Lady Louise.' Another smile. 'I can assure you that when I back him today I shall expect to get my money back ten times over. We can cheer him on together.'

She began to laugh, holding her hand across her mouth.

'Yes, I do find her hard going. She says so little, even in answer to a question. Maybe there isn't much to stimulate her mind, shut up in that great big castle in the middle of nowhere. I'd go crazy if it were me.' Her heart was still beating fast, as she walked further into the room and closer to him. She prayed that nobody else was awake and up yet; that none of the others would come down and spoil the delicious thrill of being alone with him. 'To be honest, I don't understand what Jamie sees in her.'

Waldo smiled again.

'She is . . . how do you English so delicately put it? A good match. In plain American parlance, her brother's a lord and he's got plenty of brass.'

'Jamie isn't marrying her brother.'

'No. But the brother is a widower and she's his only living relative. The rest you can work out for yourself . . . you're a bright girl.' She blushed at the unexpected compliment.

'Lord Dunroven is still quite young. He might remarry.'

Waldo's smile lessened. Yesterday, Jamie had seen them together beside the colt's paddock. Had Dunroven given her any inkling of the plan he might have in mind? It was considered the height of bad taste to indicate that you wanted a lady's hand in marriage upon a single acquaintance; but Waldo would have given anything to have overheard their conversation.

'What do you think of Dunroven?'

'He's very different to his sister . . . he has a great passion for the turf. A large stable of his own, back in Scotland. He was telling me about them. Three yearlings that his grandfather bought from mine all went on to win some of the most prestigious races in the north of England. He says that when we go to Dunroven Castle, I shall see the Turf Room . . . an enormous barrel vaulted room where the walls are covered with paintings of every horse they've ever owned. Fascinating.'

'And most obliging of him.'

'Obliging?'

'To invite me, too. To Dunroven Castle.' He smiled the smile that made her legs grow weak. 'A further opportunity to be with you.'

She stared back at him. The whole room, the clocks, the pictures, the walls lined with books, all receded from view. She shook her head, as if she had not heard him.

'Do you know what I thought to myself when I first came into this house? When I first set eyes on the painting of your great-grandmother Anna Maria? I thought, if only I could find a woman who looked just like that painting . . . the same hair, the same skin, the same eyes . . . and then the door opened and you walked in.' She went on staring at him, dumbly. 'Her face, the face in the portrait, looking at me. You took my breath away.'

She swallowed. She opened her lips to speak but no words came out. Beyond the room, people were beginning to move about the house, but she could hear nothing except his voice.

'Do you know something? I almost married a millionaire's daughter before I came back to England. A steel magnate, with a mansion in Philadelphia. I thought, I'm nearly thirty, I ought to have a wife. But I couldn't do it. I thought of you and I couldn't do it.' He made no move to come towards her. 'That face, that face that is like no other face . . . I couldn't get it out of my mind . . .'

Just at that moment the door behind them opened, and Jamie came into the room.

'Well, what's going on here? Discussing the odds?' He came over to the fire and held out his hands. 'Bloody . . . beg pardon . . . damn weather's fair ruined the course, I suppose you know that? That nag of yours will probably turn his toes up, Rebeccah . . . and Portland's filly that I've backed for the second race is well known to run like a dog when the going's too soft. Too late. I've put the bet on now.'

Rebeccah murmured an answer and ran from the room.

'What the bloody hell's wrong with her?' she heard Jamie say.

She ran across the hall; up the staircase, stumbling over the trailing hem of her grey velvet gown. She reached the landing and turned left, fled along it and found the door of her room. Inside, she banged the door shut and leaned back against it, panting, her eyes closed.

His words rang in her ears. However tightly she closed her eyes, she could still see his face, the face that had haunted her ever since she had first met him. For the first time in her life, she wanted to be loved by a man.

Slowly, she opened her eyes. She looked towards her bed. She wondered, with a thrill that made her whole body shiver, what it would be like to lie there, naked beneath the sheets; his body moulded into hers; his lips kissing her flesh, his long, elegant fingers stroking the soft skin of her face, her hair, her lips . . . no, no! She mustn't think it, mustn't allow herself to want him. It wasn't right. Wildly, she paced the room, clenching and unclenching her fists. Dear God, if only Alice were here! How she missed her, wanted her, longed to talk with her again! Only Alice would understand. And her grandmother?

She made her way back along the landing and down the stairs. Across the marble hall, to the door of the drawing room where Anna always went before breakfast.

The room was empty.

She turned away, and went into the dining room. Lady Louise and Dunroven were already there, seated at the long table. Her father at one end; her grandmother, looking pale and drawn, was seated at the other.

'Oh . . . I didn't know that you were here . . . I wanted to talk to you . . .'

Anna smiled, concealing the pain that had kept her awake since before dawn.

'Best that you all make an early start . . . you know the roads on Diamond Cup day!' She turned to Dunroven. 'Congestion of the roads is something that I'm certain is unknown to you in Scotland. All that wonderful scenery and open space. But I can promise you that if we delay leaving for the course much later than eleven o'clock, you'll have to walk across the fields to get there.'

'Is it really as bad as all that?'

'On Derby Day, much worse!'

Rebeccah sat down in her usual place, almost nervously. 'I don't think I want any breakfast, thank you.'

Her grandmother and father stared at her. Across the table, she could feel Dunroven's eyes fixed on her face.

'You're not feeling well?' Her father's voice.

Anna laughed. 'Of course she is, James. It's the excitement. Gold Bridge in the Hambletonian Stakes. One of the first big races that I entered my colt Bloodstone for.' She thought back, to a young, slim girl with stark blue eyes and wild streaming black hair, screaming him on to victory at the rails. 'He flew it. Like a swallow. Not that I ever doubted him . . . the first victory . . . there's always something so special, so magical, about that.'

'I understand exactly what you mean,' Dunroven said, his eyes on Rebeccah. 'Miss Russell, isn't your sister expected home today from Italy?'

'Alice? Yes, with my cousin Lottie Tradescant. She'll miss the first part of the meeting but, with any luck, she'll get here in time for the big race. I know she wouldn't miss it for the world. Nor Lottie. From the few letters we've had from them, I think they're both suffering from a bad dose of homesickness.'

'I should love to go to Italy again,' Louise Dunroven said, her only contribution to the entire conversation. Rebeccah looked at her, made some reply, and smiled, wondering anew what Jamie could possibly see in her. Of course, it was the money. As the others talked, she let her eyes wander back and forth to Louise's fair, pale face; despite the Dunroven fortune, the massive racing stable, the acres of land, it was impossible not to feel sorry for her. What kind of life would she have with Jamie? Maybe he was different now, maybe he had changed, renounced his gambling, his idle friends, his reprehensible ways. There was an old saying, a leopard never changes its spots; Jamie's reform had only happened after his long stay in Scotland. Rebeccah doubted it was his mother's influence. But perhaps she was being cynical and unjust. Didn't her father say that in every man there was some good, somewhere?

At that moment the dining room door opened and Jamie himself came in, and there, behind him, was Rufus Waldo. Their eyes met and held across the room. Oblivious of the others, her eyes refused to obey her will and remained latched to his face. He smiled, as he greeted everyone present in his own, inimitable, charming way.

'A toast,' he raised his tea cup towards Rebeccah. 'Too early for wine, but this will do. May Gold Bridge do justice to his beautiful and charming owner.'

There was a murmur of assent around the table. At its head, Rebeccah sensed her grandmother's eyes watching them, and she could not turn and look at her. Later, before they left the house, Anna called her to one side.

'A moment, Rebeccah, before the carriage is brought round to the door.'

'The sky looks heavy. Do you think it might rain again?'

'If it rains, then we as well as the horses will have to make the best of it.' She eased herself with difficulty into a chair and told Rebeccah to close the door. 'No, no. I can manage. I'm not helpless. Not yet. Well, there isn't much time, the guests are waiting to leave. So I might as well come straight to the point. It's best that way. And, as you know, I prefer to be blunt.'

Alarm bells sounded.

'What's wrong?'

'Rebeccah. What do you think of Rufus Waldo?'

The question took her completely by surprise. She could feel the blood draining away from her face.

'I have the same opinion of him that you do.'

'Oh, come, Rebeccah . . . you don't need to fence with me; you're my own flesh and blood. And I do have eyes. Old, yes . . . but I can still see very well with them. You're in love with him, aren't you?'

A short silence. The clock on the mantelpiece began to strike ten o'clock. She waited, until the last chime had died away, before answering.

'Yes, I think I am.'

'I've also noticed the way he looks at you. I suppose, by that, I could hazard a shrewd guess that the feeling is reciprocated.'

Rebeccah's heart began to beat very fast. She felt dizzy, light headed, as if she had drunk champagne instead of tea.

'He hasn't said so.'

'My dear girl, I haven't lived for all these years without learning something . . . particularly about men. And I think Rufus Waldo wants to marry you. Whether he asks your father before, or after you come back from Scotland . . . I think it's only a matter of time before he does.'

'Do you really think he will?' She came forward towards Anna eagerly, her eyes bright and sparkling with joy, her voice shaking, excited. 'I came down early this morning . . . before anyone was up . . . I couldn't sleep. I didn't sleep much last night. I went into the library and he was already there . . . but while he was talking to me, Jamie burst in.'

'He never did have any sense of timing.'

'He didn't ask me to marry him. I don't know if he would have done, if Jamie hadn't come in when he did.'

'Rebeccah . . .'

'. . . You do like Rufus Waldo. You said so. When he first came here, when he was representing the Merritt Company.

And now. I heard what you said to papa. That he was a man after your own heart.'

'Yes, I did say that. And I meant it. But I want you to do something for me.' A pause, which to Rebeccah seemed like an eternity. 'If that is his intention, and he does ask you . . . will you wait for a month before you give him an answer? Just a month . . . no longer.'

'But . . . but why?'

'I'll tell you then. I can't now.'

'But I don't understand.'

'You will.'

'I'm not meant to seem too eager . . . is that it? It wouldn't be ladylike!'

Anna smiled at her. No point in upsetting her, when it might all be for nothing; when that tiny seed of doubt in her own mind might well prove to be nothing at all. Better to tell a white lie, and let her go on thinking what she wanted. Not often did anyone else put words in Anna Brodie Russell's mouth.

'Yes, something like that. And I know he'll think you're well worth waiting for . . .'

24

THEY WALKED, side by side, eyes screwed up against the drizzle that had slowly begun to fall after the end of the first race, edging their way through the crowds towards the grandstand. There were no ladies out on the course, or in the saddling enclosure; the muddy ground and the rain had sent them all back to watch the remainder of the meeting from the dry and comfort of their private boxes. Though he cursed the soggy grass and the wet, Waldo was thankful for the inclement weather; stuck in the private box in the grandstand with the rest of the party, which now included the Earl of Clanradine and the Tradescants, all over from Chilworth Manor, there would have been no opportunity at all to talk with Jamie.

'Poxy weather,' Jamie grumbled, coarsely, squinting the drizzle from his eyes. 'I knew I'd go down in the second if the going changed. It was perfect yesterday. Now I'm another five hundred out of pocket.'

'When you marry the Dunroven girl, five hundred will be just loose change.'

Jamie's face darkened. They went on, picking their way through the thinning crowds.

'Nothing's got till it's got.'

'Stop complaining. She's one of the biggest catches going and you've all but landed her.' He stopped talking instantly as two men passed them that he knew. He acknowledged them and they walked on. 'Listen to me and you won't go wrong. The engagement's already official; now it's time to close the deal. At the Ball tonight you announce the wedding date and the invitations start to go out. Make it for six weeks ahead . . . not too far away and not indecently too soon . . . otherwise someone might start to get suspicious. We're nearly home and dry but we're still treading on thin ice; if anyone got wind that the old woman isn't cutting you in on the inheritance and Dunroven heard about it before we have a chance to get rid of him, we're sunk.'

Jamie glanced around them furtively and lowered his voice.

'You said nothing could go wrong!'

'It won't. If you keep your mouth shut and keep your head.'

'How are we going to do it without it looking suspicious?'

'You can leave that to me. Wishard came over two weeks ago with his coterie, and they've set up temporarily in a yard just outside York. Conveniently not too far from the Scottish border. One of his men is a particular friend of mine, and somehow I've got to get him invited to the castle.'

'Can't we handle it on our own? Wouldn't a stranger in our midst look more suspicious after it's happened?'

'Don't let your guilty conscience cloud your judgement; use your head, Jamie. My reputation's above reproach, and Ismay's a friend of mine. Besides which, his family are well respected in Boston . . . and his uncle owns one of the biggest shipping lines in America. Dunroven and everyone else will welcome him with open arms. I'll make some excuse after the big race and get away to town, then I can send him a telegram to come down. We'll meet – by chance of course – on the course here on the final day of the meeting, and I'll introduce him to your father and the old woman. They'll ask him back to the Old Brew House, and during the conversation at dinner, he'll just mention that he's working for Enoch Wishard in York. Dunroven will invite him to join the party at the Castle, and then all our worries will be over.'

'Are you sure you can trust him?'

'He wouldn't be a friend of mine if I couldn't.'

They stopped walking as they neared the grandstand entrance, and turned to survey the runners of the next race cantering down the course.

'Keep your eyes on the horses. We can't go into the grandstand yet; too many eyes and ears.'

'This Ismay. If his uncle's a shipping magnate, what's he doing mixed up with Wishard?'

'Black sheep of the family. Not interested in ships. His passion was always with the horses. But his parents died when he was five, and his uncle neglected him. So he ran away from home and did what he wanted to do. He worked for his uncle for a while, but it didn't work out; that's when I met him. He did the same job for the Belle Mead that I was doing for Merritts.'

The last of the runners disappeared behind the line of trees on its way to the starting post. The rain steadily began to get heavier.

'Come on,' Waldo said, turning away and walking towards the grandstand. 'Let's go up to the old woman's box before we get drenched to the skin.'

Rebeccah sat on the edge of her seat between Louise Dunroven and her grandmother, clutching the edge of the grandstand box, her blue eyes fixed rigidly ahead on the deserted bend of the course that was Tattenham Corner. Any moment now and she would see them, the field of fifteen horses, Gold Bridge somewhere among them; closely bunched together as they took the bend, clods of turf flying, whips cracking, a sudden flash of colours and silks.

Her mouth felt dry and hot, as if she had a fever; her heart hammered and pounded. The palms of her hands and her forehead were warm and clammy with sweat. As her ears strained for the first sound of the pounding hooves, she admonished herself. It was only a race, sport, winning didn't matter. It was different to her grandmother's day when the result of the race was a matter of life or death. Whether the colt won or lost, she would still feel the same.

She stole a quick, fleeting glance at her grandmother's face; how pale and strained it looked today. She thought of the big portrait in the drawing room back at the house, of a lithe young girl with striking blue eyes and long black hair, striding in her velvet riding habit among the shocked crowds of men, pushing them out of her way as she ran to the edge of the course, shouting her horse's name.

I'm not her, she was unique. I could never do what she did. What do I know of poverty, suffering, danger, fear? Everything I have, I owe to her . . .

She reached out her small gloved hand and held on to her grandmother's, and Anna turned and smiled, without speaking. They could both hear it now, the pounding of the hooves and the yelling of the crowds, the masses of common people on the other side of the Downs rushing from the slopes to the edge of the course like an army of multi-coloured ants.

Then she caught sight of Gold Bridge, McHeath in her tawny colours with the single baton of blue, matching stride with stride of the leading horses. Oblivious of everyone around her, she leaped to her feet and screamed his name, pulling off her new Paris hat and waving it in the air like a mad woman.

The colt shot forward, two furlongs out, and swept past the rest of the field as if he were on an exercise canter like any other day, up on Banstead Downs.

She spun round, tears of surprise and delight standing in her eyes, then she threw her arms around her grandmother's neck and sobbed. At that same moment the door of the box opened, and in walked Alice with Jamie, Rufus Waldo and Lottie Tradescant.

'You're back! And Gold Bridge won!' She hugged her and kissed her cheek. 'Oh, Alice, I've missed you so much . . .'

*

'What was she like? Whatever did you say to her?'

'To begin with, I told her exactly what I thought of her for what she did.'

'Did she explain why she did it?'

'For my own good. Because if she left me with my father, he could give me the kind of life she couldn't. Because I was his daughter and she thought I belonged with him. She wasn't even sorry.' Alice turned away and stood by the window. 'When I walked in, it all started to come back. The crumbling *palazzo*, with its half bare rooms, all big and echoing like a tomb. It was like walking out of the sunlight into a prison . . . so cold, so dark, so damp. The whole place smelt unbearably musty, like an abandoned church. I couldn't wait to get out again into the fresh air, into the daylight. I wish I'd taken Lottie with me, instead of leaving her at the hotel. Most of all,' she looked over her shoulder and smiled at Rebeccah, 'I wished that you were there with me, too.' She came away from the window and sat down on her big curtained bed. She leaned against the carved, heavy oak bedpost. 'Venice was beautiful, just as I remembered it . . . but it isn't my home any more. The only thing I felt when we left was relief.'

'Will you see your mother again?'

Alice hesitated, then sighed.

'I don't think that I want to.' A pause. 'She was such a hypocrite . . . she was trying to make herself out to be some kind of martyr, as if abandoning me when I was nine years old was a great act of painful self-sacrifice! She just wanted to get rid of me, to put the responsibility of an unwanted child onto someone else's shoulders.' Her voice became suddenly hard and cold. 'I could see through her in a moment.'

For a moment Rebeccah was silent, thinking of her own mother, the mother who never came back. She remembered the rustle of her gown on that last, long ago evening, the fragrance of her perfume as she'd stooped over her, and kissed her goodnight. She closed her eyes, blotting out the rest.

'Are you going to write to her?'

'I don't see the point, do you? It would make me as big a hypocrite as she is.'

Rebeccah came and sat down beside her. She put her arm around Alice's shoulders.

'It's something only you can decide. Like going in the first place. Somehow, it got it out of your system. All those years, thinking, wondering, trying to guess why she did it. Now at least you have your answer. If you hadn't gone, you'd have always wondered if you should have. And it would have been horrible, unbearable, never knowing, never seeing her again while you had the opportunity.' She tried to think of the right words. 'If I'd been in your place I would have done exactly the same.'

Alice suddenly leaped to her feet, her face smiling brightly.

'Let's not talk about her any more. She isn't worth it, anyway. Let's forget about her, and Italy, and everything else in the past. I want to know what you've been doing for the last three months, while I've been away!'

'Waiting for you to come back.'

'Rebeccah, be serious! And what's Rufus Waldo doing here? I thought that when he went back to America last time he didn't plan to come back.'

'He's bought a big stud in the south, and he's over here, eyeing up the English bloodstock; then he and Jamie ran into each other, just by chance. I wrote to tell you and Lottie all about Jamie and the Dunrovens; when Jamie and Rufus Waldo ran into each other in Edinburgh, Dunroven invited them both to stay as his guests in the castle, and when Jamie came down for the Diamond Cup, father invited all of them to come with him.'

'As well as the Earl of Clanradine!' Her voice had changed again, almost bitter. 'Don't think I don't know what papa's up to! I knew that, the moment I walked into the grandstand

and saw his pale, lashless eyes staring at me! I smelt a plot. Tell me, Rebeccah, has he been seeing a lot of papa while I've been away in Italy? Don't lie to me!'

'I've never lied to you! Don't you know me better than that? Yes, he has seen a lot of him. But why read something in that, that might not even be there? They both have big interests in racing and bloodstock . . . it might be just business.'

'Families like the Clanradines think of marriage as business as well as their horses. "Who'll buy, who'll buy my wares? What bid, sir? What am I bid for this fine young filly, by Russell, out of an unraced Italian mare?" '

Rebeccah stared at her, shocked.

'Crude, isn't it? But true. Strip it of all its ritual and glitter, and there you have it, the bare bones of a contract. Clanradine's had his little lashless eyes on me for a long time, and now he's moving in. I'm just waiting for papa to call me to one side, on the pretence of asking me about my trip, and what I said to my mother . . . and then he'll say that Clanradine's asked him if he can marry me, and what a wonderful opportunity that will be! I'll lay you odds two to one on I'm right.'

'You sound so bitter. Cynical. That isn't like you.'

'Perhaps I'm more like my mother than anyone thinks. I know what she would do. Marry Clanradine. Quite a coup, an Earl, isn't it? For a bastard like me.'

'Alice!'

'Well, it doesn't matter. I should be flattered, I suppose. Think myself lucky that he wants me. Half the dowagers in society will be hating my guts when the news gets out. Just to get one over the lot of them will give me acute pleasure . . . them and their plain, stupid, boring daughters, all lined up like cows at Smithfield meat market. One of the biggest catches of the season, and Alice Russell's got him!' She began to pace the room, biting her fingernails. 'I've seen them, at the house parties and the London Balls, whispering about me behind their fans. I'm sorry if I sound so bitter, Rebeccah.' She smiled, wanly. 'But I can't help it. When you hear other people talking about you, it isn't always easy to pretend that you don't know what they're saying.'

'I think you're wrong. About Clanradine. He wants to marry you because he's in love with you.'

'I'm not sure if I believe in love any more.'

'Alice, I wish you wouldn't talk this way!'

'Oh, I'll get over it, now I'm home. I've been with Lottie too much. She doesn't believe in love at all. She'd sit there, most of the day, tinkering on the piano in the hotel, making up tunes and singing them. All the staff and hordes of guests, too, used to gather round to listen to her . . . what a voice! You know how much the Italians pride themselves on their singing? They said she was another Adelina Patti. "No," she said, with a perfectly straight face. "I'm Lottie Tradescant and I'm much better".' She rocked with laughter. 'The hotel manager had another piano brought up to our room, and she used to practise on that every evening, before we went downstairs to dinner. But it was so old, and out of tune, that she spent most of the time cursing it, with language I'd have thought no well brought up young lady would have ever heard of. I do envy her. Going to live in London. Having a career on the stage. Doing just what she likes. If only I'd been born with a voice like hers, how different my life would be!'

'You might hate it. Hard work, long hours. Hordes of stage door johnnies following you wherever you go. Singing in a music hall isn't all roses, I'm sure of it.'

'At least it's a choice.'

'For a time. When Lottie gets tired of it, she'll most likely marry some rich man with a title and have half a dozen children.'

'She won't. She's adamant about that. We'd lie in bed at night and talk for hours. She just wants to be free. To have a proper career, be independent of men. I think she's right, you know . . . and she'll have the best of both worlds. Hordes of admirers bringing her champagne and red roses, being wined and dined like a princess, being able to mix in every kind of society. Not answerable to anyone except herself.'

'But what about later, when she gets old? What then? Where will the hordes of admirers be, with their bottles of pink champagne and red roses? Think about it, Alice. Wouldn't you rather be the centre of one person's life, than a forgotten, unloved has-been? Loneliness is a terrible price to pay for independence.'

It had taken Rufus Waldo more than an hour to make his way back from the course into Epsom, and reach the little post office. The crowds, wending their way back from the meeting, had already spilled into the town, packing every inn, eating house and the single hotel to bursting point. As he stood there, looking all about him to ensure that there was no one in sight that he knew, carts and carriages rumbled past, while the drizzle that had begun to fall during the racing had turned into a downpour, turning the street and single road into a quagmire.

But it could not have suited him better. In the milling, noisy crowds, the tumult and the pouring rain, it was easy to fade into the background.

Turning up his collar and pulling down his hat, he went inside to send his telegram to Cornelius Ismay.

25

THE WHOLE HOUSE was ablaze with lights, noise and music. Guests filled the big oak-panelled drawing room and spilled out into the hall and ante rooms, where long tables, covered with starched, snow white linen, groaned under the weight of an endless variety of food. The servants hovered in among the vast congregation of people, serving drinks from huge silver trays.

An orchestra played Strauss waltzes on a raised dais in one corner of the vast room, while couples danced, or stood in groups to one side, chattering of the day's events.

In a huge chair beside the window, Anna sat alone, watching them, thinking back to that other Ball, so long ago, when she and her sister Clara had gone to Ralph Russell's mansion after the Emperor Cup. She remembered the white gowns they had worn, and how the guests had fallen silent as they'd walked in, Ralph Russell at her side. She had loved him even then without realizing it; she could see his face, as clear as if he were in this room still, as he'd opened the plush lined casket that held the Russell emeralds, and placed them around her neck. So long ago.

She looked up, through the moving crowds of brightly gowned ladies and black suited gentlemen, as she caught sight of Rufus Waldo coming towards her. As their eyes met across the floor, he gave her his charming smile.

'Lady Russell . . . please forgive me. But I must leave you for a short while.'

She raised her eyebrows.

'Is something the matter?'

'No, nothing. Except that a messenger arrived from Epsom a few moments ago to deliver a telegram. An old friend of mine, who's come over with the Wishard stable to train in Yorkshire, is on his way down from London . . . the stable told him I was here in Epsom, and as he has business in the south, he thought he'd pay me a call. Would you think it very ill mannered of me if I excused myself for an hour or so to meet him and get him settled in the hotel? I haven't seen him for several months, not since I came back to England.'

'Wishard? He's the crack yankee trainer I've heard so much about? Made a small fortune, hasn't he, for his owners?'

'That's the one. Remarkable man. Just got a way with him where winners are concerned. And a special success rate with difficult horses. I have a lot of respect for the man. Something else that might interest you . . . he's brought two promising young jockeys over here with him . . . Lester and Johnny Reiff . . . you might like to see them ride sometime.'

'I'll look forward to it. But wait a moment Mr Waldo. We can't have a friend of yours spending the night in a hotel when we have ample room here. Bring him back with you as my guest.'

'It isn't necessary . . .'

'Nonsense. If he works for Enoch Wishard, I'd like to meet him.'

A pause. 'But he doesn't have evening dress. He isn't expecting to attend anything fancy like this . . . he'll understand . . .'

'I insist.'

He smiled at her, and she understood, then, why Rebeccah had fallen in love with him.

As he made his way back through the dancers and the groups of laughing, chattering people, she saw the women's heads turn as he passed. Yes, there was an irresistible charisma about him. But, she wondered, did it hide something else?

Jamie left the noise and music in the crowded drawing room, and made his way to the library on the other side of the hall, where he poured himself a large brandy and sat down. He looked at his gold fob watch, then checked the time against the mantelpiece clock. Rufus Waldo had left ten minutes ago for Epsom. In the landau, the journey should take no more than fifteen or twenty minutes. By ten o'clock he and Ismay should have arrived back at the house.

He refilled his glass and stretched out his long legs, resting his feet on the big club fender. Pity he couldn't find an excuse to have missed the Ball altogether. He wasn't in the mood for socializing with people who bored him and whom he despised. But everything was different now, now that he and Louise Dunroven were officially engaged, and the wedding date set. Six weeks from now. He smiled, letting the smugness and self satisfaction wash over him. Get Dunroven out of the way, and all would be plain sailing.

Deep in his thoughts, the sudden movement at the door made him jerk upright, muttering a curse. But it was only his sister Alice.

'You made me jump!'

'What a pity.' She came in and closed the door behind her. 'Are you sick and tired of everyone, too?'

'To the stomach. But why are you wearing a face as long as a kite? You've no reason to complain. You've hooked Clanradine, haven't you?'

She sat down on the floor at his feet and crossed her legs. 'Some catch.'

'Tell me a better one. Alice Russell, a Countess. You'll enjoy yourself spending all his money!'

She pulled a face. 'If I don't die of boredom first.'

'There's always plenty more fish in the sea, isn't there? With your looks you can take your pick.'

She laughed, suddenly. 'You'd get on so well with my mother, Jamie. She said exactly the same. Take a lover.'

'Why stop at one?'

'And if Clanradine found out?'

'You're too clever to let yourself be caught. And more than a match for a stupid oaf like him.' He gulped back the remainder of his brandy. 'Besides, everyone's at it, right from the Prince of Wales down . . . everyone knows it and they just accept it. Like dressing for dinner. You're only in trouble if you forget to be discreet.'

Alice stared into the leaping flames of the fire.

'He's marrying the wrong sister, but he doesn't know it. It should be Rebeccah, not me. She's the one who believes in love and fidelity.'

'And don't you?'

'Neither papa nor my mother were particularly noted for theirs.'

'So cynical!'

She looked at him sharply, her dark eyes almost accusing.

'What do you know about her and Rufus Waldo? He wants to marry her, doesn't he?'

'Why should you mind if he does?'

There was a long silence while she went on staring into his face, the only sound the ticking of the clock and the far off noise of the guests and dancers.

'Because I want him.'

It was Jamie's turn to be surprised. 'Does he know?'

'I doubt it. But you know him so much better than I, Jamie. If you wanted to do me a favour, you could always find out.'

There was another silence, while he wondered if he could trust her. After all, until she went away three months ago to Italy, she and Rebeccah had always been close; both of them always against him. What had happened to change that situation? Could he take what she was saying at face value, that it was only the sudden appearance of Rufus Waldo? She saw the suspicion in his eyes.

'Does Rebeccah know how you feel?'

'Don't be stupid!'

'She doesn't know. Well, I shan't tell her. Why should I? But then you've always known how I felt about her, haven't you? And you always did take her part against me.'

'Only when we were children. Everything's different now.'

'You really do want him, don't you?'

'If it wasn't for the inheritance, do you really think he'd choose her and not me?'

'A lot of men would consider Rebeccah more beautiful.' He got up, slowly and lazily, and leaned against the mantelpiece. 'The typical English rose. Anna Maria's portrait come to life. Even I have to admit that. You're beautiful, too, of course . . . but in a different way. I would think that you look strikingly like your mother.'

He could see that his answer had angered her.

'What do you know about beauty? That white-livered milksop you're marrying! For her brother's money, of course . . . and don't try and tell me any differently! I tried to talk to her earlier tonight, but she can't string two sentences together . . . my God, can't you find anyone better? All I can say is that when I look at her it makes me realize how badly you want the money!'

He rocked with laughter.

'Who looks at the ceiling when he's poking the fire? She's pretty, at least. Something pleasant to look at over breakfast. For indulging my real personal tastes, I have every intention of looking elsewhere.'

'And you accuse me of being cynical!'

'I do nothing that other men don't already do.'

She got up, smoothing down the folds of her gown and looking at her reflection in the wall mirror.

'I suppose we'd better go back to the others. It might look strange.' She hesitated. 'And where was Rufus Waldo going in the landau? I saw him leaving as I came through the hall . . .'

'A friend of his telegraphed that he was in Epsom. He's been invited to come and stay at the house.'

'But we're leaving for Scotland the day after tomorrow.'

'Maybe Dunroven will invite him to join us.'

Rebeccah was walking from the crowded drawing room into the cool and quiet of the hall, when she caught sight of them, suddenly, and instinctively stepped back. Oblivious for once of the presence of Rufus Waldo, she stared at his companion dumbly, unable to take her eyes away from his face, for she was instinctively repelled by him.

He was tall and dark with a similar build to Waldo, but with pale grey, penetrating eyes that seemed wary and cold; across his left cheek, two inches long, ran an ugly, jagged scar that disfigured his face.

'Miss Russell,' Waldo was saying to her, smiling, 'may I introduce you to my friend Cornelius Ismay . . .'

As she stayed rooted to the spot in horror, Ismay put out his hand towards her. 'Miss Russell, I'm honoured to meet you.'

'I . . . I'll take you to my grandmother . . .' On wooden legs, she somehow made herself move forward. Past the gaily dressed, dancing couples, the groups of laughing, chattering people, servants balancing trays of refreshments and wine. When she reached Anna's chair, Dunroven was already with her, and instinctively, she moved closer towards him so that he stood between her and Cornelius Ismay.

After the introductions had been performed, Dunroven turned to her, smiling, and asked her to dance.

'Yes,' she said, almost too eagerly. 'I should love to.'

'I told you that bloody Dunroven had designs on my sister!

That's three dances, in a row. What'll we do if he says anything to father tonight?'

'Shut up. Don't talk rubbish. How could he? It isn't etiquette. He hasn't known her long enough. If nothing else, fools like Dunroven play everything by the rules. He wouldn't dream of making any proposals when he's only been a guest in the house for the last few days.'

'But how can you be sure?'

Waldo scowled. 'Why don't you go in there and dance with her yourself instead?' said Ismay from across the room.

'That's exactly what I intend to do!' He went out, slamming the door so hard that the chandelier rattled and shook.

'Dunroven's suddenly become a major complication to us,' Jamie said, offering Ismay one of his father's cigars. Ismay shook his head.

'I don't smoke.'

'Please yourself.' He sat on the edge of the desk and lit up. 'It was my grandmother's idea to ask them, him and his sister Louise . . . my fiancée. Neither of us bargained on him making a play for Rebeccah.' A long blue column of smoke wound its way upwards towards the ceiling. 'Ever since he got here, he hasn't been able to take his eyes off her.'

'Does that surprise you? Your sister is exceptionally beautiful.'

'We've got to get Dunroven out of the way.'

'So Rufus was explaining to me on the way out here. But when do we get the chance to sit down and plan it all in detail? It'll look suspicious, if people remember the three of us hiding ourselves away behind closed doors, or whispering together in corners, after it's done. And Lady Russell, for one, is nobody's fool. I knew that as soon as I met her.'

'It's got to look like an accident. On a shooting party, an occupational hazard, wouldn't you say. But none of us know exactly how it can be done until we get there . . . for instance . . . what part of the estate is going to be used for the shoot, how many keepers he's taking, how many spectators. We can't afford to take any chances. And it's also a question of timing. Somehow, we have to lure Dunroven away from the main party, and make sure that none of the others follow. That might not be easy. It's essential to get him on his own at some time during the afternoon. Then one of us, who'll be waiting out of sight, can get a shot at him; but it's got to be at such an angle that it really does look like an accident. Any chances that it looks in the least like a suspicious death, and we're done for.'

Ismay looked at him levelly. 'I know what Rufus thinks. But what about you? Is it really necessary to kill him?'

'It's not only that he's been trying to get close to Rebeccah. You know the old saying, Hell hath no fury . . ? Well, if Rufus beats him to the post he could start taking an interest in his line of business, and if he digs deep enough he'll come up with the truth. As for the other reason . . . he's only agreed to me marrying Louise because he thinks I'm in for the lion's share of the Brodie Russell inheritance . . . if he found out that I don't get a penny, the marriage to his sister would be off.'

Ismay nodded, slowly. 'Yes, I see all that. But if Rufus marries your sister and you marry Dunroven's before he finds out anything at all, would it really matter if he did?'

'You don't understand! If he finds out about Rufus he'll ruin him. Rufus'll go to jail. If he finds out about me, all he has to do is get himself a wife to give him an heir, and Louise won't get anything . . . I'll have nothing but the dowry she came with. And that won't suit me, Ismay. That won't suit me at all.'

Ismay got up. Slowly, he stroked the livid scar on his left cheek. Then he glanced at the clock.

'It's nearly eleven, Jamie. I think we'd better go and join the others.'

*

'You don't want to go to Dunroven Castle? Why not?'

'Cornelius Ismay. I don't like him. I hated him on sight.' Rebeccah shivered, and turned away from her father. 'He makes my skin crawl, with that hideous scar . . .'

'That is uncharitable of you, Rebeccah. You surprise me. The man can't help his appearance . . . maybe he was kicked by a horse.'

'I still don't like him.'

'You don't know anything about the man . . . and he is a friend of Rufus Waldo.'

'That doesn't mean I have to like him.'

'He seems pleasant enough to me . . .'

'I still don't want to go to Scotland.' She stared out of the library window, her back stiff, her voice stubborn. 'Can't I make some excuse?'

'It would be the height of rudeness . . .'

'I could pretend I was ill . . .'

'With the look of you, who'd be stupid enough to believe that? Enough of this nonsense. You deliberately snubbed the man at breakfast, and again at lunch. If you go on like this people will begin to notice, and you'll embarrass and shame your grandmother and me! I won't have it. You behave with courtesy to guests that come into this house. You're old enough to know better. And to have good manners.'

'I'm sorry, papa.'

'Well, hadn't you better go upstairs and see what you need to pack? And remember, it'll be much colder than it is down here . . .'

She went, angrily, and found her maid. While the girl folded away the layers of clothes Rebeccah stood numbly at the window, looking down into the stableyard, not listening to her chatter. She could see Rufus Waldo and Ismay, walking side by side, stopping now and then to watch the horses that were turned out into the paddocks beyond. Ismay's arrival had spoiled everything. She had pictured herself, not him, strolling with Rufus Waldo beneath the trees, perhaps going riding together . . . now it was too late. In the morning they were leaving for Scotland and she would never have the same opportunities again. She almost hated him. And with Enoch Wishard training in York, when could she hope to see Waldo again after this?

'Looks like more bloomin' rain, Miss Rebeccah,' the girl said from somewhere behind her, as her small, nimble hands deftly folded and packed the clothes. 'Gives me the pip, it does!'

'Lock the trunk when you've finished, Maggie; I'm going for a long ride.'

She wasn't dressed for riding, but she didn't care. Pulling on a pair of long boots, she ran downstairs and out into the courtyard, then made her way through the evening drizzle to the stables and Gold Bridge's stall.

It was another hour before the lads gave the horses their final rub down, and fed and watered them for the day. Pulling a saddle down from the wall, she flung it across his back and tightened the girth. When his head collar and reins were on, she led him out into the yard and hauled herself onto his back.

'Come on, boy!'

At the familiar sound of her voice, he neighed and moved forward. Then she slipped her booted feet into the stirrups, and turned his head in the direction of the Downs beyond.

It was growing dark and she had ridden much further than she'd planned to do, when the rain turned from a steady drizzle into a deluge. Dismounting, Rebeccah led Gold Bridge to the nearest tree and they both sheltered beneath it. But after almost another half hour it showed no signs of lessening, so she remounted him and turned him in the direction of home.

She had no idea of time. She rode on, her eyes screwed up against the lashing rain, her long hair, soaking wet, sticking to her skin and dripping onto her face. When at long last, in the distance, she could see the lights shining from the house, her clothes were saturated.

The lads came running as she trotted Gold Bridge into the yard. She jumped down from the wet saddle.

'I'll help you rub him down. I didn't mean to stay out so long.'

'Cor, blimey, miss, you're soaked to the bloomin' skin, you are! Catch yer death! 'E's all right . . . nags are used to runnin' in the rain . . . caused a proper to-do up at the 'ouse, I can tell yer! None of 'em knew where you was till we noticed th' 'orse was missin' . . .'

'I'll help you rub him down first. I'm all right.'

'Want to catch pneumonia?'

She had begun to shiver. 'All right. I'll go indoors and change my clothes. But I'll be back to see him later.' She turned and ran across the yard, shielding her eyes from the driving rain. Something tall and hard suddenly crashed into her.

Gasping, half blinded by the water from her hair that was dripping in her eyes, she dashed the saturated strands away from her face, and stared upwards into the cold, piercing grey eyes of Cornelius Ismay.

Before he could speak, she pushed her way past him into the house and came face to face with Rufus Waldo.

'Rebeccah! We've been looking everywhere for you! Where in God's name have you been?' She stopped, dripping rainwater all over the polished marble of the hall, suddenly realizing that for the first time since she had met him, he had inadvertently used her first name, and the sudden, unexpected intimacy of it thrilled her. She smiled, taking him completely by surprise.

'You come in, from God knows where, soaked to the skin . . . and you just smile?'

Tossing her wet hair out of her eyes, she went past him to the bottom of the staircase.

'I was smiling because you called me Rebeccah. The first time that you've ever done it.'

He reached out and laid his hand on hers as it rested on the stair rail, and fire ran through her.

'That doesn't mean that I didn't want to.'

26

THE HEAVY, ORNATE SUITS OF ARMOUR which lined the long gallery in the castle gleamed in the moonlight, as it bathed the flagstones with an eerie, silvery glow.

Somewhere in the stillness of the night a door creaked, then closed again; a ghostly figure, swathed in white, moved silently along the corridor and into the gallery, the single candle in its holder flickering in her hand.

It was cold and draughty in the ante-room, where the bare granite walls were adorned with antlers and the stuffed heads of deer, as she slowly, stealthily, made her way up the narrow, winding steps, her bare feet silent on the icy stone.

Outside the heavy, steel girded arched door, she hesitated, for several moments. Then, her long delicate fingers clutching at the latch, she lifted it and went inside.

By the light of the candle she saw the huge, heavily carved bed, hung with velvet drapes, colourless in the semi-darkness; the faint light from the deep-silled, mullioned windows picked out the gilt of the paintings on the opposite wall, the porcelain jug and basin, the brass fender that surrounded the empty grate. Silently, she closed the door behind her, and turned the key in the massive lock. Then she tiptoed quietly towards the sleeping figure in the middle of the great bed.

The whiteness of the bedlinen against the blackness of his hair stood out, as she reached over and touched his face with the tips of her fingers; then he stirred, and opened his eyes; as he saw her face, illuminated by the light of the single candle, he sat bolt upright in the bed. But his face showed no surprise.

Setting down the candle, she took the pins from her long dark hair and let it fall down to her waist. Then, slowly, smiling as she did so, she unfastened her nightgown and let it fall gently to the floor, while he gazed hungrily on her nakedness.

Before she climbed into bed beside him, she turned and blew out the candle, remembering her mother's parting words.

'*Be clever, Alicia; be clever if you want things from men . . .*'

They made their way carefully, cautiously, through the thick density of trees; watching, listening, pausing when they sensed the nearness of their prey. In the distance, they could hear the far-off sound of the others' guns, the distant laughter from the women who had gathered at the edge of the copse to enjoy the picnic.

Jamie, crouched down behind the fallen tree trunk, turned to Dunroven, his voice a whisper.

'I'm certain it went that way . . . did you hear it?'

'It's an animal, yes . . . but it may not be the stag we followed. Hush, I can hear something moving . . .'

'One of your keepers went in that direction with Cornelius Ismay.'

They stood up, their shotguns held at the ready, then picked their way with infinite care across the clearing, stepping between the twigs and fallen leaves.

It was then that Dunroven saw it, its huge antlers standing proudly on the noble head, ears twitching, straining for any alien sound. Hardly daring to breathe, without turning round, he raised his arm and signalled to Jamie behind him. Then, without warning, there was a harsh, sudden rustling sound in the depths of the forest, and the great beast, sensing its danger, vanished from sight.

With a cry of dismay and disappointment, Dunroven turned around in the direction of Jamie; but Jamie was no longer there.

Rufus Waldo's dark, glittering eyes looked triumphantly into Dunroven's startled ones. Then the shot from the double-barrelled gun exploded in Dunroven's face.

The small party of women looked up, suddenly, as they saw the running figures coming towards them, shouting at the tops of their voices. The servants, busy with the picnic, stopped what they were doing and stood there, dumbly, wondering what had happened. Rufus Waldo, Jamie, two of the keepers and Hugh Glenross, one of Dunroven's neighbours, came rushing up, guns held downwards, gasping for their breath.

'Quickly, for God's sake!' shouted Waldo to one of the other men. 'There's been an accident in the forest . . . we just found Dunroven . . .'

'Go for Doctor McTaggart in the village,' Glenross said, distraught, to Dunroven's ghillie. 'Hurry, man!'

'Dear God, what happened . . ?'

Jamie and Rebeccah were trying to comfort the hysterical Louise.

'Dunroven must have stopped to clean his gun. Somehow, it went off . . .'

'Give her some brandy, quickly! I think she's going to pass out!'

Rebeccah glanced up, suddenly, as the second keeper and Cornelius Ismay came running. Her eyes met his in one single, cold, accusing glance.

'Did you see what happened, Mr Ismay?'

'I'm sorry. I did not. We were about fifty yards away, on the other side of the clearing, when we heard a gun go off. We thought nothing of it, until we heard the others shouting for help.'

'Take the ladies back to the castle,' Rufus Waldo took

charge. 'This is no scene for them. Jamie, you'd best go with Louise.'

When Dunroven's sister, sobbing and incoherent, was led away out of earshot, Rebeccah stayed behind.

'Is he badly injured?'

They all stared at her, before Rufus Waldo spoke. 'Dunroven's dead.'

Anna stayed where she was in the big wing chair, looking down gravely at the letter in her hand.

All around her on the desk, there were piles of other papers waiting for her attention; bloodstock files, foal reports, sire ratings, an estimate, that she had not even had time to read, for the building of a new, enlarged wing on the existing stables.

For the first time in her life, she felt too tired, and too depressed, to look at any of them. Best leave them for McGrath, and her son, to sort over.

She looked down again at the letter, wishing that James had not gone to Ireland for the bloodstock sales, but was here with her now. Strange, that for the first time in her life, she had felt the sudden need for his presence.

She glanced at the mantelpiece clock. John Mordaunt would be here to go over the racing entries any minute; replacing the letter in its envelope, Anna opened one of the drawers in her desk and put it away. He came in, punctual as usual, a copy of one of the London newspapers clutched in his hand.

'Terrible news, this, my lady. You've already heard, I suppose? I liked Dunroven.'

She looked up with sad, tired eyes.

'Jamie sent us a telegram yesterday. Dunroven's sister is distraught . . . as you can imagine. Six weeks before the wedding was to take place. It can't now, of course. Not for six months at least, perhaps a year.'

'Poor lassie. And he was her only living relative.' He shook his head, morosely. 'A proper tragedy, my lady. Gun going off, by accident. What could Dunroven have been thinking of, cleaning the barrels out and forgetting to put on the safety catch? I can't understand it, not an experienced man like he was . . . still, that's the trouble, isn't it? You think you know it all and then get careless. Been enough accidents that way . . .'

Anna remained silent, the seeds of doubt at the back of her mind ever since Jamie's news had arrived, growing with every moment. But she still had to be sure . . . and, as yet, she had no proof.

Mordaunt drew himself up a chair on the opposite side of her desk.

'A pretty bad shock for all the young ladies, being there when it happened; not something you'd forget in a hurry.'

'No . . . not something you'd forget. Lord Clanradine and Hugh Glenross, one of Dunroven's neighbours, are bringing them back here as soon as things at the castle have been left in order. Jamie's taking Lady Louise to stay with his mother, near Inverness.'

'And Miss Alice . . . will her wedding to Lord Clanradine still go ahead as planned? Damn shame . . . damn shame . . . spread a black cloud over everything, this has . . .'

'There's no reason why it shouldn't.' She picked up the stack of racing entries and pushed them across the desk towards him. 'The sooner we can put it all behind us, the better.'

While Mordaunt went through the papers she had given him, she lay back in her chair and tried not to show the pain that had suddenly come back, sharp and stabbing, to her chest. Like tiny red hot needles it prodded and pricked, tormenting her. Beads of perspiration broke out along her forehead; each breath she drew was agony, like bands of steel tightening across her chest.

She sat there, without speaking, for several minutes, while

Mordaunt, head bent over the papers in his hands, went on speaking, oblivious of her pain.

When he had finished the day's business, he stood up, smiling.

'Is there anything else I can do for you, my lady?'

Anna smiled, slowly, her mind somewhere else far away.

'If you will, would you have the St Simon colt brought round to the front of the house? I should like to see him today.'

'Yes, of course, my lady. Right away.' He went, papers tucked beneath his arm, whistling as he went, wondering why she'd asked for what she did. No knowing, at that great age. But even Anna Brodie Russell had her whims.

Anna sat there, hands clutching the sides of her big wing chair, gazing out through the tall wide windows, out into the gardens, at the bright, blue spring sky.

One more look. One more touch of the soft, gleaming coat, the velvet muzzle. Priam. Hope. Bloodstone. And, please God, Rebeccah . . . before it was too late . . .

27

THE RAIN HAD FALLEN DOWN ceaselessly for more than a week, filling the courtyard with dark, swirling puddles, and swelling the water in the moat. The sky was still angry and cloud-laden, threatening more rain. Gloom hung over the castle like an ancient curse. And Rebeccah had never felt so unhappy or depressed in all her life.

She glanced at Alice, curled up on the window seat, staring out at the lashing rain.

'I wonder that Jamie can ever bear to live here, after this . . . I couldn't.'

'I doubt if he'll see it in the same way as we do. Now that Dunroven's dead, Louise gets everything. And what comes to her, comes to Jamie. King of the castle.' She gave a harsh, brittle laugh. 'Just what he's always wanted.'

'I hope they'll be happy. For her sake, not his.'

'Oh . . . I shouldn't waste too much pity on Louise . . . she'll want for nothing, after all. The family town house, in the most fashionable part of London. The Castle, when she wants to spend time in the country. Winters abroad, in the warm climate. Money no object. The only difference is that instead of being Dunroven's sister, she'll be Jamie's wife.'

Rebeccah was surprised at the sharp, almost unfeeling tone that Alice's voice had lately, ever since she had come back from Italy. It puzzled her.

'She's still lost her only brother, and he died a horrible death. Nothing she has will ever bring him back again.'

'Who knows? Given the choice she might not want him back.'

'She hasn't stopped crying her eyes out since the day of the accident. And she had to be almost carried back from the churchyard after the funeral. You know that.'

'Some women cry over anything.'

'Alice, what's the matter with you? You've never been this way . . .'

Alice turned round, away from the dismal scene outside the mullioned window.

'I'm sorry. It's this place. It's so morbid and depressing. I always did hate castles. Not that it isn't impressive and magnificent . . . but it's like a prison, all the thick stone walls and the moat outside . . . as if we were all trapped, somehow . . . and the weather. You know when it never stops raining I always get depressed . . .' she sighed. 'It never rained once, when Lottie and I were in Venice. Every morning, as soon as I woke, I'd look out of our window in the hotel and see the same blue, cloudless sky. I got used to it.'

'Are you sure there's nothing else?'

'You mean have I had second thoughts about accepting Duncan Clanradine? No, it isn't that. I decided that I would even before he asked me. Of course, I guessed that he would . . . it's strange, how you can tell when men are going to do or say certain things . . .'

'But you don't love him?'

'God, no! But, to put it crudely, I won't get a better offer.'

'Why have you become so cynical? You were so different before you went away.'

'Perhaps you only thought I was. I haven't changed. I've realized certain things, that's all.'

'I don't understand.'

'We've always been so close, you and I. Like twins, almost . . . I never even thought of us both having had different mothers . . . anyway, it never seemed to matter. But when I met my mother, when I understood why she did what she did, it made me realize that we're different, now. After all, I'm just James Russell's bastard and you are the Brodie

Russell heiress. It doesn't matter, Rebeccah . . . I still love you exactly the same as I always did. Nothing could ever change that.' She smiled, sweetly, the old Alice that Rebeccah knew. 'But I have to make the best of it while I can. That's why I decided to marry Clanradine.' She laughed, almost gaily. 'That'll surprise my mother. Me, a Countess!'

'But wouldn't you rather wait, for someone you really love?'

'He might never come riding by . . . and then what would I do? Stay at home, a burden on you, and become a wrinkled, bitter old maid. I'd rather go into a nunnery!'

'You don't mean that!'

'No . . . it was just a joke. And a bad one, I'm afraid. But maybe it's really better this way . . . who knows? I might get to love him after all . . .'

For a long moment, Rebeccah fell silent. 'The house will seem dead without you.'

Alice smiled. 'I don't believe that at all . . .'

'How much longer are we going to be cooped up like chickens in this poxy castle? It hasn't stopped raining for more than a week!'

'Patience, Jamie. Where's your respect for the dead?' Rufus Waldo lay back in the chair and rested his long, elegant legs on the highly polished surface of the table. 'I thought this was what you wanted. Lord of all you survey, master of Dunroven and all its riches . . . and Dunroven's pretty sister . . .'

'She bores the arse off me!' Jamie helped himself to Dunroven's whisky. 'And she's not so pretty, either. She's been blubbering so much for the last ten days, her eyes are swollen up like a pig's.'

'In the night all cats are grey.'

'That's another thing! When are we going back to London to enjoy some real women? I haven't had one since we came . . . thanks to you refusing to come with me to Edinburgh.'

'No point in being careless. We might have been seen. After you're married, it won't matter. For now, you'll just have to grin and bear it.'

'Easy for you to say.'

Waldo's eyes were suddenly hard. 'Let's stick to our plan, shall we? As we agreed.' He glanced at Cornelius Ismay, standing across the room from them, staring down into the moat from the small arched window. Ismay was unusually silent.

'What's wrong with you? Itching to get back to Wishard?'

'No,' Ismay answered without turning round, after the single word falling silent again. Waldo got up.

'You haven't lost your nerve, have you?'

They faced each other.

'I came over here with Wishard to fix races and make myself a nice little pile of brass for a rainy day. I didn't bargain for getting involved in murder.'

'I told you, it was necessary.'

'Was it?'

'We've been through all this before. Dunroven was a danger and we had to get rid of him. And since when did you start to have such delicate scruples, after six years of working with Enoch Wishard?'

'Doping horses and killing a man in cold blood are two different things.'

There was a mocking tone in Waldo's voice. 'I didn't ask you to pull the trigger, did I?'

'You still made me an accessory before, during and after the fact. We could all hang.'

'But we won't, Ismay. Because only the three of us know the truth about Dunroven's death, and only the three of us ever will know.'

There was a long, heavy silence.

'Where are you going?' Waldo asked him as Ismay went over to the door.

'For a walk. Anywhere. To get away from here.' He slammed the door after him.

She caught sight of him at the opposite end of the long gallery, and stopped instantly in her tracks. She shivered, involuntarily, with distaste, half turning away to run back. But it was too late. He had already seen her and she was already half-way along the corridor. No doors to escape through. Too far to go back. Steeling herself, she went on walking towards him.

'Miss Russell?'

Neither of them smiled. She stared into the cold, pale eyes, at the ugly, jagged outline of the scar that disfigured his cheek. 'Is Lady Louise Dunroven any better today?'

'No more than she was yesterday or the day before. Would you be, if you'd just lost your only brother?'

'I don't know. I haven't seen or spoken to either of mine in more than eight years.'

'Please excuse me. I have to pack.' Before he could speak again, Rebeccah brushed past him and walked on to the end of the gallery. She could feel his eyes watching her as she went, and she quickened her steps, keeping in check the almost overwhelming desire to break into a run.

When she was out of his sight, she stopped, leaned back against the cold stone wall of a nearby alcove, and closed her eyes. It was still with her, the creeping of the flesh, the strange, eerie feeling that instantly came over her whenever she looked at him. She thought back to the day of the accident, when he had been the last man to return from the forest, and the strange look he had had in his eyes, almost as if he'd known what was going to happen . . .

She tried to calm herself. To tell herself that it was ridiculous to suspect him . . . he had never met Dunroven before that night in Epsom . . .

Then, from a nearby room, she heard Jamie's unmistakable voice. So he was with Rufus Waldo.

She opened the door and went in.

'Jamie!' His appearance shocked her. He lay there, full length on the couch, a cigar in one hand and a glass of whisky in the other. 'Why aren't you with Louise? The doctor had to give her another draught . . .'

'I thought she was asleep, and that Lottie and Alice were taking turns to sit with her. Is she asking for me?'

'She was, but none of us could find you.'

Slowly, sulkily, he put out the cigar and swigged back the remaining whisky in the glass. 'I suppose I'd better go then.' He went, with ill grace.

'How long has he been drinking like that?' Rebeccah turned to Waldo.

'Come, now, it isn't as bad as it looked. Jamie isn't very good at handling other people's tragedies . . . haven't you ever noticed that?' He smiled, the smile that soothed and warmed her. 'The accident, seeing Dunroven's body . . . the funeral . . . coping with Lady Louise . . . it's taken quite a toll. He pretends that he can take it all in his stride, but that's just for the sake of appearances . . . it's really quite shaken him up, if you want to know the truth.'

She sat down, and stared into her lap.

'I suppose you're right. Perhaps I'm being unjust.' She looked up, suddenly, into his dark, hypnotic eyes. 'It just seemed so disrespectful, as if what happened didn't matter any more. But then, that's Jamie.'

'Not this time.' He paused, then sat down beside her. The nearness of him made her feel dizzy, breathless. 'It was quite a vile sight . . . Dunroven's body, when we found him . . . I thought Jamie was going to be sick . . .'

'I can't believe it's happened!'

'Often tragedy strikes when we least expect it. Dunroven made a single, foolish mistake and it cost him his life. If only the shot had gone wide.'

'When we first arrived here, I thought how beautiful the castle was. Somewhere I could live, and be happy in. I almost envied Jamie. But now, when we leave, and I can't wait to leave . . . I never want to see it again!'

'I feel that way too . . . angry, almost. Because Dunroven's death has made it almost impossible for me to ask you what I'd intended to while we were here . . .' Her head jerked up. 'It would seem . . . in bad taste, somehow . . .'

Rebeccah stared into his eyes, holding her breath, almost willing him to speak the words she longed to hear.

'You know, don't you, that I've been in love with you for a long while . . . longer than you know . . . and I want you, Rebeccah. I want you for my wife.' He took her hand and raised it to his lips. 'I want you more than I've ever wanted anything . . .'

She had had them move her great wing chair so that she could sit there, beside the half-open window, looking out into the garden that she loved, to the orchards and the paddock beyond, where her horses cantered across the grass, satin coats gleaming, or grazed, idly, in the bright spring sun.

She had always loved the springtime, even as a child, when the damp, crumbling little hovel where they had lived in Suffolk had never seemed quite so cold, never seemed quite so bleak, as it did on the long, freezing, bitter winter nights when the four of them had huddled together around the dying fire, trying to keep warm.

Anna lay back now and closed her eyes, a heavy feeling of weariness pulling her back into sleep, the sounds from the outside gradually, slowly, fading away into silence.

Like images in a dream, the faces from the past came back to her in an endless procession . . . her mother, Anna Maria, bent over her sewing in the bad light; Edward Brodie, staring at her across the rain-drenched paddock grass; faithful Jessie, kind-hearted Sam Loam; loyal Chifney, her sister Clara, sitting at the piano, her long, delicate fingers moving softly across the keys . . . the soft, warm touch of the horses she had loved . . . and Ralph Russell, whom she had loved most of all, where was he now . . ?

For a single moment, Anna opened her tired eyes, and gazed at the painting of herself that hung upon the wall. That young, beautiful, striking face, the blue eyes vivid, the black hair flowing out behind her, seemed somehow to be smiling at her . . . and the slim, velvet-clad figure stepped out from the huge gold frame. It came towards her, beckoning, laughing, holding out its hands, as if seeking to release its image from the tired, ageing body where it had hidden for so many, long years . . .

A voice, the lost voice of her youth called her name. *Anna Brodie*.

She closed her eyes. At long last, she was coming.

Rebeccah let Rufus Waldo help her down from the carriage, and go with her into the house. It seemed cool and quiet, without anyone to greet them except the servants; her father still in Ireland, Jamie back in Scotland with his mother and Louise Dunroven; Lottie gone home to Chilworth Manor, leaving only her and Alice.

'Is my grandmother asleep?' she asked Anna's butler, as they came into the big, panelled hall, the men bringing in the trunks full of luggage behind them.

'She's in the drawing room, Miss Rebeccah. Asked for the window to be opened a bit, so that she could see down to the paddocks . . . right pleased to see you both, she'll be . . .'

Rebeccah opened the door of the room. Softly, quietly. There she was, in her favourite, big, wing chair, her eyes closed, a smile on her lips. The breeze from the partly open window blew the curtains, gently to and fro, and there beside her on the floor were sheets of paper, blown down from the little table at her side.

'We're back!' Rebeccah said, going over to her and kneeling down. 'And I have some very special news to tell you.' She touched her arm, gently. 'Can you guess what it is?'

It was then that she realized Anna was not asleep. Her skin was cold. Her limbs were stiff. A miniature of Ralph Russell on a single gold chain, was still clutched tightly in her hand.

Alice stood there on the threshold of the room, staring all around her. The doctor from Epsom had already gone. Rebeccah was still sobbing in her room, being comforted by Rufus Waldo.

Dry-eyed, Alice walked over to the desk and opened the drawer, feeling for a pen and paper. Someone must get word to their father in Ireland. Someone must send a letter to Jamie and let him know. If nothing else, he'd rouse himself and come back for the reading of his grandmother's will. Just in case.

The surface of the desk had been polished and the pens put away. Pulling out the drawer further, Alice sorted through the stacks of papers to look for one. It was then that she caught sight of an envelope, addressed to Rebeccah, in her grandmother's unmistakable hand.

For a moment she stood there, holding it. Then she tore it open and read it.

A smile crept across her face. Her dark eyes glittered. Pushing back the drawer, she folded the envelope in two and hid it in the bodice of her gown.

PART FOUR

The Wife

28

REBECCAH LAY THERE in the darkness, listening for his footsteps outside the door. Like all the other nights, she waited, falling asleep when he came home so late that her eyes would not stay open. Then, in the morning, she would wake to find him gone.

For nearly a whole year, she'd never complained about her loneliness; her happiness when they were together made up for all the times they were apart. But she wanted so much to be a part of everything he did, that when he smiled, with that slow, charming smile she loved, and told her it was men's business, she would become annoyed.

'Don't tell me. You're doing business with Enoch Wishard, aren't you? I don't understand why. We've had more winners than ever this season from our own stable; we don't need to send any of our horses over to his.'

'But he has a way with them. Ever since John Mordaunt left Epsom and went over to France, we've had fewer successes than we did when your grandmother was alive.'

'That isn't true. The only horses that haven't done well in our own yard are animals you bought when you must have been out of your mind.' His smile had faded; but Rebeccah had been too angry to notice. 'We've always concentrated on the Classics, Rufus. Why are you suddenly interested only in second rate handicaps?'

'There's more money to be made.'

'But we don't need it.'

'There's nobody in this world who doesn't need more money than they've already got.'

'My grandmother always put the prestige of the stable above any question of financial gains.'

'Your grandmother is dead.'

That was when they had had their first quarrel. And he had stayed away for three nights in a row.

She lay back now against the ornate carving of the headboard, listening for the sound of his footsteps as he climbed the stairs. There was the faint but unmistakable sound of the front door closing, a few moments of silence, while he took off his coat and top hat and left them in the hall. Another five minutes, and she would see the thin beam of light showing from beneath his dressing room door.

She had never liked the London house, with its tall, cold, white exterior and long windows that looked out across the square, the noise of carts and carriages rumbling by on the road outside.

She could hear him moving about in the next room. Noisily, dropping things, cursing as he stooped to pick them up. That, too, was unlike him. Frowning, throwing back the covers on the bed, Rebeccah got up and opened his dressing room door. Then received the biggest shock of her life.

His once immaculately white shirt was hanging open, the front of it stained with dried liquor and blood. His evening dress was creased and dirty, and his breath stank of whisky. She stared at him.

'Rufus? In God's name! What's happened to you? Where have you been?'

He was drunk. Drunker than she had ever seen anyone. Disgusted, unable to believe her own eyes, she recoiled from him as he came towards her, laughing wildly.

'Where have I been? On the river, in a boat, with some friends of mine . . . that's where I've been . . . down to Wapping, if you want to know!'

'Wapping?'

'Filthy hole. Dark. Dirty. Empty warehouses. That's where the fight was held. Bloody good fight it was, too. Bloody near killed each other . . . pity they didn't . . . then I wouldn't have lost all my money . . .'

She went on staring at him. 'Do you mean a prizefight? But they're illegal!'

He let out a high, raucous laugh. 'So is running a whorehouse, but they still do it! Nearly forty rounds, it went . . . blood everywhere . . .' With a shaking finger, he pointed to his shirt. 'Had a ringside seat . . . got this, all over me . . . the bastard I bet on got punched into pulp . . . lost me ten thousand!' He grimaced, with disgust. 'I didn't like the smell of it, I can tell you . . . wouldn't be surprised if he took a dive . . .'

She could feel the tears beginning to prick and burn behind her eyelids. She turned without another word, went back into her bedroom and closed the door.

This was the other Rufus Waldo; the Rufus Waldo she hated; the stranger who, unexpectedly, without warning, emerged when the husband she loved and idolized had taken too much to drink.

She sat down on the bed and wept.

At the beginning, he had been careful to hide his weakness from her; now, he didn't care. Wives put up with the shortcomings of their husbands, whatever they were; that was expected of them and they had no right to complain. Even the highest ladies in the land were in good company with the poor, the downtrodden; Alexandra, Princess of Wales, had suffered all of her married life from her husband's infidelities; just as countless women in the middle classes, in the poor, put up with theirs; maybe Lottie Tradescant's nonchalant cynicism about love had been right after all.

No. No, she wouldn't believe that. She loved him and he loved her; his faults didn't matter. The best men were entitled, once in a while, to find themselves the worst for drink. She wiped her eyes and, slowly, climbed back into bed.

It was cold, now, and she pulled the covers up close around her body. The small fire had gone out. Next door, she could hear him moving around in the dressing room. She lay back on the pile of pillows and closed her eyes.

It was then that the connecting door was flung open, and, on opening her eyes, she saw that he was standing there, staring at her.

Slowly, without speaking, he undressed. He came over to the bed and got in beside her.

No, not now, not that. Her eyes were sore and heavy, and she longed for sleep. Whispering goodnight, she turned over. But his hand lay like a stone on her shoulder.

'Rebeccah . . .'

'Please, Rufus. I'm tired . . .'

'You are also my wife.' She felt him coming closer to her, unfastening the ribbons on her nightgown with his groping fingers. She could smell the remnants of the liquor he had been drinking on his breath, the stale odour of sweat, and she turned her face away. He grabbed her and shook her, enraged.

'Don't you dare turn your back on me!'

'Leave me alone! I told you, I'm tired, I want to go to sleep!'

'You can go to sleep when I've finished.'

Roughly, he pulled off her nightgown and tossed it on the floor, while she lay there without moving. He had never done this before, never forced her against her will. But it was her duty as his wife to submit to him. She let herself go limp, as he climbed on top of her. When he had finished, she gave a low moan and rolled over on the bed, as far away from him as she could. But his hands had locked themselves back onto her shoulders, and he was pulling her round to face him again.

'I haven't finished yet.'

She stared at him through the blanket of darkness without comprehension. Weariness washed over her, her eyelids drooped.

'Please, Rufus . . .'

'Turn around, with your back to me.' When she was slow to obey him he lost his temper and pulled her into the position he wanted, roughly; she started to cry. Through weariness, through despair, through disbelief.

'Like *that*! Are you stupid . . ?'

Doing as she was told, she crouched there, shivering in the chill of the room, her limbs aching unbearably in the hateful discomfort of the position he wanted, as he forced himself into her. Clenching her fists, screwing up her face in pain, she buried it in the depths of the pillows to stifle her cries. Then, when the agony became almost too great to continue, her abdomen feeling as if it would burst, he collapsed on the bed beside her, panting.

For a long while she lay there, on her stomach, too miserable to move. Only when, at last, she heard the sound of his snoring, did she haul her body from the bed and leave him there. Fumbling in the darkness, she found her clothes, and dressed herself.

Then she went downstairs to the tiny library and sat, a book open on her lap but not reading it, till dawn.

He was a totally different Rufus Waldo at breakfast. Smiling, gentle, deferential; cracking jokes. He ate heartily and read the newspaper and the morning's mail.

'One for you, my dear,' he said, tossing the single letter to her across the table. 'It looks like your father's handwriting. And the postmark is Newmarket.'

Leaving her breakfast scarcely touched, Rebeccah took it and opened it with stiff, numb hands.

'Alice and her husband are down there for the July meeting. He wonders if we'd care to join them.'

'You may go, certainly.' The dark eyes glanced at her from the top of the newspaper. 'But I'm afraid that I shan't be able to join you. Too much business in town.'

The sudden rush of happiness his answer produced in her made her feel puzzled and guilty. She remembered the early days, the days when the mere sight of him, the sound of his voice, the prospect of being alone with him for only a few moments, would bring a hot flush to her cheeks and make her heart race with excitement and anticipation. Had being married destroyed so quickly the magic she had felt?

Where did it go, where had it vanished to, that plethora of delight and heady pleasure, when the thrill of being in his company had seemed something so special? If he had remained perfect, if he had had no ordinary faults like other men, would she then have gone on in her adoration, her head still buried in the clouds?

She stole a glance at him. Immaculately groomed, immaculately dressed. No trace of the tipsy, insensitive, panting beast of last night. Trying to blot out the memory, she shuddered and looked away.

She got up, murmuring an excuse to leave the table, then wandered aimlessly about the house. It seemed to her a prison, a prison hemmed in by tall, black, gleaming railings, from which she longed to escape. No gardens, no fields, no orchards, no rolling Downs, with the strings of early morning horses being brought up for exercise from the stables. Yes, at last she could admit it; she was homesick. For the world she had left behind her. For the life she had exchanged so eagerly, so willingly, for this other.

She pulled herself together, briskly. She was still the same person inside. She knew exactly what she wanted to do.

Going into the morning room, she sat down at her little kneehole desk, took out paper, pen and ink. Then she wrote a letter to her father. As she signed and blotted it, there was a tap on the door and a maid came into the room at the sound of her voice calling permission to enter.

'A gentleman to see you, ma'am – Mr Cornelius Ismay.'

She looked up, sharply.

'Cornelius Ismay? Did you tell him Mr Waldo isn't at home?'

'He asked to speak to you, Mrs Waldo.'

She frowned and stood up. 'You'd better show him in.'

She was standing by the window, half turned away from the door, when the maid announced him and then closed it behind her. Rebeccah's hands gripped at the window ledge, as if she could not somehow meet him face to face without its support. Awkwardly, she faced him and forced herself to meet his eyes.

The change in him startled her. Gone was the harsh, unnerving stare she remembered; in its place his eyes looked weary and sad. His face was haggard, as if he had not slept properly for a long while. Though he did not smile at her as their eyes met across the space of the room, she could not fail to notice the gentleness in his expression.

'Mr Ismay . . . I'm afraid if you came to see my husband, he has already left the house.'

'Yes, I saw him leave. From across the street.' She looked startled. 'I was waiting to see you, alone.' He made no movement towards her. 'I haven't seen you since your marriage. I've had no opportunity to say what I came here to say today. I wanted you to know how sorry I was to hear about the death of your grandmother. Anna Brodie Russell was a remarkable woman. A legend in her own lifetime. A woman I met only once but have never ceased to admire. Please accept my sincere condolences.'

'Thank you . . .'

'I would have written, when I first heard. But I wanted to tell you face to face. That evening, when I first came to Epsom and she invited me into the house . . . I've never forgotten that. I never shall forget it. She made a deep impression upon me. A lasting impression. And so did you. I thought then how alike you were.' He stopped, almost abruptly, as if he suddenly remembered that they were little more than distant acquaintances and that propriety had already been exceeded by his words. 'If there is ever anything I can do for you, you have only to ask.'

'That is very kind of you.' Her mind thrashed about for words, for the right thing to say, but she felt suddenly tongue-tied and inadequate, confronted by this new, different Cornelius Ismay.

'I must be going.'

'Please . . . can I offer you some refreshment . . . a glass of sherry, perhaps?'

'No, thank you. I must be on my way.'

He paused, at the door, and kissed her hand. For the first time since she had known him, she did not recoil from the touch.

Alice sat at her dressing table mirror in her old bedroom, while her maid got on with the formidable task of brushing out her hair. It reached down to her waist when it was unbound; thick, silk like waves that clung, with a life of their own, to the maid's fingers, as she drew the brush gently through each strand. Beautiful hair.

Alice had been unusually silent ever since their arrival; and unusually bad tempered. When the girl accidentally pulled too hard, her mistress had tugged the brush from her hands and hit her with it, savagely, across the knuckles. Then she had been dismissed.

Bursting into tears she rushed from the room, colliding with her mistress's husband on the landing outside. He entered the bedroom.

'I've just seen your maid, in floods of tears. What happened?'

Alice glared at him, sullen-faced, in the mirror. 'She hurt me and I slapped her.'

'Was it necessary to be so unkind?'

She picked up the brush herself and began to draw it through her gleaming dark hair with rapid, impatient strokes.

'It amazes me that you continually express such touching concern for the servants.' Her voice was sarcastic. 'I really don't know why you bother.'

'I was always brought up to believe that we should treat everyone, whatever their station in life, with proper deference and courtesy. Servants are no exception. And to invoke loyalty it is a mistake to treat those who serve us with unkindness and injustice.'

'Please, Duncan. I have a headache.' How pompous he was! 'I'm in no mood to listen to one of your lectures on how I should treat minions paid well to perform the most simple of tasks!'

He came over to her and kissed her cheek, while she made no response.

'I'm sorry to hear that you're not feeling well. I hope you'll feel better this afternoon, when we drive down to the course.'

'I shan't be going down to the course. All morning this headache's got worse. I shall lie down on my bed and go to sleep. I hardly slept at all last night.' There was irritation and admonishment in her voice, and he fell silent. How bored she was, how bored and impatient she had always been, at his dull, unimaginative love-making. 'You go, with father and Rebeccah. I don't think I could stand it, all the crowds and the noise.'

'I'll stay behind with you, if you want me to.'

She lost her temper. 'I don't need a nursemaid, Duncan!'

Duncan Clanradine drew up a chair and sat, without speaking, watching her. He loved to watch her at her dressing table, her long hair loose, her slim, lithe body, tantalizing in its perfection beneath the flimsy robe, as if he could not, somehow, bring himself to believe that he had been lucky enough to marry anyone so exotic and so beautiful. If only she could get on better with his widowed mother, if only she could bring herself to be kinder and more thoughtful towards the servants. He sighed.

'Is there anything I can do for you while I'm here?'

'You can go away and leave me alone!'

When he had gone, Alice threw down the brush and began to pace, restlessly, about the room. Her eyes glanced at the clock on the mantelpiece. Another two hours before they all left the house! How she wished that he could have left her in London where she wanted to be, not buried in the country that she'd quickly grown to hate and despise. But to have insisted on staying behind without him would have been too risky, too dangerous; there were unseen eyes everywhere, watching, only too ready to make mischief. Clanradine was soft-hearted and easy-going, but he was not a fool. Nor would his absurd sense of family honour and personal pride allow her to make him one. She had to tread carefully.

She had already decided what she would wear. But she would not dress herself until much later, when everybody in the house would be safely out of the way. She smiled, slowly, confidentially, at her reflection in the mirror. Then she went and lay down on the bed, and drew the curtains around her.

Rebeccah found her there, more than an hour later. Pretending she had been asleep, Alice opened her eyes, hand to her forehead as if the slightest noise was unbearable to her, and peered at her sister through the half light.

'It's worse,' she said, lying back on the pillows, before Rebeccah had a chance to speak. 'I've been getting them, bad ones, more and more lately. I don't know why. I'm sorry to spoil everything,' she smiled, weakly. 'I was so looking forward to the racing this afternoon . . .'

Rebeccah sat down beside her on the bed and laid her hand across her brow.

'Your head doesn't feel hot. Shall I get Mary to fetch you up some headache powders? You're not coming down with anything, are you?'

'I hope to God I'm not! I hate lying here, all the curtains drawn, like some pathetic invalid! And Duncan always makes such a fuss . . .' Her voice sounded almost bitter. 'If he says anything to you about him coming back from the course early on my account, for God's sake do anything to dissuade him. I can't bear it when he hovers around me as if I were a sick horse!'

'He's very devoted to you.'

'If that's devotion then I don't want it. I can't stand being constantly stifled!'

Rebeccah frowned. Alice had changed so much since those three months in Italy, since she had married Clanradine.

'But you are happy, aren't you?'

'I don't know. What is happiness? I'm not sure if I know the answer any more. If it's being married to someone rich and secure who'll give me anything I want, then, yes, I suppose I am happy. I've done well, haven't I?' She gave a small, bitter little laugh. 'She hates me, his mother. Old bitch. Always criticising me, dropping sarcastic little hints that he's too thick-headed to understand . . . but I know. She was against him marrying me from the first and that made me all the more determined to marry him. If only she'd known! It's ironic, isn't it? When he isn't there she can barely bring herself to be civil to me.'

'You have to remember that he's an only son, and her husband's dead. She sees you as a rival for his love, and she can't cope with that except by expressing pointless hostility. If you can see that, then you can easily win her round.'

'I wouldn't even bother.' She closed her eyes again, with an air of finality. 'I'm sorry, Rebeccah, but when my head aches like this I can't think clearly. Go and enjoy the racing. And cheer Gold Bridge for me.'

Rebeccah leaned over and kissed her on the cheek, and then went away again. Alice could hear her footsteps growing fainter and fainter, until they vanished into silence. She sat up, pulled aside the bed curtains and looked at the clock. Another half an hour before they all left the house for the journey to the racecourse. Another half an hour before it was safe for her to get up and get dressed.

Impatiently, she lay back on the pillows to wait.

She tiptoed to the door and opened it, then peered outside. Silence. Kind, and convenient of her father to let most of the servants have the afternoon off, so that they could go down to the Heath and watch the big race. Only Mrs Fitton, the cook, and old Harker, the butler, would have been left behind, both by choice; Mrs Fitton always had a sleep in the afternoons and old Harker would be pottering about in the wine cellar. Slowly, Alice smiled.

She crept into Rebeccah's room and opened her wardrobe.

The faint, subtle scent of violets came from the rail hung with clothes. Her dark eyes ran over them, hurriedly; then paused. Dull green silk, devoid of any eye-catching trimmings. Exactly what she wanted. Taking it down from the rail, Alice flung it over one arm and closed the wardrobe door.

It took her only fifteen minutes to get ready. The last touch, a small, matching hat with long, fluttering veil; the perfect disguise. Anyone glimpsing her, from a distance, would think that she was Rebeccah. Purposely, she let her dark hair hang loose.

A glance in the mirror. An arrogant, self-satisfied smile at the reflection. Then she drew on a pair of riding gloves and ran down to the stables.

She had often ridden bare back. No time, anyway, to bother with a cumbersome side saddle. Pulling on the bridle, she stood on an upturned bucket and raised herself onto the animal's back, urging him forward into a trot as they came out from the stall into the yard.

A rapid, furtive glance all around her. No one in sight. Slapping the horse's rump with her small whip, she turned his head in the direction of the field beyond, and headed at a gallop towards the line of the distant trees.

She slowed down as the small, deserted rubbing house, a relic of former days, came into sight. A hundred yards to its left, she could see his mount tethered, far from any chance of prying eyes, to a bush in the small clump of trees near the edge of the Bury woods.

She pulled him up, uncertain whether her lover would be waiting for her where he had left his horse, or inside the little wooden edifice as they had agreed.

She slipped down from the saddle, and led her horse by its reins towards the old, ramshackle building. As she came within feet of it she saw a movement inside, and Rufus Waldo appeared in the frame of the door. Wordlessly she ran to him, throwing her arms around his neck, covering his lips and face and hands with wild, passionate kisses. He pulled the hat from her head, winding his hands in her long, shining hair, taking the reins of her mount from her and leading it inside the rubbing house with them from the bright sunlight outside.

He kicked the door shut and pulled her down on the old, musty straw that lay scattered on the ground.

Neither of them spoke. Breathlessly, tearing the clothes from each other they made passionate and uninhibited love on the hard, dirty floor, while Alice's mount, muzzle to the ground, nosed the wisps of straw in search of some morsel to nibble at.

When it was over, they lay in each other's arms, still naked, hands linked, staring breathlessly up at the chink of sky through the ruined ceiling.

'I missed you so. I wanted you so desperately. I thought I'd go mad shut up in that house with Duncan and the servants.' She rolled over and let her hands wander across his body. 'It would have been easier if I'd stopped behind in London. You could have sent Rebeccah down here and stayed behind too. But it would have looked suspicious, too obvious. And we might have been seen . . .'

'Better this way. With nobody knowing.' He leaned over her and kissed her, lingering, his body still on fire. 'I want you again.' He touched her. 'I always want you. Once is never enough with you. Never enough.' He took her in his arms roughly, almost brutally, the way she loved, the way Rebeccah had always hated. He could feel her excitement as he flung her body backwards on the ground, holding down her wrists so tightly that she cried out with pleasure and pain. Then, as he bent his head down and his lips touched her warm flesh, he felt his, and her own passion explode into flames.

'When will I see you again?'

'Soon. When you go back to London.'

'But you said meeting in town was too dangerous. That there was too much risk. For both of us.'

'There are always ways and means.'

'If only I could get rid of Duncan it would be easy.'

He smiled, slowly. 'You must use your wiles on him and persuade him to pay a dutiful visit to his widowed mother.'

'He'd expect me to go with him.' Her face was surly. 'He always does. Even though he knows she hates the sight of me and I detest her.'

'I'm certain you can bring him round to your way of thinking. As only you can.'

She grimaced with distaste.

'I can't bear the thought of him touching me. He makes me sick . . . those white, stubby fingers, pawing me . . . it's like lying there, underneath a porpoise . . .' She was angry when Waldo laughed. 'It's easy for you! If I refused him, too often, he might get suspicious . . .'

Waldo finished refastening his immaculate white shirt cuffs.

'As I just said, there are ways and means. To get everything.'

She stood very still.

'Are you trying to tell me something?'

'You're a clever girl, Alice. Use that quick, sharp brain. A sure way to hold off your husband's unwanted attention. And for getting him to agree to anything you want.'

Suddenly, she understood.

'Do you think he'd fall for it?'

'Of course.'

'And when he finds out that it isn't true?'

'You made a mistake. Any woman can make that kind of mistake.' He kissed her, and handed her the reins of her horse. 'We can't leave together. Too much risk of one of us being seen. You leave first. I'll follow in ten minutes.'

Outside she turned back and threw her arms around him.

'But you're supposed to be in London.'

'I will be, in a few hours . . . and no one any the wiser.'

She sighed. She laid her head against his chest.

'I can't bear the thought of you being with her . . .'

Since her grandmother's death, her father had become a changed man. Years older, the once jet black hair liberally streaked with grey, the face only a vestige of the handsome face she remembered. The eyes were dull, lifeless; he ate little, spoke less. Often, when Rebeccah had come unexpectedly into a room where he was, he would not even lift his head to glance up, but remained sitting, motionless, staring blankly into space. The change in him had shocked her, as if she herself were responsible for it.

She watched him now, walking side by side with Alice's husband through the milling crowds in the paddock below the box, with a semblance of his former self. There was a slight, almost imperceptible smile on his lips; as she continued watching she saw him stop, every now and then, to shake hands with an old acquaintance or exchange words with a trainer he knew.

The atmosphere on the racecourse, the bustle and colour and noise, seemed somehow to have lifted his spirits. Rebeccah smiled as she saw him talking now to the trainer of the favourite, the strained, lined face almost taking on a changed, brighter expression.

Her blue eyes roamed slowly over the heads of the plentiful crowd below her; gentlemen in morning suits and top hats, bevies of ladies more interested in showing off their fashions than in the racing. Grooms, trainers, stable boys, jockeys in bright silks, the horses for the main race being unrugged in the paddock.

It was then that she suddenly caught sight of him, and stiffened with surprise; one face she had not expected to see, the face with the long, jagged, disfiguring scar – Cornelius Ismay. For the second time, she did not feel that same revulsion, the recoiling from his presence. Was it only their brief, unexpected meeting in London, when he had come to the house to offer his condolences for her grandmother's death that had slowly begun to change her mind about him, or was it something else, something more subtle, that she herself was not even fully aware of?

He glanced up towards the grandstand at that same moment and their eyes met, and held. He did not smile at her. She made no gesture of recognition. He merely tipped his hat towards her in greeting, then replaced it on his dark hair and was gone.

She wondered at once what he could be doing here, alone, without Rufus. Then she remembered that he worked for the trainer Enoch Wishard and Wishard had had runners in every race so far, most of them enjoying phenomenal success. But his stable would have no chance in this, the last and most prestigious race. The favourite, a bay colt from the

Welbeck Abbey stable, was now odds on to win from the highest class field in years.

Seeing Ismay so unexpectedly had distracted her from her intense interest in the race; with difficulty in concentrating now, she took up her field glasses and looked through them at the runners cantering to the start.

The crowds had begun to surge down towards the rails, the places in the grandstand and the private boxes were rapidly filling with people. Rebeccah leaned forward, the field glasses in her hands, straining her eyes towards the curve in the course where the field would thunder down. It was a sharp, treacherous bend where not only the surefootedness of the horse but also the skill of the jockey would make all the difference between victory and defeat.

The sun had gone behind a blanket of cloud overhead, the blue sky suddenly seemed dark. There was a strange, brooding heaviness in the air, as if the bright summer's afternoon was about to disappear into the abyss of a thunderstorm.

Sure enough, as the first horses appeared to the roaring of the massive crowd at the turn in the bend, great drops of rain began to fall from the angry sky.

The leading horses surged into the straight, the Welbeck favourite half a length ahead; then, to the crowd's utter dismay and Rebeccah's, the 100–1 outsider from the Wishard stable, ridden by the American jockey Johnny Reiff, passed him with as much ease as if he had been a broken down cart horse.

It galloped on like a demented thing to pass the winning post four lengths ahead of the nearest rival, then threw off its jockey and crashed headlong into a six feet brick wall.

Rebeccah flung down the field glasses and rushed out of the box. Through the crowded grandstand, hatless, pushing astonished people roughly out of her way. She almost fought her path through the solid wall of bodies at the entrance, where everyone was surging in from the course to shelter from the sudden shower of rain.

She held her hand in front of her eyes to shield her face from the downpour, when she crashed heavily into a tall, dark-suited man.

She gasped as she stared up at him.

'Good afternoon, Mrs Waldo,' Cornelius Ismay said.

The wild impulse she had always felt to run from him was curiously absent still. 'Mr Ismay! I'm surprised to see you here alone. I saw you earlier, from the grandstand.' She felt her mouth turn into a small, nervous smile. 'My husband said that he had business with you in town. That's why he isn't here with me.'

A strange expression came into his eyes. She saw a momentary hesitation, as if he was trying to think of the right thing to say.

'We finished our business sooner than anticipated. He would have changed his plans and come down with me, but something else came up that he needed to attend to.'

She tried not to stare at him too intently.

'I must find my father!'

'You're upset . . .' For the first time, she heard real emotion in his voice. 'Was it what happened in the last race?'

'Did you see it too? That horse . . . it crashed straight into the brick wall . . .'

'It must have killed itself straight away. It went berserk.'

'I've never seen anything like that happen. Not ever.'

There was a break in her voice and she struggled to control it. Not now. Not here. Not in front of Cornelius Ismay. She mustn't cry. She wouldn't. Taking her completely by surprise, he suddenly laid his hand on her arm, and she felt herself shiver; but not with repulsion.

'You're upset. Please, let me walk with you to find your father.'

'I can manage by myself.'

'I should consider it an honour to accompany you.'

She looked around her almost desperately, seeking any

face she knew. But there was no one in sight. She suddenly felt a rising panic, almost afraid, without understanding why.

Then she heard her father's voice calling to her.

29

'CORNELIUS ISMAY, HERE? In this house?' Alice propped herself up on one elbow, rubbing her head. 'If Rufus said that they had business in London, why isn't he there with him?'

'I don't know, not the truth, anyway. He said that Rufus had other business and couldn't join him on the train. Something's going on, Alice. I feel it. Something connected with Enoch Wishard . . .'

'And papa invited him to stay here for the rest of the meeting?'

'Yes . . . Wishard and the rest of them from his stable have been put up at the White Hart, in Newmarket High Street.' She sat down beside her sister on the big bed. 'Ever since Ismay came to the house in London . . . that time I told you about . . . he seems different, somehow . . . not sinister any more. I don't know how to describe it, not exactly.'

'Maybe you've just got used to that hideous scar!'

'It's something more than that. I feel myself being able to like him . . . perhaps it was the way he spoke about grandmother . . . it wasn't just politeness; he wasn't trying to be patronizing. I could tell. He really meant what he said. I suppose part of the reason I was prejudiced against him was that he always seemed to be around when some disaster struck, like Dunroven's death . . .'

'And today?'

'It must be coincidence about the accident after the race . . . him being there. This time, I could swear that Wishard managed to fix that horse that killed itself. If you'd been there, you'd understand what I mean. It was no accident.

The Wishard colt could never have beaten Portland's, not in a hundred years. I don't know how they did it, but that was a crooked race if ever I saw one . . .'

'You think Portland's jockey pulled the favourite on Wishard's orders?'

'Maynard? He's as honest as they come! And he was riding the colt out for all he was worth. That was no pull. Besides, that field was the strongest for the Cheveley Handicap that we've had in years . . . and there were twenty-five runners. You don't think twenty-four of the jockeys pulled their mounts, do you? No. It's something else. And I think Wishard has something to do with it.'

'But what?'

'Like I said, I don't know.' She bit her lip, her mind going over and over again the last furlongs of the race. 'It's just a feeling I've got, a gut feeling. And I know I'm right. What really worries me is that Rufus is involved with Wishard's stable over here, and if Wishard is doing anything illegal, he might unwittingly be part of it . . .'

'Surely not!'

'Alice, I'm worried . . .'

'But you can't prove anything. And you can't accuse anyone without proof. Besides which, you don't even know what you're trying to prove in the first place.'

'Do normal horses hurl off their jockeys and then kill themselves by running into a solid brick wall?'

'No, but some horses do go berserk from time to time. Remember when papa told us about Fred Archer, being attacked by one of Mat Dawson's savages up on the Heath? And that other one, years ago, who ran amok at stud and killed a groom? That's what must have happened today.'

'It was horrible . . .'

Alice sat up in the bed and put her arms around her.

'I wish you hadn't seen it.'

'I hope I never see anything like it again.'

*

They looked at each other, in silence, from across the room. Clanradine had gone upstairs to sit with Alice, who was still not well enough to come down; her father had been called away to the stableyard. So she, the only one left, was alone with Ismay.

When she could bear his silent scrutiny no longer, she got up and went to the window and stared out of it, watching the long shadows cast by the poplar trees across the lawn. Behind her, she could sense him getting to his feet; no gentleman remained sitting while a lady stood. Then she heard his voice, suddenly, breaking into the silence, a few feet away.

'You're still upset about the horse.' It was a statement more than a question.

'Yes, I'm still upset about it.'

'You have a special feeling for them, don't you? As if they were human. Your grandmother had it, too.' A pause. 'That was the secret of her success. They knew it, and she could do whatever she liked with them.'

She turned round swiftly, startled by what he said. She had never taken Ismay, until now, for a sensitive man. He worked for Enoch Wishard and to Wishard and his owners horses were just a tool.

'That's the truest thing you've ever said.'

He smiled. 'When I was fifteen, I saw a carter whipping the living daylights out of an old, blind horse. Skin and bone it was, all but; trying to pull a wagon loaded with bricks uphill. A job for four strong horses, not one old, worn-out one. I ran across the street and shouted at him to stop it, but he just turned and cursed at me. So I yanked the whip out of his hand and gave him a taste of his own medicine.' Lightly, he fingered the ugly, jagged scar that disfigured his left cheek. 'He pulled a knife out on me . . . that's how I managed to get this.'

She stared at him, trying to put her feelings into words. But before she could speak at all her father had come back into the room.

'Damn St Frusquin mare's gone and slipped her foal!' He uncorked a fresh bottle of brandy and poured himself a glass, then one for Ismay. 'The dam had a history of slipped foals and stillbirths, but the blood was so good I reckoned we could take a chance on it. Seems I was wrong to.' He took a long gulp of the rich, amber liquid. 'My mother and I never could agree on that one point. If she slips one, don't bother sending her back to the same stallion . . . that's what she'd always say. Try her with another and him with another mare . . . and see which one is at fault. If it's her, then she's a bad breeder.'

'It makes sound sense to me,' Ismay said.

'That jockey of Wishard's, the Reiff boy. Is he riding for your stable or can anyone hire him? I've seen him riding down here, and up at Doncaster and York . . . I like his style.'

'You'd have to ask Wishard about that.'

'He's got a brother, hasn't he? Both came over here at the same time . . .'

'Lester Reiff. Wishard brought them over with him when he came, to ride for the colony of American owners that sailed with him. Lester's always had trouble with his weight, but not Johnny; he's one of the best lightweight jockeys we've got . . . as you've already seen. He's never weighed more than five stone.'

James Russell laughed, something of his old self.

'I saw him in the paddock, being fussed over by some of the society women. In that Eton collar and knickerbockers, he looks like a funny little choirboy.'

Ismay made no further comment. 'It's a beautiful house you have here . . . near enough to Newmarket and Cambridge to be close to town; far away enough to be a seat in the country. This part of the world isn't well known to me.'

James Russell seated himself in a big, comfortable chair. 'My wife and I chose it together . . . when we were first married. It was always called Linnets Hall, for some reason, and we both liked the name. We saw no reason to change it, to Russell House, or Russell Hall, or Russell Manor . . . we saved that for the town house we bought in London. That was sold, years ago, after she died . . . never used it much, anyhow. She preferred to stay at a smart hotel whenever she went up to town . . .' He stared into his glass, Rebeccah and Ismay half forgotten, while he forced himself, almost unwillingly, to think of the past. Strange, for so long, for so many years now he had not been able to think about her, or even speak her name.

'Once, the house was always full of people. Never seemed to have it to ourselves . . . it's never seemed the same, somehow, since she left . . .' Rebeccah and Ismay exchanged a glance.

'Are you all right, papa?'

'. . .The Prince and Princess of Wales came here, did you know that? For the Moulton Cup Ball . . . that was a night to remember! He was often here, HRH. Until the scandal, when Corinna left me . . .'

'Papa . . .' Rebeccah had half risen from her place, but Ismay silently shook his head at her, and placed a finger to his lips.

She could feel her face growing hot as her father talked, almost to himself, as if neither of them were there; for more than eleven years she had never known him to speak her mother's name.

'You wouldn't think it could be the same house, if you'd been there that night . . . not the same house. Like a mortuary, now. So quiet. Hushed, silent, like when you're standing for a funeral service in church . . .' He was staring ahead of him, his mind elsewhere. 'I remember that gown she wore, the last time I ever saw her . . . the night when she caused the scene that ruined me at Court . . . the Dysarts had invited us over to their Ball . . . white and gold it was; and it glittered, like stars, when she moved. She was the most beautiful woman there . . .'

Quietly, Rebeccah got to her feet and came over to him, and laid her hand gently on his arm.

'Papa . . . shall I go and fetch Mowbray, and let him help you upstairs? I think you should rest now. The doctor said that you must get plenty of rest . . .'

'. . . a terrible thing,' he said to Ismay, as if he had not heard or seen her, 'to marry a woman just for her father's money . . . they all do it, from the highest in the land . . . but it stinks . . . I loved Isabella, but we could never have lived together . . . she would have driven me out of my mind . . . Margaret, she would have bored me in a year . . . I thought it was just Charpentier's fortune that made me do it . . . maybe it was, then . . . it was only when she'd left me that I realized the truth. I really had loved her . . . but I threw it all away . . .' The glass of brandy fell to the floor, and he drooped forward, head in his hands, and began to weep, while Rebeccah stared at him in horror. She had never seen a grown man cry before, much less her own father. The father she had once idolized, the father who had always seemed so strong, so proud, so firmly in control. She was rooted to the spot where she stood, staring down at him, this aged, sad, broken man, a shadow of his former self.

Quietly, Cornelius Ismay came across to where he sat and touched his arm. He looked at Rebeccah.

'If you'll go and fetch his manservant, I'll help him upstairs to bed.'

They looked at each other.

'I . . . I don't know why . . . I don't understand what's suddenly made him speak like this . . .'

'It doesn't matter, there's no need to apologize. He's been ill, didn't you say? Do you think someone should ride for the doctor?'

'I think he needs to sleep. If he's no better in the morning, I'll ask Mowbray to send someone into Newmarket . . .' She hesitated, as Ismay helped her father to his feet, supporting his body with his thick, strong arms. 'Thank you for helping him like this . . . I'm very grateful . . .'

He smiled, and for the first time she suddenly realized that she liked him.

'I'd do the same for anyone.'

The lights from the upstairs windows streamed down across the terrace and the lawns, as they walked side by side along the line of rose beds, past the sundial, the rockery, the sunken garden, their footsteps leaving imprints in the damp grass.

They paused, taking a last look around the peace and silence of the garden before darkness finally fell.

'I loved this house, when I was a little girl; when my mother was alive. And she loved this garden. She'd take my hand, and we'd walk together, and she'd tell me the name of every flower and every plant. She'd say to me, they don't have gardens like this in Kentucky . . .'

'Were you very small, when she left your father?'

'I was nine years old. It was July then, too . . . the year everything suddenly became different . . . the year everything suddenly changed . . . I can't talk about it very easily, not even now . . . strange, that it should still hurt me so much, after all these years . . .'

'I'm sorry, I didn't mean to pry.' Ismay's voice beside her was gentle. 'Some things we can't ever really bring ourselves to talk about. Some things we just can't face. I'm like that, too.' They began walking again, back towards the house. 'My parents died when I was five. My uncle brought me up, with my two brothers and two sisters. But he never had much time for any of us, and when I was six I ran away. Did he beat the hell out of me!'

Her head turned sharply. 'He was cruel to you?'

'Couldn't stand the sight of me. Used to lock me in the attic to punish me for this and that. Never raised a finger to his own sons.' He shrugged, as if it was of no importance. 'As soon as I was old enough, he had me sent to his shipyard as an apprentice . . . but it wasn't to my taste. I didn't want to work for him; I didn't want to have to spend the rest of my life being grateful. So I made my own way.' A short silence. 'It hasn't always been the right one.' There was a note of finality in his voice, as if he did not want to discuss the subject further. Rebeccah did not press him.

He said, suddenly, 'That door, on the other side of the house . . . where does it lead to?'

'Just to the old wing that was closed up a long time ago.' A short silence. Strange, that it should still hurt her to think about that day, so long ago, the day when she had first met Jamie. It seemed so trivial, so unimportant now, that single, ugly memory, softened by the passage of time. 'It's a very large house; when my father first came here, all the rooms were used. But later on he closed up one wing and had everything covered in dustsheets. That door is the servants' entrance, for when the maids used to carry the buckets of coal upstairs to light the fires. It was easier, quicker, than carting them all the way across the inside of the house. The rooms are all empty now.'

Ismay looked up at the dark, silent windows, and felt the brooding sadness of neglect. The house was dying, and he could almost hear it weep.

'You're travelling back to London the day after tomorrow, when the meeting is over?'

'I shall go in the morning, if my father's no worse. After what happened on the course today, I've no heart to stay and see the rest.'

'Is Rufus expecting you?'

'Not for another two days. But I shall surprise him.'

A strange look crossed Ismay's face. 'You could send him a telegram.'

'It doesn't matter . . .'

'Will your sister and brother-in-law be going with you?'

'No, they'll travel straight to Scotland. The change of air will do Alice good. She's spent so much time in bed, lately.

Not like her. Next month we're going to Dunroven Castle to stay with my brother Jamie . . .'

'Yes, I know; he invited me, too.'

'Will you accept the invitation?'

'I hadn't intended to.' He looked into her wide, blue eyes. 'But I think I might change my mind.'

The hansom cab pulled to a halt outside the tall, white exterior of the London house, and Rebeccah climbed down and waited in the porchway while her maid paid the driver. The luggage she had taken with her to Linnets Hall was to be sent on, later; all she had brought back from Newmarket was a single valise.

She rang the bell several times before Benson, their butler, came to answer; this was in itself unusual. But when she stepped inside the hall she immediately understood; coming from the dining room on the ground floor was a terrible, deafening noise, so loud that she could barely hear what he was trying to say.

'I'm sorry, madam,' Benson said, his face red with confusion and embarrassment, 'but Mr Waldo is entertaining several of his gentleman friends. He wasn't expecting you back for another two days . . .'

'So I can hear.' Tight-lipped, Rebeccah sent her petrified maid upstairs with the single valise, and made her way furiously to the room from where all the shouting, swearing, drunken singing and ear-splitting din was coming.

She stood there, aghast, eyes wide on the threshold of the room, speechless with disgust.

The table was in a complete shambles. Broken glasses, spilled wine, chicken bones, dirty plates, all strewn across the once-white linen tablecloth. Drunken men, men she had never seen before, shirts undone, jackets awry, lounged on chairs around the table, singing or yelling at the tops of their voices. And, at the head of the table, as dishevelled as the rest, but with a big, bare-breasted girl slouched against him on his knee, sat Rufus Waldo.

As she slammed the door behind her they all suddenly looked up, and everyone fell silent. Waldo stared at her, the smirking expression of a moment ago wiped from his face.

'*Get out.* All of you. Get out of my house before I send one of my servants for the police.' Outrage overwhelmed her. She strode over to where Waldo sat with the half-naked girl on his knee, and pushed her, head first, onto the floor.

He staggered to his feet, maddened. '*You bitch!*'

'How dare you! How dare you bring this whore into my house! And how dare you order my servants to wait on this drunken scum!'

Behind her, she could hear the sound of chairs scraping back, as Waldo's cronies slunk out of the room. The girl had dragged herself to her feet and found something to cover her nakedness. In five minutes, they were alone.

'What the hell do you think you're doing?' Dark eyes blazing, he came towards her, shouting at the top of his voice. 'Do you know how big you made me look, in front of my friends?' He held up a finger and thumb. '*This* big.' He stuck out a hand and pushed her so hard that she almost lost her balance. 'You've made me into a bloody laughing stock! You, my own wife!'

Furiously, she stood up to him. 'You've made yourself into a laughing stock! And me! My God, what a wolf in sheep's clothing! And I believed everything you said. Everything. I believed you when you said you loved me.' Tears of rage and anguish sprang into her eyes, and she dashed them away with the back of her hand. 'You were so clever, Rufus. So clever. With all your charm. With all your big business connections. You even fooled my grandmother. What chance did I have, a raw, naïve girl with her head in the clouds? What was it . . . the money? Or was it just the prestige of marrying into the family?' A tear welled up in the corner of one eye and rolled slowly down her cheek. 'And I felt sorry for my sister Alice. Marrying Clanradine, when she didn't love him. Marrying him just because it was a "good" match. I thought I was the lucky one! My God, how I envy her now!' She turned round and ran out of the room; up the stairs, stumbling over her long gown and cloak as she went, shaking and sobbing. Like a blind woman, she found the door of her room and fumbled for the handle to open it. Then she threw herself on the floor beside the bed and burst into tears.

A few moments later, she heard his footsteps behind her.

'Get up.' His voice was hoarse, almost a whisper. Wildly, her heart began to hammer with fear. 'I said, get up.'

Slowly, she turned her head and looked at him, through red-rimmed, swollen eyes.

'Please go away and leave me alone.'

He strode over to her, grasped her roughly by the arm and pulled her to her feet. Then he slapped her across the mouth and threw her on the bed like a rag doll.

'Don't speak. Don't say anything. Just listen.' She stared at him, holding her throbbing lip where he had struck her. There was blood on her fingers. 'You are my wife and will obey me. When you married me, your property – all of it – ceased to be yours . . . that is the law of the land and there is nothing you can do about it.' He stood over her, glaring down into her white, terrified face. 'You're my property. This house is my property. The estate, the racing stable and the stud in Epsom and Newmarket, all belong to me. And so does Gold Bridge . . .'

'*No!*'

'If I choose to sell him, to have him shot, or to send him to the knacker's yard for dog meat, I am perfectly at liberty to do so . . . and there's nothing you could do to stop me. I advise you, for your own good, to remember that. The law of the land is firmly on my side.' A smile that struck chill into her. 'Only if I treated you with such brutality that you had cause to be in fear of your life, could you go to law and obtain a divorce . . . and I warn you, Rebeccah, that if such a course ever enters your mind, you would be wise to forget about it . . .'

She struggled up on one elbow, tears running down her face. 'You wouldn't dare to have him shot . . !'

'I think you know me well enough to believe that I never make idle threats.'

'But he's the most valuable horse in the stable! You said so yourself . . !'

'Like any other piece of horseflesh I regard him as a pawn. To be used as I think fit.'

'What are you talking about?'

'Any plans I have for any of the Russell horses now or in the future, are no longer any concern of yours.' He turned his back on her, went out of the room, and slammed the door behind him. Rebeccah hauled herself from the bed and ran after him.

'You lay a finger on that horse and I swear you'll be sorry for it!'

He swung round on her, grabbed her by the wrist and flung her back into the room. Then he left and locked the door from the outside.

She called. She hammered on it. She shouted for her maid. When her voice was hoarse and her throat dry she sank down behind the door in a crumpled heap. Downstairs, Rufus Waldo rang for Benson and her maid.

'See that the dining room is cleared up at once.'

'Yes, sir.'

'And Mrs Waldo is not feeling well, after her long and tiring journey. She is not to be disturbed under any circumstances. Do I make myself clear?'

'Yes, sir.'

Without looking at them, he dismissed them.

30

ENOCH WISHARD LIT a hand-rolled cigarette and put his booted foot on top of his untidy, dusty desk.

'You're pulling the St Simon colt out of the Guineas and the Derby and putting him into the Prince of Wales Handicap instead? Have you lost your mind, Rufus?'

'Have you ever known me to do anything without an excellent reason?'

'There's always a first time. Done it to show that sassy wife of yours who's boss, eh?' He dotted the ash from his cigarette into an already overflowing litter bin. 'No call to go cutting your nose off to spite your face . . . that don't make no sense. Why, besides the big prize money from a double like that – and he'd win 'em both, I seen him run – there's all the prestige; and a fortune in stud fees when he retires. That's one piece of horseflesh that don't need no dope in him to make him fly.'

'All right. Supposing I hadn't taken him out of this year's Classics . . . what kind of brass would I rake in? Last season's Derby winner got £5,450 and for the Guineas, even less. What's five grand to me? Lost stakes on a prizefight bet. Small change. Chicken feed. Unless I back him big myself – and with his crack form, what kind of odds do you think I'd get? Not worth bothering with. Now . . . in a top class handicap, running against the best handicappers in the country, his odds'll be longer . . . just a little . . . just enough not to make it smell suspicious when he comes in a close second.'

Wishard narrowed his eyes. 'You fixing to stop your own nag?'

'It's called good business.'

'Eyebrows'll raise if you go ahead and pull him out the Classics.'

'That's been taken care of. The next two Derby trials he takes, he won't win. Loss of form. Not the nag we thought he was. Spread a few rumours from the yard. I know what I'm doing.' The slow, easy smile. 'Besides, if he stays in the Classics it means Rebeccah'll be expected to show herself. That's what I don't want, her getting us invited out to other people's houses. In a weak moment, she just might open her mouth and let something slip that I don't want her to. I won't take that chance.'

'Just tell 'em what you told 'em six months ago . . . she's still in mourning over her father's death.'

'That hare won't run. How can I say that when her brother and sister are out and about being seen in Society? Someone'll smell a rat. The English are stupid but not that stupid.'

'So she's more sensitive than they are. So she's taken her old man's death extra hard . . . stands to reason, don't it? The other two are only his bastards.'

Waldo went on toying with the chain of his solid gold watch. A legacy purloined from James Russell.

'If the bitch hadn't opposed me with the business, if she'd kept her nose out of the way I run things, I'd have been content, more or less, for us to go our separate ways, and just keep up appearances for the look of it. I'd have made her an allowance out of the estate and she could have gone on living at her father's place, while I stayed at Epsom. But oh no! She wanted the Epsom house because it belonged to her grandmother and carte blanche over all the decisions with the bloodstock. No dice. I didn't marry money to take a back seat. I've never taken orders from any goddamned woman and I don't aim to start taking them now. Particularly from my own wife.'

Wishard stubbed out the cigarette and began to roll another one.

'Does she know how much you've used up from the estate kitty to finance all your betting coups?'

'Of course she doesn't. The less she knows the better for both of us. When the old woman died and I married her, I didn't realize that she'd put two thirds of the estate assets into a trust fund . . . not a penny of which can be touched till Rebeccah turns twenty-five. That's a while yet. Too long. Clever. I managed to get rid of the Brodie accountants, but there's nothing I could do to change the names of the trustees.'

'But if you go on betting big and have too many losses, you'll run short of ready cash . . . you can't get your hands on hers while it's still tied up. True, you could sell off some of the bloodstock to raise capital. But as soon as the trustees found out what you were doing, they might start to dig too deep . . .'

'I can handle it.'

Wishard shrugged.

'OK. It's your business. You wheel and deal. But watch your back. The old woman was no fool. She set up the trust fund to protect the girl and appointed the trustees for exactly the same reason . . . the guys in charge of the pursestrings were picked for their brains. Saul Tradescant for one. Don't go treading on thin ice. If you go through what's left, then try twisting her arm to go running to them for a top up, they're going to start asking you some awkward questions. Don't forget, Rufus . . . you're involved with me; and I'm answerable to my owners. They fronted the purchase of your non-existent stud for the look of it, to help make it look like when the Russell girl married you, she was marrying big money. No trails leading back, remember . . . this operation's too big to be jeopardized. When things get too hot for comfort over here, we'll just transfer the whole lot over to the other side of the Channel . . . that way, we all stay one leap ahead.

'But be careful. Never underestimate a woman. You

might think you've got her exactly where you want her . . . under your thumb. But she's got spunk. And she's got Brodie blood. Even if she's afraid of you, or what you might do with that colt of hers, she might just get tired of keeping up the pretence of appearances. Then you'll be in big trouble.'

Wishard's unaccustomed pessimism was beginning to annoy him.

'I do know how to handle my own wife.' A hint of testiness in his voice now. 'She wouldn't dare create any scandal . . . she knows what'd happen to her precious horse if she tried it. But she won't. That bloody nag's like her own child.'

'Her mother walked out on her father, remember. Right in sight and sound of the Prince of Wales!'

'That was different; she didn't have anything to lose. She went running back to her rich, doting daddy, and Russell was left to lick his wounds. Rebeccah's got nobody to run to . . . her grandmother and father are dead. No Charpentiers left, either . . . her mother was the last of the line. She hardly ever sees the Tradescants any more; I've seen to that. And her brother and sister hate her guts.'

'Got it all sewn up, haven't you, Rufus?'

Waldo smiled. 'I planned it a long time ago.'

She stood at the tall window, staring numbly into the night. The high, Georgian buildings of the square opposite glowed white by the light of the street gas lamps; hansom cabs, the occasional carriage, clattered by along the now almost deserted road. Across the street, lights in the other houses were beginning to go out. Was it so late, now? Had she really stood here for so long, lost in her thoughts? Strange, how for the past few months she'd had so little conception of time.

She heard him enter the room behind her, but she stayed

standing where she was. She heard his footsteps, moving about the room, and without turning she knew that he was pouring himself liquor from the decanter on the little table.

'I'm waiting for you to come to bed.'

'Are you? Why not go up? I don't feel tired. Maybe I'll go into the library and read awhile.' No. No. Not bed. Beads of perspiration from panic, began to stand out along her brow. Her heart sank. She felt sick, giddy with weariness, her mind and her body longing for the sleep that he denied her. Like an animal that has been hunted to exhaustion, she craved a safe, secret place where she could curl up and hide. But he would not let her.

He was standing behind her now, reaching out, his fingers on her arm. He tightened them.

'Rebeccah. It's nearly eleven. I said it is time to go upstairs.'

'Can't you go alone? I said that I'd prefer to read awhile.'

'You can read tomorrow.'

'I have to see about the packing, then. All the luggage to be taken to Inverness . . .'

'Rebeccah. Do me the kindness of not provoking me. I said it was time for us to go to bed.'

Like a sleepwalker, she left the room and mounted the stairs. There was a fire in her bedroom, warm and comforting; she thought what a luxury it would be to go to bed and fall asleep, listening to the crackling of the leaping flames . . .

But she knew that he would not allow her to fall asleep. Not before he had forced her, as he always forced her, to do what he wanted. She could hear his voice, hushed, insidious; the voice she had once loved, the voice that had once thrilled her. Threatening, bullying. '*It's your duty, Rebeccah. You are my wife. The law says . . .*'

She could hear his footsteps on the stairs, the creak of the boards outside her room, his hand on the door. He was coming towards her now, steadily, undressing as he did so;

then he reached out and touched her, firmly, on the shoulder. Her whole body shivered.

Revulsion rising in her, she tried to stall him with conversation.

'Have you decided how long we'll stay with Jamie at Dunroven? I know he suggested a month in his letter . . . but I wanted to be back in time for the Derby trials . . .'

She could hear the sound of him unfastening his necktie.

'Derby trials? Oh . . . I believe I quite forgot to tell you . . . I've decided to withdraw Gold Bridge's entry for both the Derby and the 2,000 Guineas . . .'

She spun round, staring at him, unable to believe her ears.

'You've done what?'

'I've scratched him from both races. On the advice of your racing manager, my dear. Apparently he's had a drastic loss of form and some problems with lameness in his right hand foreleg. No sense in running him below par. Stephenson thinks it highly unlikely that he'll be fit enough to compete for any of the Classics this season, including the St Leger . . . and I know how much you value his advice. But not to be downhearted. It's a big disappointment, certainly . . . but next year we can enter him for the Ebor and the Ascot Gold Cup . . . Stephenson thinks he'll do even better as a four-year-old.'

'He never mentioned any loss of form to me when we were in Epsom a month ago.'

'He didn't want to say anything that might alarm you, knowing how much you value the horse . . . and when he spoke to me before we left, I told him to wait for a week or two and see how the animal shaped up. But next morning when they were giving him a trial on the Downs he had to be pulled up half-way. No need to tell you that if you continue to race him as you have been, regardless, you almost certainly risk giving the colt permanent lameness.' He smiled, and went on undressing as if that were the end of the matter. 'I know that isn't what you'd want to happen.'

'No, of course I don't. It's just that I don't understand it. Gold Bridge has never suffered from a day's lameness in his life!'

'It can suddenly afflict the best of horses. And often does. It's just bad luck.'

'I don't understand why Stephenson never mentioned a word of it to me . . .'

He came towards her, laying his hands on her shoulders. She stiffened under his touch.

'What's this? I hope, for your sake, that you're not thinking of fighting me . . .'

Before she could answer there was a sudden loud knocking on the street door outside. It echoed, strangely, eerily, into the silence of the house. Cursing beneath his breath, Rufus Waldo went into his dressing room and pulled on a robe, making his way onto the landing as Rebeccah saw the light from Benson's oil lamp light up the darkness of the hall.

She went out after him, staring down over the landing rails to see the identity of her saviour.

Benson drew back the bolts and opened the door, and the golden lamplight threw into sharp relief the dark, rugged features of Cornelius Ismay.

'What the hell are you doing here at this time of night?' She heard Waldo's voice as he rushed down the stairs and into the hall, gruff, with a trace of alarm in it. He snatched the oil lamp from Benson and sent him back to bed.

Rebeccah moved further out onto the landing, taking care to keep out of sight. She heard them exchanging low, rapid whispers; then both of them disappeared into Waldo's study and closed the door.

She waited there, clinging to the banisters for several minutes, fighting the temptation to creep downstairs and listen outside the study door. But just as she began to edge her way carefully down into the hall, the door swung open and both men came out.

Ismay saw her first. For a few, fleeting moments, they stared into each other's eyes; then he removed his top hat and gave a little bow towards her.

'Mrs Waldo . . . I must beg your pardon for disturbing you at such a late and inconvenient hour. Some urgent business that couldn't wait until morning.'

'Please don't apologize . . .' Desperately, she wanted him to stay. 'I'm afraid all the servants have gone to bed, except Benson . . . but if there's something he could fetch you . . .'

'We both have to leave,' Waldo cut in, roughly. 'Wait here, Cornelius. It won't take me longer than a few minutes to get dressed.'

'Rufus? What is it? What's happened? Is something wrong?'

'Go upstairs to bed!'

He pushed her in front of him up the staircase, without giving her time to bid Ismay goodnight. She sat there on the bed, shivering, listening to the sounds of him next door in his dressing room.

Hesitantly, slowly, she got up and stood in the half-open doorway connecting the two rooms.

'It's bad news, isn't it? Is it anything to do with Wishard?'

He had been kneeling down lacing up his shoes. He looked up sharply as she spoke, almost angrily.

'What business I have with Enoch Wishard is nothing to do with you! I thought I told you to get back to bed?'

He stood up, looked at himself in the cheval mirror, then grabbed his top hat from the hat stand and went out. She lingered on the landing, half out of sight, trying to catch his words as he ran downstairs.

'Did you tell the cab driver to wait outside?'

'Yes, of course I did.'

'Then let's get going.'

She turned this way, and then that. She slept, fretfully,

tormented by her dream. Ghostlike, she moved across the lawn, her bridal veil flowing, her feet not touching the solid ground but floating in slow motion, her long hair streaming out behind her, fanned by the gentle breeze. The ruins of the house, her father's house, loomed up before her eyes, the burned out shell black and gloomy in the eerie dusk light. On she glided, passing silently through the once-rich rooms, now bare and empty, unrecognizable, in their abandoned desolation.

Ahead of her, suddenly, she glimpsed the outline of a massive bed, untouched by the ravages of time that had destroyed the once-proud house, a bed of richly carved mahogany with a damask canopy, all draped in lavender . . .

Onward she glided, closer and closer, her ears, at last, catching the sound of human cries . . . as she neared it, to her horror, there, in its midst, lay the naked body of Rufus Waldo, his arms caressing a naked woman with long, black hair . . . at the sudden sound of her wordless scream they both turned, staring at her, and Rebeccah looked into the face she knew . . .

She awoke, minutes later, bathed in sweat, her heart thumping. Somebody was knocking on the front door.

Leaping dazedly from the bed, she grasped her velvet dressing gown and pulled it about herself, then ran down the stairs.

The knocking was soft, almost gentle. None of the servants had been woken. On her way to the door Rebeccah glanced at the longcase clock. Half an hour after midnight. Rufus had been gone for more than an hour.

Drawing back the bolts as quietly as she could, Rebeccah opened the heavy door gently, to let him in. But the face that stared back at her from the darkness was not her husband's.

'Please, will you let me in?' said Cornelius Ismay.

Wordlessly, she stood back as he came into the hall, closing the door behind him.

'Where is my husband?'

'I must speak to you, Rebeccah.'

She stared up into his eyes. It was the first time that he had ever used her name, and she felt inexplicably moved by it.

'We can talk in here. I don't want to wake the servants.'

Inside the chilly, dark little morning room, they stood looking at each other. Then he spoke.

'I think there are certain things that you must know. For your own good. If Rufus or Enoch Wishard knew that I was here, I couldn't answer for the consequences . . . both of them are entirely ruthless.'

Her heart began to beat very fast. 'I don't understand.'

'Enoch Wishard trains racehorses for a colony of American owners, principally the millionaires James Drake and William Gates. How they both became millionaires I'll leave to your imagination. But, as Balzac once said, behind every fortune there is a crime.' Rebeccah went on staring at him. 'Ever since he came over here to train, Wishard has had phenomenal success; and he's made a fortune for his crooked owners in betting coups. They're his speciality; not in fixing big races where any noticeable divergence from established form would attract dangerous and unwelcome attention . . . he's too clever for that. He's brought doping horses to a fine art, and Rufus has been of inestimable assistance to him in bringing inside information from other stables whose trainers and owners are in his confidence.' He paused for a moment. 'Do you remember that day when we met at Newmarket, before your father died? The 100–1 outsider who beat everything in sight by four lengths and then killed itself by crashing into a wall? Wishard had had him doped half an hour before the race.'

She clenched her fists. She closed her eyes. She tried to speak, to say something to him, but the words wouldn't come.

'I'd never seen anything like that ever happen before. Usually, the drug just wears off and that's the end of it. It was the first time, believe it or not, I've been brought face to face with the real cruelty of it . . . I never thought about it too closely before; I didn't want to. I got involved with Wishard six years ago, when I was in debt and I desperately needed money . . . and there was no other quick way to get it. I'm not trying to make excuses for myself; there aren't any. I've done everything I've done from the very first with my eyes wide open. I can't undo any of it. I've been as ruthless and unfeeling as they have. But after that day at Newmarket when that horse crashed into the wall, and I saw how much it affected you . . . for the first time I felt sickened by it all. And sickened by myself.'

She looked up into his face, the face she had loathed before that evening in her father's house when he had told her how he had come by that ugly, disfiguring scar. She made herself speak, her voice sounding hoarse, strange, as if it belonged to another person.

'Why are you telling me all this? It's something to do with tonight, when you came for Rufus?'

'The Jockey Club are launching a serious enquiry into the incident at Newmarket, and into Wishard's activities. I don't need to tell you how deeply Rufus is involved. He's with Wishard now.'

'But I don't understand . . . there already was an enquiry into the race, and they found nothing. The official verdict was that the horse had gone berserk for no reason they could make out, and since he passed the post first he was still given the race. You know that. Why would they reopen the enquiry now?'

'Because they've received anonymous information that the race was rigged, and that Wishard and Rufus were involved.'

'But who . . ?' She broke off, in mid-sentence, suddenly realizing the enormity of what he was saying.

'Yes, I did it, Rebeccah.'

She went on staring at him, without understanding.

'But if Wishard and Rufus are brought down, you're brought down too.'

'I know that. That's why I intend to leave the country.' He smiled, almost bitterly. 'Cowardly, isn't it? I'm as guilty as they are, and I leave them to face the music. Of course, by the time the Jockey Club, and the law, find out the truth, Wishard and Rufus will have discovered who betrayed them. But that's a chance I'll just have to take. I can't leave the country until after next weekend; your brother, if you remember, invited me along with you and Rufus to the shoot at Dunroven Castle. If I disappeared before that it would look too suspicious. By the time Wishard was arrested, his men would have got to me first.'

There was a long, painful silence.

'Why have you come to tell me all this?'

'Because I'm in love with you.'

When he had gone, she still stayed exactly where he had left her, leaning against the chair; unable to think, feel, move. She stayed there for a long while, at length trying to marshal her tumult of thoughts, trying to remember when exactly it had been that her feelings of revulsion and dislike for Cornelius Ismay had changed.

Had it happened that day when he'd come to the house to tell her how sorry he was for her grandmother's death? Had it been that day on the course at Newmarket, when the shock and the brutality of the violent end of the doped horse had affected them both, and, in doing so, beaten down the barrier of dislike and distrust on her part? Had it been later, in her father's house, when Ismay had told her about the scar, when he'd walked with her in the gardens that had never seemed the same after her mother's death, and brought back something in her life that she was only now aware had been missing? There was a sensitivity, a gentleness about him, when they had talked alone, that she had never seen before, and which she now knew Rufus had never possessed.

Woodenly, she made her way upstairs and went into her bedroom; but she did not get into bed. Going to her little rosewood escritoire, she took out paper and a pen and sat down, in the early dawn light, to write him a letter, her ears strained for the first warnings of Rufus Waldo's return. Too dangerous to send by ordinary mail; but she would give it to Alice. Alice whom she could trust absolutely . . .

If only she could have gone with Cornelius Ismay . . .

31

ALICE STOOD at the tall, deep-silled, mullioned window, watching her husband and her brother, and two gamekeepers a few paces behind, as they walked briskly out of the castle courtyard and disappeared into the grounds. Following on, slowly, their heads bent in conversation, she caught sight of Rebeccah – a flower basket on one arm – and Louise Russell, Jamie's wife.

'They've gone.'

'And I must follow, in a few moments . . . much as I'd prefer to stay here and make love to you.' Waldo came across to her and drew her away from the window. Then he pulled her face towards his and kissed her, lingeringly. 'We'll meet in London. When we get back. Or at the Kent house. You'll be rid of Clanradine for more than three weeks, while he's paying his filial respects to his mother!'

'You haven't told me everything, yet, about the Jockey Club enquiry and Enoch Wishard . . . are you in any danger?'

'Yes. If the Jockey Club uncover what really happened after the race at Newmarket when the bloody nag ran itself into that wall, they'll bring in the law . . . and I don't need to tell you what that means. Someone in the organization has talked; there's no doubt about that. Ismay's stopped down in London, trying to do some digging into it . . . he won't be arriving until late tonight. I may know more then. Whoever sent that anonymous message to the chief steward hasn't come forward in person because he knows what Wishard's men would do . . . but if he changed his mind and decided to risk showing his identity, he could turn Queen's Evidence . . . if he thinks he can cope with having to look over his shoulder for the rest of his life.'

'You mean Wishard would pay to have him silenced?'

'Not Wishard; his speciality is doping horses. His owners. None of them got to be millionaires worrying about other people's blood being spilled.'

Her dark, glittering eyes looked thoughtful.

'And you've no idea who it could be? Has Ismay?'

'Not yet. But it's bound to be, as he says, one of the small fry. They always start squeaking first.'

'But even if Ismay can find out who sent the letter, won't it be too late? Once the Jockey Club have been alerted, they won't just drop the whole enquiry because the author of the anonymous tip off has disappeared. If anything, they'll be more suspicious.'

'Suspicion is one thing. Getting proof of it is quite another. If Wishard packed up the whole operation and moved it over to France – which he intended to do later in any case – nobody could prove anything. The whole episode would die a natural death, with nobody else any the wiser.'

She was smiling. 'You seem very confident of that.'

'I am.'

'For the sake of argument . . .' Slowly, Alice began to walk about the room. 'If Wishard and his owners were brought down, could anything they allege bring you down, too?'

'Nothing that would stand up in a court of law. I've had one or two business deals with Wishard's owners, over sales of racehorses . . . nothing out of the ordinary or that anyone, even my enemies, could say were illegal. Gates and Drake both know that if they admit to anything that might bring me down, they're brought down too.'

'What about the sale of the Belle Mead stud, Rufus? The non existent stud they sold to you for half a million dollars?' She smiled, drily, 'The stud you let it be known you'd purchased, solely to impress my grandmother that you were a man of means, eminently suitable to be considered as a husband for Rebeccah?' He stared at her. 'You captivated my sister with your good looks and charm, yes; but did you really think you'd taken in anyone as astute as Anna Brodie Russell?'

His voice was low, thick, hardly above a whisper. 'What are you talking about?'

'Oh, come, Rufus . . . you know that I'm in love with you; I always have been, from the very first moment I saw you. I'd rather die than do anything that might destroy you . . . surely you know that? But when my grandmother died, just before you married Rebeccah, I was searching in her desk for something . . . and I found an envelope that she'd left with my sister's name on it.' She had all his attention now. 'When I opened it, I found a documented report that she'd had sent to her, from an enquiry agent in America . . . the report had been compiled by someone who had worked for Jerome Charpentier . . .'

'Where is it . . ?'

'. . . it was a complete history of you, Rufus . . . with corroborated proof of every deal you've been involved in for the past ten years . . .'

'It was a forgery! Nobody could ever have got that kind of information!'

'You knew very little about my grandmother . . . and you grossly underestimated the strength of her love for my sister. Do you really suppose she would have let Rebeccah marry a man whose entire background she hadn't had thoroughly investigated? You overestimated your own personal attractions, Rufus – did you think that that hypnotic charisma that can get you any woman in your bed that you desire, would have the same effect on a woman long past feeling any? Vanity, Rufus. One of your deadly sins.'

'Where is this report?' His voice had gone dangerously soft.

'In a safe place.' She smiled. 'Where nobody can ever find it, of course. Except me. Did you really think that I'd have shown it to Rebeccah? I could have done, couldn't I? If I hadn't been so much in love with you myself . . . after reading the truth, she would never have wanted to see you again, and you would have been free to marry me. But I knew you were marrying her for the money. For the inheritance . . . you see how devoted to you and unselfish I am? I didn't want to stand in your way . . .'

'What do you want, Alice?'

'What I've wanted right from the first time I ever saw you – you. I want you to leave Rebeccah and take me to France.'

'Don't be absurd! Things are perfect between us as they are now – me, a respectable bloodstock owner married to an heiress; you the wife of a wealthy Earl. We can meet whenever we feel like it and nobody is any the wiser. Nothing could be more convenient . . .'

She gave him a sly, sideways glance. 'But not convenient for me, Rufus. Not any more.'

'What the devil are you talking about? If I left Rebeccah and you left Clanradine, have you any idea of the scandal it would cause?'

She smiled. In that moment, the likeness to her mother was striking. 'Not so great as the scandal it would cause if the dossier I have about you were to be made public.'

He stared at her, his dark eyes narrowed. Slowly, he came towards her. '*You wouldn't dare . . .*'

'Only if you pressed me to it. You say that you love me. Prove it. In society, all that matter are appearances. You've made enough money from your illegal racing activities and betting coups with Enoch Wishard to give up everything here and start with me afresh in France. You give out that you're setting up new bloodstock interests there; I tell Duncan that I want a change of air. When you've realized as many of her assets and taken as much as you can, you can divorce her and I can divorce Duncan. Then I shall be Mrs Rufus Waldo.'

'You really mean it, don't you?'

'I want you, Rufus. I want you badly enough to do anything. I can't go on like this. The lies, the pretences; meeting only when there's no danger that we'll be seen. Always watching everything I say to other people; when we're in public together, making out you mean nothing to me . . .'

'For God's sake . . !'

'. . . It's true, damn you! But you don't care how I feel, do you? Ever since you first came to the Epsom house I couldn't get you out of my mind . . . I'd lie awake at night, thinking about you, wanting you, hating my sister because I knew you wanted to marry her instead of me. For the inheritance, you'll say. Yes! I knew that too . . . but do you think that made it any easier for me to bear? Thinking of you, with her . . . while I had to make do with that oaf Clanradine!'

'Alice, don't be a fool! If I left Rebeccah now and went with you to France . . . what do you think people would say? I don't mean the moral outrage . . . to hell with that! Who I go to bed with is no bloody concern of theirs or anyone's. Let them be outraged. It's more than that. In the light of the spy in Wishard's stable, I just can't afford to disappear . . . not yet. Because if I did then the Jockey Club would start asking questions, and that would signal danger. Think about it. If I go to prison, where would you be then?'

For the first time, Alice fell silent.

'Be clever, Alice. Let's bide our time.'

'It's the money, isn't it? You want to wait until she's twenty-five and you get the lot! Why don't you admit it, Rufus? Your greed far exceeds the love you profess for me?'

'Don't be foolish . . .'

'I'm not. But if you really love me as you say you do, I want proof.' There was a hard tone to her voice now. 'As my grandmother used to say . . . deeds, not words. Talk is cheap.'

'I'm talking about expediency! For both our sakes!'

'So you say. But are you sure that expediency is the true reason why you hesitate? Or is it that you don't want the stigma of being married to a half-Italian bastard?'

'For God's sake, do you think I care about that . . ?'

'I don't know, Rufus . . . do you?'

He came over to her and grasped her by the shoulders.

'You know the answer to that! You always have! You. That's all I've ever wanted . . . you. You in my arms. You in my bed. We're two of a kind; didn't I always say it?' His grip on her shoulders tightened. 'We both did what we had to do for expediency's sake . . . but Clanradine should have married Rebeccah, and I you . . .'

She looked up into his face. He was perspiring slightly.

'I want you, Rufus. On my terms. If you love me as you say you do, then you'll do what I want.' She moved away from him. 'I must go now . . .'

When he was alone he went over to the window and leaned against it, staring down into the dark, murky water of the moat. For the first time in his life, that quick, sharp, agile brain would not obey him; like a long disused, rusty wheel, it would not turn, and he stayed there, head in hands, trying to bend it to his will.

Dismay and fear suddenly turning to anger, he thought, bitterly, of Anna Brodie Russell; so she had not trusted him after all! Yes; he had been guilty of complacency in thinking that he had taken her in as he had taken in all the rest . . . and it had almost been his downfall. How to get his hands on the fatal, incriminating dossier that Alice had hidden? That, more than anything else, would be the most difficult task of all. But, if he gave in to her, if he did exactly what she was demanding of him, would that not save him after all?

He began to pace the room, restlessly, turning over everything in his mind. Though he desired her as he had never desired any other woman, he could almost hate her, for putting demands on him when his mind was already occupied with the danger of the Wishard spy. And was it what he really wanted, to leave England, to leave all the wealth and the prestige, the niche in Society he had carved for himself, and live in obscurity and disgrace with a woman so fiercely possessive, so totally ruthless, as Alice Clanradine? He wondered if he himself really knew the answer.

Later, when the women were in the drawing room after dinner, and Clanradine had gone down to the gatekeeper's lodge for some reason of his own, Waldo managed, somehow, to get Jamie alone.

'For God's sake . . . your face is white as candlewax. What is it?'

'It's your sister, my dear Jamie. Your sweet little sister Alice . . .'

'I thought you were sleeping with her . . .'

'I am. But she wants more than that.'

'How much more?'

'Marriage.'

Jamie began to laugh. 'How can you? You're married to Rebeccah . . . and Alice is married to Clanradine.'

'Alice wants me to divorce Rebeccah and take her over to France. Then Clanradine can divorce her for adultery and desertion.'

Jamie's grey eyes narrowed. 'But that would be social suicide. For both of you. She must know that. And the money. The remainder of the inheritance in the trust fund . . . you wouldn't be able to touch a penny.'

'I know that. And so does she. But she no longer cares.'

'I find that very difficult to believe . . . no woman alive loves her creature comforts more than Alice . . . just like that greedy, grasping Italian bitch of a mother. She'd have slit her own mother's throat for a diamond necklace . . . she almost bled father dry. He told me. Alice might despise Duncan Clanradine, but she knows that if she left him for you, everything she takes for granted now would be over.'

'She says I've made enough from Wishard's illegal betting

coups to make it all worthwhile. Especially if I start to liquidate the Russell assets that I can get my hands on right away . . . like the entire collection of bloodstock.'

'But that's madness! Why throw everything away for the sake of staying tied to Rebeccah for the next few years? When she's twenty-five, you can get your hands on the entire fortune. Isn't that worth waiting for?'

'Not according to Alice.'

'Tell her she'd better prepare herself for a long wait.'

'I can't.'

'Why not?'

Waldo told him about the secret file.

'Do you think she's bluffing?'

'I've known Alice for long enough to realize that women like her never make idle threats.'

'But what are you going to do?'

'It's what you're going to do, Jamie . . .' He stopped, suddenly, and held up a hand in warning. 'A servant?' He went over to the door and opened it a few inches. Darkness in the corridor outside. No sound, only his imagination. No wonder, with his nerves the way they were. 'You're going to find out where she's hidden it, and then leave the rest to me. I can't afford to have a lethal weapon like that dossier in Alice's hands to use against me!'

'You don't seriously believe that she ever would?'

'One thing I've learned about women . . . and I've never been proved wrong yet. If they want a man badly enough they'll do anything in their power to get him. Even kill.'

'Alice?'

'Jamie, you must talk to her and find out where she's hidden that file . . .'

'But how can I make her tell me? Alice is nobody's fool! And as soon as I mention the dossier, she'll guess that you've told me and put me up to it!'

'You must find out where it is!' He got angrily to his feet and went over to the door. 'We can't stay here talking . . .

that will make her suspicious. And Ismay should be arriving any minute . . . Clanradine's gone to meet the carriage at the lodge. God, that this should happen to me now!'

'You don't suppose . . .'

Waldo's voice was sharp. 'Suppose what?'

'Do you think Alice could have sent that anonymous letter to the Jockey Club – about the incident at Newmarket being much more than it seemed?'

Waldo hesitated, then dismissed the idea. 'It couldn't be. The dossier your grandmother had in her desk that Alice discovered after her death, only gave details of my activities up till my return to England. The rigged race at Newmarket was only a few months ago. It couldn't have been Alice.'

'Of course . . . I didn't think of that.' Jamie got to his feet, heavily, and passed a hand across his brow. He was beginning to perspire. 'I'll do my best, Rufus. But Alice is much too clever to be caught out like that; remember the old saying. You can lead a horse to water but you can't make him drink.'

'You'll have to do better than your best. Remember . . . you're in this almost as deeply as I am . . .'

When Ismay came into the room, her heart beat fast. When he looked at her, she felt her face grow hot. While the men settled down to a game of baccarat, Rebeccah got shakily to her feet and went over to the grand piano.

She had learned to play when she was fourteen years old, and played beautifully, often accompanying her cousin Lottie Tradescant when she'd been at Chilworth Manor; now, the soft, lilting popular song that drifted out from the keys as her hands moved expertly and surely across them, soothed her, calmed her, helping to stop the shaking in her wrists and fingers.

As she played, she tried to concentrate on the music and not on Ismay's profile, and, instead, focus her eyes on different objects about the room.

It was a magnificent room, a huge room, and the sound of her playing much louder than it would have been in any other part of the castle; the ceilings were high, with beautifully modelled cornices, the walls hung with damask and Brussels tapestries; family portraits, from three hundred years before, adorned the east and west walls, with an oval painting high above the doorway, by an unknown artist, of Louise and her brother Dunroven as children. As her eyes rested on it, the notes beneath her fingers died away, and she paused, suddenly, pretending to adjust the sheet music in front of her on the piano stand.

Unwillingly, she thought back to their last visit to the castle; the sudden, single shot from the forest; Rufus Waldo and Ismay running, Dunroven's blood splattered body, covered with a sheet someone had hastily borrowed from the lodge keeper, the still warm corpse carried back to the castle in a makeshift shroud. She remembered her suspicion of Ismay, and her own hostility, and wondered how she could have ever doubted him; but she had been blinded by her own unfounded prejudices.

As the last notes died away, she closed the top of the piano and remained sitting.

'You must take me to hear Lottie sing at the Empire, Duncan,' Alice said, bored with her conversation with Louise. 'You promised that we'd go before we left . . . but nothing ever came of it. As usual, you put business before your promises to me.'

'I'm sorry, my dear,' Clanradine said over his shoulder, while the others went on watching their cards, 'but it couldn't be helped. I did promise you and I mean to keep that promise. As soon as we go back.' He turned away when it was his turn, and placed down a card from the top of his hand. 'I hear Lottie was invited to a private recital at Marlborough House this weekend, to sing for HRH and Princess Alexandra. Not her usual music hall repertoire, I understand . . . something much heavier. Two arias from

Samson and Delilah, no less. I would have loved to have been there.' He turned back to concentrate on the game.

'Three Aces!' Waldo shouted, triumphantly. 'You can't top that, any of you!'

'You should have been playing in HRH's party at Tranby Croft,' Rebeccah heard Ismay comment, drily. She stifled a smile. The scandal of the Prince's friend cheating at cards was still talked over, even six years later.

'Does anyone know if HRH ever did keep to his vow about never playing baccarat again?' Clanradine asked no one in particular.

'What HRH says in public and what he does in private have always been two different things,' Waldo answered, raking in his winnings and shuffling the deck of cards. 'Who's for another game?' A murmur of assent went up around the table. 'Double the stakes. No fun playing for a pittance.' He began to deal the cards. 'That damn affair at Tranby Croft would never have seen the light of day, if HRH's fancy piece Daisy Brooke had kept her mouth shut. More fool him for spilling the beans to her. But it does prove a point.' He started to laugh. 'You never can trust a woman.'

Alice looked at him sharply.

'Or a man. If HRH had kept his mouth shut and told no one about what went on that weekend, Daisy Brooke, like everyone else, would never have known about it.'

'My dear Alice, since when has HRH ever been discreet when it comes to his women? Society didn't dub Daisy Brooke "Lady Babblebrook", for nothing; he never did know how to pick them. Look at the Jersey Lily. A classic example of put a beggar on horseback that I've ever seen. When he first noticed her, butter wouldn't have melted in her mouth; at the end of the affair she was stuffing ice down his back for a practical joke.'

'That was what finished her as a royal favourite.'

'How delicately you put things!'

Rebeccah joined in the conversation. 'Is she still living with that disgusting brute George Baird?'

'The Squire? Making hay while the sun shines, now the rose has lost some of its youthful bloom.' Waldo's voice was cruel. 'A better bet, even, than HRH. More brass. Stinking rich. Stands to reason, doesn't it? Inherited over three million from iron and coal before he was ten. His widowed mother was quite incapable of controlling him . . . the fellows at the club say he went to Eton and Cambridge but left both without a vestige of education!' He let out a raucous laugh. 'And rough riding tactics weren't in it. Threatened to shove Lord Harrington over the rails!'

'Didn't the Jockey Club warn him off for two years over that?' Jamie asked.

'He bounced back again. Better than ever. Got to admire his spirit, even if you think the man stinks. Money no object. He paid more than £17,000 to Lord Falmouth in '84 for some top class horses . . . by far the largest single buyer.' A glance across at Rebeccah. 'Your grandmother, God rest her soul, told me when I first met her that she'd never deal with the Squire, on principle.' Another laugh. 'Still, his filly Busybody did win him the Guineas and the Oaks . . . he knew his horseflesh all right. And never happier than when he was riding the winner.'

'Or beating up the Jersey Lily,' Clanradine said.

'Was that really true?' Louise Russell asked, from her place beside the roaring fire. 'I can't believe it was ever more than a rumour, put about by some of his enemies . . . and my brother always used to say that no man ever had more. Surely no woman would stay with him if he treated her so badly.'

'It depends on what you call bad. £5,000 every time he gave her a black eye is the quickest way I know of making money. Even better than long odds on a 100–1 winner.'

'I don't think that's funny, Rufus.' Rebeccah got up, made her excuses and left the room. Waldo's loud, unconcerned laughter followed her into the quiet and coolness of the stone corridor outside. For a moment she leaned there against the wall, her eyes closed, glad to be quit of that hot, stifling room, the gossip and the laughter of her husband. When she had collected herself and harnessed her anger, she began to make her way in the direction of her room.

She closed the door behind her, lay down on the soft, red velvet curtained bed, and stared up at the plain, white, barrel-vaulted ceiling, as austere and simple as a convent. It was a peaceful room.

Simply furnished, compared to many of the other, grand bedrooms, the only furniture beside the bed were two Charles II chairs, a longcase clock, and a lady's dressing table with an ornate, carved mirror. After a while she got up, reluctant to go back again into the drawing room and join the others. Instead, she walked over to the mullioned window and stared out.

There was little she could see through the blanket of pitch black darkness; the outline of the distant trees, the gate keeper's lodge, the twinkle of the water down below her in the moat. When a soft tapping on the outer door suddenly broke into her thoughts, she jumped.

'Who is it?' She spoke, nervously, her heart beginning to hammer wildly. But instinctively, she knew.

He was standing there in the dimly lit passage, the ugly, jagged scar on his cheek thrown into sharp relief by the light of the wall lamp near the door.

'*Cornelius*!'

'We must talk . . .'

'He mustn't find you here.'

He came into the room; for a few moments they stood, looking at each other. Then he leaned towards her and kissed her lips. Fire leapt through her.

'I only came here because of you. You do know that, Rebeccah?'

Breathing heavily, she leaned back against the wall.

'You must go back . . . otherwise he'll suspect something!'

'I told them I wanted something in my room.'

'He might follow you; to ask what's happening in London with Wishard. He'll wonder where you are . . .'

'I know how to handle Rufus. Just listen.' They both fell silent instantly at the faint tread of footsteps outside.

'It's only one of the servants.' He took her hand in his and began, slowly, gently, to stroke her fingers with his palm.

'I haven't stopped thinking about this, ever since I last left you. It's obsessed me, I haven't stopped turning it all over in my mind. I haven't slept. I've hardly eaten. All I can think about is you.'

'Please . . . help me . . . Cornelius, I must get away from him. Before he destroys me. Before I go out of my mind.' She fought back the tears. Too dangerous. When she returned to the others Waldo's sharp, probing eyes that missed nothing would see the reddened rims, the tear stains on her cheeks. Nothing must give her away. 'What can we do, both of us, to be rid of him?'

'Leave him, and come with me. When I've sent all the proof of his scheming with Wishard to the authorities, he'll be ruined forever.' As her face brightened his remained dark. 'But it isn't as simple as that, Rebeccah. It never is. It would mean living like a fugitive . . . maybe for years, possibly forever . . . because when Wishard's ring find out who betrayed them, my life won't be worth a cent. I'm not sure if it would be fair to ask you to share that danger with me.'

'I don't care about the danger. I'll come with you anywhere.'

'You can't decide something like that until you've thought about it for a long while.'

'I've already decided. But why should you be in danger? You can turn Queen's Evidence . . .'

'And show beyond any doubt that I was the traitor in their midst? If I denounce the ring anonymously, we at least have the chance to live something of a normal life . . . otherwise there's no hope. If the colony of crooked owners that paid Wishard to rig their races only think I was clever enough to slip out of the net and disappear, then they'll never suspect me. Plenty of others in the ring had the same access as I did to Wishard's dirty dealing . . .'

She forced her mind to think clearly. 'I'll do anything you say.'

'Then listen. When we leave the castle, I have to go to York, and you and Rufus will travel back to London. Wait for me to contact you there.' He paused. 'If it's too much of a risk for me to come to the house myself . . . is there anyone you can trust to bring you a message?'

'My sister Alice!'

'Perfect. Who'd suspect an innocent visit from your own sister? Certainly not Rufus.'

'I'll tell her. As soon as I can. So that she can help us if needs be. Tomorrow, when we have the picnic during the shoot.'

'Tell her to say nothing to Clanradine. Not a hint. Just to wait for me to give her the message.' He took her hastily in his arms and kissed her hard, upon the lips. When he released her she could only stare dumbly into his bright, grey eyes.

'I must go now.'

He was gone, before she could answer.

32

THEY TRUDGED ALONG, side by side, guns held down, keepers and dogs trailing behind them, shielding their eyes from the unaccustomed glare of the midday sun. The mist had begun to clear now, and only hovered, swirling in little patches, on the low ground and in the deepest part of Dunroven forest.

From the knoll of the hillock, where the servants were clearing away the remains of the picnic, the women gathered to watch the men stalk their prey.

All morning Rebeccah had watched for an opportunity to get her sister alone, but none came. Clanradine had stayed in bed until Alice got up; then remained with her, maddeningly, while she had been dressed by her maid and all through the long ritual of breakfast. Never one moment alone. Rebeccah watched impatiently, now, as the group of women surrounding her sister showed no signs of moving away. Then an idea struck her.

'Alice?'

The beautiful, dark, Italian eyes turned and looked into her face.

'Alice . . . let's go and see what's happening! Let's go and find the men!' The others gave her looks of shock and astonishment. 'Come on, they might even let us try our hand with their guns!'

'I really don't think you should . . .' Louise Russell started to say. But Alice began to smile.

'Why not? I never could manage to resist a challenge.'

*

'I don't believe it!'

'I tell you it's true!'

'... *Rufus*? Involved in illegal betting coups with Wishard? Do you really believe Cornelius Ismay?'

'For God's sake, Alice! Why would he want to lie about it? They were friends ...'

Alice concealed her true feelings beneath a mask of contrived surprise.

'Friendship goes out of the window when two men want the same woman. And a man will lie about anything, if he wants a woman badly enough.'

'You don't believe him?'

'I hardly know anything about him. Except that I thought he was Rufus's best friend.'

'I've already explained to you why he turned against him!'

'I thought you loathed Cornelius Ismay. Isn't that what you said?'

'I don't know when my feelings started to change ... when it all started to happen ... I've gone over and over it in my mind, and I can't remember ... I think it was after that race at Newmarket, when Wishard's horse stormed past the field and killed itself, crashing into the brick wall ... I saw it ... I couldn't sleep that night for thinking about it ... I've never been able to get it out of my mind ...'

'But there was a stewards' enquiry after the race. I can remember Duncan telling me. They came to the conclusion that the horse had simply gone berserk, that it was just something that happens from time to time. Nobody ever suspected foul play.'

'Nobody ever does ... Enoch Wishard is far too clever. But the race was rigged. Cornelius told me so. That's what started to turn him against them ...'

'Oh, come, Rebeccah. Even you can't believe anything as feeble as that? He's besotted with you and he wants to take you away from Rufus. He'd tell you anything to get what he wants from you. If Wishard was a crook do you suppose for one moment that the Jockey Club would allow him to have a trainer's licence?'

They went on walking, slowly, in silence. They reached the dark belt of the forest trees.

'He can get proof.' Alice's head shot up, sharply. 'The drugs that Wishard uses and injects into his horses to make them run faster . . . Cornelius can get samples. When the Jockey Club and the police examine them there'll be no doubt in anyone's mind that they won races under the influence of illegal dope.'

'But that would be suicide. Doesn't he realize what they'd do to him if they found out the truth? If he betrays them he'd be a marked man. Members of crooked racing syndicates have no mercy where big money is concerned. And would you be safe if you went with him? Have you thought about that?' She grasped Rebeccah's sleeve. 'Talk him out of this, Rebeccah. For your safety and his. Promise me.'

'I can't.'

'If it's just you he wants, there's another way out. Buy Rufus off. You said yourself that his one god is money. And that's why he became involved with Wishard's ring in the beginning. Then you and Cornelius can be together and nobody will ever know that it was him who wrote the anonymous warning to the Jockey Club.'

They stopped walking and looked at each other. In the distance they could hear the faint sound of guns firing.

'What Wishard is doing, Alice. It isn't only illegal. It's cruel; it's immoral. Injecting dope into worn-out, tired horses. Forcing them to run when they're not fit; they win, yes . . . but not because they're the fastest or the best. And Cornelius says it has a disastrous effect on most of them that are subjected to it – like that incident with the brick wall. Do you think after that he could go on working for them?'

'He's managed to keep his conscience quiet until now.'

'Only because of the risks! He's talked about turning Queen's Evidence . . . but I'm so afraid! If he goes to the law openly, they'll know that it was he who betrayed them.'

Alice squeezed her sister's arm even tighter.

'For God's sake, Rebeccah, think about this before you do anything at all . . !'

'I haven't been able to sleep for exactly that reason. And nor has he.'

Both at once, they caught sight of the little group of men up ahead. Alice shouted and waved. One of the keepers began to move away across the small clearing, leaving Ismay and Rufus standing there alone.

'What the devil are you both doing here?' Waldo's dark eyes held anger. 'Don't you know how dangerous it is to wander in these woods when we're all walking about with loaded guns?'

'You must blame Rebeccah; it wasn't my idea to come.'

He turned on his wife.

'I would have credited you with more sense.'

Briefly her eyes met Ismay's. 'If you want us to go then we will.'

'Hush! *Ismay, look*!' His voice dropped dramatically to a whisper. With one arm he signalled the two girls back. 'There, grazing behind that distant clump of trees . . .' His eyes glittered; he licked his lips expectantly, keyed up with the excitement of the kill. When Rebeccah followed his eyes she could see it for herself: the big, majestic, soft-eyed stag, his massive antlers pointing proudly into the sky, cropping at the rich, luscious grass. Slowly, Waldo raised his gun and placed it in position. 'Get behind, all of you . . . this one is mine . . .'

Rebeccah stood there, trying to tear her eyes away from the inevitable; she felt weak-legged, sick; longing to bang her hands together, longing to shout at the top of her voice, so that the magnificent creature would be startled, and run away. She stood there praying, her fists so tightly clenched that the nails bit into the flesh of her palms. But the creature made no movement at all.

Smiling, Waldo raised the barrel of his shotgun to take aim. Then she saw his finger moving slowly, surely, to make contact with the trigger. Just as he was about to fire she flung herself forward, knocking the barrel of the gun upwards into the air. The shot rang out into the sky, miles wide, and the startled beast vanished as if it had never been.

Waldo wheeled round on her, almost speechless with rage.

'*You bitch*!' He raised his hand to strike her, but Ismay sprang in front of him. He seized his arm.

'Don't be a bloody fool, Rufus! The keepers, the others . . . do you want them to see you strike your wife?'

'She did it on purpose!'

'All right. It's gone. There'll be others. Come on, let's catch up with the rest of the party.'

'Yes! I did it on purpose!' Her blue eyes blazed at him, all her fear of him gone, now she was in Ismay's presence. 'That beautiful, gentle creature . . . what harm has it ever done you? You can't bear to see anything free, can you? All you want is to kill and maim!'

'You wait till we get back to the castle!' He was shaking with anger. He had forgotten the others nearby. If Cornelius Ismay hadn't been there he would have given in to the powerful impulse to strike her. 'I promise you . . . you'll be sorry for this!' He snatched up his shotgun and stamped off. Ismay began to follow him; then he turned round and looked at her.

She stood there, the daylight that had filtered its path down through the thickness of the trees picking out the lights in her dark, lustrous hair and striking blue eyes. All dressed in green, she looked like some exotic, mythical creature of the forest. Ismay thought that never in his whole life had he seen anyone more beautiful.

Then Alice spoke, and took her by the hand. 'Rebeccah, we must go back.'

'Calm down, for pity's sake!'

'She did it on purpose, damn you! The bloody bitch did it on purpose! Right there, in front of everyone, turning me into a laughing stock! I'll teach that spoiled bitch to make a fool of me!'

'They should never have been in the forest in the first place. They should have stopped back where they belonged, with the other women,' said Jamie.

'It was her idea. Alice said so. It was Rebeccah who wanted to come looking. My God, if we were back in London and not in this place full of guests, I'd have given her the thrashing she deserves.'

Jamie poured himself and Waldo a glass of gin and sipped it, thoughtfully.

'You're on edge. You need a woman.' A sly note crept into his voice. 'I can always tell. And you can't go creeping into Alice's bed with Clanradine there beside her.' A smile. 'And she can't come tip-toeing in to you . . .'

'You don't have to remind me . . .'

'But there is a very convenient place I know . . . a recent discovery, as a matter of fact . . . that I think you're going to enjoy . . .'

Some of the anger disappeared from Waldo's face. 'Is it far from Inverness?'

'On the outskirts of the town.'

'Our excuse for leaving the others without inviting them to come with us?'

Jamie laughed. 'Some pressing business to do with the estate. For which I need your assistance. Besides . . . I owe you a favour. Do you remember that whorehouse near Woolwich Wharf?'

Waldo downed the glass of gin in one gulp. 'I have no objection to you repaying me.'

Alice watched them intently as they made their way down towards the castle stables, in the fading light. The mist was growing thick, now, and treacherous; it was no time to be outside. She, for one, did not believe Jamie's tale of calling on one of his tenants on the edge of the estate, to arbitrate a small but pressing dispute between him and one of his neighbours. And, even if it were true, he had no need to take Rufus Waldo with him.

'It's best if he comes with me. In the dark, no man in the highlands with any sense would go out riding alone. One of us could get bogged down, out on the moor. Besides,' he'd said, flippantly, 'best to keep him and Rebeccah apart for this evening. After what happened in the forest today, he still hasn't calmed down.'

'Why don't you take a manservant?' Alice had persisted, carefully watching her brother's face. Ever since she was a child, she had had an uncanny knack of knowing exactly when other people were lying. And Jamie was lying now.

'Not much company in that.' The charming smile she always found it so easy to see through. 'Tell Louise not to wait up.'

The sounds of the piano rang through the castle as she walked quietly, unobtrusively, down the winding stone steps towards the servants' hall. From behind one of the doors she could hear the sound of laughter; from behind another the clatter of plates and pans, the sound of someone throwing wood upon a fire. She walked along the little narrow passage until she came to the end of it, then, pausing to look around her for only a moment, Alice knocked softly upon the door.

A young manservant opened it, with dark brown curly

hair and mud brown eyes. He looked at her, startled that one of his master's guests should come down to the castle basement. But Alice smiled.

'Are you alone?'

Awkwardly, he tried to recover from his surprise.

'Why, yes, my lady Clanradine . . . I was just polishing the gentlemen's shoes . . .'

Unobtrusively, she stepped inside. The smell of leather and polish pervaded the air in the tiny room, not altogether unpleasant. She noted, for no particular reason, that it was spotlessly clean.

'I have something I wish you to do for me. Immediately. I am prepared, of course, to pay you well.' She opened the purse that she had brought with her, and tipped a pile of sovereigns onto the little work bench beside him, while he stared speechlessly. 'Needless to say, I shall expect you to exercise the greatest discretion. And to mention this . . . arrangement . . . to no one. Do you understand me?'

He nodded, wordlessly, his eyes glancing from her face to the pile of money.

'My brother and Mr Waldo left the castle a few minutes ago. I want you to follow them and find out where they're going and who they see. When you have done that . . . and you'll stay out watching them for as long as is necessary . . . you will report back to me.'

'Yes, my lady Clanradine.'

She opened the little door. 'Hide that.' She glanced towards the money. 'And take the greatest care not to be seen . . .'

33

'Mr and Mrs Rufus Waldo!'

The footman called out their name, and they stepped forward from the marble portico into the brightly-lit, chandelier hung hall, to be greeted effusively by their host and hostess.

Rebeccah, dressed in an exquisite ballgown of pale saffron silk, watched half amused, half bitterly, as Rufus lavished every vestige of his enormous charm on his vain, arrogant, overdressed hostess, a woman ten years his senior, whom she detested and from whom she would never have accepted an invitation had it not been for his almost brutal insistence.

As she moved forward into the throng, smiling at someone she knew here, nodding to an acquaintance there, she kept glancing back, discreetly, over her shoulder to see where he was. And there, sure enough, in a corner of the room sipping champagne, she caught sight of him with Lady Augusta Flynne. Every now and then her loud cackle of laughter would ring out, carrying high over the noise of the guests and the music from the orchestra.

She accepted a glass of champagne from a passing footman, then, as she was sipping it, felt a light touch on her arm.

'Lottie!'

'So you're back from the wilds of Scotland.'

'It's so long since I've seen you!' Rebeccah said with real feeling. And it was true. Months had passed since they had last met; and then only for several minutes in the foyer of the

Shaftesbury Theatre. So many times, sunk in a deep depression, she had got out her pen and paper, meaning to write; but somehow she never had.

She remembered sitting, dejectedly, in the loneliness and silence of her room, staring down at the blank sheets of paper. How even to try to explain to another living soul the depth of isolation and unhappiness that she felt? The disappointment, the dashed hopes and unfulfilled dreams. It was impossible then, and now.

'Let's find a quiet corner. Where's Rufus?' Rebeccah inclined her head in the opposite direction and Lottie Tradescant followed her cousin's eyes. 'Oh, I see. Fully occupied with charming our elegant and refined hostess. Yes, she's ghastly, isn't she? A Frankensteinian mixture of Maudie May and the proverbial Fat Lady of the circus. No woman alive was ever born with that shade of hair. And a red velvet ballgown with that figure? Even from where I'm sitting, it looks as if it's ready to burst its seams . . . like the Stour when it's almost ready to burst its bank after too much rain . . . let's hope she doesn't cough suddenly, or eat too much at dinner . . . or laugh at HRH's pathetic jokes . . .' She turned aside and looked in dismay at Rebeccah, doubled with silent laughter. There were tears in her eyes.

'Lottie . . . if only you knew how much I needed to have someone to make me laugh! If only you knew how much good you've done me! God knows, these last few months I could have done with it!'

'Are you unhappy?' Lottie, as direct and outspoken as ever.

'If I said no, then I'd be lying.'

'Is it Rufus?'

'I should never have married him . . . I see now what a terrible mistake that was. But too late.'

Lottie's beautiful blue eyes were serious as few saw them.

'I was about to ask you why you did . . . but that would be a foolish question. What you saw in him I saw in him myself, the few times we ever met.' A pause, while she sought the right words. 'He dazzles. He charms. He overwhelms with his wonderfully handsome face, and those dark, black pools he has for eyes. He'd make a marvellous actor. Totally striking. Totally irresistible. And, of course, he's very well aware of it.'

Rebeccah went on staring into the crowded ballroom.

'I often remember, when I'm alone, when I'm feeling unhappy, what you once said about never getting married. You were right. It is like walking into a trap. But the trap is so cleverly baited, and you can't step out . . .'

'You could leave him . . .'

Rebeccah was shaken out of her lethargy.

'But the scandal! Wives don't leave their husbands, Lottie. It isn't done. It never was. They can make us suffer, they can make us miserable, make our every waking hour a hell on earth, but we must suffer in silence. That's the rule. And if we ever have enough courage to run away then we need somewhere, and someone, to run to.'

'You could have any man you wanted.'

'Could I?'

'Do you really care about society? What is it, anyway?' She looked out over the milling, brightly clad groups of guests. 'This? All this glitter, all this hypocrisy, this pointless, empty charade . . . does it really matter if we're part of it or not? In fifty years nearly everyone in this overcrowded, overdressed, overrated throng, will be dead anyway . . . except us. Yes, that's it . . . laugh. Laugh at them. Laugh at it all. Your grandmother and mine were sisters, and they didn't belong to society. They fought it, they made it accept them. On their terms. You're not Anna Brodie Russell's granddaughter for nothing . . . I know that. Before your mother left . . . before she died . . . we were almost brought up together . . . remember?'

'Yes, I remember.'

'Is there someone else?'

The question was sudden, totally unexpected, and she

was completely startled by it. She looked down into her folded hands.

'So there is? Does he know about it?'

'God, no! He'd be insane with rage!'

'Insane with wounded vanity, more like! He's so obsessed with what he considers to be his own perfection, he could never imagine any woman preferring any other man . . . no matter how badly he treats them.' A frown creased her forehead. 'Does he treat you well?'

'There have been . . . a lot of arguments.' She gave a small, bitter little laugh. 'In the beginning, I wanted to please him so much . . . I wanted to do everything his way . . . what I wanted, or needed, didn't seem important any more. It was like being under a spell, somehow . . . as if somebody had waved a magic wand and I'd been suspended in time, asleep . . . then, all of a sudden they waved it again, and I woke up . . . but I didn't want to be subservient any more. I didn't want to have to agree with all his decisions. I didn't want to play at being a sweet, adoring, obedient little wife. And he couldn't understand it. I'd never argued with him before; I'd never questioned anything he'd done. And now I was. That's when it all began . . .'

Lottie looked at her for a long while. Through the middle of the crowded room, someone was edging their way towards her.

'Rebeccah . . . I never thought he was right for you . . .'

'People will only say that I've made my bed, Lottie; and I must lie on it.'

'You can't sleep if you're uncomfortable.'

'We're all expected to act a part, aren't we? It's always been that way. Happy marriages. Contented husbands and satisfied wives. It doesn't matter if underneath all the veneer, it's just a sham. That at country house parties, hostesses deliberately arrange the bedrooms so that husbands having affairs with other people's wives, and wives having affairs with other people's husbands, can have everything made so much more easy . . . that's what my mother must have hated; that must have been why she left papa . . . all the other women, the constant flirtations, the endless infidelities . . . I couldn't have suffered that, either . . .'

'Is that the reason you haven't left Rufus? Because of the way your father was ostracized after she left?'

'It isn't only myself I need to think of . . . if it was, then it would all be so easy . . . but you know as well as I do that how I behave affects other people, people that I love and care about. You, Alice . . . and if not Jamie then Louise . . . I've always liked her, even though she's one of the dullest women I've ever met.'

'My reputation can take care of itself.' Rebeccah smiled. 'Run away. Shock them all and be damned the lot of them. And, speaking of Dunroven . . . I always did think that he had designs on you.'

Rebeccah stared at her. '*Dunroven*?'

'That time when your grandmother invited them down to the Old Brew House. The way he kept looking at you. The way he followed you about. Like a devoted, faithful spaniel longing for its mistress's attention . . . I even remember Jamie making some remark about it. For some reason he didn't seem particularly pleased.' She smiled, and began, absent-mindedly, to stroke her delicate lace fan. 'I don't know what made me think of that, after all this time. You mentioning Louise, I expect. Do they still seem happy?'

'As long as she never discovers Jamie's many faults.'

'Poor Dunroven. That accident was such a tragedy. That's partly the reason I never accepted another invitation to the castle . . . cowardly of me, I know. And it was so beautiful there. Just think. If you'd married Dunroven instead of Rufus you'd have been a Countess, and Jamie would have ended up with almost nothing except Louise's dowry.'

Before Rebeccah could answer, the tall, fair haired young man who had been making his way towards the place where they sat, presented himself, and their conversation was never resumed.

'Is it true, what I've heard? That you're going to treat us all to another incomparable rendering of Saint-Saëns?'

'If you mean am I going to sing two arias from his opera *Samson and Delilah*, like I did after dinner at Marlborough House . . . then, yes, what you've heard is true. May I introduce you to my cousin, Rebeccah Russell . . . Mrs Rufus Waldo.'

'Mrs Waldo, your servant.' He turned back to Lottie. 'If I could spirit you away for a few moments to discuss the music . . .'

'Yes, of course. Rebeccah, we must talk again . . . you must call on me at the theatre, or at home, now that you're back in London . . .'

Later, seated in the grand music room, listening to the strong, sweet, powerful voice as it rose effortlessly to the cadences of the Saint-Saëns song, Rebeccah let her restless, distracted mind wander back, to those stolen moments alone with Cornelius Ismay. How much she longed, needed, to see him again. But it was too dangerous to meet at the house . . .

It was then that the idea came to her.

She joined in the applause all around her. Through the long dinner that followed, she toyed, listlessly, with the endless courses of rich food. Then, as soon as the dinner was over, she pushed her way through the press of laughing, noisy guests to where her cousin stood.

'Lottie, can I speak to you in private?'

In the ladies' deserted cloakroom, she closed the door and leaned against it.

'Lottie, please help me. I've no one I can turn to. Alice is away on Clanradine's estate and Jamie wouldn't throw me a lifeline even if I were drowning. I've no one I can turn to except you!' To her own consternation, she had started to cry.

'Rebeccah! What is it?' Lottie came to her and put her arms around her. 'I knew something was wrong!'

'I'm desperate. I'm so unhappy. I'll go mad if I have to spend another night with him in that house. I hate it so. Every room. Everything in it. It's like a prison.' It tumbled out, then, the story of her and Ismay. The illegal betting ring, Wishard, the threat to Ismay's safety.

Lottie pressed her firmly onto the nearest seat.

'Listen. Rebeccah, listen to me. You must get Ismay to go to the police. These men could be dangerous. With huge sums of money involved . . . fortunes at stake . . . do you think they'd stop at nothing to protect themselves? You must make him go, at once . . . for your own sake . . .'

'But don't you see, he can't . . . he can't do it . . . if he turned Queen's Evidence they'd know his identity, and he'd be running away for the rest of his life. They'd never let him be until they had their revenge. If he makes certain the Jockey Club and the police have the information and the samples of the drugs they use to dope the horses anonymously, he at least has the chance to pretend that he's escaped the net and gone free before getting caught. That's the way it will look to Rufus and Wishard. Rufus would never suspect him . . . unless anything happens to connect him with me . . .'

'Rebeccah . . .'

'That's why I need your help, Lottie. I must see Cornelius. I must. I'll go out of my mind if I don't. Please, can you get a message to him to meet me in your dressing room at the theatre? It's the only place in London where nobody would ever think to look . . . and we won't involve you. It can be while you're away at rehearsals . . . you need never know about it . . .'

Lottie sat down beside her. 'All right . . . yes, of course I'll help you. But I still think you're both fools to try to keep this to yourselves. If Ismay gave them the names of the ringleaders, they would all be rounded up and arrested before any of them could become a danger.'

'That's where you're mistaken, and why Cornelius can never come forward of his own accord. He knows only the names of some of them. As soon as Wishard was arrested, the others would escape from the net.'

'Yes . . . I suppose you're right. I do see . . .' Lottie put her chin in her hand, trying to think. 'And when Ismay has sent the proof to the Jockey Club . . .'

'If he could ever find out the names of everyone involved in the betting coups, he could give himself up and turn Queen's Evidence. Since that's unlikely ever to happen, all he can do is lie low after the ringleaders have been taken, and we can go away somewhere. God, Lottie . . . I don't know . . . I can't think properly, my mind won't seem to function . . . I just want to be with him . . . and I just want peace . . .'

Outside, they could hear talking and laughter, and approaching feet.

'Look. We can't stay in here . . . people are coming.' Lottie put an arm around her shoulders and helped her to her feet. 'Quickly . . . dry your eyes. Splash your face with water. Don't let Rufus see that you've been crying. Don't do or say anything to make him suspicious.' She thought quickly. 'Will he be leaving the house tomorrow?'

Rebeccah tried desperately to remember something he'd said. 'I think he mentioned that he had some business, with Wishard, and that he was going down to Epsom for two days. I wanted to go with him so that I could see Gold Bridge . . .'

'Don't go. Make an excuse. Anything. Pretend that you feel ill . . . all the rich food you ate at dinner tonight. No better reason. I'll send a note round to Ismay's lodgings in the morning and ask him to call on me at the house . . .'

Rebeccah turned to her, tears of gratitude in her eyes. 'Lottie, how can I ever thank you for this?'

Neither of them spoke in the carriage on the short ride home. Once inside the house, Rebeccah went straight upstairs and let her maid help her undress, ready for bed. Worn out with her own emotions, she lay back against the welcoming, comforting softness of the pillows, and half drifted into troubled sleep.

She jumped, suddenly, almost crying out, when she felt a hand pressing against her arm.

Eyes wide, trying to focus in the dim light, she saw his face brought into sharp relief by the light of the oil lamp he had placed beside the bed.

He was naked. Her heart lurched, and, instinctively, she pulled the bed covers up around her, as if seeking their protection.

'Please, Rufus . . . not tonight. I don't feel well. I think it was the rich food at dinner . . . I feel sick . . .'

'Take off your nightgown.'

'Rufus, please. Leave me alone.'

His eyes were cold and hard. 'I said, take it off!'

'No! Go away, for pity's sake!' She tried to fend him off, her flesh shrinking from his touch, the touch that so long ago had thrilled her, but now revolted instead. She cringed from the groping, insistent hands that pawed at her breasts, that tore at the folds of her flimsy nightgown. Despite everything that Lottie had said, her loathing and outrage overcame her caution, and she pushed him violently away.

'You bitch!'

'Don't touch me!'

'You're my wife, God damn you, and I'll do anything I please with you!' He grabbed her by the arm and twisted it savagely behind her back. Then there was a sickening ripping noise as he tore the nightgown from top to bottom.

As he pushed her down roughly on the bed, Rebeccah hit him with all her strength, with her free hand.

'Whoremonger's brat!' He slapped her, violently, across both sides of her face, and pulled her towards him by her hair so roughly that she cried out.

Sobbing, hysterical, she kicked and punched until she was exhausted; but he was too strong for her. Half conscious when he pushed himself callously into her, when he'd finished he left her lying there, half clothed, tears streaming down her face.

When he had gone, she crawled back into the bed and pulled the cold covers about her bruised body, while she cried herself to sleep.

34

SHE STARED AT HIM across the tiny, cluttered little dressing room, every space and every piece of furniture strewn with costumes, hats, shoes, and theatrical gowns.

'Cornelius . . .'

'*My God!*' He came towards her, shaking with shock and rage, the deep, jagged scar livid on his cheek. 'I'll kill him . . . I swear on my mother's soul that I'll kill him . . .' He reached out and touched the fading bruises on her face and neck, gently, tears of emotion in his eyes. '*That bastard!*'

'Please, Cornelius, don't. Don't talk about him. Don't talk about that night . . . I want to forget . . . if you went after him you'd be arrested . . . then he'd know, he'd guess, that it was you who sent that letter to the stewards . . . you can't take that risk. I won't let you!'

'Do you think I intend to let him get away with this? That I care more about my own miserable hide than I do about you?'

'It isn't a question of that . . . don't you think I hate him too? Don't you think that I loathe every day, every hour, every moment I have to stay with him, that I have to live under the same roof? If you give in to the temptation to lay one finger on him, we'll lose everything. Wishard's ring will find out that you're the one who betrayed them to the authorities. Any chance we have of being together in the future will be dashed forever!' Her voice rang out passionately. 'Please, Cornelius, don't do it, for my sake!'

He came closer to her and took her in his arms. Without

speaking he cradled her head on his chest and stroked her hair.

'Rebeccah, you can't stay with him. Not after this. Make any excuse. Go to your sister. Or your cousin. Even Jamie . . .'

'I can't stay with Alice. Clanradine only brought her back to London to attend some special function or other. In a week they're going back to his estate near Perth . . .'

'Can't she make some excuse to stay behind? You've told her the truth, everything that's happened?'

'Yes, of course I have. She's the only one besides Lottie who I can trust. Do you think I would have asked her to pass on our letters if I couldn't? I shall give her all of them, and the documents you asked me to hide for you in case your rooms were searched . . . she'll know where to put them for safe keeping. Thank God I can rely on her!'

'Rebeccah. Listen to me. When you leave here you must take a hansom cab straight to Clanradine's house. Explain everything to Alice . . . I have to go to York, today, to get hold of the rest of that evidence. Somehow, I've got to do it.'

'But Rufus will be there! He said he had urgent business with Wishard!'

'He'll be there only for a day or at most two. When he comes back to London you mustn't be alone in that house!'

She sank down onto the nearest chair, burying her face in her hands, fighting the impulse to cry.

'Cornelius . . . please, I beg of you, be careful. I couldn't bear it if anything happened to you . . .'

'No, Rebeccah. It's best if we don't stay here.' Smiling, kneeling down beside her, Alice gently wiped the tears from her face. 'Duncan left for Perth early this morning; I said nothing to him at all . . . I think that's best.' She took Rebeccah's hands in hers. 'The fewer people who know where you are, the better. Until Rufus is arrested. Who knows, if he finds out about you and Ismay, he could send someone looking for revenge. Trust me. I know exactly what we can do.'

'Alice, I'm so frightened. I'm afraid for Cornelius.'

'He knows how to take care of himself. He'll get hold of the rest of the evidence you said he needs . . . the complete list of names from Wishard's desk, and the samples of the dope they've been using; as soon as he gets his hands on those, he can go straight to the police. Now, listen to me. I've rented a tiny house for you – near Mitre Square – somewhere where nobody is ever likely to look for you . . . or expect you to be. Just for a few days until Ismay has the evidence and it's safe for you to come back again. Think. If Rufus or anyone else wanted to find you, this house, or Lottie's, would be the very first places they'd look.'

'I'm so sorry to burden you with all this. But you and Lottie are the only ones left that I can turn to. If it wasn't for you acting as a go-between, it would have been far too dangerous for Cornelius and I to have written each other letters . . .'

'I'd do anything to help, don't you know that? For God's sake, Rebeccah . . . you're my sister! Now, pull that veil down over your face. I've sent one of the manservants to call a cab . . .'

Rebeccah stood up, fumbling in her drawstring bag.

'Alice, please take these letters and hide them somewhere for me. Nobody must ever find them.'

'They're the letters I passed on between you and Ismay . . .'

'I know it's foolish of me to keep them . . . and dangerous. But I couldn't bear to destroy them! I keep thinking that if anything happened to him I couldn't bear to have nothing left at all . . !'

Alice stared down at the bundle in her hand.

'There are documents, too . . .'

'Papers that Cornelius took from Wishard's desk. Only a few, but irreplaceable.'

'I know exactly where to hide them. Come, quickly. I can hear the cab.'

When she returned to the house again, Alice sat there in the drawing room for a long while, reading through the letters and the documents, a faint smile of mockery on her lips. When she had finished, she went upstairs to her dressing room and hid them in a secret compartment in her little desk.

Then she rang for her maid.

'Lucy? I have to go out for a while. I may be late returning . . . possibly not until tomorrow afternoon or evening. My sister is going to visit our brother in Scotland, and I shall be accompanying her to the station.'

'Yes, my lady . . . shall I pack your case for you?'

Alice smiled.

'That won't be necessary. The few things I shall need I can attend to for myself.' She stood up. 'Just get Hutchinson to call me a cab.'

When the girl had gone, Alice went back to her little corner desk and opened the secret drawer. Leafing through the documents Rebeccah had given her, she selected one and then closed the drawer. Taking a pair of needlework scissors, she snipped away the lining of her velvet muff and placed the folded paper inside. Then, carefully, she found a needle and thread in her tiny workbasket, and restitched it.

As she stood up and caught sight of her reflection in the mirror, she paused and looked at herself, for a moment thinking of the striking likeness between herself and her Italian mother.

Slowly, she smiled.

35

THE SLENDER, dark-haired young woman with her face heavily veiled stepped down from the train at York station, and made her way along the crowded platform to the street outside.

There was a line of horse cabs waiting for passengers, and she raised her small, gloved hand, and hailed one.

'Please take me to Mr Enoch Wishard's stables.'

As she was shown into the untidy, dusty yard office, Alice lifted her heavy veil and laid it back to show her face. She smiled as he stared at her, clearly taken aback by her beauty. He got to his feet, trying to recover from his surprise.

'Mr Wishard?'

'That's my name, ma'am. And may I have the pleasure of knowing yours?'

'Rebeccah Waldo.'

His mouth fell open.

'Rufus's wife?' He went on staring at her. 'He was here, less than a day ago . . . are you looking for him?'

She smiled.

'No. I know that he was here . . . and that by now he would have left York. You see, Mr Wishard, he told me before he left London that he was intending to pay a visit to my brother Jamie, at Dunroven Castle.' She came further into the room. 'En route, he will have stayed at a small house that was left to my brother when his mother died . . . it used to be a hunting lodge. My brother gave him a key.'

'Forgive me, Mrs Waldo . . . but I don't quite see what this has to do with me . . .'

'It has everything to do with you, Mr Wishard. You see, I happen to know that the senior stewards of the Jockey Club were sent certain anonymous letters concerning your racing operations in this country . . . yes, I thought that would interest you. It might also interest you to know that the identity of the sender is my husband, Rufus Waldo.'

'I don't believe it.' He came forward towards her. 'Rufus would never . . . he's in this as deep as me! He told *you*?'

'I found some documents in his possession . . . by chance . . . and he had to tell me the whole story. Also, he was dissatisfied with his share of the illegal proceeds.'

Wishard's long, clever face lit with rage.

'That son of a bitch!'

'It's his intention to go to the authorities when he returns from Scotland, and turn Queen's Evidence against your betting ring. I assure you, Mr Wishard, that he means to do what I say.' She paused, to let him take in the full implications of her meaning. 'However . . . if I were to give you exact details of his whereabouts . . . the hunting lodge . . . you could ensure that he never reaches London to betray you.'

His eyes narrowed. 'I don't understand. He's your husband. And you . . . you want him dead?'

'I discovered some time ago that he was being unfaithful to me. I had him followed . . . and there's no doubt. I also know that he married me for my money . . . and that as soon as he can get his hands on the bulk of my estate, he intends to leave the country with his mistress. I think you'll agree that that is reason enough for me to want revenge.'

For a few moments they looked at each other. She could almost see Wishard's quick, cunning, agile brain thinking, cog upon cog.

'We were planning to move the whole operation to France anyway, in a matter of months . . . things were beginning to get too hot, anyhow . . .' He rubbed his chin, and began to pace the small, cluttered room restlessly. 'Once he's out of the way, it'll give us the short breathing space we need to wind up and get out . . .' He stopped pacing, and suddenly looked up at her, suspiciously. 'Just a minute. How do I know that what you're telling me is true? How do I know that you're not just trying to get my men to do your dirty work for you and get rid of him . . . because you caught him in some other woman's bed?'

Without speaking, Alice picked up a paper knife from Wishard's untidy desk and ripped open the lining of her muff. Then she took out the document that Ismay had stolen and handed it to him.

'I think that answers your question.' As she watched the incredulity on his face as he looked at it, she wanted to laugh out loud. 'Well . . . do we do business together or don't we?'

Impatiently, Rebeccah stared from the tiny curtained window, down into the street below. It was getting dark now, and she had been waiting, for several hours, for Alice to reappear. But, as she strained her eyes into the fading light, there was no sign of her sister.

Disconsolately, she sat down on the edge of the bed, her head in her hands.

She had not eaten since the day before. Fear for Ismay's safety, of what might happen, had robbed her of all peace of mind, of sleep. Her head ached, continually, dully. She felt sick and empty and weak.

When she heard the sudden noise of footsteps outside the front of the house, she leaped to her feet, her heart racing. Alice was back; perhaps she had Cornelius with her.

She rushed to the door and opened it. Then her whole body froze, as she came face to face with the two uniformed policemen standing there.

'Mrs Rebeccah Waldo?'

She nodded, through parched lips, gazing at them dumbly.

'Mrs Waldo, you are not obliged to say anything unless you wish to do so . . . but what you do say will be taken down in writing and may be given in evidence . . .' She felt the cold, hardness of metal, as the handcuffs pressed against her flesh. 'Rebeccah Russell Waldo, I arrest you on suspicion of being directly concerned in the wilful murder of your husband . . .'

36

'I DIDN'T DO IT! I didn't kill him, I tell you! I don't know who did!' Shaking, she dashed away the tears with the back of her hand. 'How could I have had anything to do with his murder? I wasn't even there!'

'Mrs Waldo, please calm yourself. Nothing is to be gained by behaving with hysteria . . .'

'I'm innocent!' She covered her face with her hands. 'I've told you what happened. I've explained why I was hiding in that empty house. My sister took it for me, for a safe place to stay until . . . until we could think what to do . . .'

The lawyer pulled out the chair for her to sit down, patiently. How much he had always disliked dealing with women prisoners; the tears, the emotional outbursts, the half irrational rantings of innocence. Already, the trial had become an overnight sensation and from the very first day every available corner in the vast court had been packed.

He looked at her gravely; at the huge, wild eyes, fearful as those of an exhausted, hunted animal; her face was white, hollow-eyed, drawn. Even when she sat, listening to what he said to her, her small, delicate hands were never still.

'Mrs Waldo, this isn't helping either of us. I beg you, please, sit down. We must talk. And I cannot help you unless you calm yourself. And tell me the truth.'

She turned and looked at him, with angry, accusing eyes.

'I already have. And you don't believe me. I can see it in your face . . .'

'Mrs Waldo . . . until the Prosecution produced those letters, I would have staked my entire reputation on an acquittal. Both your half-sister and your cousin have already testified that your late husband had treated you with extreme cruelty . . . indeed, even your own servants testified that they had overheard violent arguments between you, and that on one occasion there were bruises on your face which could only have been inflicted by your husband. You confirmed this in the witness box. Further evidence taken has confirmed that your late husband was indeed deeply implicated in the operation of an illegal betting ring . . . the main culprits of whom have gone to ground or fled abroad to escape arrest. All the available evidence pointed quite unequivocally to your innocence . . . especially the evidence of your half-sister Lady Clanradine, who testified that she took you to the empty house because you both thought you were in physical danger from your husband.' His voice changed to a graver tone. 'That was before the discovery of the letters . . .'

Her voice rang out in panic and disbelief. 'Somebody stole them from Alice!'

'However they came into the Prosecution's hands, they are fatal to your case. They show beyond a shadow of doubt that you had a lover . . . a lover who hated Rufus Waldo even more than you had cause to . . . the Prosecution now contend that his murder was planned by both of you, and executed by the man that you refuse to name . . .'

'He had nothing to do with it! He wouldn't kill in cold blood! He wouldn't! He wouldn't even kill an animal . . .'

'Mrs Waldo, you must name him. If you continue to refuse to give the Court his name, you must alone stand charged with this murder. Look at it from the Court's point of view. You both had the motive. Both of you had the opportunity. Please, I beg of you, think most seriously on this. Your lover – and I make no moral judgement – has failed to come forward to speak for you. If he alone is guilty of this crime . . . you would be most foolish and ill advised to continue to shield him.'

'You think that he's abandoned me.'

'Mrs Waldo, I am a lawyer and I deal only in facts. The facts are that you are on trial for your life and he has disappeared. You refuse to give his name. Unless you do so, it is my duty to warn you that, in the light of this new evidence, you will almost certainly be found guilty of murder.'

She fell silent. She turned away.

'I have already answered.'

Behind her, she heard him rise to his feet and tap on the bars of the cell door, for the warder to let him out. There were loud, echoing footsteps on the bare stone corridor outside, and then the noisy jingle of keys. More footsteps, dying away in the distance.

She sank down onto the hard, narrow prison bed, and closed her eyes.

Lottie Tradescant stopped restlessly pacing about the room, and turned to her mother.

'It's absurd. Crazy. Madness, to even suggest that Rebeccah could have had anything to do with his murder! Anyone who knows anything about her can testify to that! That bastard Waldo. If he'd been my husband I could have plunged a knife in him myself.'

'Lottie, you've already been a defence witness on her behalf, like Alice . . . there's nothing more that anyone can do. She might have been acquitted, but for the sudden appearance of those incriminating letters . . .'

'By themselves, they prove little. How many married women hate their husbands? How many married women have secret lovers? Neither is a crime. Because Waldo was blown to pieces in a remote hunting lodge in Scotland, there's nothing to suggest that Rebeccah might have had anything to do with it . . . but the Prosecution are now saying that the appearance of a third person . . . Cornelius Ismay . . . is sufficient to point to the conclusion that they wanted Waldo dead in order to be together. But that's insane! Can't the Court see that they could have achieved that without the murder of her husband?' She ran a hand through her long, disordered dark hair. 'For God's sake, mama, I don't know what to do . . . tell the police that I know the identity of the lover she's trying to protect, or keep silent. For the first time in my life, I don't know what I should do.'

'Lottie . . . I can't make your decisions for you. That would not be the right thing for me to do. It's for you to decide. But, for Rebeccah's sake, I beg you to try to speak to her first . . . you may be one of the very few people who can make her see reason.'

Lottie let out a deep, anguished sigh.

'*Where* is Ismay? And, if he really isn't guilty, why doesn't he come forward?'

'You seem so convinced that he's really as innocent as Rebeccah believes him to be.' A pause, while mother and daughter looked at each other. 'Perhaps all of us are about to be proved wrong.'

She stood there in the dock, flanked by two stout women warders, holding on to the sides of the box. A small, pale, dark clad figure, her face like a mask. She watched, dull-eyed, as the next witness for the Prosecution took the witness stand and repeated the oath. A tall, thin, grubby boy of about sixteen. He gave his name. His place of abode. Neither meant anything to her. Only when he answered that his occupation was stable boy in the former employ of the trainer Enoch Wishard, did she stand more erect, and take notice.

'How long had you been in the employ of Mr Wishard at his stables in York?'

'Eleven months, sir.'

'And did Mr Wishard give you a specific reason why he was terminating your employment?'

'No, sir. 'E just cleared out.'

'Would you kindly answer the question in an acceptable form of English? Please tell the Court what you mean exactly by that?'

The boy cleared his throat, nervously.

'Well sir. There'd bin rumours around the yard . . . well, that all wasn't plain sailin' . . . rumours about Mr Wishard was closin' the yard down and movin' over to France. I'd gone sick for a couple of days, an' instead of livin' over the stables, like usual, I'd stayed at me pa's public 'ouse, over on Queen Street. When I went back . . . the day after the murder . . . it was all in the papers, it was . . . the yard was empty. Horses. Men. Mr Wishard. Just gone.'

'And what did you discover was the reason for that?'

'Mr Wishard was bein' investigated by the police for illegal bettin' activities . . . fixin' races an' that . . . I never saw nothin' like that meself, sir . . . but then, 'e would 'ave bin too clever for that, if it was true . . .'

'Think carefully before you answer the next question. Two days before the murder of Rufus Waldo, did you direct a lady of quality into Mr Wishard's yard office?'

'Yes, sir. I did.'

'Can you please describe her appearance for the Court?'

'Yes, sir. She was dressed in very fine clothes. A dark velvet walkin' gown, and a dark 'at with a veil over 'er face.'

'And did she tell you her name?'

'Not me direct, sir. She asked to be taken to Mr Wishard, and I took her to 'is office. I 'eard 'er say to 'im that 'er name was Mrs Rebeccah Waldo.' A loud whisper went up among the public gallery.

'I see. And do you now recognize this lady in any part of this courtroom? Please, take your time.'

The boy's eyes went straight to the small, slight figure in the dock.

'That lady there, sir.'

Another gasp among the crowd in the gallery. The Crown Prosecutor smiled.

'Thank you. No further questions, my Lord.'

Rebeccah paced her dingy cell.

'He's lying! I was never there!'

'Mrs Waldo, what reason would he have to lie? Please, be reasonable. I cannot help you if you refuse to tell me the truth!'

She turned on him. 'I am telling you the truth! Somebody's paid him to say what he did. Somebody who wants me to hang!'

'Mrs Waldo. The boy is completely unconnected with any of Enoch Wishard's criminal activities. His record is clean. He has nothing to gain by lying, nothing to gain by distorting any of the facts that occurred. But his testimony is crucial to your case . . . please see that. It places you firmly under the direst suspicion. Why would you go to Wishard? To admit to him that you'd discovered his connection with your husband, and to say that, in return for your silence about what you knew, you wanted him done away with so that you could be free to go to your illicit lover . . .'

She wheeled round on him. 'How dare you!'

'Mrs Waldo, those are the words the Prosecution will use, not mine.'

'I want to go back in the witness box. I demand to go back. I'll tell them the truth. The truth about Rufus Waldo. How he schemed and plotted and charmed, so that he could marry me for my money. How he forced himself on me.'

'Mrs Waldo, if you do that, then you will be condemned from your own mouth. Any such outburst will only serve to convince the jury beyond all doubt that you had the strongest possible motive for murder . . . or to be a prime instigator of it.'

Her mouth was a bitter line. 'They want to find me guilty

because I hated my husband and took another man as my lover? The ultimate crime. Yes, I hated him! Yes, I wanted him dead! But, as God hears me, I didn't kill him. Nor do I have any idea who did.'

She sank down onto the plain wooden chair, and covered her eyes.

After a long, painful silence, the lawyer spoke.

'Mrs Waldo . . . for the last time I must ask you . . . is there anything in your account of what happened that you wish to change . . . before it is too late? I must tell you, it is my duty to tell you, that if you persist in keeping to your present story, you are almost certain to be convicted.'

Slowly, she shook her head.

He stood there, awkwardly, for several more minutes. Then he picked up his briefcase, and quietly left.

Outside the cell, he paused and sighed.

'A message for you, sir. From your office. A gentleman wishes to speak to you urgently . . . he says he has the necessary evidence to clear Mrs Waldo . . .'

'You're Joshua Harman? Mrs Waldo's lawyer?'

'Yes, I am. And may I ask your name?'

The man with the ugly, jagged scar that disfigured one side of his face gave a small, tired smile.

'My name is Cornelius Ismay.' He paused. 'I wrote those letters to Mrs Waldo. I was once the close friend and partner of her husband, until I discovered certain facts about his collusion with Enoch Wishard that sickened me to the stomach. No, I didn't kill him; even though when I left London, after I discovered he had raped and beaten her, it was my intention to do so. Nor did she do it or coerce anyone else to do it for her.' Harman went on staring at him, unable to speak through his astonishment and surprise. 'The reason, the only reason I have been in hiding is because I had to find the evidence to set her free. If I'd come forward when she was arrested, I too would have been arrested.' He took a deep breath. 'I can prove that she's innocent. And I can prove who is guilty of the crime.'

The whole Court was silent. Then, Rebeccah watched her Defence Counsel slowly stand up.

'My Lord, the Defence is in possession of new evidence, and additional witnesses which are imperative to the presentation of its case. I ask permission to call the first of these.' After the necessary assent, he cleared his throat; the whole Court leaned forward, expectant, avid, curious. 'I call Cornelius Ismay to the Stand.'

'*No!*' She sprang forward in the dock, clasping the hard, cool edges of it. The warder stepped forward and laid a hand on her shoulder.

Their eyes met and held. As he took the oath, he kept his eyes on her face. Then, he smiled.

'Please state your name.'

'Cornelius Ismay.'

'Mr Ismay, will you please state your relationship to the deceased?'

'I was once his friend and partner.'

'And your relationship with Mrs Rufus Waldo?'

For a moment he hesitated.

'I love her.' Loud murmuring rippled through the court.

'Are you the author of several letters which have been offered to this Court in evidence?' An usher stepped forward, and held them up to him.

'Yes, I am.'

'And the remaining letters . . . do you recognize those?'

'They were written to me by Mrs Waldo.'

'Will you please tell the Court why you have only now come forward to speak in her defence?'

'A week before the murder of Rufus Waldo, I met Rebeccah Waldo in secret in the dressing room of her cousin

Charlotte Tradescant, who, I believe, has already testified to the Court. She will confirm that this is true.' A pause. 'Rebeccah was in a state of extreme misery and fear . . . she still bore the physical marks of the beating her husband had given her the night before, when he raped her in her bedroom.' He paused, until the gasps of horror subsided. 'It was then that I made up my mind to kill him.' The noise from the public was so loud that the Judge called for silence. 'I already knew, because I had been a party to it, of the illegal betting coups which took place between Rufus Waldo and Enoch Wishard. Up till the incident at Newmarket, when a doped horse ran into a brick wall and killed itself, I acquiesced in their criminal activities to rig races. I admit that to the Court. But after that incident, I made up my mind to get out. Also, I was the anonymous writer who sent a warning to the stewards of the Jockey Club about Enoch Wishard's criminal activities.'

'Please go on, Mr Ismay.'

'Rebeccah told me that she would go to her sister, the Countess of Clanradine, whose husband was away from London. She was terrified of being in the Waldo house by herself, and she said that her sister Alice and her cousin Lottie Tradescant were the only two people she could trust. That was the last time I saw her until today.'

'You went after Rufus Waldo with the intention of killing him?'

'Yes.'

'Did you kill him, Mr Ismay?'

'I did not.'

'When you reached York, in fact, did you not find that you had arrived too late, and Rufus Waldo had already left the city?'

'Yes.'

'And what did you do then, when you discovered that he was already gone?'

'I went to Enoch Wishard and demanded to know where

he was. I told Wishard that if he refused to tell me, I would go to the police immediately . . . before he had time to leave the country.'

'And will you please tell the Court what Mr Wishard said?'

'He said that Rufus Waldo had gone to see his brother-in-law, Jamie Russell, at Dunroven Castle. And that he intended to break his journey at the hunting lodge near Inverness to which Jamie had given him a key after his mother's death.'

'Will you please also tell the Court what other information Enoch Wishard gave you.'

'He said that he had already had a visit, the previous day, from Rufus Waldo's wife.'

'And did that greatly surprise you?'

'I found it impossible to believe. Not only because I had left Rebeccah in London, frightened out of her skin, but because Wishard told me that the woman he spoke to, the woman who told him that she was Rebeccah, showed him a document which proved his complicity in the illegal betting coups he set up for his crooked owners with Rufus Waldo . . . she told him that in exchange for her silence, she expected him to get rid of her husband.' Again, the Court erupted. 'From my knowledge of Rebeccah Waldo, I know that she would never have done such a thing.'

'Mr Ismay, the murder of Rufus Waldo took place the following night. That same night, in the early hours of the next morning, Enoch Wishard and his associates fled the country and are now believed to be somewhere in France. Will you tell us if you recognized the document he showed to you and which Mrs Waldo used to threaten him into arranging this crime?'

The usher brought the document, folded and crumpled, to the witness stand. Ismay looked at it.

'I took the document, some time ago, with a number of other documents, from Enoch Wishard's desk. I showed them to Rebeccah, and she pleaded with me not to turn

Queen's Evidence because Wishard's employers would have had me killed for betraying them. If you ask her again on oath, she will tell you that she gave them to her sister for safe keeping, together with the letters.'

'Mr Ismay. You tell the Court that in your opinion the woman who went to Wishard's office shortly before the murder, was not the defendant.'

'I know now that she was not.'

'And can you also tell us if Enoch Wishard gave you another reason for her wanting her husband's death?'

'He told me that she had had Rufus Waldo followed, and discovered he was being unfaithful to her.'

'Mr Ismay. Will you now tell the Court why that woman could not have been the real Rebeccah Waldo?'

Ismay paused, while he looked across the crowded courtroom to where Rebeccah stood.

'Because Enoch Wishard told me that the woman he saw that day had brown eyes.' He turned. 'Rebeccah Waldo's eyes, as the Court can see, are blue.'

Rebeccah stared, across the blurred, jumbled faces that separated them. Alice stared back without blinking, almost without surprise. A small, twisted, mocking smile played about her lips.

Rebeccah went on staring at her, as Ismay stepped down from the witness box and someone else took his place.

'Are you William Smith, a hansom cab driver in the city of York?'

'I am.'

'And on the day in question, did you take a lady of quality from the train station to the stableyard of Enoch Wishard on the outskirts of the city?'

'Yes, sir. I did. An' a very handsome lady she was, too.'

'Was she wearing a hat with a veil?'

'Yes, sir. She was. But at the end of the journey when she was looking in her purse for the fare, she pushed it back off her face.'

'And did you get a clear look at this lady's face?'
'Yes, sir. I did.'
'Mr Smith, if you see that lady now in this courtroom, will you please be so kind as to point her out . . .'
He shifted himself round in the witness box, then stuck out his thick, craggy, work-worn finger directly at Alice Clanradine.
'That was the lady I took to Enoch Wishard's place. Without a shadow of a doubt.'

Epilogue

Rebeccah sat, in the big, wing armchair where her grandmother had once sat, staring out over the gardens and the Downs beyond. Slowly, as if waking from a long sleep, she laid her head back against the leather and looked around her at all the old, loved, familiar things.

Nothing had changed in the big, oak panelled room that Anna Brodie Russell had loved; sitting there, in the chair where she had once sat, Rebeccah felt a strange, calm, curious kind of peace settle over her at last. As Lottie Tradescant came back into the room, she glanced up, and smiled.

'I'm grateful, so grateful, that you've come down to stay with me from London . . . I know you've always preferred the town to the country . . .'

Lottie sat down opposite her, and held her hands out towards the blaze of the fire.

'I've always loved this house . . . ever since I was a child . . . there's always been something special, something magic about it. No wonder she loved it so.'

Rebeccah was silent for a moment.

'We used to sit here, right in front of the fire, Alice and I, at her feet . . . and she'd tell us stories of when she was a girl, when she first saw the house, the drive all broken and covered with weeds . . .' She looked down into her folded hands. 'I always felt so close to Alice . . . from that very first night when my mother left, and the woman Maria brought her here . . . it was as if . . . as if there was always a very special bond between us . . . when I saw her in that courtroom, when she stood in the witness box and I saw hate pouring out of her . . . it was like looking at a stranger . . .'

'Rebeccah, I know it's easy for me to say this . . . but you must forget. You must think about Cornelius and the future. Alice, Jamie, Rufus Waldo – they're all part of the past.'

For a while, they sat in silence.

'I will. I will try to. When Cornelius comes back after Jamie's and Alice's trial. Dunroven's death . . . I still can't believe that Jamie could have played such a part in it . . .'

'I always thought that Jamie was a bad lot . . . papa always used to say so . . . he wasn't surprised when it was proved true. He was always uncle James's favourite, wasn't he? And for the life of me I could never understand why . . .'

Rebeccah got up, and went over to the window. There, across the stableyard, she could see one of the grooms leading Gold Bridge into his stall.

'By the way . . . while you were in . . . while you were waiting for the trial . . . your grandmother's lawyer asked me to hand you this . . . it was something his clerk had forgotten to give him, when he came to the reading out of her will. It was an envelope they found among her private papers, addressed to you . . .'

Rebeccah turned away from the window, and took it. 'There was another envelope that they found with my name on among Alice's papers . . . a copy of a report my grandmother had commissioned on Rufus Waldo, when she realized that I wanted to marry him . . . if only she hadn't died when she did . . .'

'Put the past behind you, Rebeccah. She always did.'

Rebeccah gazed down at the yellowing envelope, at her name, written in her grandmother's tall, bold hand. Slowly, she tore it open. Then, she smiled.

It was a verse, from the pen of an anonymous poet, copied in Anna's own handwriting. Tears stinging at the back of her eyes, Rebeccah read.

'If I should die and leave you here awhile,
Be not like others sore, undone, who keep
Long vigils by the silent dust and weep.
For my sake turn again to life and smile,
Nerving thy heart and trembling hand to do
Something to comfort other hearts than thine.
Complete these dear unfinished tasks of mine,
And I, perchance, may therein comfort you.'

She folded it and placed it back inside the envelope. Then she glanced up at the portrait that hung there on the wall, the portrait of the girl with long, dark hair and striking blue eyes.

Perhaps it was a trick of the fading light; maybe a fancy of her imagination. Certainly, it was smiling at her.

The Hawthorne Heritage

Teresa Crane

'A finely crafted romantic novel.'
Yorkshire Evening Post

Jessica Hawthorne grows up a strange, isolated child in the sumptuous beauty of her family's home, Melbury New Hall, in 19th-century Suffolk.

Robert Fitzbolton, a young aristocrat, is the companion of her lonely childhood, her comfort through family tragedy and the heartache of young love.

But is the support of Robert's friendship enough? Locked together in a disastrous marriage, they flee to Florence searching for freedom and fulfilment.

Robert finds what he is seeking, but Jessica is a true Hawthorne and is drawn – inevitably – back to Melbury, to her destiny . . .

FONTANA PAPERBACKS